Z-Rated

Also by Zane

Edited by Zane

Zane Presents

Z-Rated

Chocolate Flava 3

The Eroticanoir.com
Anthology

ATRIA PAPERBACK

New York   London   Toronto   Sydney   New Delhi

ATRIA PAPERBACK

A Division of Simon & Schuster, Inc.
1230 Avenue of the Americas
New York, NY 10020

ATRIA PAPERBACK and colophon are trademarks of Simon & Schuster, Inc.

Manufactured in the United States of America

ISBN 978-1-62090-390-2

Copyright Notices

Contents

Z-Rated

Come See a Man About a Horse

Zander

Damn, she's got a fat-ass pussy! I was sitting at my desk at 10:15 a.m. with some morning wood that wouldn't go away. *Shit!* This chick, Nadine, was making my blood boil. If I actually ever got my hands on her, she was getting the dick-down of the motherfucking century.

"Wes, you there?"

Aw hell, now she was bending over so I could view her pussy from the back. *Umph! Umph! Umph!* Wes Holmes pressed over some pussy? Never that, but . . . *damn!*

A tap came at the door. "Wes, you there?"

It never failed. Whenever I was locked away in my home office, trying to watch my morning virtual pussy, here Lisa would come.

"I'll be right out, Lisa!" I yelled, though that wasn't even necessary. As thin as our walls were in our crib, I could've whispered and she would've heard me. That's why I always kept my speakers on mute. Lisa and I had enough damn drama without her knowing about my computer pastime.

Nadine was now sitting on her bed, playing in that fat pussy for me. She had her head thrown back and was holding her pussy open with one hand while digging herself out with the fingers of her other hand.

Yeah, pull all that juice out, baby! I licked my lips once . . . twice . . . three times. I wanted to taste all that, suck on that thick clit, and bury my nose in between her juicy pussy lips.

I desperately needed to jack off real quick and release my built-up nut but Lisa wasn't about to leave me alone for another ten minutes and whatnot. She was excited about going to pick out a wedding cake.

I understood it was fucked up. Engaged to my college sweet-heart, planning a big wedding because she insisted on one, and sweating Nadine's pussy on the Internet all at the same time. It was never my intention but shit, reckless behavior rarely is intentional. I kept telling myself that it wasn't doing any harm. It's not like I could get to the pussy. Nadine lived in Jamaica and there wasn't a chance in hell of me running into her ass in the dirty Bronx.

"Wes, the baker insisted that we be there by eleven. We need to go."

I could hear the irritation in Lisa's voice. I loved her and never wanted to hurt her but, truth be told, Lisa's pussy couldn't hold a candle to Nadine's. Even though I got to fuck, suck, and lick all over Lisa's pussy every night, Nadine's was calling my name all the way from Negril. What was a horny Negro supposed to do?

"Give me two minutes, Lisa. I swear, I'm coming."

Nadine was sucking her pussy juice off her fingers and I damn near could taste it through the computer screen. My eyes were as wide as saucers.

I wanted to tell her how I envisioned nailing her against the wall and pumping my dick into her from the back, but I couldn't risk saying it out loud so I typed it.

BIGWES6969: Damn, you got a fat pussy. I wish I could take all that shit doggy-style.

Nadine must have heard a beep or something on her computer because she stopped playing with herself, licked her fingers again, and then typed back.

PHATNNEGRIL: Funny you should mention that. I'm coming to NYC next week for my job.

I damn near busted one right then and there. My dick got even harder as I scooted up closer to my desk. I took my dick out of my sweats and started working one hand up and down the shaft while I typed back with the other. Lisa was going to have to wait.

BIGWES6969: Damn, for real? When you going to be here? I've got 11 inches calling out your name.

PHATNNEGRIL: I know all about that horse between your legs. I'm coming to get it.

True enough, Nadine had seen my dick plenty of times. When Lisa was fast asleep, I'd be in my office jacking off on the cam and exploding all over the laptop screen. I couldn't explain it but for some reason this chick had my nose wide open. Maybe it was the fact that she was out of range. A lot of my buddies were feeling the same shit; wanting to conquer some pussy that they couldn't realistically get to.

It's not that men are bad; it is the nature of the hunt. When we already have a woman that we used to think was the shit before we got her, then we want the next one. Let me try to explain. A man sees a Lamborghini Superleggera and says to himself, "Damn, I gotta have that sexy motherfucker!" He sacrifices and saves up to put a down payment on it, even if it takes years, and then he is beaming like a lighthouse when he pulls out of the lot. All eyes are on him as he cruises in his whip and every woman wants to fuck him because they think he has money. He gets so much pussy that he has to drink a gallon of water twice a day just to keep himself hydrated.

Fast forward a few months and the thrill is gone. He sees a Bugatti Veyron dip past him going 85 mph on the highway and all of a sudden, his Lambo might as well be a hooptie. He no longer feels like the man. So what does he do? He decides that he has to have a Bugatti and starts figuring out how much he can get for a trade-in. Or he desires to have them both; one to keep in the garage and the other to sport around in, depending on his mood of the day.

It's the same way with women. Most men want a main chick or, like they say in pimponics, a bottom bitch. But we also want something in the garage to toy around with when the mood strikes us. And it is always, always about the hunt. When I was little, my mother made me read "A Sound of Thunder" by Ray Bradbury, a short story about men who always wanted to hunt the next big thing, so much so that they paid to time travel and go back in history to hunt dinosaurs. They had hunted, and killed, every modern animal in existence. They had to stay on a path and not disturb anything or it would fuck up the equilibrium of history. So they could only kill dinosaurs that were about to die anyway, from fallen trees or whatnot. One dude, Eckels, fucked up big-time and caused a snowball effect that changed the course of history upon their return.

I mention that to say that I realized good and damn well that making plans to fuck the snot out of Nadine when she came to New York could upset the equilibrium of my relationship with

Lisa. As I sat there, whacking off, common sense told me that holding on to the Lamborghini that I had sacrificed so much for was the right thing to do. But glancing at the screen, Nadine had gone back to playing in her fat pussy . . . that damn Bugatti.

I could feel my cum building up, like a balloon expanding in a wooden box, and Lisa was tapping lightly on the door again.

"I'm coming!" I yelled out, telling the damn truth. I was coming, all right.

"I'll go wait in the car. Hopefully, we'll get there in time," she responded through the door. I heard her huff off down the hall and, a few seconds later, the front door slammed.

I took that opportunity to turn up my speakers and microphone.

"Nadine . . ." I could feel it about to spurt out and grabbed a golf towel from on top of my set of clubs so I wouldn't make my typical mess on the screen. Then I stood up and starting jerking off right to the cam, so she could see it. "Come see a man about a horse!

"Awwwww!" I came like a clap of thunder as Nadine giggled with delight. Even her laugh was sexy. "Shit! Look what you do to me," I said as I caught about a pint of my nut in the towel.

"I wish I could swallow that down the back of my throat." She touched the screen like she was trying to get ahold of my dick. "What a damn waste."

"So what day you getting here?" I stuffed my dick back in my sweats. "I need to run. I'm headed to the gym." It was a lie but I couldn't say, "Thanks for letting me jerk off to your fat pussy. Now I need to go check out wedding cakes with my fiancée."

"I'll be there to ride that horse next Wednesday. Make sure you're ready for all this." Nadine spread her pussy lips open so I could get a clear visual of her clit. "I hope you can back all this talk up. I can see the dick is big, but I hope you know how to use it."

I chuckled. "I'm going to fuck you so hard, you won't ever want to leave me."

She grinned. "You might be right."

I cut off the cam real quick before I started talking too much shit. I didn't want Nadine catching feelings. It was all about the Bugatti and once I tapped that ass, she could head back to Jamaica and never hear from my ass again.

I was a pitiful excuse for a man; I'll admit that. On the day Nadine arrived in New York, I was scheduled to go get a tuxedo fitting with my groomsmen. I told my best man and road dawg, Tony, to cover for me. If Lisa asked him how it went, he was all set to tell her that it went great and the fellas and I decided to go get some beers after the fitting, allowing me to stay out until bar closing time. In the Bronx, that could vary from one a.m. to all night. Matter of fact, Tony and the others did hang out that night, so I later discovered. They went to a new titty bar, though. I wasn't mad at them. If I didn't have a booty call waiting for me at the Marriott Marquis in Times Square, I would've been right up in there getting some lap dances my damn self.

Women never seem to understand why men go to strip clubs. It's simple. We can go in there with fifty ones and have a good time, have some titties rubbing up against our noses and some asses clapping in our faces, as opposed to going to a regular bar, looking at sports, and hoping some thirsty chick might suck you off in the men's room or out in the alley for a few minutes. I'm not complaining about getting head; you can get all that in a titty bar and then some, if you feel like shelling out that dough. No attachments, no pressure to hook up later, no drama.

But fuck all that. I was all about clapping Nadine's ass cheeks together my damn self while I rammed my billy into her thick, juicy pussy from the back. As I arrived at the hotel and waited for an elevator, I was hoping she had some lube with her and wouldn't mind some anal. Lisa wasn't even having that shit . . . never. I figured I might as well get all my fetishes out my system while my Internet jump-off was in the country.

Damn, you about to nail a chick from another country! I thought, as an elevator finally arrived that I could cram my six-foot-two frame into. I'd never seen a hotel with so many fucking elevators, and yet the average wait was at least five, ten minutes. This exotic-looking babe got on the elevator after me and we were forced to press up against each other because it was so crowded. She had skin the color of henna and these big, sexy-ass eyes. She looked like she was Liberian or Dominican or some shit.

She grinned at me over her shoulder and then, by the time we reached the tenth floor and stopped to let an elderly couple off, she was doing a reach around and feeling up my dick. She must've felt the mass on her ass and wanted to see if it was all me.

I whispered in her ear. "Big Wes 6969 at planetzane dot org."

She giggled and replied, "Liberian Girl 2010 at people dot net."

Shit, I knew she had that Liberian feel!

She got off at the next stop and now my dick was cramming my pants. I scanned the elevator to see if there was any other potential pussy on board. Naw, all the rest of the chicks looked like they lived in caves. I sighed and pulled some mint breath spray out of my pants pocket. After a couple of squirts, we were finally at my stop.

Nadine was in Room 2418; the number of times I intended

to stroke her pussy. I knocked and heard her heavy accent telling me to give her a second. I heard some heels clicking on the floor and then she opened the door, butt-ass naked except for a pair of six-inch stilettos.

I looked her up and down while she stood there with her hands on her hips, staring at the bulge in my pants.

"Nice shoes." I grabbed her by the throat and rammed my tongue in her mouth. She was all over me, trying to break some damn records yanking my clothes off.

I picked her up, walked over to the bed, and tossed her on it as she pulled my wife beater off. Then I lifted her legs in the air and spread them wide open.

"Damn, look at that fat pussy," I whispered.

"It's all for you, Daddy!"

I wasted no time digging right in. I was starving like Marvin.

Fifteen seconds in and Nadine's thighs were trembling like a contestant on *Fear Factor*. She had no idea what her ass was in for. I grabbed her left pussy lip into my mouth and sucked on it like a tit. She couldn't take it and tried to push me away.

"Hell no, you're not running from this," I informed her. "You've been teasing me with this pussy for months and now it's all mine. Lie back and let me eat my dinner." I slapped her on the ass. "Like a good girl."

Nadine was incoherent and managed to get out a moan while I went back to work. I stuck my tongue in her pussy and pushed it as far up inside her as I could. My tongue isn't a joke either; it's longer and thicker than normal. Women love it!

Now, all women have a different taste. Fuck what you heard. Pussy isn't sweet and it doesn't taste like chicken. A lot of chicks don't want to experiment and taste themselves so they get to lying about how sugary their juices taste. If a chick wants to know what her pussy really tastes like, she needs to swipe a finger over her armpits after a minor workout and lick it. That's what her pussy will taste like, nine times out of ten.

Nadine surprised me. She did taste better than most but, then again, as much as she finger-fucked herself for me on the webcam and sucked her fingers, she had probably decided to step up her game by eating a lot of sweets. I tore into my Bugatti like it was a slice of heaven and hoped my Lamborghini wouldn't try to track my ass down anytime soon.

I yanked a pillow off the head of the bed and told Nadine, "Turn over."

She was dazed and confused but managed to flip over as I placed the pillow under her stomach.

I grabbed her ass cheeks roughly and pushed her ass up as I climbed on the bed behind her. "You thought you were going to come over here to the States and pussy-whip me, didn't you? Opening the door naked like you were running things. I'm the king of this motherfucking castle."

"You're the king, Wes," Nadine blurted out as I buried my face in her ass and pussy.

Within seconds, she was bucking and catching a rhythm with me, pumping that pussy up at me. I grabbed her right ankle and lifted it up while I pressed my left leg against hers. Then I ate her ass good and she was creaming all over my tongue. She must have come three times before I stopped eating and decided to fuck her brains out.

I stood up while she tried to recover, and took off my pants and boxers. She looked over her shoulder. "Damn, it looks even bigger in person."

"You can handle this dick," I said. "You come from Jamaica and American women are always bragging on Jamaican dick."

She propped up on her elbow. "Hell no, that's a thing of beauty right there!"

"Don't call my dick beautiful." I turned her on her back and pushed the pillow up under her head. "Call it handsome."

Before she could respond, I was already fucking her face. I got on my knees, grabbed her head gently with both hands, and started feeding her all eleven inches. She gagged at first but she got the hang of it.

"That's right, Nadine. You came to see a man about a horse. Well, giddy up. Suck me dry. I know you want this dick."

"Um, hmm," she mumbled.

Now of course, I wasn't expecting her to devour my entire dick. Even if she'd had her tonsils removed, that shit wasn't happening, but she got enough of it in to please me. I took her hand and guided it onto my balls. She started squeezing them just right and I felt a nut building up.

"Where do you want me to shoot the first load?" I asked her.

I took the head of my dick out long enough for her to answer, "On my tits."

Now you're probably wondering why I never mentioned Nadine's titties. She had a fat ass and a hefty pussy but her tits were barely more than nipples. Still, if that was where she wanted my cream, there it was going to go.

I stuck my dick back in her mouth and a few minutes later, I announced, "I'm cumming!"

There's an unwritten code that a man should announce when he's about to bust a nut. No one ever told us that but if you watch enough pornos, it just catches on. Plus, it gives chicks a warning so they can figure out where they want it. Some swallow, some spit. Some want it on their tits, others on their ass. Some want to hold it in their mouths and snowball. Fuck if I'm down with that nasty shit, though.

I pulled out and let it rip all over Nadine's chest and she rubbed it in like cocoa butter. *Well, so much for me licking over that part of her body*, I thought. *I'm hitting her shit from the back!*

I told Nadine to suck me hard and then I turned her over yet again. I was orchestrating our fuck session like a director at a Broadway play. I had her push up on her palms while I lifted my left knee and pulled her leg over my thigh so it could bend behind my back and then I nailed her.

She screamed when I rammed my shit all up in her pussy and then froze, like I was trying to feel her uterus. I had impaled her ass. I held her there for a moment, her leg suspended in air, giving her a chance to get used to my size. Then I commenced to delivering those 2,418 strokes at varying speeds. A little more than halfway through, around 1,276, Nadine couldn't take it anymore and collapsed on the bed and just relinquished the pussy to me. I pounded her ass to sleep. I decided to give her a break on the anal action. I didn't want the front desk to have to call an ambulance for her ass, and I do mean "ass" literally.

Nadine returned to Jamaica a very happy woman and I married Lisa the following month. Our parents, relatives, and friends doted all over her on our special day and it was all good. We honeymooned in Canada and fucked day and night for ten days straight; we didn't give a damn about sightseeing.

Winter flooded into New York and it was cold as a mug outside. Lisa and I went to see the lighting of the Christmas tree at Rockefeller Center and then went home to cuddle up for the night.

I couldn't sleep and went into my home office to browse the Internet. I had grown bored with looking at Nadine play with herself and cut her ass off. I had conquered the pussy; moving on. Much to my surprise, there was an email from the Liberian chick from the elevator that day. I had forgotten all about her.

What's up, Big Wes? I was wondering if you wanted to hook up. I've been fantasizing about that humongous dick I felt through your pants that day on the elevator. I want to get up close and personal with it, if you feel me?

I licked my lips and pondered. I had the Lamborghini in my bed, wearing my ring, and the Bugatti had served its purpose.

I started typing.

Hey you, with your sexy Liberian ass. I want you to meet me tomorrow, the same place we first laid eyes on each other. Room 2418, if I can get it. I want you to come see a man about a horse.

"Fuck it," I said as I hit SEND. "I've never had a McLaren F1. Now that's some exotic shit right there!"

Dick Tease

Allison Hobbs

Three times a week, I wake to the rich aroma of coffee, and other pleasurable sensations. Today, my senses are further aroused by the determinedly firm grasp of a woman's hand. Wrapped around my shaft, her palm feels like a velvet glove.

"Good morning," Marcelle greets me, bringing me into sharp awareness. With her dark skin, her exotically slanted eyes, and silky lashes, my housekeeper, Marcelle, is a rare beauty. Her full, sensual lips are painted bright red. They entice me, and send my imagination into overdrive as I picture the ring of her lipstick stain encircling the base of my hard-on.

My shaft lengthens and thickens inside her satin clutch. Involuntarily, I begin to thrust.

"It's so big . . . and powerful," she utters, staring provocatively at my dick. Her grip tightens, providing perfect friction.

My face contorts as I forcibly shove a raging erection in and out of her closed fist. It is possible that the early-morning hand job she's giving me might be the only way for me to get off. I struggle to reach the finish line. At any moment, Marcelle might decide that exercising her wrist is too much work.

As expected, she announces her boredom with a long, dramatic yawn. She releases my erection and covers her mouth, muffling the sound.

"Don't stop," I say in a gruff whisper. She's such a dick tease, and her antics distress me. Prompting her to continue, I hump the empty air. But Marcelle is a willful woman, and I realize I can't coerce her into doing anything she doesn't want to do.

"I have something else for you," the dick tease says, wearing a taunting smile.

Marcelle lifts her billowy white dress and straddles me. Her thighs press against mine. Her skin is soft and luxurious—heavenly. It's hard to keep my hands to myself, but I have to. She'll let me know when the time is right to indulge my cravings.

Slowly, tauntingly, she unbuttons the top of her dress. She cups cocoa-colored breasts. Fondling her perfect mounds, she entices me. Bending forward, squeezing her breasts together, she offers her chocolate peaks. "Suck," she tells me.

My lips pucker around the dimpled flesh. My tongue whisks against one dark bud and then the other. She loves nipple play; she has orgasms when I tug her nipple with my lips while lathering it with my tongue.

The smell of her . . . the texture of her skin is intoxicating. My dick swells to an enormous size, and I moan from a mixture of pleasure and pain.

I'm ready to fuck. I want to lodge my hardness deep inside her. But she won't let me. I have to wait for her command. I cater to Marcelle's every sexual whim, and I love pleasing her. At times like this, it's difficult to concentrate. I so desperately want to mount her, and stuff my dick inside her teasing pussy.

She slowly extracts her nipples from my mouth. Unhappy, I make a whining sound.

Feeling deprived, my lips remain parted . . . openly yearning for more licking and sucking. But most of all, I want to fuck her.

Her long, sepia fingers travel to her panties. Working at the side of the crotch, she pulls the elastic aside, exposing a forest of pitch-black hair. I wait for permission to bury my face inside the darkness.

She clasps my dick, guiding my bulging erection between her legs.

Her pussy emanates heat; it warms the head of my dick. I grimace as I wantonly plunge into scalding juices.

"I'm not ready," she says breathlessly and pulls away.

"Don't tease me, please," I say in a tone that begs. "You're torturing me."

Marcelle responds with a wicked smile. She scratches a trail down my chest, causing me to wince as her fingernails cut into my skin.

I endure the pain because I want to fuck her. Trying to get into her panties, I attempt a different approach. "Take your dress off," I cajole. "Let me see your naked beauty."

An exhibitionist, she complies. She slips out of her dress and panties, and tosses them to a nearby chair. In all her naked glory, she once again straddles me. We're both naked now; her dark sienna skin against warm brown.

She reaches downward and separates her folds, proudly showing off a gash of soft flesh that glistens with arousal.

Yearning to taste her, my mouth waters.

"Hungry?" she asks.

"Starving," I murmur in the voice of a haunted man.

Marcelle inches forward and places her pussy on my eager lips. Grasping the headboard, she makes her hips swivel. I inhale her musky, womanly scent. I taste her pungent cream. My tongue becomes overactive, stretching, undulating, greedily eating all the pussy that I can get.

She lifts up, repossessing her pussy while giving me a disapproving look. She shakes her head. "What am I going to do with you? Where are your manners?" Tsking, she wags a finger.

Contrite, I look away.

Marcelle glances down at her watch. "I have tons of housework."

"Can I help you with your chores?" I ask desperately. I'll do whatever it takes to stay close to my housekeeper.

"No. You know the rules. You're confined to this room. Stay put," she warns and narrows an eye at me.

I sit upright and reach for her. "I don't want you to leave." I'm choked with emotion.

Leaning away, she smiles as she eludes me. "I have to get started." Marcelle gets out of bed. Tall and stately, she towers over me as I sit on the bed.

I want to appear somewhat cheerful, but I can't change my sorrowful expression. Giving me an exasperated look, she crooks her finger. "All right, you can have a quick suck."

Grateful, I scurry to the edge of the bed. She steps forward, allowing me to encircle her thighs and firm buttocks with my arms. Lowering my head, my puckered lips fasten onto her erect clit. It soothes me like a pacifier. I moan with appreciation as I suck her elongated clit.

She taps the top of my head. "That's enough," she says and backs away.

Left with a hard, pulsing dick, I dejectedly cup the sides of my face with my hands and watch my dick-teasing housekeeper disappear through the door. There are consequences for violating Marcelle's rules, and so I sit still for a while. Then, like a disobedient puppy, I sneak down the stairs, following behind her.

I can hear Miles Davis playing in the background. Marcelle

enjoys listening to music while going about her chores. My careful steps are concealed by Miles's screaming trumpet.

I creep about, spying on her, taking notice that she's no longer naked and is now dressed in her housekeeper's uniform.

Stroking my raging erection, I play voyeur as she pours herself a cup of coffee, and then sits at the kitchen table, perusing a fashion magazine. Her foot pats to the jazz rhythms that blare. She's often told me that music stimulates her; gets her in the mood to dust, mop, and clean.

There's a hard knock on the back door. I pay keen attention as Marcelle admits a strapping delivery guy. He's hefting a five-gallon water bottle upon each shoulder, moving effortlessly, as if the heavy bottles are as light as feathers.

Skulking in the shadows, I watch her interact with the deliveryman. It pains me to see how flirtatious she is with him, and how overly familiar he behaves in her presence. *How long have they known each other?* I wonder. Judging from the sensual way that she moistens her lips with her tongue and the way that his eyes undress her, I get the distinct impression that these two have something going on.

Jealousy burns my face. My heart is thumping as loud as the drumbeats that boom from the speakers.

The water bottles have been set near the pantry door. The delivery is complete, so why doesn't Marcelle send the arrogant brute on his way? It takes all my restraint not to burst from my hiding place and eject the blue-collar oaf from my elegant home.

I hold back a gasp when Marcelle slips into his arms. She kisses him with a lustful urgency that I wish were reserved for me. A murderous rage overcomes me. I want to shoot them both. Anguished, I fall to my knees. Though consumed with pain, I have to conceal my presence.

I've taken a great risk in defying Marcelle. The woman has a spiteful temper. If she discovered that I've been stealthily moving about and snooping on her, I'm sure that she'd slap my face and curse me out. Even worse, she might give me her notice, and that would be tragic. I don't know if I could recover if Marcelle quit her housekeeping position due to my rebelliousness.

Losing Marcelle would bring unimaginable anguish, and so I become still and quiet as I clandestinely observe her unzipping the water deliveryman's pants. He closes his eyes, throws back his head, and moans as Marcelle gropes inside his fly.

With a hand stuck inside his briefs, she struggles and wrestles as if trying to capture a vicious reptile. With a triumphant expression, she brings out a monstrously large penis. She imprisons the deliveryman's enormous dick inside both of her hands, giving it a double-handed stroke that is unlike anything she's ever done to me.

My face flushes with envy. My dick throbs with desire. I give it a comforting caress . . . a consoling squeeze.

A delighted squeal escapes Marcelle's lips, drawing my attention away from my pulsing erection. Squinting, I focus on the activities in the kitchen. The deliveryman is lifting Marcelle in his arms. His muscles bulge as he crosses the room. I watch with resentment as he gently places her on the granite counter.

I should be sequestered in my bedroom, and not nosing around in Marcelle's personal affairs, but I can't help myself. I'm obsessed with her. Consumed by lust.

I rise to my feet, determined to be the well-trained and obedient employer that I've promised to be. Before I can slip away, I notice that Marcelle is offering her swollen breasts to the deliveryman. She's a shameless hussy. How could she present him with the same treats that only a short while ago, she shared with me?

It's shocking, the way this beast of a man is ravishing her tender breasts. Lashing them with an angry tongue . . . nipping, biting in a savage manner.

And Marcelle seems to love it. She's writhing and moaning. Coaxing him to bite her nipples. Demanding that he suck harder. Now she's speaking softly, whispering in his ear. She lifts her uniform, welcoming him between her legs.

Marcelle has always enjoyed the flirtatious advances of men; still, I never expected her to take it this far. I shake my head regretfully as it dawns on me that every man that enters my home—service workers, business associates—has enjoyed the pleasure of my maid.

I've done everything to keep her happy. I bow down to her and worship at her feet. For her to fuck another man in my home, right under my nose, is unconscionable. Her deceit is unforgivable. We had an agreement that as long as I obeyed her, she would eventually allow me to fuck her. But she's nothing more than a dick tease; she never intended to make good on her promise.

I gaze with contempt in my eyes as a stranger sticks an unworthy dick inside her, impaling her with a violent thrust.

It's cruel. Unfair. I can hardly bear to watch, but I'm morbidly fascinated. The deliveryman is ramming Marcelle, pulling her close and pounding her possessively, asking if her pussy belongs to him.

I'm incensed, yet my dick betrays me; it stiffens when I hear Marcelle murmur, "This pussy is all yours, baby."

I can no longer witness this atrocity. With my head hung in

sorrow, I turn away and woefully climb the stairs. Back in my position on the bed, it is clear to me that I've allowed Marcelle to play me for a fool.

When Marcelle finally returns to the bedroom, her uniform is crumpled and her hair is tousled. A taunting smile curves the corners of her mouth. "I'm tired from cleaning." She stretches out on the bed. Lying on her back, she places her hand on her head, feigning exhaustion.

I'm appalled. She reeks of sex. She's covered with the masculine sweat of a brawny laborer. Sad as it may seem, I still want to put my dick inside her. I yearn to penetrate her whoring pussy, and so I have no choice but to go along with the ruse.

"I'm so tired. I need a back rub, darling," she tells me, pretending to be frazzled from hard work. I know what she's really been up to, but I can't divulge the fact that I've violated her rules.

She comes out of her uniform and lies on her tummy. I'm relieved that her lovely back has not been defiled with that man's sweaty stench.

Adoringly, I caress her skin, rubbing gently, kneading the imaginary knots. All the while, I'm secretly hoping that I've finally earned the right to penetrate her pussy.

"Feels good," she says, enjoying my touch. I smile with pride.

"That's enough foreplay," she says suddenly. Without warning, she gets on her hands and knees. "You've been a very good boy. You deserve a reward. Fuck me," she orders.

Delighted, I oblige. I grab her hips before she can change her mind. Frantic, I quickly slip my knob inside her slit. Her pussy is overly wet and juicy. It feels as if I've plunged into a wonderfully slimy abyss.

"Like it?" she murmurs as I deliver dick strokes into a pussy that's saturated with a combination of female juices and masculine cum.

"Love it," I respond breathily, steadily stroking through the pool of lust.

"Was this pussy worth waiting for?"

"Yes," I honestly admit. The pussy that the deliveryman has prepped for me is the best I've ever had.

The CD is playing a live John Coltrane session. While Marcelle lounges, sipping champagne, and eating chocolate-covered strawberries, her foot wiggles to the sound of Coltrane's saxophone.

I cheerfully don her work uniform and do housework with a smile on my face. After I finish dusting, I carefully close the parlor door. I don't want to disturb my mistress with the roar of a vacuum cleaner.

A noise from outside distracts me. Peeking through the curtains, I see that the grocery van has arrived.

Another delivery; I smile.

Unashamedly wearing Marcelle's uniform, I open the back door and admit yet another muscular man.

I knock on the door to the parlor. Marcelle tells me to come in.

"Mistress, there's a deliveryman in the kitchen."

"Did you tip him?" Her eyes glimmer with interest.

"No, not yet."

Marcelle waves her hand dismissively. "I'll handle it; send him to me." She points a manicured finger at me. "I expect to have privacy while I'm taking care of the tip."

"Yes, ma'am," I agree. "I'll be fully absorbed in my chores."

"Good boy," she says with a brisk nod.

My maid and I have a better understanding now. No longer a dick tease, she lets me have sloppy seconds three days a week.

Through the cotton fabric of Marcelle's uniform, I stroke my dick in anticipation. After the grocery man finishes making his delivery, Marcelle will graciously spread her legs for me.

Meat Me

Lynn Lake

She pushed open the wooden door with the cracked pane of glass and walked into the dingy shop. Inside, pornographic DVDs, magazines, and books were stacked three wire racks deep; sex toys and dolls of all makes and models lined the walls. The place smelled of stale cigarette smoke and spunk.

The woman strolled around the racks and past the glass counter full of lighters, rolling papers, pipes, and dildos that ran along the far wall. She was tall and slender, in her mid-forties, dressed in a dark-blue business suit, slim legs sheathed in metallic blue stockings that spilled out of her knee-length skirt and into three-inch black heels. Her raven hair was carefully done up; her light-brown, aristocratic face tastefully made up with blue eye shadow and black eyeliner; plush lips glossed to glistening.

"Hiya!" the man behind the counter said, leering; a little guy, pitch-black, with horn-rimmed glasses and a shaved skull. "They're waitin' for ya."

She slowed momentarily when he spoke, then coolly nodded and walked past, through the red velvet curtain that cordoned off the video and peep show booths from the rest of the store.

"Bitch!" the man swore under his breath, balling his little fists. He watched the woman's trim buttocks shudder from side to side under her tight skirt as they and she disappeared behind the curtain.

The smell of spunk was stronger in back, the raucous moaning and groaning of video porn stars and live peep show performers rising and falling in rhythm to the heated slap of flesh against flesh, both on-screen and in-person. The woman's heels clicked briskly along the tile corridor, past the booths and through the swinging door at the end of the hall.

There were three stalls inside the "washroom"; the green metal doors of two of them closed, the middle one hanging open. She didn't hesitate, entering the middle stall and then closing and securing the door.

There was a padded stool on wheels where the toilet should've been; a roll of paper towels where toilet paper normally hung. Two holes had been cut into the side panels of the stall almost dead center, five inches in diameter and foam-padded around the edges. The woman sat down on the stool and crossed her legs and waited, ice-green eyes flicking back and forth between the holes.

A cock suddenly speared through the hole to her right; a fully-erect cock, vein-striped shaft and mushroomed cap shining licorice-black under the stuttering fluorescent lights; pube-pebbled balls crowding the bottom of the opening. A tight smile flashed across the woman's lips.

She appraised the cock at eight inches long and five inches in circumference. Years of experience had honed her measurement skills. She made no move toward the twitching dong, however; waiting, watching the other hole.

A cock thrust through that opening as well. A pink-shafted, purple-headed, vein-ribboned cock, as clean-cut as the other, but jutting slightly upward like a fleshy horn. She appraised this one at nine inches in length, six inches in circumference. She allowed herself another brief smile, eyes darting from one huge, disembodied cock to the other.

Then she stood up and removed her jacket, her white satin blouse, and bra. Her large, brown, mocha-tipped breasts spilled out and swayed as she slipped off her skirt and panties. Naked now except for her nylon stockings and patent leather high heels, she carefully placed the tailored outer garments and silken undergarments on the floor in a corner. Her body was tight and streamlined, belying her age, her pussy shaved clean for maximum sensation, flaps shining and aroused.

She sat back down on the stool and pushed herself forward, grasping the two straining cocks in her manicured hands. Groans erupted from behind the panels as she clutched, felt, weighed the pair of pulsing erections, lightly stroking for texture and firmness. The one in her right hand was smoother and straighter; the one in her left longer, heavier, and thicker. They both pushed urgently at her hands, their throbbing traveling right through her down to her pussy.

She held the pink one and stroked the black one, swirling her soft, warm, brown hand up and down the pulsating length of the impressive dong, around and about the bloated blue-black cap. The cock jumped in her pumping hand, swelling higher and harder. She stared as she stroked, eyes locked and unblinking, hand and fingers deftly tugging and caressing while she held tight to the other big penis.

The grunts and groans behind the right panel became more animated, the wall shaking as she stroked harder, faster, really pulling on the vibrating cock. Her hand flew up and down the raging length of shaft, up and over the glans-split hood.

Perspiration dappled her forehead and upper lip, her tits

shuddering with every heated stroke, her body flushed and pussy sopping. She could feel the dong seize up iron-hard, and she gasped when a pearl of pre-cum surged into the gaping slit at the head of the pipe. She thrust her own head closer and flicked out her tongue, snatching the drop into her mouth.

The panel shook with the weight of the body behind it. The woman engulfed the leaking cockhead with her warm, wet mouth, then the shaft, easily and expertly consuming the cock, her cheeks puffing out and her throat widening to accommodate the enormous erection.

Until her nose pressed right against the partition, lips kissing her hand still gripping the base, mouth and throat packed full of cock. The owner of the dong yelled, "Fuck!" The other cock jumped in her hand, desperate to know what was going on.

She kept the tremendous member locked down in her mouth and throat for ten torrid seconds; hot, humid breath steaming out of her flared nostrils and dewing the green metal. Finally, slowly, she pulled her head back, the dripping shaft oozing out of her mouth until she clung to just the meaty cap with her teeth.

Then she pushed her head forward again, swallowing the over-engorged cock, breathing deep of the musky scent of the tightened balls, feeling the blazing appendage beat all through her trembling body.

"Fuck, I'm gonna come!"

She pulled on the dong a couple more times with her lips and mouth, taking it to the back of her throat and beyond, bathing the sensitive underside with her tongue. She jerked her head all the way back so that the ebony snake popped right out of her mouth and hung there, gleaming and twitching and ready to burst.

She grabbed on to it, sliding closer, pointing the throbbing tool at her bared chest and fisting. An agonized groan, and semen dribbled out of the slit in the well-formed hood, then sprayed. Six bursts of hot, sticky spunk splashed against her chest, showering her tits. Her hand milked the jerking cock, her pussy shimmering with the shooting sensation and the wicked feel of the heated semen on her tingling skin.

It was over in less than ten seconds. She dropped the spent dong and pivoted around to face the other cock, which she had never let go of.

She grasped it now with her other hand as well, and pumped it with both, softly and lightly, then harder and tighter. She reveled in the bumpy texture of the shaft, the incredible curving length of the cock. She tugged so hard that blond-fuzzed balls spilled out of the hole, which she briefly cupped and squeezed.

Then she stood up, sent the stool careening into the wall. Holding the up-thrust prong around its thick, furry base, she backed up to it, long legs slightly parted and back slightly bent, sticking the swollen hood into her moist pussy lips from behind.

Fingernails scraped against metal on the other side as she brushed the purple cockhead against her pussy lips, washing it in her hot juices, before popping it right into her pussy and recklessly pushing back until her taut buttocks touched the panel, embedding the turgid dong inside her.

She finally unhanded the prick at that point, grabbing up her sperm-slick tits and squeezing them, pinching her rigid nipples. Her butt cheeks were pressed almost flat against the partition, the long, hard, thick cock filling her cunt. Gritting her teeth, she rocked back and forth on her high heels, impaling herself on the pole.

The heated grunts and groans from behind the metal barrier

mingled and melded with the woman's own breathless gasps and moans as she rocked faster, fucked herself more urgently; the cock thrusting back now, matching her rhythm.

Her buttocks smacked briskly against the partition, the stall shaking, the mammoth cock sluicing back and forth in her sucking pussy, swelling her twat and bum and body with shimmering heat. She felt the churning member stiffen still further inside her, heard the cry of "Here it comes!" Felt the scalding splash of spraying semen—dousing her pussy.

The wildly thrusting cock pumped her full seven times.

But she didn't come herself.

She still had a number of swingers clubs and dogging sites and filthy back alleys to visit that evening—promising even longer, thicker, more massive cocks.

The man leered when she answered the doorbell. "Bit of a size queen, huh?"

He was a little guy, pitch-black, with horn-rimmed glasses and a shaved skull. She regarded him coldly. "Who are you?"

He snorted. "Don't even see me, huh? Got your mind on big dicks all the time." He tried to step inside, but she blocked the doorway, tall and slender and cool in her sky-blue stockings, wraparound cobalt-blue skirt, and pearl-white satin blouse. "I'm the guy from Brownbaggers—the guy behind the counter. You know, the place with the glory holes—"

"What do you want?"

He smirked. "It's not what I want, baby. It's what you want."

She started to close the door.

And he shoved his sweatpants down, exposing a deep-black cock that dangled five inches long, unerect from a thicket of dark pubes.

Her ice-green eyes locked on the slab of meat, and her hand tightened on the doorknob.

"Twelve inches, if you treat it right, baby," he oozed.

Like the rest of the spacious house, her bedroom was done up in subdued shades of silver and blue, elegant and tasteful, if somewhat cold. She dropped to her stockinged knees in the shag and dug her glossed fingernails into the elastic waistband of the man's pants.

He grinned down at her as she pulled down his sweatpants and grasped his cock. "Yeah, that's the way!" he grunted. "That's what pretty mama wants."

She lifted the heavy, hanging piece of meat, then stroked the smooth, shifting foreskin, anxious to grow the dong as long as the man had promised. It would be longer than she'd ever had before, in all her years of searching and stroking and sucking and fucking.

"You got a pretty fancy place here, Vanessa," he said, glancing around and licking his lips. "Guess you ain't out chasing dick *all* the time, huh?"

His voice grated annoyingly in her ears.

But his cock *was* growing in her soft, damp, caressing hand, stiffening, thickening, lengthening, rising up like a hooded cobra rises up out of its wicker basket when its master plays the proper tune. She grabbed on to it with her other hand, pulled with the pair, watching the darker head swell out of the dark foreskin, the huge, dangling, black sack tighten.

"Name's Leonard, by the way."

It was almost parallel with her parted lips now, throbbing hotly in her tugging hands at ten inches long and seven inches around, and still growing, swelling obscenely and sizing up between the little man's loins. Right before Vanessa's fixated eyes.

"Name's Leonard, I said!" He snatched his cock out of her grasping hands and took a step back, then furiously fisted the final two inches himself.

Then he stepped forward again, and held the mammoth appendage over the kneeling woman's flushed face like a club. He slapped her cheek with his cock, the other cheek. "Notice little 'ol Leonard now, huh, bitch!?" he growled, smacking her forehead and nose and mouth with his meat.

She closed her eyes and stuck out her tongue, and he spanked her moist, pink, budded tongue with his thunder cock. Then he jammed the mushroomed hood into her mouth, pulled it out again before she could seal her glossy lips around it.

"Think you can handle this much cock, Vanessa!?" he snarled. "Even you ain't never had this much cock before, have ya, Vanessa?"

She clutched the taunting man's skinny buttocks and flung her mouth open as wide as it would go. He wagged his dong over her mouth, keeping her in quivering suspense. Finally he grabbed the back of her head and shoved his cock right into her maw.

He grunted at the wet-hot impact, and she gagged, just a little, as he sank his entire foot-long slab into her mouth and down her throat. He pulled her head forward and thrust his hips out, stuffing his whole suffocating cock inside her.

"Motherfucker!" he marveled, staring down at the woman's glowing face, her lips kissing up against his balls, his cock gone, disappeared inside her mouth.

Her cheeks bulged outrageously and her throat stretched obscenely. Her body burned and head spun with all that solid rod locked down in her mouth. Hot, triumphant puffs of breath blew out of her flared nostrils, her pussy gone sodden in her panties.

"You *are* a fuckin' snake charmer!" Leonard rasped, sweat sheening his face. He grabbed her head on either side and pumped his hips, surging his cock back and forth in her mouth.

She clung to his clenching buttocks, rocked to and fro on her knees by the man's massive dong plunging her throat and pistoning her mouth. She stared up at him, urging him on with her watering eyes. Snot bubbled inelegantly out of her nose and streamed down onto his shifting shaft. His dirty fingers dug into her soft hair, pulling the carefully coiffed, silken strands apart, sawing away at her bouncing head.

Until, at last, he pulled out of her mouth and throat and staggered backward, humongous cock glistening and bobbing. "Want it in your pussy, bitch!?" he gasped, wiping sweat off his face.

She jumped to her feet and tore away her skirt; skinned off her panties. Then she ripped her blouse and bra open and flung the garments aside. Standing there naked before him and his monster cock, she was four inches taller than him even in her stockinged feet.

He gaped at her well-preserved, caramel-colored body, her large, hard-nippled breasts. "Want me to stick this thing in your pussy and split you in two, huh?" he said, regaining some of his composure, waggling his prick at her.

She fell back on her bed and spread her legs, cupping and squeezing her splayed breasts. He didn't bother stripping off his pants or his T-shirt, crawling between her long legs and slapping her shaven mound with his dong.

She winced with pleasure as he smacked her pussy and clit

with his heavy cock. Finally, he brutally shoved his boiled-up hood through her gleaming pussy lips and plowed his cock into her cunt.

She moaned, clutching her tits and holding her breath, deeply, soulfully feeling inch after swollen inch of meat slide in and in and into her pussy. Soon he was sprawled on top of her, huffing and puffing between her breasts, his club of a cock buried to the hilt in her stretched-out cunt. She rolled her head back and forth on the pillow, reveling in the wicked, burning, full sensation of having that much cock wedged and beating inside her.

"You—you like it, huh, baby!?" he wheezed in her face, grabbing on to her tits and roughly squeezing.

She dug her nails into his buttocks, spurring him on.

He drew back, pushed forward, pumping her hot, wet, gripping snatch with his huge prick. Again and again and again. Faster and faster.

"Mmmm!" she moaned, her eyelids fluttering.

He sucked on a nipple, the other one, groping her boobs and churning his hips, relentlessly pounding her pussy with his battering-ram cock.

They bounced up and down on the bed, the hard-breathing man fucking the gasping woman as hard and as fast as he could. Vanessa clenched her teeth and set her lips in a grim line, absorbing the thundering cock, body and soul. Leonard strained and thrust to meet her massive need.

"Up the ass! I'm gonna fuck you up the ass!" he cried, his balls boiling with imminent release.

"Yes!" Vanessa hissed, blind to the man, full of his cock.

He tumbled over to the side, drawing his dripping pipe

with him. She rolled over onto her stomach, reaching back and smearing dripping pussy juice between her butt cheeks.

Leonard sucked humid air into his billowing lungs and mounted her again from behind. Sweat poured off his contorted face and onto the silken skin of her gracefully curved back. He prodded his bloated cockhead between her mounded buttocks, found her bumhole, and pressed in.

She instantly pushed her butt up and back, enveloping the enormous tip of his cock with her anus. He fell on top of her, his wrist-thick shaft delving deep into her chute.

"Motherfucker! You never had it like this before, huh, baby!?" he gritted into her ear, moving his hips up and down, cock back and forth in her ass. "You never had it so good, huh, bitch!?"

She bit into the pillow and pounded the mattress with her fists, the man reaming her chute with his giant cock, blowing her ass apart. The bed and her body bounced in rhythm to his frantic thrusts, her raw moans sounding even above the tortured creak of the bedsprings.

He slammed against her shuddering cheeks again and again, ruthlessly plundering her ass with his cock. "Fuck, baby!" he screamed. "You can't take me no more! I'm gonna come!"

He spasmed. And his cock exploded in her bum, dousing her chute with heated semen.

She felt the searing spray of cum against her bowels five times; the man's sawing, shooting cock filling her to bursting.

But she didn't come herself.

They briefly lay together afterward, Leonard's flaccid dong spooning between Vanessa's legs.

"You think you got 'room' for me here?" He laughed, kissing

the soft skin of her long, slender neck. "Now that you know who I am?"

"Get out," Vanessa responded, shocking the presumptuous little big man right down to his softened penis.

She still had a number of bathhouses, escort agencies, and strip clubs to visit that evening. Because for her, bigger wasn't better; it was only the beginning.

Choices

Tenille Brown

Adrienne was nervous, although she knew she had no reason to be. It wasn't like she had a problem eating alone, but eating alone hadn't been the plan.

Adrienne was a woman who worked hard and liked treating herself and, tonight, she had planned on treating herself to an orgasm. That was nothing out of the ordinary, but how she had come to this point—well, *that* was new.

His name was Darrell and she met him on some website where you posted your pictures and talked all day about what you were doing, what you were wearing, and whatnot.

One day he flirted, and Adrienne bit.

Sure, the social networking thing was a new venture, and maybe she should have thought twice about it, but she had been careful.

There had been an entire two months of exchanges between them. Two months of chatting, emailing, and talking on the phone. Two months of sexting and sending each other naughty pictures. And eventually, there was phone sex at one in the morning.

Adrienne thought they were clear on what they both wanted.

She knew *she* was.

But now, sitting alone at the table in a far corner of the room, she tried to remember if anything she had said or done had led

Darrell to believe she wanted more; if she had somehow exuded desperation when she thought she was being coy and flirty.

Adrienne looked around the dimly lit restaurant. She was beyond restless. And the waiting was breaking down her confidence minute by minute.

Couples came in and went out as Adrienne sat there, waiting.

And maybe it was the waiting, the posing with her clasped hands propped beneath her chin, the polite smile and subsequent "no" every time the waiter came by to ask if she wanted to go ahead and order, that made her so aware of her solitude.

She'd given Darrell a thirty-minute grace period because, after all, she was a little early herself. But at nine-fifteen, a full hour and a half after their agreed meeting time, Adrienne was fed up.

She was looking around her and eyeing the door, trying to plot a graceful, yet subtle exit; something hard to do in a crowded restaurant, dimly lit or not.

And there was also the matter of the vacant room upstairs.

When she had gone up to take a look at it earlier, it was every bit what she had imagined it would be—a king-sized bed, a whirlpool in the center of the room with enough room for two, a balcony with a view of the city.

There was expensive champagne in a bucket full of ice with a flute on either side—her added touch. And lavender-scented spray on the crisp white sheets—her touch as well.

Now Adrienne cursed herself for having been so forward, for assuming things were going to go so well between her and Darrell that the natural progression would be to hightail it upstairs to a room rented for the night. Even though they had discussed it prior. They had talked thoroughly about how Adrienne would be all kinds of naughty for him and Darrell would worship her body until she could no longer stand it.

Maybe Adrienne had scared him off.

Maybe Darrell really wasn't used to a woman so forward, even though he had given her the impression that he was. He had said he liked a woman who knew what she wanted and wasn't afraid to go for it.

And go for it Adrienne did, dropping nearly three hundred dollars on a suite in a posh Chicago hotel.

The entire thing was making a mockery of her now.

Her hair was extra curly and flowing right past her shoulders; all the bullshit magazines she had been reading said the look was romantic. She wore a purple dress with thin straps that clung to her curvy body and stopped directly above her knees. High heels finished the look, strappy and colorful; the best accessory she was wearing and Darrell wouldn't even get to see it.

I can stay here alone, Adrienne thought. *I could order up a bottle of wine and a dirty pay-per-view movie. If nothing else, I could take care of myself and call it a night.*

But the more she thought about it, the more pathetic it seemed; even more pathetic than meeting a man on the Internet and agreeing to meet him for dinner, drinks, and fucking.

What had she been thinking?

Fed up, Adrienne signaled the waiter and ordered a dirty martini, extra dry.

He nodded.

She drank it quickly and was thankful for the rush it gave her.

She pulled out her wallet to pay, but the young man held up his hand, shook his head, and pointed to the left where a dark-skinned man in a dark-gray suit was sitting at the bar.

Adrienne was prepared to nod her appreciation when he turned around in his chair, but she was taken aback by his familiar face.

Leroy!

And he was drinking his favorite drink; scotch and ginger ale.

He hadn't changed a bit.

He came over, just as Adrienne knew he would.

"Waiting for someone?" Leroy asked, though Adrienne was pretty sure he had been watching her the entire time and had figured out her story from the way she sat tapping her foot and throwing quick glances at the door.

But Adrienne humored him and said, "I was."

"No show?"

"Something came up," Adrienne said quickly.

"I see," Leroy said, though Adrienne was convinced he didn't believe it.

He was straightening the collar of his jacket, smoothing his thick sideburns that Adrienne noticed had started to gray.

It looked good on him.

When had she seen him last?

Two years ago? Three?

Yes, it was shortly after the divorce; they were both still pissed about it all and avoided each other at all costs.

"So, you're leaving?" Leroy asked.

Adrienne reached for her purse. "That's right."

"Not hungry anymore?"

She could smell his cologne. "Not really."

And suddenly Adrienne was even more pissed that the whole thing had taken such a toll on her, that she actually had lost her appetite and was considering going home and sitting in front of the television with a bowl of ice cream on her lap.

So, just like that, Adrienne changed her mind.

"You know what? I think I will have a bite, after all."

She set down her purse and picked up her menu while Leroy took the seat across from her.

Adrienne scanned the list of entrees. If Darrell had shown up, she would have ordered a salad, but this was Leroy. She had no reason to impress him, so she got what she wanted.

Chicken Marsala for her, stuffed flounder for him.

Halfway through the meal, Adrienne felt Leroy's leg brush lightly against hers under the table.

Was he getting fresh with her?

She let it slide.

"You look good," Leroy said, leaning back in his seat. His brown eyes were bright with sincerity.

Adrienne smiled slightly. "Thank you."

"He sure missed out."

"I appreciate that."

It felt nice to relax, to stop caring whether her new hairstyle was still intact or her perfume had worn off.

It was nice to put her elbows on the table and answer texts and emails while she ate her chicken, and to burp without saying, "Excuse me."

After all, it was just Leroy. They had been married eight years and he had seen her at her worst. And it was funny how some things with Leroy were still a natural reflex for her, like handing him a napkin and telling him he had crumbs in his beard. How she ordered water for him because he never seemed to remember that scotch wasn't a good thing to chase your food with.

His food half-eaten, Leroy asked, "Was dinner all you had planned, or was there something else?"

He had that shit-eating grin on his face like he already knew the answer.

Adrienne didn't want to give him the satisfaction. "No, there was nothing else."

Leroy looked her up and down then, from her come-fuck-me heels to her cleavage-baring fuck-me dress. He knew. He had to know.

Adrienne was serving pussy on a platter tonight and it was obvious.

"I'm merely saying, if there was something else on the agenda, like bowling or miniature golf, I've got some time on my hands."

No, it had been neither, but she had intended to show her athletic ability tonight, and it was a shame that it wasn't going to happen now.

The quick shifting of her eyes gave Adrienne away.

Leroy crossed his arms over his chest. "What? Were ya'll going to his place or yours?"

"Fuck you, Leroy."

"So, you were going to get a room?" Leroy was on a roll now.

"Fuck you, Leroy."

Leroy leaned forward and whispered, "I could rent a room, you know, with a view."

Adrienne sucked her teeth. "You're too damn cheap for that. You forget I know you, Leroy."

If Adrienne didn't know better, she'd say that Leroy had planned the entire thing to make her look bad, but it was hard to believe that even he would stoop that low.

Adrienne dabbed at the corners of her mouth and threw the napkin on the table.

She had a choice; it was obvious. She could either take her ass home and leave an angry message on Darrell's voice mail, or she could go upstairs with Leroy.

She looked to her left where the revolving door spun slowly.

It would be a cliché to take him upstairs, to fuck him in the bed that she had anticipated fucking Darrell in . . . so . . .

She turned right.

She said, "I'm going home, Leroy, and I'm going to need a lift."

Randy Crawford was playing on the car stereo. Leroy sang softly along to "Street Life."

Adrienne looked at him out of the corner of her eye. "Oh, you're a songbird now?"

"I'm a lot of things you never thought I was," Leroy replied with a grin.

She let the words pass between them. She knew better than to dwell on any of it. After all, she had been married to this man.

And she didn't dwell on Leroy's hand reaching over now and then either, resting on her bare thigh and knee. Except she was getting warmer sitting next to him and she wasn't sure why, and trying to be cool while discreetly adjusting herself on his leather seats proved to be quite difficult.

Adrienne pulled at her dress because the cocky mother-fucker that Leroy was, he'd probably think she was trying to en-tice him.

"You okay over there?" he asked.

The question startled her.

"Yes, I'm just fine," Adrienne said through gritted teeth.

"Thinking about your . . . *date?*"

Adrienne could feel Leroy's eyes on her.

"No, Leroy, I'm not thinking about anybody."

"Okay, okay. I was just checking on you. I do worry about you, Adrienne."

"You don't have to worry about me. I'm fine."

"Oh, no doubt," he said.

And there was Leroy's hand again, and as if he was realizing it for the first time, this time he snatched it away.

"Damn, Adrienne. I'm sorry about that. I wasn't trying to cross any lines. I was just driving and vibing, you know and . . ."

"And?"

"Well, your legs; they're soft."

Adrienne felt her confidence returning. "Weren't they always?"

"Yes, they were."

Adrienne could have left it at that, could have left the conversation right there, but she didn't.

Instead, she leaned back in the comfortable leather seat and let her dress rise farther up her smooth, mocha thighs.

Let him have a look at that.

Leroy glanced at her legs and stared at her.

He turned his car into her driveway.

It took a minute for Adrienne to get out. She had to readjust her dress, but she soon gathered her bearings and opened the car door.

She said, "Good night, Leroy," as nonchalantly as she could muster.

But Leroy didn't say good night back. In fact, he didn't say anything at all.

Instead, Leroy got out of the car, leaving the engine running. He looked at the house, hands in his pockets. "Did you get new shutters?"

"Yes, along with a new roof and storm windows."

Adrienne knew stalling when she heard it.

Leroy nodded slowly. "And that dress. Is that new?"

"Yes, Leroy, it's new. As if you'd be able to remember it if it wasn't."

There was nothing stopping Adrienne from going inside the house, nothing at all, except Leroy pulled her into his arms and held her tight.

Of course, Adrienne wouldn't have had to wiggle much to break free, but she didn't. She stood there and let him pull her to him.

Leroy leaned against the front of the car, pulling Adrienne along with him. Her back rested on his chest.

Leroy spoke softly in her ear. "Didn't it strike you as odd that I was sitting in one of the snazziest places in Chicago and I was all by myself?"

Adrienne nodded slowly. "*You* had a date?"

"You got it," Leroy said.

"And she cancelled." It was a statement rather than a question.

"No, she came." He cleared his throat. "Came and left."

He laughed that throaty laugh of his.

Adrienne laughed, too. "Well, now I don't feel so bad." And that was when she chose to whisper, almost into the night, "I was going to fuck him after dinner. I was going to fuck him good, too."

Her spontaneous truth caused Leroy's dick to rise against her ass.

It was an Adrienne that she was sure Leroy wasn't familiar with; raw and up-front, no holds barred.

"I was planning on getting lucky, too," Leroy said. "It was supposed to be a 'no-strings' type thing with a lady I met a couple of weeks ago."

"I think my date got scared," Adrienne said.

"I think mine did, too," Leroy added, his head nodding.

"But I'm not scared." Adrienne's voice was soft and raspy now, so much that she barely recognized it.

"I'm not scared either, Adrienne."

"No strings?" Adrienne asked.

"None whatsoever."

Adrienne began to grind against Leroy's stiffness.

Had he ever been this hard before? Even when they were newlyweds in their twenties, he was always so frisky and she was always so ready.

Leroy lifted Adrienne's dress and pushed aside her panties with his fingers.

She was alarmed at her own wetness, but she welcomed it. And at this moment, she didn't need more than Leroy's fingers . . . didn't ask for more than him working them in and out of her warm, wet pussy.

Adrienne's eyes were half-closed, her back arched while Leroy explored her.

He finger-fucked her with one finger, then two, and finally three. And just when Adrienne was close, when she was sure she would come right there, Leroy gently moved her aside, adjusting their positions.

He reached around and squeezed her breasts and nipples that were now hard and pressing against the thin material of her dress.

She heard Leroy unzip his pants, heard him fumbling to set himself free from his boxers.

Her dress was up over her hips, her ass exposed to the night. Leroy slipped inside her easily. Adrienne was reintroduced to the generous length and girth of his dick as he started fucking her slowly, steadily, right there in her driveway, bent over his Cadillac.

Adrienne's mouth hung open; words caught in her throat that couldn't escape because she was so enraptured.

She planted her sharp heels firmly against the concrete to maintain her balance as Leroy pushed against her, filling her with the sweet thickness that was his dick.

The hood of the car was warm against her breasts; the vibration of the humming engine caused her body to tremble.

The crisp September night air rested on Adrienne's bare brown ass and legs, but Leroy kept her warm.

Adrienne liked that she couldn't see him; that every move took her by surprise.

Was he going to move this way or that? Was he going to kiss her neck or reach around and fondle her breasts some more?

Leroy's fingers lightly brushed the side of her face and Adrienne took one in her mouth and sucked gently.

He moaned.

Always a man with a bag of many tricks, Leroy turned her over then and lifted her legs so that they rested on his hips. He hovered over her and slipped inside her deep.

Fucking him this way had always been more intense and Adrienne kept her eyes on Leroy's face. She watched the many ways his expression changed as he fucked her, the look of ecstasy washing over him.

Looking into his eyes, Adrienne knew Leroy was going to come soon, but she also knew that her ex-husband would never let his go until she exploded first.

And explode Adrienne did, coming so hard that her stomach tightened and her thighs trembled relentlessly as she gripped them tighter against his hips.

Leroy pulled out seconds before he came, leaving Adrienne dangling somewhere between passion and exhaustion. He finished himself off with his hand and squirted the result of their coupling on her exposed pussy.

His come was hot against her skin.

Adrienne's breathing came fast and heavy.

Leroy helped her off the hood of the car and onto her feet. She straightened her dress while he zipped his fly.

They exchanged their good-byes with a quick kiss on the lips, Adrienne going inside her house, Leroy backing slowly out of her driveway.

It was past one in the morning and Adrienne was lying on the bed, naked, when her phone began to vibrate on the nightstand. She hadn't bothered to turn it off.

When she picked it up, a text message from Darrell crossed the screen.

Got caught up in a meeting at work and couldn't call. Sure sorry I missed you.

It almost made her smile. Almost made her want to slide up her phone and type back the words *I'm sorry, too* . . .

Almost.

But she put the phone down.

Placed her hands behind her head and stretched.

Darrell had missed his chance. She'd call him in the morning and tell him all about it.

Then she'd call Leroy and ask him over for breakfast.

And maybe, if she chose to, they would do it all over again.

The Night Game

Patt Mihailoff

It was a summer day that started off brutally hot and extended into a steamy, irritating afternoon that ended in a white-hot night.

Jaleel, or Jai as he liked to be called, watched Nyrah Manning with annoyance as she moved her sometimes jiggly, sometimes not, body around the dugout—talking to, but most often yelling at, a youngster preparing to go out onto the field. If he was to go for a heavy-breasted sort of woman, his tastes leaned more in the line of Star Jones *after* the surgery.

Jaleel wasn't happy that, in the interest of political correctness, Nyrah had been chosen as the assistant coach of the Haverford Middle League alongside him. They were always butting heads about who had the best strategy on the game or what position a certain kid should or should not play. Now the team was vying for the state championship, and he did not want to hear anything from this mouthy bitch.

It was the third inning and the bases were loaded. Jai whistled and called out encouragement to his team, noticing that Nyrah glared back at him as though he was disturbing their brooding concentration.

A loud pop sent the ball flying through the air. Everyone was cheering as the fleet-footed youngster ran around the bases. Jai had been watching a series of approaching clouds and hoped that any rain would hold off until the game was over. No such luck! A large, angry, gray cloud rushed in and let go a downpour so swift and so hard that they all grabbed as much gear as they could and ran for cover under the dugout.

With two teams and a bevy of sideliners who hadn't made it to their cars huddled in, everyone was scrunched together in soaked clothing, pushing back as even more teammates and parents rushed in.

Jai found himself right behind Nyrah and raised his eyes upward with exasperation. He hoped she wouldn't turn and begin castigating him, in front of everyone, about what *she* thought proper Little League protocol was. *Bitch!* he thought unkindly.

Nyrah chastised two boys who were trying to shove each other out into the downpour.

"Stop it, you knuckleheads!" she said, leaning forward to tap them both on the shoulder.

Her ample backside rubbed ever so slightly against Jai's middle and he tried to move back, but there was nowhere to go because he was already flat against the back wall.

"I said, stop it right now!" she yelled.

But the boys continued laughing and shoving each other and, when she leaned over farther to try to separate them, her plump ass rubbed right into Jai's crotch.

Shit! he thought and willed himself *not* to have an erection. He kept thinking that even if it did happen, it would have less to do with her, and more with his need for the sex he wasn't getting lately. *Think about something else! Worms, dogs, ice cream.* It wasn't working. Worms were long and squiggly, dogs were in heat, and ice cream was thick and creamy just like . . .

He shook his head to clear it of the sexual comparisons and

tried to think of less tempting things. But that ol' sex goddess tramp, Venus, was in a teasing mood and his dick leapt to full and solid attention. He didn't move but his cock twitched like it was palsied against the softness of her ass cheeks. As much as he didn't care for the brassy woman, he had to admit this didn't feel half-bad. He saw her stand up ramrod straight, but she didn't turn around. He could only imagine the shock that must have been on her face. After all, they really *didn't* like each other and their only interaction had been arguing over something that happened during the games.

The fickle California rain slowed to a drizzle and everyone began leaving the dugout, hurrying to their cars before it started again.

He couldn't imagine why, but he was a little put off that Nyrah hadn't looked back, even to give him her best bitch-witch glare. She left the dugout area screaming at her two boys who were horsing around on the muddied field to get their gear and *move it*!

Alone in the emptied dugout Jai shook his leg and clenched his fist to try to alleviate the ache in his almost pained, rock-hard balls, hoping the thought of what a total bitch Nyrah was would help to ease his raging hard-on.

Slowly and thankfully, it began to ebb. *Good! Because I don't want her—or anyone like her.* He preferred the elusive, faceless cyber partner he chatted with who could make him come with the mere sound of her voice during their secret bouts of phone sex and exchanges of titillating emails.

He looked up in time to see Nyrah collect her kids and hurry to her van. The shapeless blouse she wore was now soaked from the rain, clinging haphazardly, and he could have sworn he glimpsed her large, dark nipples pouting through it. Again, his dick betrayed him. "Will you behave," he murmured, looking down at it.

At home, Jai tried to work but something had him rattled. Dinner had been eaten; the kids, not his, were in their rooms; and his girlfriend was ignoring him as she usually did now that she'd *captured* him, as he'd heard her say to friends many times. He was beginning to resent her and he blamed himself. When he'd first seen her, he thought he'd died and gone to the Playboy Mansion in the sky. She was beautiful, with long, dark hair and a figure that said she'd had no kids, wasn't about to have any kids, and no kids would ever stretch that flat stomach out of shape. It was a complete surprise when he'd found out later that she, in fact, had two children and had suffered two miscarriages prior to her divorce. He wondered how in the hell some women could be graced with such killer bodies while others . . . he didn't want to think about Nyrah and her soft curves that were nothing like his girl's. The memory of her soft backside pressing against him, and the fact that it was done innocently and without immoral thought, made his dick begin to twitch and awaken.

Again he tried to reassign his thoughts, and he wondered if he should stay in the confines of his man-cave and download a little cyber porn or just go to bed and read until he fell asleep.

The phone rang. He didn't bother picking it up. It was usually for his girl and he presumed the rest of the evening would be filled with her idle chatter and irritating laughter.

"Pick up, Jai!" she yelled out to him.

He picked up the receiver.

"Um, Mr. Williams, it's Kareem Manning. Did you take the two new bats? We can't find them."

"I don't think so, but I'll have a look." He checked, but didn't have them. But it wasn't unusual for gear to get lost or misplaced when there was so much equipment and two or more teams were playing. Their team didn't have that kind of money to waste and he knew he'd better backtrack and try to find them.

"No, son, they're not here."

"Okay, Mr. Williams. My mom just left for the field to look for them. Thank you. Good night, sir."

He acknowledged the pleasant child and wondered why his girl's kids didn't have manners like that.

He was about to go to bed, but a thought suddenly hit him. It was late and dark and Nyrah was out there searching for two Little League bats that some thug could easily take from her and use to kill her. *Would serve her right for all the lip she's been giving me for the last two months,* he thought irritably. Then he went to the hall and grabbed his car keys.

"I have to go to the ball field! There's some equipment missing!" he yelled to his girl as he headed for the door. He sighed heavily when he saw her merely wave him off as she continued her cell phone chat and stared at the muted *Dancing with the Stars.*

The ball field was closer to his house than to Nyrah's, and she drove up as he was getting out of his car. *What the hell is she wearing?* he thought as he walked toward her.

"Your son called and said you were out here looking for the new bats," he said.

Now that he was up close, he saw that she wore a knee-length, cotton nightgown with a large sweatsuit jacket over it. It was truly the *un*-sexiest outfit a woman could wear.

"He shouldn't have done that. I told him I'd come and look;

there was no need to bother you." Her voice held that surly, aggravated lilt he hated—or thought he did.

"Well, as long as we're here . . ." he said, ignoring the way she tried to pull the jacket down over the nearly opaque nightgown.

There was no moon but, under the dim and sporadic park lights, he could see the outline of her face and the harsh slash of her mouth as she pinched it even tighter before walking into the game grounds. Her determined gait indicated she didn't need any help in locating two wayward baseball bats.

Yeah, well, a big thick dick is exactly what you need between those prissy lips of yours, he thought meanly.

As she walked in front of him, her opaque gown revealed her thick but strong legs moving toward their destination with irritated purpose and, for some reason, he didn't exactly hate the way it looked.

They finally reached the dugout, feeling around the corners and against the walls for the bats. Neither had thought to bring a flashlight, although Jai did have one in his car. But his eyes had gotten used to the dark as soon as his night vision kicked in.

From the opposite corner, he watched as she leaned down and looked under the bench.

"Here's one," he heard her rasp as she struggled to get it.

"Here, let me," he said, moving behind her.

"I got it," she hissed back, sternly.

"Fine!" he shot back.

From his angle, he could see that her arms weren't long enough, but he didn't care to be chastised for trying to help again. She bent to one knee and stretched. He watched as her

nightgown inched up her thighs, then her hips, exposing her very *un-sexy, serviceable*-looking underwear.

Suddenly, it was like the world clouded over and he was cocooned in a vacuum of space far away. Even as it was happening, Jai felt as though he was someone else and leaned down and ran his hand over her ample ass cheeks, first one, then the other. He heard her gasp, then bump her head as she tried to get up, but by then his fingers had moved between her cheeks and down to massage the soft, fat crevice through her panties. He felt her shudder and couldn't believe it when her legs opened an infinitesimal inch. The movement was slight and could almost be missed, but his fingers knew an invitation when they felt one. A tiny moan escaped her as he worked them against her flesh. And then he felt it, the unmistakable movement against his hand as her pussy began to ride against his rubbing fingers. It was a slow motion at first, then it increased until she was moving with such friction he could feel the moist heat through her panties. He maneuvered his forefinger so that it angled in between her covered lips, and then he just let her ride.

She was moaning quietly, with a little hiss thrown in when it really felt good to her. He didn't dare touch her anywhere else and break the magic of the moment, but he could tell she was reaching her peak from the shudder she gave and the guttural growl that whooshed from her lips like the sound of an alley cat in heat.

She came in a hard rush and everything her underwear didn't capture slathered over his fingers.

He smiled. *She was a squirter!* His cock hardened and it was a big one.

He removed his wet hand and straightened and watched her get up using the bat as leverage. *What if she brains me with it?* he

thought. But in the dim light, he could see her face was flushed with—exertion? Embarrassment from her massive cum? What did one say at a time like this? *Was it good for you?* Or, *You really needed that, didn't you?* But then it was something he needed, too—that and more, but never in his wildest dreams did he think it would be with *her.*

"Look, I'm sorry, I don't know what came over me," he tried to explain.

"You never struck me as a chubby chaser," she said.

"Don't say that." His voice was low. He didn't want her misplaced attempt at humor to break the mood.

"I felt your cock against my ass this afternoon and I realized it wasn't your fault; things like that happen," she said, looking at him earnestly and then shrugging as though it didn't matter.

Is she apologizing? he wondered. Where was the hard, brash *she-bitch* he was used to? That was the person he could handle. Not this woman who didn't seem so large now, and whose face seemed softer in the darkness. Even her voice, with that Kathleen Turner sultriness, was gentler now.

"It felt good—*you* felt good," Jai said.

She laughed and her breasts jiggled a little, and to him it seemed so natural and tantalizing. He suddenly felt an urge to clamp his mouth on them, to suck her nipples until she moaned with delight.

"Yeah, that's what my kids' dad said right before he left me for someone who was a size four."

"You shouldn't put yourself down."

"I'm not. I was never actually thin, and after two kids, a full-time job, and a shitload of housework to do, going to the gym wasn't on my immediate priority list." She switched the bat to her other hand and pulled her sweatshirt closer around her.

"I have to ask you something," he said, keeping his eyes above nipple level. "Why do you always give me a hard time on the field?"

"Because you suck as a Little League coach."

"I do not!" he said defensively, then noticed her teasing grin.

"Well, you don't *actually* suck. I guess it's because people never expect women to be Little League coaches and well, I suppose my attitude is more of a defense mechanism. Besides, come to think of it, you never actually went out of your way to make me feel welcome."

She was right; he hadn't.

There was a long pause as she saw him staring at her. Not her body, but her face; almost like he was seeing something beyond her, something that softened him.

"I'm sorry you had to come out," she said, clearing her throat.

"Are you sorry *you* came?" The question had a double meaning and he knew she was smart enough to catch it.

"No, I'm not."

Another long moment passed between them. It was as though everything that *wasn't* being said was being shouted at them like a chant at a playoff game.

"I better get going. No telling what my boys are tearing up," she said, breaking the silence.

"Nyrah . . ." He said her name gently. "Stay a minute."

"Why?"

"To talk."

"About what? About you wanting to see me open up and cum again? Is that it?"

There it was—the brash ball field witch again, but it wasn't really her; he knew that now. It was the mask she hid behind for emotional protection.

"Yes, damn it! That's exactly what I want. But I want it on my face. I want to eat your pussy right here and right now."

He had no idea what he was saying, or why, but knew that in spite of all the barbed words they'd had in the past, and all the moments each of them disagreed and glared at each other with guarded apprehension; and although each of them must have known they could never be attracted to the other, here he was craving her like a vampire yearning for human blood.

"Stay because I want you to," he said.

Nyrah's breasts heaved as she struggled for something to say, but no words came out.

Jai watched as her expression went from austerity to confused need. He pulled the bat from her hand and let it fall to the ground.

Without a word he laid her gently back on the table that usually held the water keg and Gatorade cups, and pulled her legs up and spread them. Her panties had a wide, wet stain from her earlier release and he liked the way her fleshy pussy strained against the material.

He leaned in, the high muskiness of her sex invaded his nostrils, and like a kid lapping an ice cream cone, he took a long, hard lick over the moist material with the flat of his tongue. Her moan of pleasure made him push his face in and suck. There was something he liked about eating her through her panties and, with his tongue, he traced up and down, like he was sketching. Every few licks he pointed his tongue to stab at her clit button. She was so hot, her flesh soft and pliable in his hands. He heard her hiss and knew she liked what he was doing.

Her panties became too much of a barrier. He wanted flesh— *her* flesh. He wanted to taste her, inside and out. He wanted to move his nose into her cunt crack and lick her dry. He had to find her clit nub and expose it, tease it with his teeth, until she screamed his name.

Sliding off her panties, he found—to his delight—that she was shaven and it drove him wild. He touched her, spread her, opened and closed her. He pinched her pussy lips together with his thumb and forefinger, then flattened his tongue and licked her, stiffening it and moving it inside.

She was writhing under him but he felt she was holding back, trying to control it. He didn't want her to. He wanted her to writhe, moan, to open up to him.

He stopped sucking and whispered to her. "Open up to me; let me love it."

He didn't know if she would and was giddy with blissful desire when she shifted and reached down to open her pussy lips to him. She spread them wide and, if there was a way he could crawl in and eat his way out, he would have.

The pink maw of her wet hole called to him like only a sweet song could. He wanted to devour her like a madman—but this was not *that* kind of a moment. He pressed forward and pushed his face against her open pussy and tongued her until he felt her tense, losing all control, and let her hot juices cover him.

How he loved that feeling, so creamy, so hot, so wonderfully soft, and her acidic musk that had a hint of fruitiness of mangoes and pineapple—the usual diet food of every weight-conscious maven in the state. He couldn't get enough and he wanted more of it.

His tongue went wild inside her and he felt her hips move up to give him as much access as he could take. He adored a woman who loved to get eaten out good—and *he* was good at it.

He was still slurping her hard, holding on to her ample thighs and enjoying her yielding abandon as her gritty voice groaned her complete delight and she ground her pussy against his face.

"Turn over for me," he said, breathing heavily.

She did, raising her full, tawny ass up to him. He squatted down and opened her and tongued her once again, squeezing her ass cheeks in unison with the tongue bath he was giving her.

Nyrah bit her lip to suppress a loud wail of pleasure when she felt his tongue enter her, once, twice, three times; then push so far into her, it felt like a fat, wiggling snake. *He's tongue-fucking me,* she thought with silent ecstasy. *He's tonguing my pussy so good.*

It had been so long and he was giving it to her as hard as he could, and she loved it.

The tightening of her body alerted him. It was happening again; he could feel it. He loved that about women—all women—that they were capable of coming over and over, and his special talent was that he was able to *make* them do it over and over. He'd made her do it once, and he would again.

She was moaning louder now and he was glad they were in such a remote part of the ballpark.

She was close; he could tell. Then, like a geyser, she let loose her body milk and to his utter amazed delight, he realized she was not only a *squirter,* but a *creamy cummer,* too, as wave after creamy wave oozed out of her like lava from a volcano.

He wanted in. His dick was hard and wanted to be someplace hot. He needed to feel her stout pussy lips close around him, but he wasn't sure if she was feeling him for that right then, and he didn't want to ruin this moment by pushing her too far.

But he needed release and he had to do what a man had to do.

He moved away from her, unbuckled his pants, and let them

and his underwear slide down his legs as he took hold of his stiff cock.

Closing his eyes, he began to jack off, losing himself in the imaginings of her big, soft pussy lips, her hot, wet hole, and her sweet cum. He bit his bottom lip as he shut his eyes and dreamed of everything he had been missing.

A scant second later, he felt the warmth of her wet mouth close around the head of his cock. His eyes popped open and he looked down and saw her squatting—not kneeling as one would think a woman of her size would do—but squatting with the agility of an athlete preparing for a sprint. There was no preamble to her game as she deep-sucked him all at once, taking him to the back of her throat until he heard a small but controlled gag.

He wanted to cry with joy when he felt her hands, small and pudgy-soft, as they massaged his heavy ball sac, then moved around to grip his ass to pull him forward even more. *She's swallowing me!*

She had him so deep, he felt engulfed and let out a teeth-gritting moan. Everything she was doing to him orchestrated the massive orgasm building inside him.

"Nyrah, you got to stop . . . Nyrah!" he hissed.

But she just squeezed his ass and sucked him harder and deeper.

"Nyrah, I've got to come. I can't hold it."

Her answer was her mouth clamping onto his cock like an octopus. Pulsating him like a hundred little suction cups.

His jism roared through him like a high-speed freight train and shot into her mouth. He looked down to see her swallow his juice like she was drinking a Pepsi on a hot day, taking every bit of his thick hot sap, then stop to lick him clean.

He was still hard, and he knew why. He still wanted to be inside her. He would be able to fuck her for a long time now that he'd come. *But was she up for it?*

He stared at her, and the unspoken request made her do what he wanted. She lay back on the long table and opened her legs, her pussy wide and exposed. He moved forward but waited until *she* took hold of his dick and guided it in.

She was tight, a sign that no one had hit that sweetness in a while, but once he was in, there was room. She had muscles and she knew how to use them as she kneaded his dick like an award-winning masseuse on a reality show.

He moved inside her hard and deep, then yanked her sweatshirt aside and pulled her breasts out of the top of her nightgown, and just as he'd thought, her nipples were large and tight. He nibbled them with the tips of his teeth, and he could tell she liked that. He sucked them hard as he pummeled her pussy until finally she moaned his name. It sounded passionate and true coming from her lips, and he liked that.

Deeper and deeper he pushed into her flesh, making her take every inch of his cock, enjoying the way her hands roamed up and down his muscled arms almost like she needed him, wanted him.

Keeping his rhythm, he wondered what else he dared to do. *Should I talk to her? Should I say things to her?* He didn't have to, because she did.

"Oh, yes, give me that sweet, thick cock. Push it in. Fuck me as hard as you want; just fuck me!"

Her husky voice that was now somewhere between Kathleen Turner's and Kim Carnes's of "Bette Davis Eyes" fame, made him slam into her even more.

"My cock needs your wet pussy," he hissed back. "I want to

lick you everywhere, up and down your legs, up to your ass, anything—everything you want, everything *we* want."

It was nasty, it was wrong, he knew, but he couldn't stop.

She answered by widening her raised legs, giving him access to every last bit of her.

He rocked inside her until they were both about to come.

She could feel him tense, ready to spill, and she pushed him off and sank down to take him once again in her mouth. She felt him stiffen, then moan in howling, pleasured ecstasy as she let his juice slide down her throat like smooth, melting ice.

Spent, he leaned back on the table, his breath still coming in bursts as she gulped in the night air. He looked at her as she began adjusting her clothes, picking up and balling her damp panties and shoving them into her jacket pocket.

"I didn't mean for this to happen," he said.

"It was a moment, it was just sex," she said, picking up the discarded bats and turning to look at him. Her hazel eyes seemed a little sad to him but the tiny smile that curled her lips seemed to be saying, *thank you.*

When she turned and left the dugout and started toward her car, Jai ran behind her and caught her. He pulled her around and tried to kiss her, but she turned her face away.

"That's personal and not part of what we just did."

"No," he said as he pushed his finger up her nightdress and gently circled her asshole. "This is part of what we just did. This . . ." he murmured, pressing his lips gently against hers, "is a kiss." And he slipped his tongue gently into her mouth as his finger rimmed her.

Her lips were soft, her kiss sweet, and he knew it was not good-bye.

Twenty emotional moments later, each of them was in their own car as they headed out in different directions, to different houses on different streets. Their thoughts, however, remained on the same erotic road.

It was never going to be the same with anyone else for Jai. He realized it that night when he got home and his girl was still on the phone talking to her friend. He stared at her almost-perfect body. As she motioned for him to get her a bottle of water from the fridge, he knew that somewhere along their journey her affection for him had waned.

He knew right then that it was over for them, and just the beginning for him and an unlikely woman who had brought back his passion.

Tomorrow, he would call her. He would try to make her understand that he was what she needed, because he needed her.

He was going to do everything he could to convince her that he was not about to try to change anything about her, but he'd be willing to change into anything *she* wanted him to be.

Sex might have started this, but it wouldn't end there. There was so much more to her that he needed, and wanted, to know; much more. For the first time in a long time, he slept the uninterrupted sleep of a man who had found his loving destiny.

Control Freak

Candy Jackson

CHAPTER 1

I think I'm going out of my mind.

It's been exactly one year, three months, two days, three hours, six minutes, and four seconds since I've felt the heat of a man. His lips on my lips, his legs tangled with mine, the weight of him lying on top of me, or my ass pressed against him, doggy-style.

"Shit, I've got to do something about this self-induced torture."

Why I'd decided to abstain from sex is beyond me.

At first it made all the sense in the world. I mean, I'm military, a soldier, and I had the kind of job where mistakes could cost lives, careers, and sometimes the presidency, so for me, it was a no-brainer. I had to be focused on bringing in aircraft, early mornings, late evenings, and sometimes in the middle of the night. There was no room in my life for sex. Yet, at the rate I was going, an airplane was sure to fall from the sky and it would have my name written all over it.

The problem was, I was missing Terry.

Lieutenant Terry Williams had been my poison of choice, had been my freaky lover, and I had come really close to doing something extremely foolish. I was falling in love with him.

I had to transfer; had to get away. I couldn't risk my career, my future, and my heart for a man who I knew would never marry me.

While lying with him on what is now known as "our last night together," I listened as he told me, not in so many words, that we couldn't be together. As we spooned in bed and while he made excuse after excuse on why he wouldn't commit, I thanked God my back was to him so he couldn't see the disappointment; so he couldn't see my tears.

"Baby, you know how I feel about you; how we feel about each other." At that moment Terry turned me to face him. I tried burying my face in the crook of his neck, but he wasn't having it.

"Look at me, Danny. Our jobs are demanding. I'll be transferring soon, and then what? I can't have you losing control of all you've trained for. It's bad enough we're doing this.

"I could be discharged for seeing one of my students. You're twenty-three years old, for heaven's sake. I'm thirty-five. It would never work out. Surely you understand that?"

With his eyes beautiful and sincere, he penetrated my heart with his words and I ached even more.

We went on that night, making passionate love.

I cried when I came, and cried when he came inside me.

But the next day, I put in for an emergency transfer and took my air traffic controller skills all the way to Washington, D.C. I knew he wouldn't look for me; he didn't love me the way I loved him.

During the two weeks it took the military to approve and provide my paperwork, I avoided Terry. I asked for and received permission to teach a class off base and, whenever it was time to turn in for the evening, I bunked with a friend to avoid going to my room. I couldn't chance seeing him; I didn't want him to talk me into bed.

The cat and mouse game worked to my advantage. By the time I boarded the aircraft to Washington, D.C., I hadn't had any contact with Terry. My heart ached, of course, but I needed to do it my way to keep him from pitying me. I felt like he thought I was a silly little girl.

Now, I'm sitting at my post with my mind full of nasty fantasies, wet panties, and my commanding officers are looking at me as though I have two heads.

One year, three months, two days, three hours, eight minutes, and forty seconds.

"Petty Officer Sanders." The moment I heard that deep baritone voice, the one belonging to Captain Charles Tiller, I realized that my mind had been elsewhere. I immediately tried to snap out of the erotic scene that was floating around in my head, and pretended my attention had been on the unit flying in from Cuba.

"Sir. Yes, sir."

I looked to my left, and with a quick nod of his head, Sarg gave me the okay to leave my air traffic post and let him land the plane safely. I hadn't been in control of my position, or my nasty mind, anyway.

"Oh, God, I need to get laid!"

"Excuse me, Officer Sanders?"

Oh, God, may the heavens strike me down if I said that out loud. I turned in my seat to stand and Sarg looked as though he wanted to fall to the floor in laughter. But this wasn't funny, and I had about thirty seconds to replace my lustful thoughts with my game face.

"Sir?"

I stood, my five-foot, four-inch frame straight as an arrow, looked him directly in the eyes, and then saluted. But his eyes were on my breasts. Then they traveled upward and landed on the mole that graced my upper lip. He licked his lips. He was such a freak'n pervert!

"You're going on detail training, starting tomorrow."

I opened my mouth to say something, but then closed it, knowing I had no excuse for the way I had been conducting business.

I had become a total mess.

Sooner or later Sarg was going to snitch on my comings and goings and, evidently, I had been right or else I wouldn't be standing here getting papers handed to me about where I would report in the morning.

"You will report to the landing strip classroom at zero five hundred, and if I hear you were late, it's your ass, young lady."

It was my ass he watched as I returned to my seat.

Right before I sat down, I heard his "Uhm, uhm, uhm."

CHAPTER 2

I dared not try and go to my usual hangout when I got off. Nope, couldn't risk the Captain spotting me at the NCO club. So, I headed back to the barracks with a bottle of white wine and a porn flick featuring two dudes and a girl.

I reached under my queen-sized, down-covered bed, opened up my box of toys and, with my body freshly bathed and oiled, the mood in my room set, I imagined I was the girl.

I used Terry's face for the guy who was stroking me from behind, and yes, the man who had his dick in my mouth was Captain.

In my mind, it was a very satisfying, perverted scene, and reminded me of the time I went down on Captain, my first day here. Couldn't help it; he was fine as hell and he kept making passes at me. I tried avoiding him that day, but he kept following me around the base.

First, he appeared at my lineup. I was checking in, waiting for my room assignment, and I was more than pissed that my room wasn't ready. Of course, the Air Force had a great reason for the imposition. Hell, I had basically shown up out of nowhere. But I was tired from the flight, and was ready to pull off my clothes and take a long nap. Captain offered me his office sofa.

I'd accepted his offer, lay down, and began to dream about giving Terry head.

Then, I felt his hands on me.

I woke up to real hands and a real dick in my mouth. The only part that had been a dream was Terry's handsome face. Captain had skillfully managed to get me to do to him what I promised myself I wouldn't do anymore.

But, since I had started, I finished him off.

Later, after the deed was done, I explained right to the Captain's smooth, caramel face that it wouldn't happen again. It was difficult, partly because Captain's dick was perfect, his body firm and tight. His six-foot, five-inch frame of delicious caramel latte was one I would have gladly introduced myself to without hesitation. But first I had to get Terry out of my system, my mind, and yes, my heart.

Captain wasn't kind with his words to me and told me that I was to watch my step around base; that he would be watching me.

CHAPTER 3

I woke to the sound of my alarm clock. I forced myself to look over at my nightstand and there they were, the bold numbers telling me that I was only thirty minutes away from losing my job, or worse, being court-martialed.

I pushed the toys out of my way, threw the remote at the TV, probably breaking something in the process, and quickly jumped into my fatigues. There was no time for a shower and, while tossing out everything in my dresser drawer from socks to head scarves, I realized I hadn't washed clothes in almost two weeks. I thought about rummaging through my dirty clothes hamper for underwear, but the heat and stank panties wasn't going to happen. I stepped out into the August summer only having washed my face and brushed my teeth.

"Oh, well, it'll have to do."

I did a quick jog to the other side of the base and walked into class two minutes late.

The officer was standing at the front of class, facing the chalkboard. I wanted to thank the heavens above; his ass was fit for a magazine. My nipples stood to attention.

"Good Lord, help me survive this class."

"Excuse me?"

"No, no, no, this is not happening, I did not say that out loud." He couldn't have heard me; his back was to the class. With my head down and on a serious mission to find a seat, I heard his footsteps.

"Indeed, you did, officer."

Before I could slide into my seat, the man was standing directly in front of me. I raised my head and my hand in salute. When I looked up, I was face-to-face with Lieutenant Terry Williams. "Oh, no."

Terry looked at my very erect nipples, pretending his eyes were on my name tag.

"Officer Sanders, get to the front of the class." All I could do was follow his orders.

Standing in front of the twenty-something cadets who were fresh out of boot camp, with my breasts screaming to be suckled, was embarrassing as hell and Terry knew it. But he wouldn't smile; he hardly looked at my face. Then it dawned on me; he was upset.

It had nothing to do with me being late, and everything to do with me cutting out of Texas like a thief in the night.

"Officer Sanders, please tell the class why you're late." I opened my mouth but he shut it for me. "No, don't tell them; show them how we do fifty push-ups while you give them your job description."

I didn't dare hesitate; I wouldn't challenge him because I knew what would happen. Terry wouldn't hesitate to write me up. He stood over me the entire time; he even had the nerve to put his foot on my back for a couple of those push-ups.

"I control the route and the terminals used for air traffic."

Up, then down.

"And what else, Officer?"

Up and down I went, seven more times before I caught my

breath and summoned the strength to proceed. "I do this using visual, radar, and non-radar means."

Oh, God, I thought he was trying to kill me in the process of punishing me. "I supervise and manage air traffic control, better known as ATC, and its facilities."

Finally, I had finished both the job description and the push-ups while the pimple-faced cadets took pleasure in my pain.

When I stood to go back to my seat, he hit me on the ass, causing the class to burst into laughter.

All day Terry called on me to answer the questions from the manual he used to teach the newbies. He drilled me, challenged my answers, and insulted me when I couldn't solve a problem. By the time class was dismissed, I was more than ready for another emergency transfer.

"Class, that's it. Pick up your details out front. Petty Officer Sanders, I need to see you, now." The rest of the class filed out while I stood in place, afraid to move.

I was nervous; scared even. I began to make my way to the front but Terry told me to go to the door and lock it.

"For what?"

"Because I said so, Petty Officer, and as long as I'm your commanding officer, don't question me."

Yep, he was angry, but God, I had missed him. My skin had tingled the whole time his tight ass was facing the class.

Terry was a good-looking man. When we were together, I thanked God every day for his parents because they made such a scrumptious-looking person.

I stood directly in front of him, remembering his kisses, the feel of his hands, the way he made me cum just by licking my body into submission when he wanted me to give him oral sex.

Terry snapped his fingers in front of my face.

"Snap out of it, girl, and tell me why you left me. Explain why it was you picked up and moved without even a good-bye. You had better start talking."

He said all of this while pulling my T-shirt over my head. Before I could say a word, his mouth was on mine, his tongue slipping in and out, causing me to moan.

"I can't hear you."

I tried, I really tried to speak, but he had unzipped my baggy fatigues and his fingers were playing in the small patch of curls that covered my kitty. "Please . . ."

"Please what, Danny? Huh? Please don't fuck you 'til you tell me what you were thinking?"

He now had me lying flat on his desk, my pants being moved down my body, my mind begging for Terry to hurry, but he continued to talk; to punish me. "Where the hell are your panties?"

I wanted to answer, but his lips were on my thighs as he untied my boots. Everything hit the floor at once. The moment his mouth touched my kitty, I realized that he would smell my self-induced orgasms from the night before. Terry nudged me open with his nose; I was already cumming.

He raised his head slightly and I noticed the corners of his mouth edge up in a sinful grin. "What's this I smell, little girl? Somebody's been eating my porridge?"

My body was trembling as he lifted me and carried me to the big leather chair that sat behind his desk. Straddling him, I tried to position myself for penetration, but Terry was being mean; he wouldn't let me feel his girth.

"Answer me! Captain been hit'n this?"

I laid my face against his chest.

"Don't get all bashful on me now, Danny. I was going half-crazy missing you and I get here and this self-righteous bastard tells me how good you give head. What's that all about?"

I had to tell him the truth. "It was a mistake; a huge mistake."

Panting now, I tried again to get him in my spot, but with his hands on my waist, he moved me back.

"So, Cap's been tasting my pussy, huh? I'm disappointed in you." He really didn't want to hear about Captain and what I had done with him. He lifted me slightly and brought me down hard on his ten inches of hard flesh.

"Oh . . . my . . . God." It took me a few minutes to adjust to him again. I was so tight that Terry knew he didn't have to question me again about the Captain.

"Mmm, girl, damn you're so tight; so wet."

I moved against him; I rocked him. Terry's mouth grabbed one of my nipples and his middle finger entered my ass.

I exploded.

"Yeah, Danny. Give it up, baby."

I screamed out, and came again, but this time with a force I'd never experienced.

I vaguely heard a knocking sound at the door, and I was too far gone to care.

Terry's mouth was all over me and then he moved his mouth against my ear.

"You were expecting somebody, Danny? Yeah, I bet you got 'em lined up for some of this sweet honeypot. You better be quiet before they come in here and find me hit'n my pussy."

Terry's dick became still, yet remained hard inside of me. He rose from his sitting position without breaking our connection and laid me flat on the desk.

He began to stroke me, hard.

I couldn't help but moan his name and the more ugly sounds I made, the harder he stroked.

Then he took my legs and placed one on each side of his shoulders and I immediately wrapped my ankles around his neck. Terry knew me; he knew what I wanted. I loved when he fucked me in this position. He knew that when he was all the way in, with each stroke, his dick kissed my g-spot. "Mmm."

"Oh, God, I've missed you, Terry."

My words of passion caused my freaky lover to lose control. With a simple lick of my tongue against his ear, he changed up his pattern. Terry pushed his dick all the way in, and then pulled it all the way out. He did this over and over while someone banged on the door.

I placed my hands on Terry's chest to try to move him, but he refused to let go.

It was clear that he was on a mission.

"I'm about to cum, Danny. Cum with me, baby."

I was also on the verge of cumming, but I wanted Terry to know how much I'd missed him. It was my turn to bring the heat and my turn to lose control. So, I begged him.

"Please, let me taste you, baby." My legs fell from his shoulders and I began to slide to my knees.

Terry grabbed my hair as he slid his dick into my mouth. I pulled once, then twice, and Terry delivered the very thing I was after. As he came, I suckled and swallowed at the same time.

I drained him dry, but that wasn't enough for either of us.

Terry lifted me again to the desk and with his oh-so-perfect lips and tongue, he licked me, he suckled, he nibbled and kissed me until my honey flowed easily into his mouth.

"Damn, baby, this pussy is still sweet."

I smiled at his beautiful face. "I've missed you."

"Good, because I'm here to stay. Now, we'll finish this later. Right now we better get our shit in order, 'cause somebody's on their way in here."

Quickly, we hustled on every stitch of clothing we could find.

It was the sound of keys, then the opening of the door, that prevented Terry from taking that last sloppy kiss that was on its way to my neck. So, instead we stood straight, brought our left hands to our foreheads and with a smile, saluted . . . the Captain.

Swirl

N'Tyse

Can somebody say, "horny and desperate-ass female!" Yes, I'm referring to myself right now. There I was, in a wide-open, dimly lit room—surrounded by dick. Massive, chocolate, send-your-ass-to-the-emergency-room–type dicks, to be exact. Yet with all the eye candy swinging in my direction and hanging at my mercy, I chose to play it safe—at least for the night. After all, it was my first time. Now don't get it twisted; I was no virgin. In fact, I was incredibly experienced in the sex department. However, it was my first time inside Purgatory since becoming a member. I had joined online immediately after having one of my . . . *moments*. I discovered the site as I was searching for local nightclubs that catered to women like me—single, voluptuous, thrill-seeking sex kittens who didn't have either the time to date, the patience to date, or the self-confidence to date. Surprisingly, I happened to fall in each category. That explained why I had resorted to searching for dick—not love, but dick—online.

On the web, dick came in varieties. They were convenient, readily available, and I didn't have to worry about any drama. Yes, I admit it; I was a cyber-ho. I'd spend hours at a time surfing the Internet, reading some spicy erotica, and viewing pictures of hot, butt-ass naked, well-endowed men. Then, once my pussy started percolating, I'd whip out my bunny rabbit, climb into bed, and pleasure myself until I'd calmed those urges. I did all this every single night. And that's only half of the story. I'd done the unthinkable, had made a believer out of the impossible, and had flirted with the forbidden. I would do *anything* for dick! So it was merely a matter of time before I found Purgatory.

It was an upscale nightclub centered in the heart of the city. But it wasn't just any ol' nightclub. It was exclusively for single, plus-sized women. There was a lengthy application process as well. I had to create a profile, submit my picture, and . . . get this . . . I had to wait until I was *approved*. I mean, damn, you would have thought I was applying for a Lane Bryant credit card or something. I had to sign a waiver of liability and everything. On top of having to go through all of that, I was still put on their "waiting list." This made me even more anxious to experience the place for myself.

Two months later, I learned that my membership had been granted. The membership dues varied depending on the levels. Level 1 was Heaven, level 2, Hell, and level 3, Purgatory. And I can't forget about VIP, which they called the Champagne Room. Of course, I had full access. Horny . . . desperate!

The impeccably decorated 10,000-plus square-foot venue was a secluded loft situated in the Dallas warehouse district. Valet parking, male hosts, escorts, movie theater, private shows and showers, voyeur closet . . . you name it and they had it, including naked men sprawled out on banquet tables serving as fruit and vegetable platters. All in all, Purgatory was the perfect grown-and-sexy atmosphere for releasing your inhibitions or satisfying that starving libido.

Before leaving my house, I promised myself that I would just observe, get a feel for the club and its festivities, before partaking in any of the events. And I was doing exactly that as I sat at a cornered table, in Heaven (the upper level of the club), sipping on a glass of pink champagne. I was dressed to kill, if I should say so myself. My only complaint was that my girdle was too damn tight. I should have worn the Spanx instead; although I couldn't deny that while I was in temporary discomfort, the undergarment held everything together and accentuated my curves nicely. The new black dress I wore also hugged my body. It wasn't easy trying to hide the ten extra pounds I had gained over the holidays, but judging by the way these men gawked at me, I didn't have a damn thing to worry about. My naturally long, flowing hair was pulled back in a chignon, revealing more of my smooth, mocha complexion. My skin and exotic features were illuminated by a single vanilla-scented tea light, and my narrow, brown eyes glowed as I sat in awe of everything taking place around me.

"Did you come to *swirl,* or are you going to continue to sit there and miss out on all this fun?" I heard a voice say.

I looked to my right and my eyes almost popped out of their sockets. Good lawd! All I wanted to know was whether it was real. I had only read about Mandingo, never imagined I would be meeting his back-breaking, pussy-beating, booty-spanking ass tonight. I swallowed the last bit of champagne that was marinating my tongue. My lips moved but I couldn't hear myself speak. I was *dicknotized*! After a minute or so, I was able to come to my senses. "I'm sorry. What did you just ask me?"

The host, the man with the colossal, hooked dick and potato bags for nut sacs, smiled at me. His smile was definitely a blush. I figured he was used to this type of reaction from women; especially after walking up on them with all his goods hanging out. He moved closer; my drifting eyes broke their fixation. I finally admired his oiled, bald head and bulging biceps. His skin mirrored mine and his eyes were the color of cognac. Being as fine and meaty as he was, I was able to look past his five-foot, four-inch height.

"I was just asking if you were going to swirl with the rest of us. A lady as beautiful as you shouldn't be sitting here all alone."

This time I smiled, blushed. My nerves were starting to embarrass me. My eyes roamed again, back to his midsection. I gathered my horny thoughts. "It's actually my first time here. Normally, I'm not this . . . shy."

"I see," he replied, licking the lust off of those chocolate full lips. "Well, do please allow me the privilege of showing you around."

No harm in that, I figured. "Sure. I'd like that," I said.

I rose from my seat, towering over him in my heels. I felt like a giant standing next to him. He placed his hand on the small of my back and led me through the club. I would not have believed anything I saw that night had I not witnessed it for myself. There were men and women engaging in hot, passionate sex in every direction my heels clicked. There were women sucking dick, fucking dick, and jacking off dicks, just as there were men eating pussy, fucking pussy, and fingering pussy. I had seen it all, or so I thought.

Mr. Five-Four led me through a side entrance of the club, the Champagne Room. R&B music wafted over sexually induced lovers, intermingled with glorious cries of hot erotic pleasure. Candles burned, contributing to the heat radiating throughout the sex room. My attention immediately turned to the couple in the back, fucking in open view on a makeshift bed. I nearly swallowed my tongue, rendered speechless.

"Are you okay?" Five-Four asked me. I nodded, again speechless, but horny and desperate to feel what every woman in that room was experiencing at that very moment. "Well, I'm going to go back upstairs for a minute. I'll be back to check on you."

This time when he spoke, I heard my pussy say, *"Please, don't leave us."* My facial expression and body language said the same. As he turned to leave, I made my way to a comfortable spot arranged with a black velvet chaise and a mini fruit tray accompanying a bottle of chilled champagne. I took a seat and poured myself a drink, never taking my eyes off the X-rated entertainment playing before me. I watched in envy, silently wishing that I could trade places. It was torture, sitting there watching, and from the looks of it, I was their only audience.

On the makeshift bed, the woman's head bobbled on her partner's dick, causing her wild, two-toned spiraled curls to stand out like a 1970's Afro that had been mingling with the wind. They were indeed creating their own remix of Kama Sutra, because as her long, talented tongue slid up and down his stiff length, two of his fingers were penetrating her asshole. I shifted in my seat, my hot and throbbing pussy growing wetter by the second. I took another sip of my drink, expecting the bubbly liquid to cool down my furnace, but instead, all it did was make me hornier and more desperate than I already was. So horny that I wanted to rip my clothes off and join the action. So desperate that I wanted to shove her off his dick and stuff it in my dripping pussy, then demand him to finger-fuck my asshole.

There were sex shows going on all around me but there was just something special about the thick and sexy sistah that had realized by now that I was watching her . . . them. The way she licked and curled her lips intrigued me. The way her ass jiggled with every movement aroused me. And the way she deep-throated his dick inspired me. Finally, her smile landed my way. I returned the gesture, feeling somewhat embarrassed by being caught red-handed watching them in the act. I hadn't realized how relaxed I had appeared or how intoxicated I might have been. All I knew for certain was the obvious—I needed to get laid.

No sooner had that reminder settled in my mind than she began sauntering in my direction. Her flawless latte-colored skin, almond-shaped, bright brown eyes, and full luscious lips were the incarnation of natural beauty. Her walk was like moving poetry; fluid, liberating, and extremely enticing. I could feel my heart pounding in my chest, unsure of the actual reason why she had interrupted her fuck session, hell, *our* fuck session.

"Hello, I'm Leo," she greeted me right off the bat. I was taken aback because she damn sure didn't look like a Leo. Leo was a guy's name. "My zodiac sign is Leo, but it's my handle when I'm here, as well," she added, reading my mind.

"Oh. Very pleased to meet you," I said, shaking her hand, wanting to skip the formalities. I tried to remember what name I had put in my file, but couldn't, so I gave her my real name, figuring she probably wouldn't have believed me anyway. No one did. "I'm Scarlet."

"The newbie," she acknowledged. A sinister look washed over her face. I chuckled.

"Wow, is it that obvious?"

She nodded her head vigorously. Again, I chuckled.

"So tell me, Scarlet, did you come to swirl?"

This time I skated around the question, trying to see where it would lead me.

I looked Leo deep in her eyes, slid my tongue across my bottom lip and said, "Depends." Yes, I was flirting with the idea of fucking Leo, although I had never been with, or thought of being with, a woman. I could easily justify why my thinking had suddenly been altered. I was horny . . . desperate . . . inebriated.

"Depends," Leo repeated, seduction lurking in her voice. Her eyes smiled as they traveled up and down my body. I'm not sure why I cared whether she found me attractive or not. I had come tonight for dick. Not pussy. So her opinion of me should not have mattered. But it did.

Leo motioned for her partner. He joined us, his dick still hard as a rock. Leo dropped to her knees and began sucking his dick as if her life depended on it. She started off slow, massaging his balls at the same time, and then quickened her pace. My pussy begged to come out and play. Before I knew it, my racing hormones had gotten the best of me. I began inching my dress above my thighs and proceeded to shed my undergarment.

Leo was still going to work but I couldn't suppress my needs any longer. I joined her on the floor. With his full-grown dick still in Leo's mouth, he reached over her and assisted me in pulling off my dress. I had never experienced a threesome before but I was sure that somewhere in the crevices of my wild imagination that very fantasy existed.

Now that I was completely nude, the insecurities I normally had when it came to my body vanished. Leo didn't mind sharing her space and escort with me. She slowly withdrew his dick from her mouth and gave me a reassuring smile.

"I saved the best for you," she said. Without wasting another second, I gobbled his dick like it was a stuffed turkey. I could feel Leo's hands caressing my huge ass and that drove my pussy insane. I had mastered the art of fellatio. All those erotic books and sex videos had taught me everything I knew.

Seizing the moment, I curled the tip of my tongue and slowly swept it across the head of his dick before tracing it with my lips. I then bottled as much of him as I could, which to my surprise, was the entire thing. My lips blew kisses to his twins while my tongue gave him the best dick bath he'd probably ever had in his entire life. I could feel every ounce of his excitement pulsating through my mouth. His pre-cum tasted like honey barbecue sauce. The hint of champagne I still savored on my tongue gave it the perfect amount of zest. I simply loved a tasty dick.

My pussy purred for attention while my chocolate nipples grew into bullets. I opened my eyes when I felt Leo slide in between us. She took his balls into her mouth and commenced to outperform me. A hum was coming from her throat and when I looked up, the man's eyes were rolling to the back of his head.

"Don't stop," he told Leo. "Just like that, baby." My left hand found its way between my sticky thighs. I could no longer deprive my pussy.

I slid one . . . two . . . three fingers inside my warm opening. I was so wet and slippery, my own fingers began paddling through the waves.

"I'm about to cum," I heard him say. I almost gave myself whiplash. There was no way he was busting a nut before me. I jacked my fingers out of my juice box and instantly stopped sucking his dick. Reading my mind yet again, Leo discontinued her little thing as well.

I turned and kneeled over the chaise, my juicy brown ass in the air. I arched my back and spread my glistening swollen lips for the two of them to notice. Before I could say one word, he entered me in my new position. I was sure he felt the tension in my pussy—the abandonment. He stroked me like a faithful lover, slow, deep, and with dedication. This stranger fucked me like he had known me all my life. Like he appreciated every second of being inside of me.

I squeezed my nipples before taking each of them into my mouth.

"This what you wanted?" he asked, slapping my ass. It bounced back like Jell-O. He spanked it again.

"Fuck me harder!" I panted, losing my breath. He obliged. He drove his dick farther inside me, waxing the floor of my kitty cat. I looked to my right to find Leo at the foot of the chaise, masturbating. Our eyes connected briefly as I watched her fingers move ferociously in and out of her wetness.

"Oh, shit!" I sang, nearing my peak. He lifted my ass cheeks to take some of the weight off his dick. Then, just when I thought it was almost over, he eased one finger inside my virgin anus. I could no longer hold it and, before I knew it, I was cumming all over his dick. I could hear Leo reaching her orgasm as well, but our dear friend was still going with the same stamina as earlier. Still fucking me double-dutch style. I was being jumped by his dick and his finger. Yes, my pussy was being hijacked.

Leo got back on her knees. I could feel her warm breath blowing over my pussy. She took his nuts back into her mouth. Doing that fancy thing she had done earlier.

"That's right, baby," he praised. She began tugging on his balls. My head drifted back and that's when I noticed the mirrored ceiling, the mirrored walls, all for the first time. I watched him fuck me hard . . . fast . . . just like I liked it. Shortly after, he and I exploded all over each other.

As I was leaving the Champagne Room to get cleaned up, I walked past a half-opened door. The soft jazz music playing was what lured me in. Following the concoction of cigars and perfumes, I stood frozen as my eyes feasted themselves on a room full of mostly women, watching, imitating, and enjoying every single activity taking place next door. What I had mistaken for wall mirrors had instead been a showcase window. On the other side of it was the Voyeur Closet. I was stunned as I realized they had been watching me. I tried to leave before anyone could notice, but not before peeping behind the red velvet curtain on my left.

The club owner's hand was sliding up and down his banana-shaped dick as he held one of the several folders piled on his desk. The folder had the name Jade written on it. I strained my eyes, trying hard to see exactly what it was that he was looking at. I took another step. And then another, being as quiet as I could possibly be. He began chanting something. "Horny . . . desperate."

The closer I got, the more was revealed. Five-Four was masturbating to something in that folder. His breath quickened. My heart raced and my skin crawled as I broke out in a hot sweat. "Horny . . . desperate." Thick and creamy cum erupted from his dick, filling his hand. The folder fell out of his hands, landing faceup. As he reached to pick it up, a picture . . . my picture . . . slipped out.

Tight Jeans

Giselle Renarde

The moment she slid them up her thighs, she was sixteen all over again.

Ryan laughed as he joined her in the bedroom. "Did you ever think the eighties would come back to haunt you?"

"Oh, it'll be fun. You'll see." Zipping up her acid-washed jeans, Angelique let the denim close in around her hips. They were tight. Oh, God, were they tight! The seam between her legs rode her clit hard. The crotch was already wet against her bare flesh. It wasn't normally her style, but tonight she was going commando. Without meaning to, she writhed against her wonderfully tight jeans. This was high school all over again. This was adolescence in all its nymphomaniacal glory. This was ecstasy in pants.

But Ryan didn't seem to notice the full extent of her rapture. "Chaperoning a gym full of horny kids . . . in costume! Yeah, sounds like a blast."

His sarcasm couldn't put her off entirely, but their joint laughter doused a touch of her arousal. "An eighties-themed high school dance sounds like the perfect way to spend a Thursday night."

Picking the sleeveless denim vest off the bed, Ryan held it against his naked chest. He wrinkled his nose. "You said you were going to buy me a *Miami Vice* outfit. I wanted to look like Don Johnson."

Angelique gave him a good once-over and tried to conceal her smirk. He was scrawny, pale, baby-blond, and cute as a button. She crossed the room to kiss her husband's bare shoulder. Her thighs brushed each other with every step, driving the seam of her jeans deeper into her wet slit. "Thrift Store was all out of white suits," she said. "Anyway, I didn't want to be your Philip Michael Thomas."

Grabbing her fluorescent green, paint-splatter, bat wing T-shirt from the shopping bag, she pulled it over her head and clipped it at the side with a vintage plastic ring. "Just be happy I didn't put you in bicycle shorts."

He slipped his ripped jeans on over blue boxers. "Or MC Hammer pants."

"I bet if we brush all your hair to the front, we can get a Flock of Seagulls look going on."

Ryan laughed. "Break out the hair spray, babe. We're gonna do this thang!" Strutting into the bathroom, he reached for a comb and his precious products. "Hey, who did you idolize back in the day? I thought David Bowie was God. But I was a science club geek, so that probably doesn't say much."

"Oh, I wanted to be Vanessa Williams—first black girl to win Miss America. I begged my mom to let me straighten my hair, but no. I was just ten years old. I had to suffer all those little braids, the click-clacking beads . . . well, you've seen the pictures."

"You looked adorable," he said, combing his hair to the front and gelling the hell out of it.

Angelique joined him in the bathroom and pushed her kinky hair back with a headband. Rolling on her plastic jelly bracelets, she looked at the pair of them in the mirror: grown-ups attiring themselves in the costumes of their forgotten youth. Still, they were a good-looking couple.

Maybe she was just seeking reassurance when she asked, "We're going to look ridiculous, aren't we?"

"Oh, Angie . . ." Ryan chuckled. "My students look at least this ridiculous every day."

How comforting.

The school gymnasium was hot, even before the lights went out and bodies flowed in. *Like a Virgin*—the first cassette tape she'd bought with her own money—echoed off the painted concrete walls. Until mere months ago, this music relived its former glory only in gay clubs. Now the eighties were back and better than ever.

The girls had gone all out in their Cyndi Lauper–esque outfits, while the boys put on baggy jeans and Metallica T-shirts and called it a day. The girls didn't seem to care, though. Angelique knew very well that dressing up was a form of masturbation for teenage girls, anyway. They didn't need the guys to participate. Not until they got out on the dance floor.

God, it made her head spin, the way these kids danced—bumping and grinding, stroking and groping, riding each other's thighs to bliss. Had she danced like that when she was young? Her only school dance memory involved standing about five inches away from Andy Twyford and setting her hands on his shoulders while he set his fingertips on her hips. *Awkward*—especially since Andy was shorter than she was and the music was too loud for them to hear each other talk.

Angelique found herself tapping her authentic eighties jelly shoes to the beat of "Material Girl" before realizing she found the lyrics mildly offensive. Was she getting old, or what? Compared to these wild creatures of flesh, she would have been old ten years ago. At thirty-six, she was ancient.

When she spotted Ryan on his way back from talking shop with the school principal, she ran to him. Her stupid shoes were digging into her heels already, but she bore the pain with pleasure as she pulled her husband onto the dance floor. She pulled him . . . *close*. Tossing her hands around his waist, she straddled his leg and let her pussy take the reins.

Behind his Flock of Seagulls hairdo, Ryan's eyes shot wide open. "What are you doing?" He chuckled with nerves and looked around the gym. "Angie, I'm a teacher at this school—"

"So let's show these kids how it's done." She grabbed his ass with both hands and squeezed those delicious cheeks. A surge of sexual energy coursed through her arms, and then through her core as she pressed her pussy down against his ripped jeans. The seam dug into her clit a little bit harder every time she slid down Ryan's thigh.

He was freaking out—"Angie, come on, this isn't funny!"—but her pussy didn't give a fuck and her hands wouldn't let go. She was possessed by the demon of high school hormones. They hung heavy on the air, along with the lingering scents of sweat, fruity perfumes, and cheap cologne. Angelique admired teenagers. They were shameless. She could be shameless, too. She would drink from their cups and dig her nails into her lover's fine flesh. His energy was hers for the taking, and she would take it and transform it. Her pussy would be his desire and his home.

God, she wanted him.

Angelique was vaguely aware of the cries twinkling like strobe lights all around them: "Go, Lambert!" and "Nice dancing, Mr. Lambert" and "Who's your bitch, Mr. Lambert?" The air hung heavy but electrified, like the calm before a lightning storm. Any other time, she would have been pissed that some little punk called her a bitch. Now their squeaky voices disappeared under the beat of music she'd danced to in her bedroom twenty years ago. She'd been alone then. Now she was with Ryan.

"Is your wife drunk, Mr. Lambert?"

Only on the heady dose of teenage pheromones surging through my sweaty skin! She threw her head back and wiggled her body for Ryan. *Watch my tits! Get a load of this! Don't you want me, baby?* When she shot upright, dizziness destroyed her, and she giggled as an electric tornado touched down on her pussy. Her insides swirled as Ryan spoke—she couldn't hear what he was saying—and dragged her unwilling ass into the hallway.

It was bright out there. She shielded her eyes against the fluorescent lights and the lockers painted shades of turquoise and peach. Ryan started to scold her, but there were too many students milling about. Grabbing her around the waist, he dragged her up the staircase and unlocked the door to his classroom. She laughed the whole way there.

"Are you drunk?" he hissed.

She felt eighties pop music booming up the girders. Its muffled beat rocked the floor beneath her pink jelly shoes and carried with it the spirit of torn fishnet stockings, cone bras, and messy crinolines. Those kids . . . their energy was inside her. Her jeans pressed hard against her clit and her body surged with hot, liquid sex. The trippy show downstairs hadn't just been driven by a desire to fuck. No, it was rebellion. *Against what?*

The classroom was dark—Ryan hadn't turned the lights on when they came in—but the streetlights outside lit a path. She pressed her lips to his and pulled him toward the teacher's desk, but he pulled away.

"What is going on with you?" Ryan snapped. "You're going to get me fired."

His brow furrowed, but she leaned back against his desk and winked. As she gazed at him through star-colored glasses, his expression slipped into concern. "Angie," he said, shaking his head. "Are you high?"

Clapping her hands, she laughed, then wrapped him in a hug. "You know very well I've never even smoked a cigarette." She kissed his neck. He smelled like skin and hair gel. His whole body felt like denim. "It's these tight jeans, baby. I'm high on acid wash."

The heat of his angry body radiated from his sleeveless vest. As his breathing regulated, his cock grew in his jeans—she could feel its hardness assaulting her thigh, and she crept up like a night stalker. Her juicy crotch, nestled into infinitely tight jeans, was desperate to meet him head-on.

When her hand rode down his chest, down toward that delicious dick she knew so well, he swept it away. "I've got to get downstairs. This is my job we're talking about."

She caught him before he could back away, and she knew he wouldn't dare fight her off. Using his shoulders as leverage, she hopped up on the teacher's desk and squealed as her jeans wrapped snug to her mound. She kicked off her jelly shoes. Her denim camel toe glowed by streetlight. When she leaned back and opened her legs, setting one foot up on the desk, Ryan was powerless. He stared at the denim mystery between her thighs as she slid her fingers down the fly.

Ryan took a big breath in, like he was going to say something, and then he let it out. Muffled music rose through the floor like a highway mirage. It thumped through her body with the energy rushing to her clit. "Lick me," she said. "Kiss my jeans."

Like a prophet before his savior, her husband fell to his knees. He cupped her ass in his hands, pulled her pussy close, and inhaled. As he released that breath, passionate reverberations ran through her body. He sniffed her crotch like a dog, and she loved it, but she wasn't satisfied. "Lick me," she repeated.

He did her one better—he attacked her cunt, biting her jeans like a rabid mongrel. Pangs of sexual electricity shot through her, from her clit to her tits, and all the way out to her fingers. Even her scalp buzzed in response to his animalistic zeal.

What could she feel through the thick denim seam pushing into her slit? Wetness—her pussy juice combined with his saliva to soak the crotch of her jeans. Warmth, too—she felt the heat of her seething pussy join his scorching breath. Her bare arms sizzled in waves as she sent her hand on a mission to find scissors in Mr. Lambert's desk. Crazy to think that only hours ago those desks had been occupied by horny little high school students who saw her husband as nothing more than a straight-laced teacher. Imagine what those kids would say about him after tonight! She should feel guilty for making a scene, but as she pulled a pair of black-handled scissors from the desk, she felt only lustful adoration.

"Cut them," she instructed, setting the scissors on her belly, blade facing away from him. "Make me Daisy Dukes."

He looked up at her, bright-eyed and bushy-tailed, but he shook it off. "I'm not going to destroy your jeans . . . at my school . . . in my classroom!"

"Okay," she said. She could be reasonable. "Then I'll do it myself."

Hopping down from his big desk, she tossed her foot up on one of the smaller student desks and started cutting from the bottom hem.

"What are you doing?" Ryan cried. "You're ruining your jeans!"

A chuckle rumbled deep in her throat and, even knowing it might piss Ryan off, she let it out. "I think you answered your own question there, Sherlock." She cut fast. Once she'd finished, he'd forget his objections.

He stood in the center of the floor at the front of the darkened classroom. His breathing seemed to grow deeper as he watched her cut off two entire legs of denim. All she left in the middle was the seam digging into her slit. That band of tough fabric kept her wet throughout the destruction of personal belongings. Now her trim black hair and her dark pussy lips were plain as day in the V of her thighs.

She'd cut her jeans off almost all the way to her hip bones on either side, but left the bluish-white cotton pockets hanging down. Around back, things got messy—it was hard to see what she was doing, and harder still to control the cuts. They were jagged, but they did a fine job of showing off her ass.

He barely blinked as she approached him in her T-shirt and barely-there cutoffs. "I have to . . ." He never did finish that thought.

"You have to take good care of your wife," Angelique cooed. Unbuttoning his denim vest, she slipped her fingers inside and slid her hands down his chest. It was hot and damp with sweat. Her knees nearly gave out at the scent of him—man and hair products. She pulled him back until her butt met his desk and then she spread her legs. Wide. She took his hand and forced his fingers down her front. The waist on these jeans rested above her navel. They sucked in her belly like a corset. No way she'd be taking them off. Anyway, these tight jeans got her hot and horny as a teenager. Ryan could work around them.

When his fingers met her exposed pussy lips, she gasped and then stopped his hand from moving any farther. "Grab it," she said.

He grabbed her pussy and squeezed. She grabbed the table to support herself. His touch made her weak as a kitten, but she knew what she wanted. "No, baby, grab my crotch!"

"I am!" He looked so puzzled, and his uncertainty warmed Angelique's heart.

"Sorry." She shook her head, smiling at his mystified expression. "Grab the jeans—the crotch of the jeans." Weaving his fingers between her bare skin and the denim seam, she formed his hand into a fist.

After so much instruction, Ryan finally seemed to realize what she was after. He straightened up like his muscles were possessed by the spirits of the throbbing teenagers downstairs. Grabbing an ass cheek in one strong hand, he pulled up on the crotch of her jeans until he'd lifted her bare feet off the floor.

"Yessssss!" Angelique hissed as the sopping wet seam of her cutoffs dug into her clit. He rested one of her thighs on one of his, and the feel of his denim on her naked skin made her melt. The garbled music from below pumped through her veins. When she closed her eyes she saw strobe lights.

Ryan had her totally in his power. As he pulled her forward, the denim seam felt fatter and wetter and her clit grew bigger and harder. She hadn't felt so engorged since she was sixteen, walking around all day and all night in tight jeans like these, feeling how wet her pussy got every time she sat down in class . . .

All she'd ever wanted throughout four years of math classes, English classes, sciences classes, and all the rest, was for some guy with strong hands to grab her by the fly and get her off on her own jeans. Why could nobody damn well figure that out?

And, hell, for that matter, why could she never tell anybody what she really wanted? But that's what girls were like at that age—they strived to meet the man's needs.

Now she was older. Now she was a woman—strong, powerful, and opinionated. Her husband didn't mind indulging her cravings, but in all the years between then and now, she'd forgotten about this deeply held love of denim.

Angelique still had her hands back against Ryan's desk as he rocked her back and forth, alleviating the pressure on her clit before laying the force on strong. Back toward the desk, and then forward toward Ryan's bare chest, he compelled her to ride her jeans like a bull. He tossed her around at varied speeds, at varied pressures. One hand at a time, she reached up and grabbed hold of his neck. She clung to him, panting and whimpering as he rocked her body in time with the 1980s dance beat downstairs.

Ryan swung around until he was the one leaning back on his desk. And then the hand on her ass started to move. He slipped his thumb in between her flesh and the denim until he was holding her jeans at the back the same way he was holding them at the front. The seam now pressed against not only her throbbing clit, but against her asshole, too.

"God!" she whispered, clinging to him. Was she more awed or turned on? Hard to say, until he pulled her up high enough for their lips to meet. When he drew her tongue inside his mouth and kissed her, Angelique became his wild woman. Shifting her suspended body on the miracle denim, she thrust her hips. Ryan responded by bouncing her on her own jeans. Grasping his shoulders, she threw her legs around his waist. He rose to that challenge by flossing her wet slit with denim. The closer she got to her husband, the closer she came to orgasm.

Some might say she'd lost control downstairs at the dance.

Angelique knew this was her moment of abandon. Her body bucked and thrust against Ryan and the denim. That wonderful seam slid to the side of her clit, and she struggled in his arms to land it smack on top of her pounding bud. Boy, she would be sore in the morning, but right now she didn't give a flying flock of seagulls. She was going to come, and it was going to be huge. There was so much pent-up energy inside her body she could feel it sizzling in her fingers. Her heart beat as erratically as her lunges against Ryan, and she didn't call it quits until all the throbbing warmth in her pelvis banded together to erupt in the most volcanic super-orgasm she'd ever experienced.

Ryan held her until she couldn't stand the pressure against her clit. It was too much now. Any more of this and pleasure would turn to pain. He laid her out on the table like a crying infant and cut off the seam of her jeans with that same pair of black-handled scissors. Her body pulsed and seized, and she latched on to her husband's hand and kissed his palm again and again. "Thank you. Thank you. Thank you."

Tossing the scissors in his desk, he cupped her face in his hands before bending to kiss her forehead. When he pulled away from her, every bone in her body felt the loss of him. Even this stark room of washed blackboards and generic desks spoke little of Mr. Lambert, her husband, the teacher. She'd always been so proud of him, and look what she'd gone and done! Embarrassed him in front of his boss and his students and his colleagues. After all that, he'd still indulged her denim fantasy. This man was perfect. He was perfect, but was he angry?

From his cupboard by the classroom door, Ryan pulled out a long raincoat and used it to cover Angelique's half-naked body. "Put this on and wait for me in the car," he instructed. "I need to talk to the principal." His face was stone, utterly unreadable. "You stay in the backseat under the blanket. Once I've made our excuses, I'm taking you to Makeout Point . . . and that pussy better be hot for me when we get there."

When he'd slipped out the door, Angelique set her fingers on her lips and smiled. Who could resist tight jeans?

The Pussy Pleaser

Cairo

Pussy, in my opinion, is one of the most preciously delicious wonders of the world. Real shit. Muhfuckas have lied for it, cried for it, and ultimately died for it. So why most cats don't cherish it is way beyond me. But, hey . . . it's not my issue and definitely not my worry. See, I'm a connoisseur of pussy—good pussy, that is, no ifs, ands, or buts about it. Real talk, I can spot . . . uh, sniff out . . . good pussy a mile away. Call it a gift. Call it a curse. Call it whatever you want. Fact is, I can tell whether a woman has that goody-goody-make-a-nigga's-knees-buckle type of pussy, or if she has that Run-Forrest-Run-I'ma-strip-the-skin-off-ya-dick–type shit instead.

I've been fucking since I was fourteen. And over the course of twenty-two years, I've sampled, savored, and slayed enough pussy to know when a woman has that bomb-ass pussy neatly tucked in between her thighs. How? I can't answer that. It's a knowing. Because of that knowing I can tell exactly what her body needs way before she opens her mouth to tell me. It's like I have this telepathic connection to a woman's pussy. It speaks to me. It calls out my name. And I can tell when it wants, needs, to be fucked, or simply yearns to be made love to.

Like right now, which is why I'm sitting here, licking my thick pussy-eating lips at these three honeys sitting across from me in the American Airlines waiting area for flight 1879 to the beautiful island of Curaçao. Hands down, Curaçao—situated slightly off the coast of Venezuela—is one of the Caribbean's best-kept secrets. Whew, beautiful peeps, beautiful weather, good food, and no damn hurricanes. It can't get any better than that. Although considered a part of South America, it's also a part of the Dutch Caribbean. And it's my secret hideaway spot, where I go when I wanna escape the hustle and bustle of life and bullshit. It's my time to do me, solo. In the last four years that I've flown to the island, I've fucked some of the most amazing women. Some locals, but mostly tourists, like me. Chicks I either met on the plane en route to Curaçao and vibed with—if they're sitting in first-class, that is—or those I've met at one of the bars at the hotel where I always stay. Either way, I'm guaranteed to sample a sweet, sticky dish—or two, or three—of piping hot, wet pussy.

I gaze at the three beauties as they situate their handbags and carry-ons in front of them and take their seats. They're all sexy as fuck. One has a caramel complexion. Another's skin is the color of molasses. But the one who really catches my eye is the one sitting in between her two girls, with the smooth, dark-chocolate skin and long, thick eyelashes wrapped around doe-shaped, brown eyes. Her V-neck blouse is showing an ample amount of cleavage, and the way her cantaloupe-sized tits are sitting up all nice and perky tells me she's rocking a good bra. There's something sexy about a woman who takes pride in her undergarments. I try to picture what type of panties she has on; something lace, maybe silk. I imagine them to be thongs, neatly pressed up against the mouth of her pussy, the place where my tongue wants to be.

I take in her long, slender fingers and manicured nails. Glance down at her strappy-heeled feet and see mouthwatering toes peeking out. Subconsciously, I lick my lips. Yeah, the chick is bad. And I *know*——without a doubt——that she has some good-ass pussy.

My eye catches hers. In a flash, I imagine her swirling her pussy on my tongue, tossing her head back and moaning. I envision her sweet jewel stretched and open from hours of fucking. I breathe in, deeply, imagine her smell; the tangy scent of her pussy stained on my lips, tongue, and fingers. I can visualize how her pussy is: wet and tender from an early morning fuck; glistening cunt lips splayed open by her long fingers, beckoning for my dick to enter. I grin, blinking back all the nasty shit I wanna do to her if the opportunity presents itself. Damn, how I hope it does.

She shifts her eyes. I shift in my seat, pressing my legs shut, hoping to pinch off the slow swell of my cock before it starts to brick up. I'm not the longest-dicked muhfucka there is, but at seven-and-a-half very thick, meaty inches, I'm damn sure not the shortest either. Still, I don't want my shit getting hard when there's only fifteen minutes before boarding. The last thing I wanna do is stand up and give onlookers an eyeful of fat cock bulging from my baggy sweats. Advertising my hard dick in public isn't how I like to do mine.

I decide it's best to click off my overactive imagination now before I awaken the "Pussy Pleaser." Yeah, that's what they call me. A muhfucka who knows how to use his tongue, fingers, and dick to please the punany and make that shit weep. It's also the nickname given to my dick by a chick I once rocked with. Whew, she had that goody-goody. But shit, she was a nutcase! Now that I'm sitting here thinking about it, it seems like most of the good pussy I've sampled has been attached to a nutty-ass broad. Go figure. I shake my head, glancing over at the Chocolate Beauty one last time on the sly. *I wonder if she's a damn nut, too!*

I pull the rim of my NY fitted down over my eyes, slipping

the buds of my earphones back into my ears to finish watching the rest of *Columbiana* on my iPad until it's time to board.

Two hours and fifty minutes later, we are making our final descent into Curaçao International Airport. Yo, real shit, I can't wait to kick back and unwind for the next ten days. No cell phone, no emails, no Twitter or Facebook updates; just sun, fun, and, hopefully, a whole lot of good pussy.

Once the cabin door opens, I quickly grab my shit and dip out toward customs to get my passport stamped, then head downstairs to baggage claim for my luggage. I spot the three beauties as they're coming down the escalator and making their way over to the carousel. Chocolate Beauty catches my eye again. This time, I wink at her. And she smiles back, blushing.

I grab my bag, hop a taxi, and make my way over to the Renaissance Hotel. As the driver makes his way around the island, I stare out of the window, taking in all of its beauty. Somehow my thoughts drift back to Chocolate Beauty. I squeeze my dick, deciding that once I get to my room, busting a quick nut is well deserved and much needed.

After I finish checking in, I get to my room, strip down, beat my dick, then drift off to sleep. I don't wake up until almost eight p.m., pissed that I missed out on Happy Hour from six to seven down at the Infinity Bar. The bar is located down on the third floor where the Infinity pool and man-made beach are. I jump in the shower real quick, dry myself off, then throw on a pair of Polo cargo shorts and a white V-neck tee.

The minute I make my way over toward the bar and see three women sitting there talking along with a few other hotel guests, I glance up at the starlight sky, smiling. I know without seeing her face that Chocolate Beauty and her girls are staying right here in the same hotel.

The bartender looks up and greets me with a smile. "Welcome back, my friend."

"Wyndel, my man," I say, reaching out and shaking his hand. "It's good to be back." He asks if I want my usual, a Sunburn: tequila, triple sec, and cranberry juice. Although I'm not much of a drinker, I make an exception to have at least one drink, maybe two, a night while I'm on vacay. "No doubt," I tell him.

I catch all three beauties watching me in the wall mirror, seemingly on the sly. I can tell they're digging what they see. At five foot eleven, 170 pounds of gym body, the body's right. I look over at them and speak. They speak back.

As Lady Luck would have it, there's an empty bar stool right next to the one I have my eye on. I snatch it up. Shit couldn't get any better. "So how are you ladies enjoying the island so far?" I ask as Wyndel slides me my drink.

"From what we've seen so far," Caramel says, craning her neck to look at me since she's farthest away, "it's a beautiful island." Molasses and Chocolate agree.

"Yeah, I love it," I say, taking a sip of my drink.

Chocolate Beauty shifts her body slightly toward me. "Sounds like you come here often."

I smile. "Yeah. I like beautiful things. And Curaçao is full of beauty." I lick my lips.

She smiles. "Nice."

Molasses looks over at me. "So what do you recommend we check out while we're here?"

I ask how many days they'll be on the island. "Five days," she says.

"I tell you what. How about tomorrow I show you beauties around the island?"

I can tell I've surprised them. Shit, I surprised my damn self. But, hey, if I'ma get up in Chocolate Beauty's hips, I gotta do what I can to expedite shit. All three of 'em are down.

I smile. "Cool-cool; by the way, I'm Markeith." Molasses, Caramel, and Chocolate introduce themselves as Alicia, Mya, and Jade, respectively. "Nice meeting y'all."

"Same here," they say in unison.

I glance at my watch, tossing back my drink, standing. "So, tomorrow morning, cool? Say, ten o'clock?"

They look at each other, then me, nodding. "Sounds like a plan," Caramel says. We exchange room numbers, then decide to meet down in the lobby. I toss a Ben Franklin up on the bar.

"Leaving so soon?" Chocolate Beauty asks, eyeing me. I can tell she's feeling right from her Happy Hour drinks.

"Yeah, I have a date with three beautiful women in the morning, so I gotta get my rest." They smile. And the minute Chocolate Beauty seductively licks her lips, I know I'ma be buried balls-deep inside her, sending her back to the States with a permanent smile on her face. "Yo, Wyndel. This is to cover these beautiful ladies' drinks. Whatever's left, keep the change." I say good night, then head back inside the hotel.

At ten a.m. next morning, they're already downstairs sitting in the lobby. We say our greetings, then head out the door. I decide to take them over to Punda, the shopping district, then over to St. Anna Bay Channel. We walk through Fort Rif, which has shops, restaurants, and bars, to get to the Queen Emma Bridge into Punda.

"So where you beauties from?"

"Well, I'm from Jersey," Molasses says.

"Oh, word? What part?"

"West Paterson."

"Oh, aiight; that's wassup." Caramel tells me she's from Philly. And Chocolate says she's originally from Brooklyn, but lives in Arizona. Although I'm looking at Chocolate Beauty, I ask them all how they know each other.

"From college," Molasses answers.

"We're sorors," Caramel adds.

I smile and for some freaky reason Zane's book *The Sisters of APF* comes to mind. I blink back my dirty thoughts.

Once we get to the shopping district, I let them do them while I find a spot to listen to my iPod. Once they've finished picking up souvenirs and whatnot, we head over to Plasa Bien for some local island food, then back to the hotel.

"Whew, that was delicious," Chocolate Beauty says, rubbing her belly as we walk back over the bridge.

"Yes, it was," Molasses agrees. "Thanks so much for showing us around. We really appreciate it."

I smile. "No problem. I'm glad you beauties enjoyed yourselves."

"We definitely did," Caramel says.

Once we get to the hotel lobby, we hop on the elevator together, exchange more small talk until they get off on the fourth floor.

"Hopefully we'll see you tonight at the bar," Chocolate Beauty says.

I wink. "No doubt." I keep my eyes locked on her ass until the elevator doors close. *Four days to go before that pussy gets back up on that plane. I gotta fuck her tonight.*

• • •

I don't get down to the Infinity Bar until after nine. And I definitely don't expect to see Chocolate Beauty still there, but I'm pleasantly surprised that she is. She smiles when she sees me.

"Where are your girls?"

"Down in the casino."

"Oh, aiight. You didn't wanna get ya gamble on with 'em?"

She shakes her head. "I told them I'll meet up with them a little later. It's too beautiful out to be sitting up in a casino."

I agree. Glad I don't have to worry about them cock-blocking. I order a cranberry juice. We talk a bit. I'm digging the vibe. But after an hour into the convo, I'm getting restless. The clock is ticking and I need to get them damn panties off.

"Yo, real talk," I say to her in almost a whisper. "I wanna feel your warm pussy wrapped around my dick."

She looks at me, startled, shifting in her seat. She gulps down the rest of her drink and signals for another. "Wow" is the only thing she says at first, taking me in. "You waste no time, huh?"

"Nah, I definitely don't. I see what I want and I go after it. And right now I wanna spend time tasting you, caressing you, and slipping my dick into you." I lock my gaze on hers. I can tell by the way she's blushing that I've made her pleasantly uncomfortable.

"No need to be acting all shy," I say to her. I pause when the bartender returns with her drink. I wait for him to bounce, then continue. "I'm grown, you're grown. I'm here, you're here. I'm unattached, you're . . ." I pause, giving her the chance to fill in the blanks.

She swallows back her drink. "Married," she pushes out, staring back at me. I guess she's waiting for me to shift gears with that knowledge. I don't.

I shrug. "Okay, so you're married. That says and means nothing to me. And, no disrespect, but obviously it no longer means much to you, either."

She shifts her eyes, slides her straw in between her lips, and takes a slow sip of her drink. I wish that straw was my dick instead.

She sets her drink back down on the bar, then starts toying with her napkin. "Is it that obvious?"

I nod. "Something like that. But it's all good, baby. I'm not here to judge." *Just to hit them walls right.*

I order her another drink and order myself another cranberry juice. "But obviously shit's not right at home, 'cause if it were, you wouldn't be sitting here without your wedding ring on."

She glances down at her hand. "It's in the safe."

I laugh.

"What's so funny?"

"When I spotted you at the airport in Miami, I noticed you didn't have it on then, either. So . . . that says to me, beautiful, that your little getaway with ya girls is really for something more."

"Listen . . . look. I'm really flattered, but—"

"Hold up, ma," I say, cutting her off. "I'm not looking to wife you, or disrupt your life. All I'm saying to you is I like what I see. You sexy as fuck. And I wanna swirl my dick all up in that sweet chocolate of yours."

She almost chokes on her drink.

I stand up. "Damn, you aiight, ma?"

She pats her chest, then gulps down the rest of her drink. She's staring up at me.

"Look," I say in almost a whisper. "I want you to feel something."

"What's that?" she asks cautiously.

I glance down at the bar and notice she and I are the only ones still out here. Wyndel is too busy cleaning up to even notice us. I take her right hand, lift it up to my lips, then gently kiss the inside of her palm. Then I take it and place it on my hard dick. Surprisingly, she doesn't snatch her hand back.

"You like how that feels?"

She sheepishly grins, nodding.

I lean into her ear. "Yo, tell me something. And keep it a hunnid."

She eyes me. "What?"

"Is your pussy wet?" She nods again. "Good." I take her by the hand, gently pulling her. She wants to know where I'm taking her. "Back to my room."

The minute we step inside, I pull her by her hair toward me and slide my tongue in her mouth, massaging her titties. She moans; tries to pull away from me. I hold on. Nibble on her earlobe, then kiss the side of her neck. "You know you wanna ride this dick." She moans again. I lift her short skirt up over her hips, carry her over to the desk, then sit her up on it.

"Oh, God . . . I don't know what you're doing to me. You have me about to do things I never thought I'd do."

"Oh, word? Like what?" I ask, sliding my hand between her legs, pulling at her G-string. I pop it up against her clit, then slip my middle finger into the center of her goodness.

"Like this . . ." she pants. "Cheat on my husband."

"Obviously, the nigga isn't handling his business right," I whisper in her ear. "'Cause if he was, you wouldn't be sitting here with ya legs spread and ya pussy all hot 'n wet, now would you?"

I pinch her clit. She lets out a gasp.

"Yeah, that nigga isn't hitting this pussy the way you want, is he? Hell, he can't be. This hot pussy needs to be stroked e'ery night, baby."

She moans.

"Oooh, aaah, mmmmm . . . Wait, wait . . . aaah, mmmm . . . I can't."

"Yes you can, baby," I say, unbuckling my belt, then letting my jeans drop down 'round my ankles. I'm standing in front of her with my dick thick as steel. I pull her G-string, let it pop against her pussy, again. I reach over for a condom on the dresser, then roll it down on my dick before pushing it up into her. She gasps, grips my arms, digs her nails into my skin. I lift her hips up off the desk, then give her everything she isn't getting at home—thick dick, waves of orgasms. I make her feel everything her husband can't or won't—wanted, beautiful, sexy. She throws her head back, closes her eyes. Lets my dick take her on a journey she's never been on before. She screams 'til her body starts to tremble. I pick up my pace; speed-fuck her with half my dick, then slow fuck her with all of it. She wraps her arms 'round my neck. I take in her face. Eyes rolled back, bottom lipped pulled in.

She moans louder.

"Tell me. He isn't giving you the dick like this, is he?"

"Uh . . ."

"That nigga probably gotta little-ass dick, doesn't he?" I thrust my dick up into her, stabbing at the roof of her pussy. She matches my thrusts, slipping her tongue back into my mouth. She groans.

"Aaah . . . oooh . . . aaaaah."

"This is my pussy now, baby," I whisper in her ear.

She moans again.

"Tell me this good pussy's mine."

I suck on her earlobe, kiss her on her neck, her lips, then suck on her bottom lip. We fuck 'til we're hot 'n sweaty; 'til she's dripped and gushed and stained up my dick; 'til I've flooded my condom with a thick nut.

By Monday, I have Chocolate Beauty sprawled out naked on a beach towel at Playa Kenepa Chiki with me, one of my favorite island beaches. Weekends the small cove is packed, but on days like today, this gem of a beach is practically empty. Today, there's only one other person out here, snorkeling.

Our bodies, slick and shiny with coconut tanning oil, are baking under the sun. Her succulent pussy lips are warm and sweet and sticky against my lips as I kiss and lick and tongue her slit. "Yeah, baby. You like that shit, don't you?" I whisper in between wet tongue strokes.

She arches her back and moans. "Ohhhh, yesssss . . ."

I flick her clit, slipping my middle finger inside her slippery cunt. Her insides are hotter than the sun blazing on my muscled back. Yet, the ocean's breeze cools my skin and defies the heat. My dick aches. And I can feel pre-cum seeping out of it. She begs me for the dick, and I oblige her.

"Open up for me, baby," I urge, slow winding my hips into hers. She spreads her legs wider, invites me deeper into her wetness. I give her what she wants: deep, steady thrusts. Then ease my dick out to the head. "No, baby," I whisper in her ear. I suck her earlobe. Tip drill her slit. I ease back and watch her pussy milk the head.

I plunge back in. Then pull back out. Watch as her juices coat my dick. I plunge back in again.

She gasps. Reaches for me, tries to pull me into her. I grab her by the wrists, extend her arms up over her head, pinning her hands down into the white sand. "You want this dick?"

"Yes . . ."

"Then you're gonna need to open up and release."

She pants. "It is . . . I am. We are . . . oh, God, it feels so good. I am open . . ."

"Nah, I'm not talking 'bout your pretty-ass legs being opened." I lift her left leg up and place it over my shoulder. "I'm talking 'bout you letting go. Release them inhibitions, baby."

"I am . . . uhhhh . . . I have . . . mmm . . . how do you want me to open up?"

"Let your pussy enjoy this dick. Let me please your pussy."

"Ooooh . . . my pussy is pleased."

I thrust harder. "You sure?"

"Oh, yes . . . my pussy's . . . so . . . fucking . . . pleased . . . mmmm . . . aaah . . . you make my pussy feel sooooo good . . ."

Her cunt muscles clamp around my dick.

I grip her by the hips, and under the heat of the Caribbean sun, pound her pussy, until it is quivering and erupting into multiple orgasms, coating my dick. She yells out, not caring who hears her. She begs and pleads for me to keep fucking her with this dick.

Yeah, this beauty will return to the States in two days well-fucked. And on them lonely nights when she's lying in bed, feeling alone next to her hubby, her thoughts will drift back to her time here on the island of Curaçao being fucked under the sun. She'll smile, always remembering the Pussy Pleaser.

The Brother

Alegra Verde

He thought to punish her, but she was slick with need. So, he surged forth, the eager head of his penis ramming and thudding against her welcoming womb. Her thighs tightened around his. She mewled into his ear, the heat of her breath a caress, her fingers on his shoulders tugging the stiff cut of his suit coat tighter over his shoulders. He could feel the cloth, taut, straining against the skin and muscle of his arms and back, the sleeves pulling, trying to restrain him. The seams could rip, the jacket could tear straight down the center for all he cared, but he wasn't going to stop.

His fingers clutched the firm flesh of her ass, trying to hold her steady for his assault, but she squirmed. The wet lips of her sex gripped him tight, hugging, holding him as he tried to pull away in preparation for another thrust. With her eager little pussy lapping at him, he couldn't bear to pull too far out. He pushed forward again into the lava-coated cavern. Eyes closed and mouth open, she ground herself against him, even as a tear slid over her cheek. He licked it off and covered her mouth with his, his tongue claiming all that it touched in a wild siege.

Suddenly, her eyes opened and she sucked on his tongue as her sex quivered around his straining cock. She raised her haunches higher and he lurched forward, sinking further into her, onto her, his chest heavy on the cushion of her breath. The tie that he had tugged loose because he couldn't breathe when he'd first entered the church was suddenly far too tight.

Then she was on top. His head was pressed into the aging, wine-colored carpet. She was riding him, sliding her heat up and down the sensitive skin of his pulsing rod as the soft pads of her ass slapped against his straining balls every time her hot, wet pussy slid down his cock, taking him completely; the slick lips sliding against his groin in a musky kiss.

Her dress must have felt confining, too, because she was pulling the slinky black fabric up like she wanted it off now. As she did, she exposed a line of thigh, the deep side curve of her waist, the flatness and the dimple at the pit of her stomach, and then the plump mound of her pussy with its sparse, dark curls as she slid forward. He held on to her hips, his grip increasing as he watched her tightness consume him.

There was a fleeting glimpse of the rounded underside of her high breasts, then the fullness of glowing skin, nipples tight and puckered, eggplant purple against her smooth brown skin as she pulled the slip of black cloth over her head. She pressed forward, taking him in again, her pussy swallowing his heat, her juices flowing free, her nether lips making a smacking sound.

He was so hard he couldn't breathe, the slide of her tight, wet sex down his an aching bliss. His hands caught the curve of her thigh, the dip of her waist, stroked the flat of her stomach as he strained toward her, lifting to meet her as she leaned in to him, surging forward. Her body was hot and he wanted to cover her, to feel her beneath him, to bury himself face-first in the sweet heat of her searing body.

A hand at her back and another cupping her ass, he rolled her over onto her back before she could toss the dress away. The sheath of black trailed off one of her arms, obscuring a hand as he pounded into her, the long, hard length of him pinning her down, legs splayed and arms flailing. His hips and thighs surged forward, forcing her thighs wider. Nearly oblivious to the rub of the coarse hair that peppered his thighs as it grated against the tender skin of her inner thighs, she squeezed, contracting her muscles around his length, tightening and tugging as he surged forward. His swollen flesh burned and rasped against her walls. The stiff muscle of his sex pounded and lashed even as it grew, lengthening and becoming more inflexible as it rubbed and stroked her sensitive inner flesh. Her mouth opened as buds of heat ignited trails of light until she was consumed. Deep in her throat, a sound fought the waves of heat, trying to come forth as she bathed his cock in her come. He jerked within her, trying to surge forward again, but it was a wild push as his penis twitched, spurting seed and spraying her walls until he finally slid forward, seating himself fully within her to spend the last long rush against the base of her womb as he collapsed onto her.

"Bitch," he said a long while later as he pulled himself up, staggering as he rose to stand over her. He wasn't sure what he meant by it, only that now, after that, after some of the best sex he'd ever had, he was angry. When she said nothing, he reached for a neatly folded altar cloth that rested alone on a nearby table. After using one of its pristine ends to wipe at the shiny wetness that coated his spent penis, he began to right his clothes. He dropped the cloth into her lap and then pulled his shorts up over his still damp sex and stuffed his shirt into his pants. With a soft sardonic chuckle, she closed her legs and pulled the dress back over her head. She sat on the floor in a sprawled heap like a once well loved but newly discarded rag doll. The skirt of her dress was rucked up around her hips, and other than the short laugh, she was silent.

"You didn't even wear any panties?" It was more accusation than question.

"Like that would have stopped you," she spoke to her lap.

"You've always been a whore." He meant it as a slap, but she didn't seem to feel it, so he continued. "Dressing like a *puta*, breasts hanging out, and those sly looks across the dinner table. Even that first day, the first day he brought you home."

She laughed again, the same mocking sound.

"You never loved him. Why did you marry him?"

"I loved him."

"Then how could you seduce me, his *brother*?"

"Seduce?"

"Look, Mígda. He's been dead less than a week and you come here in that dress with no panties, and no bra."

When she didn't respond, he nudged her with the toe of his shoe. "How could you come here dressed like some brazen whore?"

She looked up at him as though searching for something, but when she realized he expected an answer, she said in a voice almost too low to hear, "I don't like bras. They're too tight, and I didn't want to have a panty line under my dress."

He smirked, "*Puta,* I told him not to marry you. Coming from that family, what could anybody expect?"

She righted herself, smoothing the dress down, and as discreetly as possible, used an unsoiled end of the cloth to wipe away the wetness between her thighs before putting on her shoes, a pair of black high heels. Then she wrapped the altar cloth into a manageable heap and dropped it back onto the table. He watched silently as she tried to right herself. The high heels made the muscles in her legs clench. In that dress, with those shoes, her ass seemed to ride higher, to plump up. She smoothed the dress down over her hips again. It really wasn't very revealing. In truth, it was rather demure with its modest V-neck, but the faux wrap at her waist made the dip at the small of her back incredibly tempting. He wanted to put his hand there.

His groin tightened again. "Shit." He'd just had her; the bitch was a *bruja*. She ran her fingers through her dark, straight, shoulder-length hair. It was a good cut and fell easily back into place. She looked like the good, Catholic, grieving widow again with the tiny golden cross just below her throat, but he knew she wore nothing beneath that slip of black cloth. He knew what those breasts looked like without the covering, that they rode high and buoyant without aid. The image of her nipples, the dark purplish shade they became when they were aroused and puckered, assailed him. His penis rose and twitched anew when he remembered how she'd bathed him in her wet heat when she'd come. He could smell her, not just the fertile scent of her sex, but also the subtle sweetness of some flower as the cologne she wore heated against her skin. He was covered in that scent.

"*Puta,*" he said again to her back as he willed his stiff cock to quiet.

"You've always been an asshole, Julio. Luis was sick a long time, and I never fooled around. I was there for him. Even through that long, horrible sleep."

Another tear. He wanted to taste that, too. He wanted to follow its trail down her cheek with the tip of his tongue.

"You've always tried to tempt me, even before Julio got sick."

"That's a lie."

"Wearing those blouses that hugged your *tetas*. Hugging and rubbing against me."

"Wishful thinking, *pendejo*."

"I wouldn't take what you offered when he was alive, but

since you're giving it away now that he's gone I might as well take my fill," he said, pulling her toward him.

"I never offered when he was alive," she said, trying to dodge his hands, but he held fast. She struggled silently, not wanting the mourners gathering in the chapel to hear. He was a head taller and a good fifty pounds heavier, so restraining her was not difficult. Before long, his hand was under her skirt and his fingers trailed through the still sensitive lips of her sex, toying with the rampant clitoris that protruded just there. It was still damp and slippery from their mingled juices.

He pushed her roughly over the armrest of the ornate wooden chair that probably served as the priest's resting place after a strenuous mass. The armrest caught her just at her waist; her hands splayed, grappling against the velvet of the seat's cushion as she tried to balance herself.

Julio was behind her, pushing her skirt up higher until her ripe bottom was on display to him. She could hear as he unzipped his pants and as the cloth fell to his ankles. He leaned down, his teeth grazing, then nipping the smooth flesh of one cheek as a finger teased and tested her moist sex. He stood again, kneeing her legs, opening her wider. Then, with no further preamble, he was pushing into her, the distended head of his penis bumping and grazing the engorged labia, finally slipping past and into the newly made wetness that greeted him. She grappled for support, her hands slipping over the plush fabric as he rammed himself into her, the hard length of him heaving and shoving its way to her center, his hand gripping her hips.

"You bitch," he said as he pounded into her. "You fucking bitch."

Her muscles clenched around him involuntarily, sucking and straining against his rapid thrusts, his insistent intrusion.

"Fuck," he groaned as she tightened around him. "Fuck," he said again as she slid back against him, all wet and juicy. And then, he couldn't say anything else. He could only continue to give her all he had as he pounded into her, the rasp of each thrust sending shooting sensations that caused his groin and his thighs to tighten and tremble. He held her hips firmly, his fingers denting her skin. There would be bruises later, but she let him grip and hold her, tight and still, just the way he needed to.

He took her hard, aiming himself so that each time he drove into her, he slid all the way, the head of his penis nudging at her womb like that and like that. She mewled and moaned beneath him, her pussy holding him fast like it was made for him. She was so wet and hot and tight and her ass was so soft and buoyant, he gripped her hips harder trying to hold on, to maintain his stance. The sweat and a shattering light filled his eyes and his head, and he was coming into her, long and hard. He wanted to paint her pussy with his seed, to tattoo his mark inside her. His seed gushed forth, filling her, filling *his* pussy, *his* "Mígda," he cried out. "Mígda." The echo was torn from him as the muscles of her canal trembled hard, squeezing him, milking the last of his seed from his spasming cock.

He wanted to kiss her, to slip his tongue into her mouth, to hold her and maybe there would be tears, his. Instead, he pulled out of her and turned his back to her as he pulled the rumpled altar cloth from the nearby table. Without looking at it or her, he wiped himself before pulling his pants back up and making the necessary adjustments to his clothing.

"See," he said, tossing the thick white cloth back onto the table, *"una puta."* He'd stopped himself from pulling her dress down, from covering her. He wanted her to feel the shame, to feel exposed, to feel what he'd been feeling long before he stumbled upon her in this room. He couldn't look at her.

She said nothing, but he thought he heard a whimper.

"Fix yourself up. We have to bury my brother."

He didn't look back at her when he reached for the door of the sacristy.

"I'm glad that you never had kids with Luis. Now, I can truly be rid of you. There is nothing else."

"Julio," she called to him. His hand gripped the doorknob, but he didn't turn around. "I really loved Luis. I've been missing him for a long time," she said, her words soft, trembling.

His hand tightened on the knob. He turned to look at her. She was still a little tousled, though her hair and skirt had fallen back into place, more or less. She leaned against the wall, hugging herself. Tears made her face shiny and her nose a little red. The smell of what they had done filled the small room. He looked away, ashamed.

"He loved you, too." He looked at her as he spoke, wanting her to understand the truth of his words. The tears ran down her face now, and she was nodding her head up and down. He wanted to go to her, to comfort her, but he remembered how she felt, her breasts against his chest, her thighs cupping his. Shaking his head, he gripped the doorknob harder and closed his eyes, squeezing the lids tightly. When he opened them again, she still stood there, face wet and hands gripping her upper arms. They stood like that for a while, not saying anything. He sighed.

"Come on." He held his hand out to her, palm up. "You'll need water for that face and new lipstick."

She looked at his hand suspiciously, but the tears seemed to slow a little.

"Luis would want you to look your best with this crowd." He lifted his hand and extended it farther toward her.

He waited, and when she didn't move, he said, "Come on, Mígda. It's okay. You can do this. . . . We can do this."

She looked at him, measuring his words, the look in his eyes. But she didn't move, the fear of further censure evident in her eyes. He waited, trying to look . . . not sorry, because he wasn't sorry that he'd taken what she'd readily given. He wanted to show that he was at least penitent because he'd shown so little grace in accepting it.

"*Lo siento, Mígda. Estoy aqui para ti.*" His words were spoken softly as he lifted his hand to her again and smiled, his damp eyes seeking her watery ones. She watched, assessing him, her arms dropping to her sides. "*Venga, Mígda,*" he coaxed, his voice a gentle whisper, his outstretched hand beckoning. Then slowly, almost bashfully, she made her way across the room to slip her small, cold hand into his much larger one.

Trapped

Pat Tucker

The cabdriver took off before I could close the car door completely. It was raining buckets—no, make that barrels. A flash of lightning bolted through the dark sky. I barely made it inside the hotel. I was drenched and tired. I wanted a hot shower and a warm bed. Inside the hotel lobby, I heard music, loud chatter, and laughter floating in the air, but I wasn't in a festive mood. I tugged at my roller suitcase and made my way to the front desk.

"Oooh, are you okay? May I help you?" the friendly clerk asked.

"I'm not. I'm tired, soaking wet, and ready for a good night's rest." I chuckled.

"Well, let's hurry and get you checked in," she said. "Is the reservation under your name?"

"Yes. Ulysses Washington," I said.

Her acrylic nails clicked and clacked as she typed on the keyboard.

"Umm, spell your name, please," the clerk said. She seemed confused.

"U-l-y-s-s-e-s Washington. Do I need to spell Washington?" I asked, trying to mask my building frustration.

With her eyes glued to the screen and her fingers dancing on the keyboard, she frowned. "No, it's just I don't have a reservation for you. But it could be our system. With this storm, our power has been going out and I'm not sure what's happening with the backup generator." She tucked her red hair behind her ear as she studied the monitor.

I sighed long and hard. My teeth were already chattering because I was still wet and cold.

"*Ohmygod!!!* Is that him? Hurry, get the camera! Get the camera!" a woman screamed.

I whipped my head around to see two women howling with laughter and falling all over themselves digging into their bags. When I caught a good sight of them, I was embarrassed. One was dressed in a pair of stockings held up by a garter belt with a matching lace bodice. The other wore a sheer bodysuit with knitted flowers strategically covering her nipples and her crotch.

"Oh, my effin . . ." one screamed. "Flex!!! I'm your number one fan! I can't believe it's you, right here in the flesh!" she cried.

When my eyes focused in on this Flex, I could've sworn my coochie twitched. He was a statuesque mass of chocolate muscles perfectly distributed over a six-foot-three-inch frame, and he looked delicious. If only I wasn't so tired, I may have been willing to be his number two fan.

"Um, Mister! Mister!" the other woman yelled at another man who was walking by. He was wearing a pair of leather chaps and a jock strap with a fishnet wife beater.

What kind of party are these people going to?

"Please, can you take a picture of us with Flex?" She all but shoved the camera toward the man, grabbed her friend by the arm, and snuggled up next to Flex with a massive grin across her face.

I turned back to the clerk. "You find me yet? And what's going on here tonight?"

She finally looked up. The expression on her face was as baf-
fling as it had been from the moment she started typing. "Oh,
we're hosting an adult entertainers' convention. Did you not
see it when you booked the reservation? We were required to
post it."

"Ah, no, ma'am, I did not," I said, flustered.

She stopped typing. "Well, is that going to be a problem for
you? Most years they book the entire property, but this year they
had quite a few cancellations so we have vacancies. But things
can get pretty wild," she said, with one eyebrow raised.

I swallowed hard, glanced back at the group posing for pictures, then said, "Ma'am, I don't care what's going on here. I
really am just tired, wet, and ready to relax." I added, "Inside my
room."

Nodding her head, she returned her focus to the computer
screen. "Yeah, I don't understand. I have nothing booked under
your name. You know what, why don't you go to the restroom at
the end of the hall and change into some dry clothes. This might
take a few minutes. So you go get comfortable, let me search for
you, and that way, by the time you get back, everything should
be worked out."

What choice did I have? I wanted desperately to be in my
room, but it didn't make any sense for me to stand there soaking
wet while she searched, so I turned to leave.

The minute I pushed open the door to the ladies' room, I
heard the moaning sounds. There was no confusion about what
I was hearing.

"Oh, yes, yes, right there," a woman cried.

I rolled my eyes and sighed. *Really?* At a hotel, and you two
couldn't take it upstairs?

Just as I was about to turn around and walk back out, another woman wearing a sequined tank top for a minidress strolled in and walked into a stall. There was no way she didn't hear what was going on, so it was obvious she didn't care.

I eased into the second stall and started to change clothes.

"Good for you?" the man asked.

Sounds of skin slapping, heavy breathing, and more moaning filled the room. But it was obvious they weren't concerned with the toilets flushing, doors opening, and water running into the sink.

"Right there! Right there!"

"Tell me where," he groaned.

I grabbed the first items of clothing I could find, and rushed to change. Listening to two people have passionate sex worked like an instant aphrodisiac and I didn't want to be in *that* kind of mood.

I walked out of the bathroom and turned left instead of right, where double doors to a grand ballroom were wide open. What I saw stopped me in my tracks. I couldn't help but gawk.

Men, men, and more men!

And these were not your ordinary men either; these were the kind wet dreams are made of—sexy hunks! They sported ripped midsections, six- to eight-packs, with pecs large enough to catch any eye. These men were various hues of chocolate—milk, dark, or whatever was your pleasure. And their assets were on full display because they moved around wearing silk pajama bottoms, boxers, or anything else that showed off the results of routine hours spent at the gym.

"C'mon in," someone said.

I jumped and realized what a fool I must've looked like standing there, clearly out of place, staring like a kid in the candy store.

"Excuse me, sweetie, you coming in?" The female voice from behind startled me even more. I threw a hand over my chest to calm my heart. She was nearly naked!

"Oh, um, no. I'm sorry. I was looking for the lobby. I must've taken a wrong turn," I said. I kept my eyes up; she wasn't the least bit shy.

"Oh, yes, opposite direction," she said and pointed back the other way. "If you change your mind, the party goes on 'til two," she sang.

I grabbed my suitcase and pulled it in the right direction.

Back at the desk, the clerk Tiffany looked as confused as she had before I left.

"Please tell me you found my reservation," I said as I approached.

"No, nothing. You sure you're booked at this hotel, and for tonight?"

"I'm positive." I placed my purse on top of the suitcase and started digging through to get my wallet. "I have a copy of my reservation right here."

"Okay, good."

I found the paper and gave it to the clerk.

She looked at it, then said, "I see the problem right here. Ma'am, your reservation is at our property on *South* Fairfax Avenue." She smiled.

I looked around, confused. "What do you mean? I told the cabdriver to bring me to 2347 Fairfax," I said in a huff.

"Yes, and that's where you are. But your reservation is at 2437 South Fairfax." She extended the paper toward me. "See, it's right here." She pointed at the address. I felt warm with embarrassment washing over me.

I closed my eyes. Breathe, breathe, breathe.

"Oh, okay, so what do I need to do?" I asked. I opened my eyes and looked at her, hoping for mercy.

"Well, with the way it's coming down out there, I don't recommend you trying to go to the other property, and we do have vacancies, but I want you to be comfortable. Our guests can be boisterous," she warned.

"You know what, after what I've witnessed in the bathroom and down the hall, if that's the worst you've got, I think I'll be okay. I just need a place to lay my head," I said.

"Okay, I'll tell you what. Since it's our sister property, come down at checkout and I'll see if I can credit the old room to your account."

"Bless you!" I leaned on the counter as she typed and found a room for me.

"Okay, you'll be on the twelfth floor. Will you need one key or two?"

"One should be fine," I said.

She swiped the key card through a machine on her desk, then pulled a paper sleeve and wrote my room number on it. She leaned in as if to whisper. "Because you've had such a difficult time, I upgraded you to our junior suite at no extra cost. I hope you enjoy your stay." She smiled.

"Thank you so much!" I took the key and turned toward the bank of elevators. I pressed the button to go up and stood waiting for an empty car to come down.

The sound of the elevator's ding was music to my ears. The doors opened, I stepped inside, and quickly pressed number 12. I released a huge sigh as the doors began to close. But just as the doors were about to shut, a massive hand slid between them.

"Hold it!" a deep baritone demanded more than asked.

I quickly reached for, and pressed, the button to stop the doors from closing. As the massive steel doors quietly parted, the vision that appeared between them made my legs go weak.

Our eyes met, he smiled, and I just about melted.

Up close, he was a pretty boy, chiseled and even more muscular, if that was possible. His square jawline tightened when he smiled, and his features were exotically beautiful.

"Hi." He grinned. "Thanks for holding it." He floated into the elevator with me and suddenly my horrible day took a turn for the better.

But my tongue chose this moment to turn to rubber.

"Uhh, ah, yes. Hi." I shook my head as if that could make me any less silly.

I remembered him being the man the two women were swooning over during the impromptu photo shoot earlier in the lobby.

"Can you press number twenty-seven for me?" he asked.

Yes, and would you like my panties with that?

With shaky fingers, I reached over and pressed the button to the floor he'd requested.

He even smelled good. He was tall, and stacked in all the right places. Being so close to him made my mind race with endless naughty thoughts of the things I would do with him, how many times I'd do them, and how much I'd enjoy it.

The doors closed, and we stood inches apart with our eyes focused upward. I leaned against the elevator wall and waited for it to start moving. It did, then suddenly it jerked hard, and screeched to a stop.

"What the . . ." I frowned.

"These damn elevators," he said.

I turned to him. "Should I press the help button?"

His forehead creased, and his pretty brows came together. "Yeah, maybe you should."

But just as I was about to, the lights went out. Instinctively, I jumped and landed into the stranger's strong arms.

"I'm so sorry!" I jerked away from him. "I'm so sorry. I don't like elevators and this is—oh, God! I'm so embarrassed."

"Don't worry about it. It's gonna be fine."

I could smell his breath. It was fresh, laced with a hint of mint. But what I remember most was how smooth and taut his soft muscled skin felt. I wanted an excuse to touch him again but didn't have one.

Thirty minutes passed and we were still stuck in the elevator. Our cell phones couldn't get a signal so we used them for lights.

"I'm gonna sit down. I'm tired," I said.

I stooped down and took a seat on the floor. Soon, he eased down next to me.

"I'm Flex," he said.

"Flex? I'm Ulysses," I said.

"Wow, what a sexy name," Flex said.

"Sexy?" I chuckled. He had no way of knowing just how wild the butterflies in my belly had gone.

"Yes, and the name is quite fitting." He could recite the alphabet and I bet it would sound great.

Being trapped for two hours in the elevator with Flex wasn't as bad as it could've been. He was sitting with his back against the wall, his legs extended forward, and I lay with my head across his lap. We were becoming fast friends.

"I can't believe you don't like sex." He laughed.

We'd been talking about everything under the sun, and had somehow landed on his work as a porn star.

"As sexy as you are, you just not gettin' it right," he insisted.

"How could you go wrong?" I asked. "I mean, it's putting something in a hole, taking it out, and putting it back in again," I joked.

That made him laugh.

"Oh, my dear, my dear," he said.

A few minutes later, I was sucking his tongue like my life depended on its taste for survival.

We kissed with such passion my blood was boiling and I was ready.

The battery on my cell phone, which had been providing what little light we had, was starting to die. Flex used one hand to pull me up and he kissed me like the couple on the cover of a raunchy romance novel.

When I pulled back to catch my breath, my nipples were hard and I was wet. He took my hand and eased it down to the bulge in his lap.

"Oh, wow! Is that you?"

"No, that's *you;* that's what sexy does," he said.

We kissed again.

By hour four, I was naked, spread-eagle on my back, and watching as Flex struggled to squeeze into an extra-large condom.

"Hurry," I begged like I was in heat.

He finally got it on, but when he used his massive hands to lift me up by the waist, I thought he was trying to enter me. Instead, he licked the palm of his hand, then used that hand to rub from my clit to my crack so hard and forcefully, I thought I'd combust.

No one had ever done anything like that to me, and it felt so damn good.

I moaned and squirmed, then bit down on my bottom lip to avoid screaming too loud.

Flex guided me back to the floor, then adjusted his body between my thighs and proceeded to suck me until my eyes began to water. The more I squirmed and wriggled from the pleasure, the harder he sucked.

"Oh, sweet Jesus! Oh, yes!"

Flex was packing *more* than eight inches. And I felt every single inch as he entered me. He hovered over my body as he moved his hips in sync with my rhythm. I glanced down to see his thick, glistening dick drilling its target with experienced precision.

I looked up at him in the dim light, and even when he frowned in deep concentration, he was still drop-dead gorgeous.

An hour and two orgasms later, he finally announced his plans.

"I'm about to cum," he whispered, like he was straining.

That made me excited all over again.

Flex came hard. He felt good. He gave me unspeakable pleasure and made me understand the truth in his previous statement that someone hadn't been doing it right.

"Whew! That was incredible," I said.

He smiled.

After fifteen minutes, he turned to me and said, "Why don't you come over here and sit on my face?"

"You want more?" I asked, unable to believe he wasn't finished.

"I wanna make you feel good," he said.

"But you have, you have. How long do you think we've been in here?" I asked, looking around.

He shrugged a shoulder. "I don't know, but I'm glad I'm here with you."

"You probably say that to all the ladies when you're trapped in an elevator together," I teased.

Flex reached for me and I snuggled up next to him. He started kissing my neck and my earlobes. Before long, I was climbing onto his face. Hell if I know how he was able to balance my body on his face, considering the way I was wiggling my hips as he caressed my breasts. The man was talented.

Despite my constant moving, he was still focused on his target and I couldn't be happier. His sweet assault against my clit didn't last long. Unfortunately, orgasm number four wouldn't wait. When I came with a gut-wrenching scream, I could hardly catch my breath before Flex flipped me over and mounted me from behind.

"Oh, Jesus!"

"He can't help you right now; this ass is mine," he said.

I was raw but still enjoying the mixture of bliss and pain. Flex was doing everything right and he wasn't easing up.

"Damn, you're so good," he said.

I couldn't believe a porn star was calling me *good*. I was beaming on the inside.

When he hiked up my right leg and started slathering it with hot wet kisses, I didn't know what to focus on, the pleasure from his lips or what was coming from his hips.

A short while later, we collapsed again and I thought I'd die if he wanted round five.

"How you feel?" Flex asked.

I eased my head up slightly and said, "I'm sore!"

"Here, lemme help you."

Before I could adjust myself in a good position, he spread my legs and started kissing me tenderly. I couldn't even complain. He used his tongue to lap my juices like a hungry puppy.

He was the most incredible lover I'd ever experienced.

When the elevator jerked hard, my heart dropped to the bottom of my stomach. I thought it was the delayed reaction from having more orgasms in a span of several hours than I had experienced in nearly all of my adult sex life.

"Oh, looks like we're finally moving again," he said.

The lights came on and I sat, stunned.

Flex stood in all his naked glory, his ripped chest heaving as he held on to the side wall. His massive dick was still wet. I must admit, it looked delicious and inviting. He slipped on the silk pajama bottoms he had been wearing.

I scrambled to throw on my clothes as the elevator took off.

When it stopped on the twelfth floor and the doors eased open, I looked at Flex. He smiled and shrugged a shoulder.

A small crowd was standing outside the elevator.

"Are you guys okay?"

A short, chubby man wearing a suit pushed through the crowd. "Flex! Flex! We've been worried sick!"

"What time is it?" Flex asked.

"It's six-thirty in the morning," Tiffany said. "I'm so sorry about this. We couldn't get the technicians over here fast enough. Because of the storm and malfunctions all over the city, they made it as fast as they could," she stammered.

"It's fine. Really, it's not a problem," Flex tried to assure her.

"Please speak to me. I'm Flex's agent. We're gonna need to talk about this; he missed several appearances while stuck in there," the man said.

Finally, Tiffany looked at me, then she looked back at Flex. I remember the confused expression from the night before. But I was completely stress-free.

People flocked to Flex, and aside from the man in the suit,

Tiffany and I were standing alone. "I'm headed to my room," I said.

"If there's anything you need? Anything at all?" she asked.

"I'm fine, seriously." I headed up the hall to my room, figuring I'd have to rent a flick if I wanted to see Flex again.

But deep down inside, I was okay with that. He had helped me immensely. I figured I'd get a few hours of sleep in before I had to rush to the airport for my flight. But thanks to Flex I knew I'd sleep like a well-fed, newborn baby.

Klepto-Collecto

Thomas Slater

Canderick Mann was an ebony Adonis. He was refined chocolate that had been poured into a frame of ripped muscle and stretched to average height with a mustache being the only hair on his boyish face. He was a shrewd, thirty-year-old businessman that could back up his game with the hefty one-hundred-thou-a-year salary he pulled down as a bank senior exec.

It would appear that, on paper, Canderick Mann was in possession of the perfect life. But nothing could be further from the truth. He harbored two deep, dark secrets: Canderick was a diagnosed kleptomaniac, and had an incurable obsession with eating pussy belonging to the beautiful and desperate. He also celebrated the scent of their juices settling into his mustache and would go for days without washing.

His many visits to a half-dozen shrinks couldn't yield a definitive reason as to why he'd been stricken with what the medical world referred to as "multiple disorders." Lexapro, Zoloft, and Prozac formed the short list of antidepressants he'd been prescribed by high-end shrinks to control his impulses. The quacks could kiss his ass. He wasn't taking crazy pills, as he called them. He was simply a nigga in possession of a powerful position, making plenty of money, with a hearty appetite for eating punany and a rock-hard dick for committing larceny.

Canderick's kleptomania went way past the regular clinical definition of stealing little objects that held no significant value. He left shrinks baffled because Canderick's condition compelled him to take much bigger items with no monetary value to him and eat as much pussy as he possibly could along the way.

Canderick functioned in a white-collar capacity at Servicing Our Community Bank & Loan. It was a huge, black-owned institution that was independently owned and operated by Harry Reynolds. The bank had been servicing an upscale, black suburban Detroit community for three decades. Canderick was senior exec of operations with a special interest in the loans and collections department. His job provided him access to a countless number of women that kept both of his so-called "disorders" fed.

The country's stormy economical climate offered him a powerful tool to fish in a lake of poor, unfortunate women who were behind in their mortgage payments and desperate for some type of a solution. Canderick provided that solution. He was able to grant special privileges to those women looking to take advantage of the mortgage modification program. Being senior executive of operations afforded him the power to bypass the hair-pulling red tape faced by normal people to get his clients' paperwork pushed through for a small price. The fee called for Canderick's clients to allow him to eat their pussy until he was good and satisfied.

He thought of himself as the ultimate human stimulus package. The women that he chose had to be gorgeous. Canderick didn't do women that looked like sea-donkeys. His aggressive screening process kept out the undesirables. A single picture-text of the talent was required to get the ball rolling. Canderick was very particular in his selection. Single-woman pussy was far too easy to come by and the women were too eager to please, but married-woman pussy always raised his eyebrow. It was always a challenge to see if he could get her to betray her husband. And he always went after those couples that were struggling financially.

Canderick's larcenous heart went way beyond the normal boundaries of kleptomania. He couldn't feel complete until he could steal the cookies belonging to another man. He often professed that the love tasted better when it came from a married woman because her pussy had been marinated in the juices of marital stress. He figured married women to be ticking time bombs, ready to have a betraying orgasmic explosion over the face of Mr. Opportunity. And Canderick was just the man to wield the magical tongue that had inspired many pleasurable fantasies.

Monday mornings were the busiest time for Canderick. He always spent the first part of his day discussing alliances, mergers, and acquisitions with the board of directors. Meetings were a way of life for a big-time executive like him. There was always something to do—whether it was training juniors by guiding them through the various banking processes, or meeting and setting objectives with key executives and forming strategies to meet those objectives. He was also responsible for the acquisition of new business.

He was inside his office, dressed in navy-blue slacks, polished loafers, and a crisp, white dress shirt, leaning on a Honma brand golf putter made in Japan. Honma was a very expensive brand with a distinctive 24-carat gold plate on the clubhead. The price: a whopping $52,000 a set. He was staring out of his corner office window at one of the finest views in the building. His exquisitely furnished office overlooked a beautiful five-acre lake surrounded by pine trees and lush green grass.

"So, Mrs. Twissle," Canderick said into his Bluetooth headset. "I can push through the paperwork for your loan modification. I'll cap the monthly payments to a percentage of your household income. And just to sweeten the pot, I'm willing to waive the late fees." Canderick had made it a hard and fast rule to never use the office phone when he was setting up MWP—married-woman pussy.

The lady named Sasha Twissle considered the offer. "I don't know. I love my husband and I can't imagine going behind his back to do something like this."

"I promise," Canderick said in a smooth baritone as he flashed his picture-perfect smile in the window's reflection. "This is a win-win for you. It's a damn good deal. You can't do better than that."

"So let me get this straight" was her incredulous reply. "You're gonna grant these privileges to me . . . and eat my pussy?"

Canderick simulated the putting of a golf ball as he smiled.

"Yes, ma'am! Let me know the time and place and I'll lick you there." The hunger inside Canderick's soul was insatiable. He was an addict whose one wish was to live eternally inside a moment in time where existence depended on exposure to the tantalizing aroma of female pheromones.

"Okay. Here are the directions. My husband will be out of town visiting family," Sasha finally relented. "Be at my place this Friday at twelve midnight."

Canderick was writing down directions with his back to the door when he heard the sound of a woman clearing her throat. He recognized her perfume way before he saw her reflection in the window. She was Claudette Reynolds, the wife of his boss, Harry Reynolds.

"May I help you?" he asked in a voice brewing with agitation.

The middle-aged, mocha-complexioned woman, with salt and pepper hair, dressed in a black business suit, put her hands on her hips with attitude and whispered, "When are you going to stop using our female customers as your dirty little doggy-bone toys?"

Canderick bagged the putter and threw his navy-blue blazer over his shoulder. He walked up to her and leaned in close enough to smell her breath.

"You're not thinking about growing balls and running to Harry, are you? You wouldn't want Harry to come across our dirty little sex DVD, taped to his desk, of this dog lapping up your sweet juices that belong to him, now would you?"

"I know about your little operation, Canderick. You're sick. It's not enough that you force these women into having sex with you, but sending your goons to break into their houses afterward is just plain sick."

"I don't have sex with them—well, maybe some I do—but I eat their pussies. And how many times must I tell you that it's not what you know, but what you can prove."

"Canderick, you're a black-hearted, self-serving narcissist. One day you're gonna reap what you sow. Trust me, boyfriend, I will have my happy ending."

"What is it, *Mrs. Reynolds*? Mad because I'm not eating your geriatric pussy anymore?" He didn't give her a chance to respond. Canderick laughed in Claudette's face before he walked off.

Sasha's picture text proved her to be a dime. She was what you called "ghetto-gorgeous." Sasha was caramel-complexioned with a shoulder-length weave and long, fake eyelashes. She was slim but filled out in the appropriate places. Canderick usually turned his nose up at ghetto chicks, but Sasha was tight. Besides, he'd never eaten the pussy of a stripper before. On her mortgage modification application, she listed "secretary" as her occupation. It wasn't revealed until later that to make ends meet, she moonlighted as a dancer under the name of Twizzler at a trendy bar called Dick & Jane's. The paperwork had already been approved and it was too late to back out. Although she'd admitted to being HIV-negative, Canderick had her fax over the results of her latest test—which was negative.

He wasn't some new kind of a fool. He was thoroughly acquainted with the fact that, in some cases, "stripper" meant "hooker." But that wasn't Sasha's deal. She was a pretty nice girl who'd wedded a loser. Her husband had been a washout on the police force and a relapsed alcoholic who had gambled away their nest egg on the craps table at the Motor City Casino.

It was Friday, midnight—straight up. Sasha opened the door of her suburban home to Canderick. At the foot of the stairs, just outside the foyer, Canderick removed Sasha's red silk bathrobe. She was completely naked. The garment hadn't hit the floor good before Canderick scooped up her soft, naked body into his arms and carried her up the stairs while their tongues loudly sloshed around inside each other's mouths.

He gently placed Sasha on the earth-tone comforter of a king-sized bed and followed as she ferociously snatched the opening of his button-down shirt so hard that buttons popped everywhere. Canderick was starting to slowly recognize that his power to push modification loans through wasn't all girlfriend needed. Her need for affection was obvious as she savagely tore at his clothes like a lioness ripping open the belly of a fresh kill.

Canderick rose to his knees, towering over her small frame, and finished removing what was left of a Hugo Boss shirt, exposing a muscular mountain range of chocolate that could rival Hershey in the war for best ingredients.

Canderick was naked from the waist up as he lowered himself down by his powerful arms and passionately kissed her thick and juicy lips while the index finger of his right hand teased her rigid nipples. He broke contact just to take in all her womanly attributes. The heat from the supernova growing hotter beneath Sasha's damp skin was calling to be extinguished. Using his tongue, Canderick started at the neck and worked his way down her center, leaving a trail of warm saliva to her belly button. He circled and teased until he got the right response.

Canderick removed his tongue from her boiling skin and that's when he saw it. But he couldn't properly make an approach until her legs were spread, opening up her airport. The loud, hot aroma of her female pheromones rushed out, triggering activity behind his zipper. Canderick's dick was pulsating as he zeroed in and made a tongue-landing on her strip. He slowly poked his index finger into her mouth. Her lips closed around his finger as he moved the joint in and out, testing her dick-sucking suction.

Canderick took his time as he lathered Sasha's runway, letting his tongue glide over her folds until he found her swollen clit. He danced around it, lightly sucking, releasing, and sucking it back in, then teasing with the tip of his tongue. Sasha's body shuddered and Canderick could hear her call on her savior as an orgasm tore through her body.

He licked and sucked until she was begging him to fuck her. Canderick had only been there to eat monkey but he obliged. He stood, stepping out of a pair of black Giorgio Armani slacks, and rolled on an XL Magnum, while enjoying her scent that was trapped inside his mustache.

Canderick's dick wasn't even halfway in the pussy when the

fucking dogs started barking and growling like they were warning somebody or something not to take another step.

"My pitbulls don't usually sound like that," Sasha informed him as she attempted to get up and go to the window.

"You live out in the sticks," Canderick tried to explain. He was breathing heavily; his dick so hard it could easily win the title of America's newest brick-breaking sensation. "It's probably a possum or something. Can we get back to what I'm here for?" Canderick went back to work on Sasha with his XL. As she yelled the name of her savior, the dogs sounded like they were mauling the shit out of something, but one other thing was on Canderick's mind: Sasha had some pretty nice shit inside her crib.

Monday morning found Canderick at his desk. He'd skipped the board meeting and canceled all his appointments for the day. He kept on thinking about how nice a girl Sasha had turned out to be. It almost pained him to think of what he'd done to her. Sasha had some nice things inside her crib, too—according to the crew that he'd ordered to clean her out, two hours after the lights went out inside her house for the night. They called themselves "Our Gang." They were a couple of grimy cats that even had the nerve to nickname themselves Spanky and Buckwheat. The two had been breaking into houses for Canderick for two years now. Sasha's crib was just one of many they'd hit. That was Canderick's operation. He would push his victims' mortgage modification paperwork through, eat their pussies, and then steal their asses blind. Hell, Canderick couldn't figure out his disorders, nor was he trying to at this point. His disorders had come with a built-in excuse to steal. He was a diagnosed kleptomaniac and as far as he was concerned, there was no cure. So inside his mind, the Holy Divine had given him a gift of superiority over women. They had been put on this earth to entertain his pussy-eating pleasures.

Canderick was just confirming a one a.m. Sunday morning pussy-munching reservation with a Samantha Peterson when a man who resembled Richard Roundtree's character Shaft barged into his office, wearing a black suit and producing a gold badge.

"I'm detective Clifford Bruckheimer," he announced. "I have a few questions for you, Mr. Mann."

"Sure, detective," Canderick said, waving to one of the two chairs in front of his desk. "Have a seat. How might I be of service?"

"I'll get straight to the point. I'm investigating a series of home invasions."

"I'm a little confused, detective. What does that have to do with me?"

"The victims all have one thing in common," he said before dropping the bomb. "They all have mortgage loans with this bank, even the latest victim, one Mrs. Sasha Twissle."

"Well, Detective, if I can be of any assistance in a possible arrest, please let me know."

"Mr. Mann, I'll be in touch." The detective stood and left.

Canderick made sure the detective was gone before making a cell phone call.

"Spanky," he whispered into his headset with his eyes glued to the door. "Did y'all get rid of the shit yet?"

"Boss, why didn't you tell us that bitch had pitbulls? They almost chewed Buckwheat's balls off."

"How was I supposed to know Sasha had dogs? Anyway, we have trouble. A detective just left here snooping around. Now, I lined up one more job with this chick, Samantha Peterson, and then we lay low."

"Canderick, I'm not complaining about the money you puttin' in a nigga's pocket, but what the hell are you doing this for? It's not like you need the money. You're an executive of the collections department—"

"Not just collections, but senior executive of operations," Canderick corrected Spanky.

"Whatever. The point is, you making plenty of bread there. I know we don't get into each other's personal lives. Is it the rush that drives you? They got a name for people like you—kleptomaniac. A klepto that's over collections—"

"Senior executive of operations."

"Whatever. Buckwheat and I got a new name for you. Your new handle is Klepto-Collecto. Get it? It's a play on your kleptomaniac tendencies and you being a supervisor over the collections department."

"That's senior executive of operations," Canderick reminded him. In some kinky kind of way he liked how the new name sounded. Yeah, that was him: Klepto-Collecto.

He'd gotten a picture-text of Samantha before the detective's intrusion. On his BlackBerry, Canderick pulled up the picture-text of her rocking a string bikini. She was a forty-something-year-old housewife who looked late-twenties, with the body of a video vixen. Usually, Canderick would have his secretary draw up the mortgage modification papers, but this time he wanted to work them personally. He set to work, fantasizing about eating from Samantha's honeypot while still trying to sniff Sasha's scent in his mustache.

• • •

Samantha Peterson had negotiated her own terms: It was to be an oral-only affair with a two-hour time limit. Letting one of his MWPs dictate terms was a first for Canderick. He couldn't give a good got-damn about her terms and conditions because Samantha looked too pussy-licous for him to waste the precious little time she'd allocated him by sticking dick to her. This was some pussy he was gonna enjoy sucking on.

It was one o'clock Sunday morning and Canderick wasn't wasting any time. When he'd arrived at Samantha's crib she tried to give him some old melancholy musical about her husband losing all their savings in a Ponzi scheme. But Canderick wasn't Oprah; he wasn't there for a boo-hoo session. Canderick was there to eat pussy. And he was doing just that, with his head between her voluptuous thighs, lapping at her pudding like tomorrow wasn't his to physically call home.

To be forty, Samantha was in shape. Not one stretch mark in sight. Her six-pack abs almost mirrored his. Samantha's skin was the color of toffee. Her toenails were polished to perfection, and they were now raised as high as she could get them. Canderick was tongue-fucking her like his dick had traded places with his tongue. When they'd first started, Canderick noticed that Samantha was trying hard to fight it. She wasn't super-religious, but she kept on chanting about burning in hell for dealing with the devil. And now here she was, hot, sweaty, moaning, and playing with her nipples as Canderick sucked hard enough to dislocate her clitoris.

Samantha clenched, pulling the back of Canderick's head deeper into her na na as a tsunami of an orgasm washed her away. But Canderick kept on sucking until his time was up.

• • •

It wasn't until Tuesday that Canderick got a phone call at the office bringing horrific news.

"Boss," Spanky said in a voice filled with panic. "I think Buckwheat killed that bitch Samantha."

Canderick just sat there, not saying a word.

"We were up inside her crib when Buckwheat knocked over a glass shelf. Samantha got out of bed to investigate and Buckwheat panicked. He cracked her over the head with the pistol—fucking blood was everywhere. We dragged her to the closet and stuck her in."

"Is she dead?" Canderick asked, holding his breath.

"Don't know, but you better get lost. The police picked up Buckwheat and—"

The phone dropped the call.

At that moment, Claudette led Detective Bruckheimer into Canderick's office with two beefy uniformed officers in tow.

"Canderick Mann, get up. You are under arrest in connection with the murder of Samantha Peterson," the detective announced.

"I didn't kill anybody," Canderick boldly protested while one of the officers handcuffed him.

The detective went on to say, "We just picked up Butch McCoy. I suggest the next time you pick your crew make sure they're not stupid like Butch McCoy, aka Buckwheat, and Calvin Reed, aka Spanky. Your two geniuses left their prints all over the closet door where they stuffed Samantha Peterson's body. Butch McCoy gave you up, *Klepto-Collecto.* Gentleman, take this bad boy away."

Claudette waved as they led Canderick away.

"I told you that I would have my happy ending." Claudette was only too happy to gloat.

With no emotion, hands behind his back, Canderick walked, trying to sniff Samantha's scent from his mustache. He wore a stupid little grin on his face. Kleptomania had robbed him of a promising career and was about to steal his freedom. Canderick knew he was headed to prison, where the musty odors of inmate ass and feet were the only scents that would settle inside his mustache for a long time.

The Ultimate Affair

Rae

Tandy walked into the bathroom. She watched Darryl as he stood in front of the sink, splashing water on his face. She made her way over to Darryl, then dropped down to her knees. She spread Darryl's cheeks apart and blew into his asshole. Darryl moaned as his knees buckled. Tandy began flicking her tongue back and forth over Darryl's anus. Tandy had never done this before, not even for her husband, Omar, who was Darryl's brother.

Darryl grabbed the bathroom counter as his legs began to shake. It felt good to have Tandy's head buried between his ass cheeks, lapping his anus. It felt like Tandy knew he was the one for her.

She was one of those prissy women. She was a light-skinned black woman with pineapple-colored skin. She had a cute face with tiny features, except for her big, round chestnut-colored eyes. The way she pranced around made a nigga think he could only have her missionary style.

Darryl listened to Omar brag about how good Tandy was in bed. How she could make him—who had fucked damn near every women in Richmond, Virginia, and had been sucked off by some of the best—cum in a few seconds whenever she slurped on his dick. He bragged about how they had porn-style sex. When Darryl first saw Tandy, he thought his brother had been lying about how she got down in bed but later found out everything he had said was true. Hell, Omar even left out some details.

Darryl enjoyed the wetness between his cheeks but he was still tired from the three times that he and Tandy had romped between the sheets earlier. He knew Tandy was bucking for round four and he didn't have the energy to deliver. He reached down to grab Tandy's hands and pull her to her feet but, before he could blink, Tandy slid her tongue down to his genitals and began sucking on them. Darryl became aroused by the sound of Tandy greedily sucking his scrotum.

"Damn, you sucking the hell out my nuts. You nasty-ass bitch."

Darryl's words made juices ooze from Tandy's snapper. After the first time Tandy and Darryl had sex, Tandy told him how she liked to be called derogatory names during sex. At first Darryl was uncomfortable about calling Tandy names but after he had done it a few times and seen how hyped up Tandy became when he did it, he was thrilled with the idea. Darryl understood the only place where it was acceptable was in the bedroom, unlike Omar, who felt obligated to tell Tandy how much of a dick-sucking bitch she was whenever they were out in public.

Darryl groaned, "Damn, girl, I swear your mouth gets just as wet as your pussy." Tandy began to play with her nipples as she sucked rapidly on Darryl's scrotum. "Oh, shit," Darryl squealed. "I'm about to cum."

Tandy didn't bother to position herself in front of him before putting her mouth on his tool. She grabbed his dick and sucked it from the back. She stopped sucking when she felt it pulsate and slapped it up against her juicy lips until he ejaculated. Darryl grunted as he covered Tandy's lips with cum and his tool became limp. He looked down at Tandy as she licked his semen off her lips and he became aroused again. As much as he wanted to fuck Tandy breathless, he couldn't. He was on the verge of exhaustion. He turned around, grabbed Tandy's hands, and pulled her to her feet before she could put her mouth on his tool again. He picked Tandy up by her waist and sat her on the counter.

"Look, baby, I don't have enough energy to go another round," Darryl said with a smile on his face. "You sucked it all out of me. Besides, I have a few runs to make."

Darryl looked closely at Tandy and noticed that her thighs, hips, and her waist were thicker than usual. "Damn, ma, you getting thick."

"You think I'm putting on weight?"

"I *know* you're putting on weight," Darryl said.

Tandy sucked her teeth.

Darryl leaned over and planted a kiss on Tandy's lips. "You still look good, though."

Tandy sat on the counter and watched as Darryl got dressed. Darryl put his shirt on, then looked over at Tandy again and shook his head.

"What's wrong?" Tandy asked.

"I don't know how much longer I can do this."

"It's been a little over a year and you're tired of fucking me already," Tandy joked.

"I'm not joking," Darryl said. "I can't keep holding back my feelings for you, pretending we're just fucking, when I'm in love with you."

"So what are you getting at?"

"What I'm getting at is, I'm tired of keeping this a secret," Darryl said. "But you know my family gonna carry on like we on some *Jerry Springer* shit."

Tears welled up in Tandy's eyes. Creases formed on her face like it was a balled-up picture. Tandy looked away from Darryl. "So what you saying?"

Darryl didn't answer. He gathered his long black hair together and put it in a ponytail.

"If you don't want to be with me anymore, just say so," Tandy said as her voice began to crack.

Tandy knew Darryl was still messing with Shay, his babies' mother, whose mind was so screwed up she thought they had a monogamous relationship. But Darryl had led her on by moving in with her, by occasionally sleeping with her, and by getting her pregnant twice.

Tandy never forgot the night Shay got hold of Darryl's phone and read the text messages they'd sent each other. Some of the messages were friendly, Tandy commenting on how beautiful Darryl's children were. Some of the messages were about Omar, how he had came home high again and she didn't know if she could deal with it anymore. Some of the messages were about how they couldn't wait to make love to each other again. Shay called Tandy's cell phone at two o'clock in the morning. When Tandy answered, she could hear Shay cussing Darryl out.

"Hello," Tandy answered.

"I knew something was up with y'all," Shay yapped into the phone. "I read y'all text messages. You a nasty bitch; how you fuck ya husband's brother?"

Tandy sighed and looked over at Omar, who lay in the bed beside her, asleep. Waking him was like trying to wake the dead. Tandy screamed into the phone. "The same way I'm fucking ya man, bitch. Now shut ya damn mouth and let him get some sleep so he can fuck me tomorrow." Tandy powered down her cell phone and went back to sleep. But when Darryl fell asleep,

Shay called Darryl's mother and told her Tandy was having an affair with Darryl.

Early the next morning, Tandy heard a knock on the door. She got out of bed, walked into the front room, and glanced through the peephole in the front door. She saw Darryl and Omar's mother, Reverend Moore, standing there holding a Bible in her hand; with her were her daughters, Benita and Melissa.

Damn, I don't feel like being bothered with them today, Tandy thought. She slowly backed away from the door until she passed the kitchen, then walked into the bedroom to wake up Omar.

Tandy gently shook Omar. "Omar, ya mother and sisters are at the door." Omar didn't answer, so Tandy continued to shake him. "Omar, ya mother and sisters are here to see—"

Omar grabbed Tandy's arm and squeezed it. "What I tell you about bothering me when I'm 'sleep?"

"I know, but ya mother—"

"I heard you the first time," Omar said, as he squeezed Tandy's arm tighter. "Don't make me slap the shit out you. Just tell them I ain't here."

Tandy walked back into the front room.

Reverend Moore began to pound on the door. "Tandy, open this door! I saw your car parked outside so I know you're in there!" she shouted. "Shay told me you're having an affair with Darryl and I need to find out what's going on!"

Oh, shit, Tandy thought. She closed her eyes and took a deep breath to ease her nervousness.

"Come on and open this door!" Reverend Moore's voice sounded from the other side. "I just want to talk to you!"

Tandy rested her hand on her chest. Her heart thumped fiercely, causing her head to ache. *How the hell am I going to get out of this shit?*

Darryl pulled up in his gold Escalade and walked to the door. Ten minutes earlier, Darryl had looked at his cell phone and realized he had missed a call from his mother. He'd listened to the message his mother had left him, telling him that Shay called and said he was cheating on her with Tandy and how she was on her way to see Tandy to get her side of the story. As soon as Darryl finished listening to the message, he'd gotten in his car and sped over to Tandy's house.

"What are you doing here?" his mother asked.

"I came to see Omar and apologize to him and Tandy for the stunt Shay pulled this morning." Darryl knocked on the door. "Hey, y'all up in there? It's Darryl."

Tandy exhaled, relieved to hear Darryl's voice. She made her way over to the door and opened it.

Once everyone was inside, Darryl made up some story about how Shay misinterpreted a message that Omar sent him and went ballistic. As soon as Darryl cleared things up, he left with his family as if he was on his way home. Five minutes later, Darryl was back at the door. Tandy let him in and pecked him on the lips.

"Thank you for getting us out of that mess with your mother."

"Anytime," Darryl said. He ran his hand over Tandy's breast. He could feel his blood race to his dick as it stood at attention. "Where's Omar?"

"He's in the room asleep."

Darryl thought about the possibility of his brother waking up and catching him having sex with his wife, but the desire to drive his tool deep into Tandy and be gripped by her warm supple walls outweighed his concern. He began to unbutton Tandy's shirt. "Let's get you out these clothes so you can show me how thankful you are."

They quickly undressed each other as they took turns kissing and licking each other's lips. Tandy thanked God that she was finally able to enjoy Darryl's flesh and cure the hunger that had been building in her all night as she lay beside Omar and fantasized about Darryl. She traced Darryl's lips with her index finger, admiring the smoothness and fullness of his lips. Darryl took her manicured finger into his mouth and began to suck it. Tandy let out a moan; the sensation she got from her finger being in Darryl's mouth had awakened her clit and it was begging to be devoured by his lips. Tandy slid her finger out of Darryl's mouth. She sucked his earlobe as she caressed his hips. Darryl quivered with anticipation.

"Aah . . . don't tease me like that," Darryl groaned.

Tandy planted a kiss on Darryl's lips. "You want it now?"

"Aah, yes, give it to papi."

Tandy slid the finger Darryl lubricated with his saliva into his anus and Darryl shuddered with pleasure.

"Aah, shit. That's right, baby, fuck me. Fuck papi."

They kissed each other fervently. Darryl began to suck Tandy's tongue. The faster Tandy stroked his anus, the harder he sucked her tongue.

Darryl's stiff phallus pressed against Tandy's stomach, smearing secretions onto her navel. Tandy eased her finger out of Darryl's anus and began stroking his shaft.

Darryl let drool fall from his mouth onto his shaft as Tandy stroked it. He pinched Tandy's nipple as he whispered in her ear, "You ready for this dick?"

"Yes, papi," she cooed, rubbing her hands over her pussy.

Darryl smacked Tandy on her ass. "Bend over."

Tandy bent over and grabbed her ankles, bracing herself against the wall. Darryl knelt down and planted kisses on Tandy's hips. He licked her anus, then ran his tongue down to her clit and flicked his tongue against it.

Tandy bit down on her bottom lip. "Aah . . . I love the way you eat my pussy."

"And I love to eat your pussy."

Tandy's legs quivered, weak from the delightful sensation she felt as Darryl's tongue danced on her clit. She couldn't wait any longer; she was ready to cover his vessel with her wetness. "Put that fat-ass dick in my pussy and fuck me," she demanded.

Darryl did as she ordered; he stood up and placed his hands on the wall and shoved his erection into her hot spot. Tandy oohed and aahed as Darryl fucked away at her pussy. The thrill of having sex with Darryl while Omar was in the bedroom sleeping intensified Tandy's pleasure, making her insides so wet her juices ran down her legs.

"Oh, yes, beat my pussy up," Tandy wailed.

"Shh, before you wake up Omar," Darryl grumbled.

"Fuck him, this yo' pussy," Tandy cried out. "He can't beat it up like you do."

Darryl felt the pressure build up in his sac and knew he was about to explode. His thrust quickened and Tandy's moans became louder. A few seconds later Darryl filled Tandy's insides with cum.

Now, Darryl slapped Tandy on her thigh. "Why you always thinking like that? I ain't trying to end this. I'm just tired of all the secrecy."

"Well, why put it out there if we're just fucking?"

Darryl sighed. "Woman, did you hear anything I said? I love you. I want to make you my wife one day. But I need to find a way to break it to my family; especially to Omar."

After hearing what Darryl wanted for them in the future,

Tandy wrapped her arms around Darryl's neck and they traded kisses.

"Don't worry, babe, everything will be alright," Tandy said.

Tandy and Darryl held each other for a few minutes before Darryl made his way to the door.

"Damn, ma, I swear you getting thick."

Tandy sneered at Darryl. "Yeah, you already told me, remember?"

"I'm just a little concerned, that's all."

"Concerned about what?"

Darryl shook his head. "Maybe it's nothing. We'll talk about it tomorrow, okay?"

Tandy nodded.

Darryl walked back and kissed Tandy on her forehead before making his way out the door.

Tandy lay in bed, watching TV. She hoped Omar was on one of his binges, getting high and tricking with women who shared his habit, and wouldn't come home for a few days. Tandy couldn't wait to see Darryl again.

Tandy remembered the first time she saw Darryl. It was on Easter. Tandy sat at the table with Omar's mother and his sisters, listening to his mother discuss Bible scriptures. Tandy felt like she was in Sunday school. Darryl walked into the dining room still wet from his shower, wearing only a white towel around his waist. He had just gotten back in town from a business trip. Drug trafficking was Darryl's father's profession and he'd brought up all his male children to be a part of it. Water dripped from Darryl's wavy black hair onto his chiseled, pecan-colored body as he nodded at everyone at the table, greeting them. Tandy couldn't keep her eyes off him. The passion that stirred in Tandy at the sight of Darryl soaked her panties. How dare he come around her looking like that? He reminded her of the painting of Jesus that hung in her bedroom during her childhood—the painting she bowed down in front of as she said her nightly prayer as a little girl; the painting that she lusted over when she was a teenager and her hormones overpowered her; the painting she wanted to reach her hands into and pull Jesus out and on top of her so they could make love until her body gave out and then he could resurrect her by placing soft kisses all over her body.

Tandy leaned over and whispered in Omar's ear. "Why does your brother look so different from the rest of y'all?"

"His father isn't black like ours, he's Spanish," Omar answered.

Darryl grabbed the suitcase containing his clothes that he had left in the front room and made his way back to the bathroom to get dressed.

After seeing Darryl on Easter, Tandy started to see him on a regular basis. He came over her house at least four days a week to see Omar. Whenever Darryl walked past Tandy, he would brush against her and she could feel his manhood on her hip. She wished it were inside her.

When Omar got locked up for a few months, Darryl called to check on Tandy every week. One day, when Darryl called, Tandy was crying. Her yearning for companionship and sexual pleasure had brought her to tears.

"Hello," Tandy answered.

Darryl could hear the sadness in Tandy's voice. "What's wrong?"

"Nothing, it's just not a good time," Tandy whimpered, and then hung up the phone.

Later, there was a knock at Tandy's door. Tandy looked

through the peephole and saw Darryl. She wiped the tears from her eyes and opened the door.

"Yes?" Tandy said.

"Is everything okay?"

Tandy nodded.

Darryl looked Tandy up and down, wondering if she was wearing anything under her plush red robe. "Can I come in?"

"Sure."

Tandy turned around and made her way to the sofa. Darryl grabbed Tandy by her waist and licked the inside of her ear. Tandy turned around to face him and they kissed. Tandy sucked Darryl's tongue and Darryl slid off her robe and let it drop to the floor. Darryl picked Tandy up and carried her to her bedroom. He laid her down on the bed and looked over her body, admiring her 38DDD breasts. He sucked her nipple like an infant hungry for his mother's milk. Tandy gasped as Darryl twisted her other nipple between his thumb and index finger. She raised herself up on her elbows and cupped her breast, deciding to aid Darryl in pleasing her. She licked and sucked her breast as Darryl pinched on her nipples.

Pre-cum oozed from Darryl's dick as he ran his tongue from Tandy's breast to her belly button and tickled her outie with his tongue. Tandy's toes curled from the erotic sensation. She spread her legs apart, inviting Darryl to her flower bud. Darryl placed kisses on her thighs, then made his way to her clit. He covered it with his saliva, then used the tip of his finger to softly rub her clit in a circular motion. Tandy's legs began to tremble. She ached for Darryl's soft, moist tongue to slither against her throbbing clit.

"Eat it for me," she whined. "Please eat my pussy."

Darryl did as Tandy requested and flicked his tongue back

and forth against her clit. When Tandy began to moan, Darryl engulfed her clit with his mouth. His lips closed around her clit like a suction cup. Tears ran down Tandy's face as she whimpered and called out Darryl's name. Darryl pushed Tandy's legs up toward her shoulders and ripped through her walls with his tool. The sweat from his pecan skin and her pineapple skin mixed together and their sweet juices dripped onto the sheets.

Darryl grunted in Tandy's ear. "Do you know how long I've wanted this pussy?"

The louder Tandy moaned, the harder Darryl banged on her pussy until they both climaxed. They lay in bed, panting, as they drifted off to sleep. Ever since that night, the two couldn't get enough of each other.

Omar walked back to his bedroom and undressed. He looked over at Tandy, who was lying on her side, asleep. Omar slid under the blanket, lifted Tandy's leg up, and shoved his dick inside her. Tandy jerked away and then sat up in the bed.

"Damn, I missed you," Omar said, before trying to kiss Tandy's lips. Tandy pushed Omar away. "What's wrong with you?"

Tandy sighed. "I don't feel like it tonight."

Omar yanked the blanket off Tandy and threw it on the floor, exposing her nakedness. He got out of bed and stood there, looking down on Tandy. The sight of her naked body and his rage made his dick hard.

"What you do that for?"

"Are you fucking another nigga?"

Tandy sucked her teeth and grabbed the blanket off the floor and covered herself up.

"You don't feel comfortable around me naked anymore?"

"Come on with that, Omar," Tandy whined. "I'm trying to get some sleep."

Omar banged his fist against the wall. "Man, I swear, don't let me find out you fucking someone else."

Tandy turned her back to Omar and pulled the blanket over her head.

"Oh, it's like that," Omar said, before grabbing his belt and striking Tandy on her thigh.

Tandy yelped.

Omar grabbed Tandy's ankle and dragged her out of bed and into the living room while whipping her with his belt. Tandy's legs were on fire. She pleaded with Omar to stop but he whipped her mercilessly.

Omar let go of Tandy's ankle when they reached the front door. Omar opened the front door and pointed outside. "Since you ain't giving a nigga no ass, get the fuck out."

Tandy didn't move. She just lay on the floor, sobbing.

"I know you heard me." Omar grabbed Tandy's leg and started to drag her out the door. "Get out."

"No, please," Tandy wailed.

Omar looked down at Tandy's legs and became sickened by the purplish bruises that covered them. He realized he had gone too far, something he always did when he was high on crack.

Omar shut the door, then got down on his knees and leaned over Tandy. "Boo, I'm sorry. I don't know what came over me." Omar bent down to kiss Tandy. "Give me a kiss."

Tandy didn't oblige him. She covered her face with her hands and continued to cry.

"Oh, you ain't gonna give me no kiss?" Omar yelled. "Fuck you, then. I don't know what I'm sweating ya' chunky ass for anyway. I got bitches that look like models that would chop off their arms to be with me." Omar went to the room and got dressed and walked out the door, leaving Tandy there, crying.

Darryl knocked on the front door, waking Tandy up. Tandy pried herself up from the spot on the floor where she had lain all night after crying herself to sleep, and opened the door.

Darryl walked in the house and looked Tandy over. "Dag, it's not that I don't like seeing you naked, but next time put some clothes on before you come to the door. What if I had somebody with me?" Darryl's focus quickly went to the bruises on Tandy's legs. "What happened to your legs?"

"Omar," Tandy answered. "He came home drunk and high again and he beat me." Tears welled up in Tandy's eyes. "He even tried to drag me outside naked."

"I'm sorry," Darryl said, as he hugged Tandy. "Let's get you cleaned up."

Tandy got out of the shower, dried off, and put lotion on. She then grabbed her clothes, ready to get dressed.

"Before you put on your clothes, take this for me," Darryl said, as he handed Tandy a pregnancy test.

"But I don't think I'm pregnant."

"I know a pregnant woman when I see one," Darryl said. "Take the test."

Tandy squatted over the toilet and positioned the pregnancy test downward between her legs as she urinated on it. Before Tandy could lay the pregnancy test down on the counter, a blue plus sign appeared. Tandy nervously put on her bra and panties.

Darryl looked down at the test and smiled. "Come on, let's go in the bedroom. I want to talk to you for a minute."

Darryl and Tandy sat down on the bed and began to talk about Tandy's pregnancy.

"So do you know who the father is?"

"It has to be yours," Tandy said. "I haven't had sex with Omar for damn near three months."

This made Darryl more upset about Omar beating Tandy. Not only had Omar beaten the woman he loved, he had beaten the woman carrying his child. Darryl got down on his knees and began kissing the bruises on Tandy's legs.

Omar pulled up in front of his house and saw Darryl's Escalade parked outside. *What the fuck is he doing here?* Omar got out of the car, leaving the leather jacket he had bought to buy Tandy's forgiveness inside the trunk.

Omar unlocked the door and slid it open. He quietly made his way back to the bedroom, listening to Darryl and Tandy's conversation.

"Give me a few weeks to gather up some money and I'll move you anywhere you want to go," Darryl said.

"What about Shay?"

"Fuck Shay!" Darryl exclaimed. "I love my kids and will always provide for them but that bitch has made my life hell."

Omar pulled out his .45 Magnum and cocked it. Darryl jumped to his feet. Omar fired a shot, shooting Tandy in her neck. She fell to the floor. Omar then pointed his gun at Darryl.

Darryl knelt down beside Tandy and checked her pulse. "Look what you've done," Darryl wailed. "I can't feel her pulse. I think she's dead."

Omar shook his head in disbelief. He didn't mean to. He didn't want to kill her. His eyes bulged, revealing his feelings of terror and remorse. He thought about all the times he'd savagely beaten Tandy. How could he have done that to her? She was his high school sweetheart. Things had gone horribly wrong and he couldn't fix them. Omar put the gun to his head.

"Brah, no," Darryl shrieked.

Omar pulled the trigger and his limp body fell to the floor.

Tears ran down Darryl's face. He pressed his face against Tandy's face and cried.

Tandy opened her eyes and then grabbed her stomach and sobbed.

"Thank God," Darryl said. "Hold on, Tandy. Please stay with me."

Darryl called the ambulance for Tandy. He then called his mother to tell her that Omar had killed himself. His mother and two sisters arrived as quickly as the ambulance and police. They walked into the bedroom as Tandy was being put on a stretcher. Darryl gave his statement to the police and explained why he was there. He conveyed what he had been hesitant to tell his family all along.

Benita collapsed to the floor after hearing that Omar had turned his gun on himself after finding out Darryl and Tandy were having an affair. Melissa attacked Tandy while she lay on the stretcher, helpless. Darryl's mother beat Darryl with her Bible as she screamed Leviticus 20:21. "And if a man shall take his brother's wife, it is an unclean thing; he hath uncovered his brother's nakedness. They shall be childless."

The officer questioning Darryl restrained Reverend Moore and another officer restrained Melissa, then put her under arrest for assaulting Tandy.

Darryl's mother disowned him.

Tandy miscarried on her way to the hospital. The bullet in her neck couldn't be removed. Tandy thought the bullet protruding from her neck was God's way of reminding her that she'd committed adultery. A year later, Darryl and Tandy got married and Tandy became pregnant with Darryl's son. Darryl decided that his son's name would be Damar, a combination of his name and Omar's. Tandy thought Darryl wanted their son to bear the name because he felt guilty about betraying Omar, but she agreed to it. She would do anything to ease Darryl's conscience. Sometimes Tandy found herself feeling guilty about her infidelity but she managed to convince herself that she didn't do anything wrong; that all's fair in love and war.

The Jewelry Dreamer

Kweli Walker

It was impossible not to notice the only man in a Metrorail car, especially a fine, tall, well-built, impeccably dressed, clean-shaven, attaché-carrying man who jumped to give his seat to a sixty-something black woman with obviously bad feet. You could smell the estrogen filling the car. Once standing, he became the center of all—and I mean *all*—attention. Bras got readjusted, skirts got hiked, legs crossed, perfume sprayed, eyelashes batted, smiles went off like the Fourth of July, and hair (real and synthetic) got flipped, shaken, and smoothed. If the Metro car was a universe, he was surely its sun!

His lavender-blue silk shirt was expertly tailored and fit smoothly across his broad, firm chest. With even his slightest movement, it peeked seductively through his unbuttoned trench coat. His beautiful, honey-colored face smoldered in a quadrant of golden morning light, while his dark-brown eyes darted through the Metro car like two wild birds of prey, shamelessly feasting on the candy-box assortment of tits, asses, hips, and legs. Unexpectedly, they locked on to my smooth, African agate necklace, but only after devouring every square inch of my 38DDs, jiggling and swaying with the motion of the car. His unbroken gaze was unapologetic and lusty.

Being a stickler for fairness, I ogled his upturned cock, rigid with desire. Finally, he smiled and started finessing his way through the Monday-morning mob toward me. He settled so close, I could feel his body heat and smell the breathtaking scent of his earthy cologne wafting from his stylish coat. It was then I noticed his incredible choker, made of very rare, Neolithic, clear quartz beads. He began his cunt quest with some interesting gemstone lore about my beads. I didn't expect an ordinary line from such an extraordinary man, and he did not disappoint!

"Botswana agate can be helpful for those struggling to be genuine. It also protects a wearer from bad dreams."

"Genuine? I'm probably one of the most real people you'll ever meet, Mr.——?"

"Todd Oliphant." He extended his hand. "And you are?"

"Lisha Lane."

I held out my hand to shake his, but, instead, he wove his fingers through mine and drew our joined hands to his solid chest. It was an extremely intimate gesture from a stranger, but I found it sexually thrilling.

"You're a very attractive man, Todd, but I'm really not into all that mumbo jumbo about stones and dreams. I love beautiful beads, but I just string 'em up and wear 'em. And as far as dreams go, I haven't had a dream since grade school; let alone a nightmare."

"Really?" His smile never wilted. "How do you know *this* isn't a dream?"

I don't remember blinking or looking down, but I must have. When I looked up, our car was empty. I looked into the adjoining car and it was also empty, except for Todd. There he stood, smiling and signaling me to join him. I couldn't resist.

"Is this a d-d-dream?" I stammered.

"*You* tell me."

I shrugged, feeling foolish. "I'm not sure."

"But you're so sure dreams are all 'mumbo jumbo.' Ever heard of Oliphant's Beads of Antiquity on Lake Avenue, in Old Pasadena?"

"I've heard of it, but I've never been."

"Perhaps I can persuade you to visit," he said, gazing hungrily into my eyes. An elegant white business card with crisp, jet-black ink appeared between his fingers. "I'm a certified gemologist, jewelry designer, and metaphysician. I've spent most of my thirty-five years studying and lecturing about the power of stones and the meaning of dreams. My two brothers do most of the actual jewelry making. Our family has sold the rarest beads and made the finest jewelry for hundreds of years—since my great-great-great-grandfather arrived in New Orleans from Senegal, as an enslaved African."

"Are you going to teach your sons?"

"I have a daughter, fifteen, successfully selling her own line of semiprecious earrings. Her mother and I parted, as friends, years ago, but I cherish the dream of having another little me. Do you have children?"

"Not yet," I said, thinking, *But I cherish the idea of fucking your fine ass up and down this empty railcar, trying to make one.*

His head pulled back slightly and his thick, chiseled lips formed an "O," as if he heard my thoughts.

"May I take a closer look?" he asked.

He didn't wait for permission; just slid his cool, smooth fingertips onto my throat, beneath the necklace, lifting it into the lavender daylight pouring through the large, smudged windows. He held it for nearly a minute, gently shifting it this way and that, causing the hairs on my neck to send a four-alarm fire to the delta above my thighs. My pussy pulsed with a craving to be crammed.

He spoke softly but firmly, "Eleven minutes to the next stop, Lisha.Yes . . . or no?"

"Yes!"

I had barely tacked an "s" on the end of "yes" before my skirt was scrunched in a roll beneath my full breasts, the damp crotch of my panties had been yanked aside, and my naked ass was smashed against the metal wall, nearly six feet in the air. His perfectly round head was vigorously gyrating between my thighs, and his strong tongue was pummeling my stiff clit like a punching bag in an anger management facility. My strong thighs rested on his stone-hard shoulders, and my helpless calves flopped rhythmically against his strong back until he slid his cool fingers into my hot, juicy, waiting pussy.

Suddenly, my body quickly stiffened as he sucked and licked harder and faster. I slowly spiraled into a long, luscious cum. Once I was done, he removed his fingers, lowered me to his lap, and gently plunged inside me with his large, hard cock. He started pumpin' me deep and slow. I yelped and moaned with intense pleasure until I felt him rumble within my taut walls. We remained joined in an intimate embrace for a few seconds, but soon rushed to straighten ourselves.

As our train rolled to a stop, he sighed. "Yes, you *are* genuine, Lisha Lane. Promise you'll visit me soon."

"Promise!"

"Sweet dreams," he whispered after hungrily kissing my lips, oblivious to the fresh horde of onlookers boarding the train.

From the train to my office, I mentally replayed the sexy railcar encounter over and over. It kept me so aroused, I headed straight to the executive restrooms on the seventeenth floor, where I massaged myself into another spine-whippin' orgasm. I quickly showered and changed into my low-cut, curve-hugging, chocolate jersey dress, reserved for such emergencies. I craved more of his scent, his strength, and his manly wildness. I promised myself that next time, I'd be the "giver," and that "next time" would be very soon. I imagined walking into his shop, dropping submissively before him, and giving his long, gorgeous black cock a generous serving of my most exotic head, with my smooth agate necklace wrapped snugly around his balls.

After a morning that sexy, trying to focus was futile. I floated, dreamily, from one assignment to the next with little success. I ended up hunting down my personnel file to check out how much leave I had on the books. I discovered a week's worth of sick days. I dabbed a little toothpaste in my eyes, rubbed my nose until it glowed cherry red, made a series of Oscar-worthy sneezes, and my coworkers couldn't get my ass out of there fast enough. People with children in college can't afford to get sick.

Once outside, I dug through my purse, frantically searching for Todd's business card. It wasn't where I remembered placing it. You would have thought I was looking for a donor organ. In a frenzy, I dumped my whole purse onto a Classified section someone had abandoned on the bus bench. Most of my belongings were still in a pile when my bus arrived. The driver shot me a look of disgust as I boarded. She was being seriously harassed by a quartet of foulmouthed, wannabe bad girls. They were acting loud, rude, angry, and crude, and became increasingly agitated as I searched my purse for my Metro pass. Finally, at the bottom of the heap, I found my pass and hurriedly swiped it.

Once seated, I found Todd's card lodged in the shank of a stunning aquamarine ring, which I immediately slipped on. The teenage girls abruptly settled down in the back of the bus and began quietly amusing themselves with their bejeweled phones and iPods.

"You must be my lucky charm." The driver sighed, glancing up into her rearview mirror in complete disbelief.

Even a block away I recognized Todd, moving about near the large window of their upscale storefront. He smiled as I walked nearer, but it seemed vacant. He had changed into a sheer, white and beige, oversized, silky, button-up shirt with no collar and relaxed, matching slacks—quite a departure from the stately trench and executive tailoring.

"Nice to see you again," I said, "and by the way, thanks for this beautiful ring. How did you know I was a Pisces?" I held out my ring finger.

Todd's dark, leopard-like eyes sprang wide with surprise. He said, "I actually made that ring for one of our important clients, as a peace offering for an unavoidable oversight, but my brother thought it was inappropriate—'too intimate' were his exact words. Anyway, I'm glad *you* like it."

"Well . . . let's see what makes Oliphant's Beads so special."

He led me through a pair of taupe velvet curtains, down a short hallway, and into a large, stylishly lit showroom. Everything was displayed in intricately carved cases. I had visited many bead stores, but this was clearly the *crème de la crème*. Everything was color coordinated and displayed categorically, but the arrangement was definitely not stuffy or museum-like. Everything could be touched and examined. It was hard to believe so many beautiful beads could be found in one shop. Bead-buying is one of my many passions, but I didn't come to buy beads, at least, not today. I came to be the giver of immense pleasure.

I gently closed the large, ebony, hand-carved door behind me and quietly turned the dead bolt. By the time he turned around, I was butt-ass naked with my little brown dress draped neatly on my arm, next to my purse. His eyes drank in the sight of my smooth, blueberry-brown skin, and his lovely cock executed a stiff salute. Playtime!

I moved toward him in a kind of slow-motion, runway stroll. Leaning in, I gently nibbled his full lips and slid his pull-ons to the floor. He playfully kicked them aside. Off came my Botswana agate necklace and, as planned, I knelt before him and used it to lasso his large, velvety balls. Once I tightened the necklace perfectly, he moaned deep and arched his heavily muscled back against a large glass menagerie full of ancient amber and silver amulets. Since morning, he had changed to a light and grassy scent and shaved himself to satin smoothness, almost as if he knew I was coming to suck his cock in appreciation for the sexiest morning of my life.

I captured his throbbing cock and flooded it with my wildest kisses. Within the warm wetness behind my brilliant, merlot-colored lips, I swirled his smooth mauve dick tip in circles, until his muscular thighs started trembling. His strong hands passionately clenched my shoulders. I sucked him completely inside and stroked his whole dick with rhythmic swallows. I guided him in and out of my mouth, steering him with one naughty finger buried deep in the pillowy flower of his tight, round ass. Back and forth . . . in and out . . . deep and deeper . . .

In one sharp motion, he pulled me to my feet and growled, "Ride it!"

I climbed up on him, and he effortlessly lifted my cunt into alignment with his ready cock.

"Whatchu waitin' for?" he asked sternly. "Fuck me! If you want your necklace back, you gonna fuck me like you ain't never fucked before! Something tells me you're the kinda sexy-ass bitch who'll fuck me just right to get it back."

I took him to the roof of my vagina and began snapping my hips into him.

"Work it, girl! Awww, yeah, you workin' that pussy on me now!"

What can I say? He got rough, so I got rough. "Say my name, you Coke-bottle-cock—slingin' muthafucka!"

He looked stunned for a few seconds but finally muttered, "You ain't runnin' shit! If anybody gonna call out a name, it's gonna be you! What's *my* name?"

What can I say? Some guys need to have the upper hand, so I cranked my pussy into fifth gear and started fuckin' the livin' shit out of my railcar lover. Every time I took him to the top of my pussy, I'd grunt his name and tighten around his shaft with all my might.

Barely conscious, he asked, "Who has the sweetest, tightest, juiciest pussy in the world?"

"Lisha Lyric Lane, that's who, muthafucka!"

He released in a long series of pulsing waves. Then, and only then did he call my name again . . . and again, plowing deeply into me with the last of his hardness.

Afterward, he trapped my wrists with his large strong hands and pulled me in tight for several long, passionate, tongue-dancing kisses, and said, "This hasn't happened in a long time."

"This has *never* happened to me," I admitted reluctantly.

"Well, the damage is done." He sighed, pressing my agate

necklace into my palm, along with a rare African amber amulet. "I have a lot of new items to put in stock and a ton of online orders to fill, Lisha. When can I see you again?"

"How about tonight, in my dreams?" I teased.

"Can you handle that? Dreams can get really wild sometimes."

"Wild's my style. Boring is what I can't handle. I handled your wild ass in the Metrorail car this morning, didn't I?"

"Um . . . I know you did. Let me call you a cab, Lisha." He wasn't asking.

The cab he called was more like a limo. The driver refused to let me pay or tip him, and walked me to my door. As I fished for my keys, he handed me a jewelry box wrapped in lusciously textured matte black paper, tied with a silver metallic bow. Inside was a delicate platinum neck chain with a striking emerald pendant and matching pear-shaped earrings. On the tiny attached gift card, in brilliant blue ink, was penned:

> *Wear this tonight, and I'll cum with you in your dream of dreams.*
>
> > *In lust,*
> > *T.K.O.*

I set that gift card down, put on my running shoes, and jogged three vigorous miles through my neighborhood. I showered, exfoliated myself to a satiny sheen, and adorned my naked body with only my emerald necklace set. Ordinarily, when I don't have to work the following day, I might stay up until one or two in the morning, but I couldn't wait to go to sleep.

When eight o'clock rolled around, I started sipping hot

chocolate and reading the most boring literature I could find. Those were my last conscious thoughts, and I remained sound asleep—until I heard a frantic series of police-like raps on my front door. I snatched a lacy robe from the arm of an overstuffed chair in my room and bounded downstairs, taking two steps at a time. It was Todd, dressed exactly the way he had on the train, standing next to . . . Todd? In the white silk Indian leisure suit, and a third . . . yes, third . . . Todd? . . . Beside the first two identical men. "Railcar" Todd spoke first.

"Ummm . . . you better sit down, Lisha. There's been a huge mistake. We came to straighten things out. If you never spoke to any of us again, I'd understand, but I hope you'll at least hear me out."

I was dazed when I answered the door but became suddenly lucid as my eyes ricocheted among the three identical men. "Let's hear it."

Railcar Todd was obviously distraught but continued. "I should have told you that my brothers and I are identical triplets. I should have made a date with you right then, instead of just giving you a card. I never imagined you'd come by so soon."

"I'm Todd's identical triplet, Tyson. I should have said something once I realized you thought I was Todd, but, like I said, 'The damage is done.'"

"And what about you?" I asked the third identical brother.

"I'm Tariq, and I ain't sorry about shit! I sent you that emerald necklace set so I could come fuck you tonight in your dreams. I liked what I saw when you were suckin' and fuckin' Ty in the display room this morning."

Todd's and Tyson's heads turned in unison.

"I don't know why you fools are lookin' at me like that. This woman's a **stun**ner—a stunner with mad skills! Ain't no need to be all proper now. I'm the only one who hasn't had the pleasure of gettin' all up in that good pussy! Let me tell you something else, Ms. Lane, we have fucked the same woman too many times to count. Sometimes they knew, and sometimes they didn't. Sometimes we let each other know, and sometimes we didn't. Am I lying?"

Todd hung his head in shame. Tyson just shook his head.

Tariq continued, "The truth is, we're three certified freaks who've done just about everything three identical brothers can do, sexually. The only thing we've never done is a three-on-one. I say we drop all the bullshit and let this be that special occasion. What do you say, Lisha?"

"Yes!"

What were the chances of having *this* kind of fantasy come true? What woman hasn't imagined being thoroughly fucked by two or three men? Watching the three of them remove every stitch was enough to blow an ordinary woman's mind, but today was not an ordinary day, and from this day forward, I would never be considered an ordinary woman. Watching them parade over to my bed with their dark honey skin, freshly showered and glowing like polished copper, was breathtaking. Their three long, thick, identical cocks bobbed with excitement. While I set out an assortment of toys, towels, and lubricants on my nightstand, they murmured in a tight huddle. I couldn't resist sliding my fingers in and out of my hot pussy and rubbing my clit into a feverish red peak. Once they realized how excited I'd become, it was on!

Like synchronized swimmers, they methodically changed positions. I stroked two of them, while another identical cock stroked me deep inside. Todd curled me into a helpless ball and fucked me slowly and gently. Tyson drove his cock into me like a fucking machine. Then there was Tariq . . . mmm, Tariq was so hot!

While Todd and Tyson nibbled my earlobes, licked and sucked the tender skin of my throat and full breasts, their thick fingers hunted between my legs to find my lower lips and pulled them wide apart, exposing my sensitive inner skin to the cool air. Tariq began a long, undulating, and masterful grind. Next, Todd and Tariq gently chewed and vigorously sucked my erect, dark chocolate nipples, while Tyson's hot mouth alternately sucked my clit and whipped his long, thick tongue deep into my pink-pillowed folds. The sexual scents of our quartet filled the air. My climb began. It was like nothing I had ever experienced. Suddenly, to Tyson's dismay, Tariq seized control.

Tariq sat me on his lap, facing out. He guided his stiff cock deep into my folds and gently bounced me up and down, while I moaned with pain and pleasure. Todd knelt before my splayed cunt and put his Metro car sucking to shame. Not to be left out, Tyson climbed up, straddling my gapped thighs, and started sliding his rigid cock in and out of my mouth until I convulsed fiercely, with triple pleasure.

The sun trailed its fingers of warm, rosy light through the blinds, across my plump, round ass. I love waking up whenever my eyes happen to open and despise the obnoxious blare of an alarm.

Was it all just a dream?

Not one thing was out of place.

Maybe I was just imagining sexy things.

On the way to the shower, I whispered to myself, "Maybe it's time for psychotherapy."

In my mirror image, I noticed a long, delicate, platinum

chain and pendant between my pendulous breasts—three huge diamond peas, peeking from a vaginal-like slit in the exquisite platinum pod. When I touched the top pea, a hazy image of Todd appeared.

"When you want any one, two, or all three of us, that's all you need to do."

Yes!

Atlanta Proper

Tabitha Strong

Where do I know him from? Mr. tall, bald, and sexy was making rounds across the room, shaking hands with all the right people.

"Kellie . . . Kellie, look at Precious Wilson." Gabby tugged on my sleeve, trying to get my attention. I was too busy eyeing him. "Ooh, girl, the years have been kinder to some of us than others."

"Huh?" I answered finally.

"Over there, on the dais. She looks fifty, not thirty-five. Didn't she graduate a year before us?"

"I don't know. Who can remember? That was almost fifteen years ago."

"When she finds out you're back in town, she'll be all over you to join her women's group."

"Oh, great." *What could be better? A root canal?*

Precious stepped up to the podium. "Ladies and gentlemen, if you'd be kind enough to take your seats, we'll start the program."

I took a deep breath and sat down with Gabby and her husband, Chuck, at our assigned table.

The two hundred dollars I'd spent on the ticket was for a good cause, community development, even if it had been years since anyone in that room set foot in the 'hood—myself included. The air was dense with perfume and spotted with proper ladies' hats, each more elaborate than the next. Reflexively, I sat up a little straighter, shoulders back, head tilted slightly upward, mirroring the image of all the other good Christian women with their respectable upbringings and superior educations.

"Thank you all for coming to Friendship Tabernacle's Fourth Annual Youth Center fund-raiser, honoring Atlanta's Black business leaders who are as generous with their time as they are with their donations."

Clap and look interested, Kellie.

"Our first honoree is a man who came to Atlanta with a good idea and unstoppable determination. Today, Mr. Roderick Tyler is the founder and CEO of Tyler Foods."

Time to clap again.

"And ladies, he's single."

Oh, that was the punch line. Small laugh; more clapping. I wonder if I'll get home in time to catch the end of the basketball game.

"Good afternoon, everyone." His voice was velvet, catching my attention for real. There he stood, the vaguely familiar specimen I'd noticed earlier. "I'm humbled by this honor and share it with my two senior vice presidents. Without them, I could not do the good work I try to do."

That voice buttered my skin. "Gabby," I whispered. "Did we go to school with him?"

"No, he graduated from T.U."

Rick from Tennessee. Suddenly, I wasn't sitting so straight in my chair. I wanted to slink out of the emergency exit. I bit softly on my lip, trying not to indulge the memories, but that voice, damn it, was bringing back every delicious detail with each rolling word.

· · ·

"You could crash at our place, if you want." Gabby made the suggestion from behind her third Rum Runner daiquiri. The noise in that slushy bar was so loud she had to repeat herself. I wasn't too surprised. Gabby was always the more outgoing one among us, dragging me along for the ride under duress. But that night I was too drunk to care that she hadn't bothered asking me before offering up our floor to some guys we'd just met. Besides, it was Freaknik weekend, a 200,000-strong college block party where anything goes. Not to mention how fine these men were—three flavors; chocolate, caramel, and butterscotch. I wouldn't have minded a taste of any of them.

When the place closed, we spilled into the street with the rest of the crowd. Rick drove and we passed plenty of chicks acting a fool—booty-poppin' on the back of pickup trucks and flashing everything you could imagine.

The thought blew past: *I don't even know these dudes. My mother would kill me.* But I'd turned twenty that week and as far as I was concerned, I was grown.

What were the rest of their names? *Sean? Sam, no, it was Sam. And the light-skinned one was Jeff, I think.* They were cousins, both on the basketball team, giving us something to talk about back in our apartment. I acted like the night would end with some friendly sports talk and extra blankets. But Rick's cornrows and smooth, onyx skin had me stealing looks when I thought no one would notice. Sitting on my desk with his feet in the chair, he had plenty of swagger and was all about letting me know it.

"You got a light?" he asked me, producing a freshly rolled blunt. The bass in his voice only made me want to do his bidding.

"Gabby's the Newport fiend. Gab. Hey, Gabby." I tapped her shoulder, but she was passed out cold on the sofa. Shaking my head, I fished a lighter from her purse and handed it over. I'd only smoked weed one time before and was looking forward to the second.

"Looks like your roommate is going to miss out," Rick noted through a plume of smoke, then passed the blunt my way.

I took it strong, like I did that kind of thing every weekend, and shrugged. "Her loss."

Rick smiled at this, a smug smirk with his tongue making a tantalizing appearance. Then he nodded in his friends' direction. "We're fixin' to play a game. If you can handle it, that is."

"A game? What, like Truth or Dare?"

Rick laughed. "More like just dare."

Sam took the blunt next and dragged on it slowly while my skin started to prickle and burn. Was it the weed, or the anticipation of what he meant? I couldn't tell.

"Jeff, you want to tell her how it goes?" Rick asked.

Jeff choked out a laugh after taking a hit. "Sure. You see, there's only one rule: Try to say, 'Stop.'"

"Stop?" The word made me nervous, Rick could tell.

"Hold up, Jeff. Don't scare the girl, damn." He jumped off the desk and raised his hands. "It goes like this: You say stop, we stop. You say it, and we lose."

"And if I don't tell you to stop?" I pressed, curious to say the least.

"If you don't, then we win."

Sam slapped Jeff's hand with a sideways grin. "Yeah, and she wins, too, right, cousin?" Jeff slapped him back, nodding in return.

And then they were all quiet, waiting on my response. "Okay, so the big question is . . . what are you going to do to me?"

Jeff began to slip off his belt. "See, now that's the hard part.

You won't know until it's happening." He let the belt drag on the floor and reached for my hand. "Come on, pretty girl. Let's see how you **do.**"

Already the word was on my lips. I could have won the game right then and there with the way my chastity was pounding in my ears. **But** no, I was following Jeff into my bedroom, with Rick slipping his hands under my shirt and Sam closing the door behind us.

I turned on the light, but Rick shut it just as fast. He went to the window and raised the blinds instead. Just outside in the quad, the streetlamp blinked and stuttered, washing the room with an erratic strobe.

In my bra, I sat on the edge of my bed, my heart in my throat, and tried to think of something to say. "That thing is annoying as hell. Keeps me awake every night."

Rick moved next to me on the bed, dragging his finger over my lips. "No, it's perfect. Just enough to see what we're doing."

He was so close to me, a dark silhouette cut in sharp angles. With only the slightest hint of pressure, his finger glided over my bottom lip, curling around my teeth. Grinning with moistened lips, he let it wander along the rim, encouraging me to open wider. It came slowly at first, his tongue sweeping past my trembling lips with deft restraint. He was easing me backward and I expected to feel the cool of my sheets underneath me. Instead, the bed dipped and I landed in Jeff's lap.

"You ready?" Jeff asked me.

But I couldn't answer that question. I didn't have a clue.

Rick inhaled sharply, sucking the breath from my lungs, and whipping his tongue against mine while Jeff lifted my arms into the air and wound his belt around my wrists.

My eyes snapped open. I was scared shitless, mostly because

the fear turned me on. *I should tell them to stop. I should . . . oh, but damn, that feels good.*

Sam was kissing my stomach. Twirling licks dancing across my skin made my hips roll in a request for more. Jeff nibbled at my fingertips two at a time, watching Sam go to task on my belly button.

Rick placed his lips at my ear, toying with my earring between his teeth. "Just say the word, Kellie. Say it." His voice quaked through steamy breath, blanketing my neck.

No. I didn't want to say it, even if the leather was cinching my skin. Instead, I welcomed Rick's hand on my thigh, pulling one leg apart from the other and challenging the elasticity of my miniskirt as it retreated above my crotch.

Sam didn't skip a beat, placing his fingers flat against my cotton panties, tapping on the heat and moisture seeping through. He looked up at me with those bedroom eyes and I watched his chin disappear beyond my skirt.

Thick lips wrapped over my cunt like a perfectly rounded cup of warmth while he sent a long, hot surge of breath leaking through my panties.

I thought that I would fucking explode.

Arching against Jeff's thighs made him tighten his grip on the belt, wrapped tight enough already to ache. Rick swallowed my moan as soon as it left my mouth, kissing me more deeply than before.

And then Sam exhaled again, this time with his broad tongue pressed against my clit through the fabric. I cried out and Sam still didn't remove my panties. He kept them intact, torturing me with that brilliant tongue, soaking them as the fabric slid over my hungry pussy while he lapped at me steadily. Stop? I had forgotten the meaning of the word. It wasn't in my vocabulary.

Three tongues were having their way with me—and what now? Switching positions? The idea alone had me stirring on the bed like an epileptic in heat. Everything I had been taught, every lesson in dignity and self-respect my parents grilled into me, was dulled under the weight of my desire.

When Rick stood up, the others followed in a routine choreographed to the second. Jeff kept hold of my wrists and plunged his tongue into my mouth while Sam scooped one of my breasts from my bra. Rick pulled the soaked crotch of my panties to the side and blew. The cool air made me whimper. His hot, tender licks made me delirious.

I could hear Gabby's voice. "Chuck played golf with him a few weeks ago." She had that pleased-with-herself look on her face as she folded her napkin on the table.

"What are you talking about?" I asked her, all the chatter of the reception room suddenly present. People were busy mingling and only the two of us were left at the table.

"Don't get cold feet on me now, Kellie. Five minutes ago you said you wanted to meet him."

"Who?"

"Roderick." She sighed. "Were you even listening to me?"

"Gabby, no—"

"Too late," she muttered from the side of her mouth and then produced one of her winning smiles. "Ah, here he is; the man of the hour."

Rick smiled back. "Chuck, your woman greets you like that every time you see her?"

Gabby tossed one of her flighty laughs into the air and Chuck cleared his throat. "You remember Gabby, of course. And this is her old college roommate, Kellie Pierce."

"Who are you calling old, Chuck?" I quipped. *Oh, help me, Jesus.* Rick smelled delicious and looked even better.

"Kellie is heading up distribution down at C.C. now. Maybe she'll do a brother right and cut you in on a better soda deal," Gabby purred, trying to hook me up, but having no idea it was the second time she'd done the honors. "Chuck, come bid on something for me in the silent auction," she cooed, pulling him away, and flashed a wink over her shoulder. How did she always manage to get me into trouble?

"Remind me to thank her," Rick said once they'd left.

"Well, I'm not exactly sure if I can do anything on your beverage contract."

"No, this thank you is about fifteen years overdue."

Oh, shit.

He lowered his voice and stroked his goatee. "Kellie, with those big green eyes. If I tried, I bet I could still remember how you taste." All the blood rushed right to my toes and back to my head. *How dare he talk to me like that? How dare my body react the way it did?* "We have some unfinished business, don't you think? Our game ended in a tie."

I cut my eyes. "I was drunk. I don't even remember what happened that night."

Rick laughed. "You wanted us to dig you out; all three of us. You were begging for it." Then leaning closer, he added, "But, baby, that's no way to lose your virginity."

My jaw clenched. "That wasn't for you to decide."

"You were in over your head, Kellie. Even now, you won't admit that?"

I'd spent a whole lot of nights imagining it ending differently. I wanted them, all right—in my mouth, in my pussy . . . every one of them. I copped a sly grin, remembering their exit. "Your boys were mad as hell."

"Yeah, left with blue balls. Both of them tried to kick my ass."

I laughed and then paused, just looking at him. "You ruined me anyway, you know."

He frowned.

I'd had my share of romantic trysts and long since said farewell to my hymen, but nothing, no one had come close to what they did to me. "How can one man ever compare with three?" I questioned.

"Let me take you out and we'll put that to the test."

"You mean a proper date?"

"I don't know how proper it'll be. I'll leave that up to you."

Damn him. Rick had me trippin' over how to play this. Do we go out for sushi and have a respectable conversation or screw the pretense and just throw down in my hallway?

When the doorbell found me still in my robe trying to choose what to wear, I decided to just say, "Fuck it."

"I know I'm not early, Kellie," Rick commented when I opened the door. "That's a very nice robe."

"Silk. Hermès, actually." I leaned casually against the door frame, trying to tuck my heart back in my chest.

"You going to invite me in?"

"Have a seat on the sofa," I offered. "I'll only be a few minutes." I led, he followed; the silk flowing as I walked.

He sank into the leather and snatched my wrist, pulling me onto his lap. My robe fluttered and fell away from my thighs, leaving me bare from the waist down, and his hand slipped readily between my legs with a probing finger circling my clit.

"You don't want to go out to dinner," he declared, simply.

"No, I'm not really hungry," I breathed, licking my lips just inches from his.

"Is that right?" he said, sliding his finger deep inside me. "You seem pretty hungry to me."

"What about you?" I asked, squirming against his hand.

"Me? I'm fucking starving," Rick growled and flipped me onto my knees. I held on to the back of the sofa, steadying myself as he tugged my belt loose. First one wrist and then the other was wrapped in the silk before he tied the belt in a bow behind my back. He moved so quickly, I could barely keep up.

"You going to say it, Kellie? Can you?"

There I was, picking right up where we'd left off so many years ago. Still tingling over the control he had over me. Still creaming with anticipation for what was next.

Rick was busy burying his face in my ass and sliding his tongue back and forth under my clit when the doorbell rang again.

"Who the hell?" I wasn't expecting anyone else, though maybe I was hoping. He left me limp against the sofa to open the door. Jeff and Sam walked in, looking as tasty as ever.

"I see you already started," Jeff said, undressing as he came closer. I gasped when he dropped his pants; a thick, sand-colored cock was rising before my eyes. He spoke to me. "You should see how beautiful you look. All grown up now, huh, pretty girl?"

Sam walked over to me, too, and dragged his finger down my back, sending a shiver over my skin. "The one that got away," he said to no one in particular.

I couldn't wait one second longer. I popped my head onto that beautiful dick bobbing in front of my face.

Rick pulled his cock free from his fly and rushed on a condom. He placed his hands on my hips and plunged into my dripping pussy, rolling inside me like a tidal wave. Jeff guided his cock to the back of my throat and out again completely.

I sucked the hell out of that cock like that blowjob had been fifteen years in the making. Jeff took one hand to toy at my ass. Rick moistened me right up by dripping his warm spit on the tight ring just as Jeff's finger slipped in, followed closely by another. Across the room, Sam plucked a tube from his pocket before discarding his jeans, then took a seat on my club chair and slickened his latex-covered shaft.

Before I knew it, I was being whisked off the sofa by my bound wrists and scooped up by Rick. He placed me into Sam's outstretched arms, my legs draping over them and spread as wide as possible. I was open. Everything was wide fucking open, including my eyes, and I watched keenly as they went about adjusting themselves for the perfect angle.

"You ready?" Rick's voice was smoky and sweet.

"Hell, yes!"

Sam was first, lowering me onto his cock and pressing into my ass with slow precision. With patience he filled me with what I asked for, claiming each inch I gave him. I would lose my virginity to them after all—at least in that way.

Rick watched my face, giving me a moment to get used to Sam stroking my ass. Until it made my eyes roll back. He waited, rubbing his purple head on my clit for the sign, and took me deep when it came.

I stared right back at him with the same intensity, my mouth round with a kind of pleasure I didn't even know existed. They were fucking me, and teaching me, both at the same time, exchanging turns churning in tandem. I was the novice; they were apparently the experts, rolling ever faster into my depths, revving me like an engine 'til I was humming. Rick groaned, a low, dull rumble from deep in his chest—music to my ears against the backdrop of Sam's heavy breaths. I knotted my hands together as they racked against his flexing abs, my shoulders crying out for release as much as my pussy.

Jeff took a step closer then and pushed his cock into my moaning mouth. It was more than I imagined; more cock than I'd thought I could take. But the three of them flowed in and out of me, smooth like hot chocolate in the dead of winter. They had me, finally, the way it would have been. *Should have been.*

In a show of force, Jeff thrust his cock forward and I gagged on it as it choked back the words in my throat.

"Hold on, she wants to say something," Rick said and Jeff withdrew just as quickly. Everyone froze.

"Don't . . . don't . . ." I gritted my teeth. "Don't fucking stop!"

Don't Open Until Ramadan

Abdul-Qaadir Taariq Bakari-Muhammad

In the name of *Allah*, the Beneficent, the
Merciful, All Praises are due to *Allah*!

Dear Diary,

*I am writing to you because Ramadan this year will be quite
different. My man, soon-to-be "husband," will be working a
different shift at his job for the next six months. You see, he's a
security officer and every six months, his job rotates everybody's
shifts. So, to make a long story short, I won't be getting any dick
on the regular, which is normally during the daytime. As them
white girls used to say, "Bummer." Ha, ha. His name is Taariq
Kareem——dark skin, intelligent, thick, and sexxxxxxy in all the
right places. Like I said, he's smart and thoughtful, I might add.
He knows I like to film myself while I masturbate in various
positions. So, he went and bought me an unusual vibrator. He
knows I like movies that are considered swashbucklers. There is
just something that opens the floodgates seeing men swinging
their swords in the air, all in the hopes of fucking some damsel
nowhere near distress.*

*Men love their "cat fights." I luv a nigguh shaking a piece
of "steel" in his hands. I would say that's about even on the
physical attraction scale. Now, because of this attraction, he
went out and bought me a Black Diamond Rabbit Pearl that*

has a swashbuckling theme to it. Not only that, the color of this
vibrator is the same shade as his dick—a rusty-colored black
that's very hard to lubricate. I remember one time I sucked his
dick for about twenty minutes straight, trying to spit-shine that
mutha-fucka with my saliva and the gallon of cum he shot in
my mouth, to no avail. It looked like I hadn't even started. This
nigguh had somehow managed to swell my upper lip and it did
not look like I had done a damn thing. This shit made me mad
as hell. It made me so mad that I reverse cow-girled his ass so he
could see my other lips that needed swelling. There was no way I
was gonna half-ass good dick. Especially when I know Ramadan
was approaching and there would be no sex of any kind during
the daytime.

Adhering to the rules during the month of Ramadan is
sometimes difficult. We both work the graveyard shift. I am a
support technician for a major cable company. In other words, I
help male customers who accidentally download viruses to their
computer while stroking their dicks to porn in the wee-hours of
the morning. They always call around 3:30 a.m., mad because
their dumb, cheap asses let their virus protection plan run out.
I mean, if you will spend money on lube to jerk your cock, why
not add a few more dollars so while you are doing that there will
be no interruptions? Please don't get me wrong; Ramadan ain't
even here yet and I will be glad when it's over. A whole thirty
days of this shit will pluck a sistah's nerve in all directions.

Last year, during those nighttime hours of Ramadan, we
spent hours redefining that little, but so precious, act called sex.
There was one time that we had introduced sex toys into our
screw sessions. Funny how he managed to find a dildo his exact
size. He's six inches, by the way. Humph! Six good inches. He
told me I could practice deep throating it.

I told him, "Thanks, baby, but ain't nuthin like the real thing."

"So what, you giving it back?" he said.

"Nope, just making a comment."

As the daylight hours approached, we said a very long goodbye. I was so intrigued by that particular night, the next day I sat down and wrote this story. Mainly to remind myself of how far I have come to being both mature and comfortable with my own spirituality and sexuality.

THE EIGHTIES

Well, where should I start? How about introducing myself? Yeah, I think that would be appropriate. My full name at birth was Felicia Cassandra Washington. It's now Saleema Kataanah Washington—my legal Muslim name; at least, most of it. I wanted to change the entire name but declined, due to the fact I wanted to get married one day. I am five feet, eleven inches, dark-skinned, and a 100 percent plus-sized diva in my own right. As you can probably guess, I wasn't always Muslim. My roots are in Christianity; particularly Baptist. In my household there was one basic rule for the seven of us concerning religion and God. You simply had to believe in Him. Anything other than that, you couldn't stay in my momma's house. Unless you were my father.

Mommy begged him to go to church many Sundays. Yet, he always said no. I never fully understood why until I got older. However, when we were young, she made all of her kids attend every week. Again, as we got older, she didn't press the issue at all. Now don't get me wrong, church was religiously enlightening, but getting up early in the morning on a weekend to go to Sunday School, plus church later that same day, was something totally different. I guess it had something to do with Mommy being the teacher for Sunday School?

A funny thing happened one Sunday morning. I remember the day clearly; it was me, my sister Cynthia, my brother William, Taneesha, Robert, "Nay Nay" a.k.a. Gloria Stevens, and of course, Meez. Shawn Cortez. Now that I think about it, Sundays always had their moments. Even though we were still kids back in the late seventies, early eighties, all of us still remain in contact with one another, believe it or not. Anyway, my mom was teaching us about Sodom and Gomorrah. Such subjects concerning the Bible, she was very brief and vague on the matter. Like clockwork, in her conclusions——I always wondered where she even began most of the time— she would say, "This was that and let us go on."

Nay Nay stopped her that day and asked a question.

"Yes, Gloria. What is it?"

"Well, Mrs. Washington, I wanted to know what is Sodom and Gomorrah?"

Before she had a chance to respond, everybody's hand went up except mine. Mommy gave me one of her looks to say you better not raise it. She always treated me different than William and Cynthia. You see, she didn't give birth to them. They were my father's "chirn," as she would put it. She didn't really treat them any less favorably, but let's just say she really couldn't keep tabs on them like she did me. In some aspects, I hated her for it.

So, hands were up and the words "Ooh-ooh-ooh, I know."

"Calm down, one at a time. Okay, Shawn, do you know?"

Shawn stood up and said in her New York Puerto Rican accent, "Yah, Meez Washington; that's when two people get together and fuck, for real, for real."

The moment she said that everybody said, "Ooo oohhh."

My mom said,"Girl, watch your mouth. Don't you know this is the Lord's house?"

"I'm sorry, Meez Washington."

Mom was one of those old-fashioned, churchgoing, deep Southern women; from Georgia, to be exact. Shit, if she only knew what goes on in the South nowadays; especially in Atlanta. Dah durty, durty. Sexually, I miss that place.

Anyway, before I get off track. As Shawn sat down, ghetto-ass Robert stood up. "But look, Mrs. Washington, it's tru doe. My cuzin be knockin off honeys left and right. Err Saturday night. When I'm over his house, I peep in the room, he got honey in there bent over saying fuck me, fuck me, fuck me."

"Young man, you need to sit your hind pots down before you make me come over there!" Mommy just hated Robert. He was just too ghetto for her. True as that was, Robert was a trip. He had that class falling out that day. Yet, Mommy meant what she said. If you didn't do as she said, you were liable to get slapped across the head. I knew and they knew. Needless to say, Robert sat his ass down quick.

You see, it was things like that that just got to me about Mommy. Now, granted, she was in church all day long on Sundays and was a Bible-toting sister and yes, she knew how to keep a man (my father) home. Still, how many Saturday nights went by and I heard her in there getting her "boots knocked off," as we used to say. You know I did my lil' Peepin Tom thing, too. I'm sure we all did. I mean, late at night, when they were supposedly watching Saturday Night Live. *All I saw was my father pumping her from behind, moaning and groaning, while Mommy was saying, "Oh, Jesus! Thank you, Jesus! Oh, Jesus!!!!!" It must have been a good thing she was calling on the Lord.*

Besides, Daddy never got upset when she called another man's name. Daddy's name is Kevin.

That was my rationale anyway, when I was younger. Mommy was so frustrating. She refused to keep it real. From that Sunday School on, she stayed clear away from anything that could be considered "sexually oriented." Thus, fast forwarding me to more modern times.

THE NINETIES

It was the summer of 1991 and I had just completed one year of college at Virginia Union University. Mommy sent me there to study Theology. I put "Undecided" down as my major on my application. A lot of things went on at Union, but I prefer to let my man tell that story at a later time. I came back home to Hampton Roads having that one year of official adulthood under my belt. I wondered to myself, Where is everybody? *A year ago, right after graduation, everyone promised that they would keep in contact with one another. Yeah right! Come to think of it, Taneesha was the only one who did keep her word.*

Taneesha is so honest and trustworthy. Just why in the hell she chose to become a lawyer, I have noooo clue. She always sends me emails inviting me to come party with her and her sorors up at U. VA. Maybe one of these days, I'll take her up on that invitation.

I missed last Easter Sunday with Mommy. Thank God, I did. I know you are probably thinking, What an awful thing to say. *Humph, you just don't know. It wasn't a month that had passed and Mommy was like, "You ain't too grown to go to church with me this Sunday, are you?"*

Now that I was older, she always tried to get me with the guilt trip. I wasn't having it. I didn't feel like hearing any of Mommy's bullshit. I carried my black ass out in the street. I was bound to find something to do.

While I was driving toward the oceanfront to have some quiet time to myself, it dawned on me that Cynthia and William, my older brother and sister, were both stationed overseas somewhere in the Middle East. Now that I think about it, with all of those suicide bombings going on, Mommy probably wanted at least one of her kids to be with her during the holiday. Sometimes, I unintentionally think only of myself.

Well, there I was down on Atlantic Avenue on a Friday night alone, with nothing to do. Even though it was tourist season, I did manage to find a place to park. Surprisingly, the oceanfront wasn't that crowded, so finding a parking space was easy. It was about 10:30 at night. So, off to the beach I went. The beach was always the place where I went when I wanted some "me time." A few minutes later, I was interrupted by a very peculiar sound. I know I wasn't hearing things because a white couple had just walked past me, giggling about the same noise I heard. Something told me to investigate and walk a little bit farther to my right. I didn't have anything else to do.

The noise was off and on and becoming more defined. No doubt someone in the distance was fuckin'. To be exact, as I looked further, someone was giving some good head and, for damn sure, someone was receiving it. I said to myself, "I'll be damned. At least somebody's having fun."

My curiosity plagued me; I just had to know. So, I waited a while and listened to the sounds of oral sex that filled that little space on the beach. Don't ask me how but I knew these things about the couple that was getting it on.

As I approached the steps that led onto the sand, I took my sandals off and sat down on the first step. The railing to the right of me obscured my view somewhat, but that was cool. I didn't want them to notice I was watching. So there I sat, so bored, I was listening to strangers having the type of fun that I wanted to have. That and my lil' freaky curiosity would not let me leave. On the count of five—one, two, three, four, five—I looked directly in their direction. From what I saw, she was giving brother man some serious head problems. The brother was a fairly large man with a big gut. Every time she would go down on him, it seemed like she was trying to nail her forehead into his pelvis. She must have been doing a good job; all I saw was his head moving left to right like he was having a nightmare. You know how they show someone in a movie lying down and they're having a bad dream? They start saying, "No, no, no," and then they wake up from the dream? Well, that's how she had brother man. Almost screaming, if you ask me.

Whoever they were, they did not give a fuck about who was in their vicinity. Didn't they see me sit down not twenty yards away from them? I guess not! I could have been the police. In Virginia Beach, the cops will lock your ass up for doing some shit like that out in public in a heartbeat, as is. Now here was this bitch twice my size, wearing a hot pink short skirt, with no bra on, and titties damn near touching the sand, sucking dick. Then she had the nerve to have a tattoo on the right side of her ass of Fat Albert's face with his tongue pointed toward her asshole. I don't know what tripped me out the most, the tattoo or the fact she wasn't wearing any drawers. As for him, imagine a sumo wrestler with a bald head and black, instead of Asian, but butt naked. Yeah, it was going down in Virginia Beach on that night. No-shame-in-the-game.

Still, with that said, while I watched her go down on him,
I became somewhat stimulated and taken by their brazen
sexuality. Then I stopped and thought about how long she was
sucking him. It seemed like it was about an hour. Whatever
it was, she had beaten my record by a mile. By now my pussy
was so wet, I could smell the aroma coming out of my jeans,
hypnotizing me into sending my middle finger on a mission.
The mission was to lead the other fingers into bringing me to an
orgasm. I placed the tip of my middle finger beneath the orange,
floral lace micro-bikini I was wearing on a direct route to my
clitoris. Tonight was about direct stimulation. No long, drawn-
out masturbation sessions that I normally preferred. Ah yeah,
that's it. That's my spot. *Nothing would stop me until I was*
in orgasmic bliss.

I looked over at the couple and saw that bitch still sucking
that nigguh's dick. She was about her business. No licking balls,
talking dirty, fuckin' or nothing. Just straight up and down
"Omma bust this nigguh's drum" kind of an attitude. Shit, I
didn't know a man could last that long, considering the speed
and ferociousness that she was inflicting on him. I just knew
her lips were swollen. They had to be. Her ass needed to be
doing porn. The average woman would have gotten tired by
then.

As soon as I made that comment to myself, at that exact
moment, they both got up and removed the rest of their clothing.
She wasted no time climbing on top of him. By this time he was
lying horizontal and, like clockwork, she started thrusting her
hips back and forth. This sister put a nice rhythm on this nigguh.
Who in the fuck said a big girl did not have the stamina or
aggressiveness to fuck like anyone else? I would like to meet their
men, team up with home girl, and show them all that a big girl

will fuck a nigguh right into a coma. This is no bullshit. Just keeping the shit real. Anyway, after I had pondered that thought, I noticed her lean forward a bit and place her hands on his chest.

As she looked him in the eye, she stated, "Yeah, this some good dick . . . yeah . . . good dick."

That threw me for a loop. By now the juices were dripping from my bikini through the jeans and onto the sandy concrete. I never knew public masturbation could be so good! I positioned not one, but three of my fingers directly on my clitoris. I rubbed it ferociously. Oh, I wanted so much to be in her shoes at that very moment. It had been a while since I'd had some decent sex. Tonight, I would have to settle for this escapade.

Her nigguh must have been on Viagra, 'cause he had not come as of yet. The next position I saw them get into was doggy-style. The brother wasted no time hitting it from the back. He tightened his hands around her waist and commenced to drilling. These mutha-fuckas were doing some serious fucking and didn't give a damn who saw it. I'd never seen a man with his weight move with such fluidity and passion. Then I thought to myself, Damn, how long can they continue this? Especially without getting caught?

As soon as I thought that, I heard him say, "Here it comes, girl! Here it comes! Ahhhhh!!!! Shit!! Shit!! Shitt!!"

When he came for the first and last time, I was on my fourth and final orgasm. It looked like I had pissed on myself. Exhausted, I rested my head on the railing, feeling dizzy but well satisfied. Fuck, my ass was out of it, feeling good as shit. I was so out of it, I didn't see the couple walk in my direction. They had dressed and were headed up the steps.

She glanced back at me and said, in a very deep Southern accent, "Gurl, you should've jown us."

He was like, "Yeah, fow-reel." Then they left the beach.

As they walked away, I noticed she still had some of his cum leaking from her ass down to her ankles. She didn't even bother to clean it up. Damn, that is what you call doing the damn thing and not giving a fuck who knows it!

After that, I headed toward my car, not giving a fuck if somebody thought I had peed on myself or not. People should know the difference between piss and cum!

So there you have it, diary. A moment in time from years ago that I can reflect upon that was instrumental in my quest for total sexual maturity; a maturity that would combine both my spiritual and sexual worlds into one. I figured to title this section of you with this heading during the month of Ramadan when I desire sex the most, but can't have complete access to it like I would like. I suppose if I write about it and the experiences that I have witnessed and have partaken in, it will help me not to stray away from my discipline. Well, until next year, diary. I will stop here. I hear my husband, Taariq, calling me. Salaam (Peace).

Selective Memory

Tigress Healy

Lorenzo claimed he would've broken my fall if he could have, but now I'm not so sure. He said he didn't know I had fallen until he came out of the room and found me slumped at the bottom of the stairs. This was all a bit crazy because memory loss was to be expected since I'd hit my head, but three days later, I still couldn't remember some of the things that happened prior to the fall. My doctor said I had a type of temporary amnesia and that I would be fine, but in the meantime, I had to rely on Lorenzo to remind me of things. When I told him I didn't completely remember him, much less being married to him, he showed me our marriage certificate and wedding album. Then he reminded me of something else: That I am a highly sexual being that likes men *and* women. I definitely didn't remember that.

Nine days after the injury, most of my memory was back and I could go to work, but I still didn't remember being bisexual. I remembered feeling jealous of beautiful women when Lorenzo complimented them, but I never wanted them for myself. To that, my husband explained that I was repressed, succumbing to society's disapproval of same-gender attraction. He said I was hiding myself from their rejection. He said my amnesia enabled me to try being "normal," but that I had always hated normal things, and that normal just wasn't fun. Moreover, he said he had married me because of my liberal sexual views and would feel differently about me if I changed them now.

So my amnesia had the potential to ruin my marriage if I was going to be prudent. I wasn't feeling sexually free at all, but I wanted to be myself, and would try to dig up the old me in order to save my marriage.

"I invited a friend over," Lorenzo told me twelve days after the fall. We were in the bedroom getting ready to change out of our work clothes. "She's in town for a conference. You know how every company loves to come to Atlanta to host events. Well, I met her at the food court in the CNN Center."

My heart started a cadence at the thought of them flirting over lunch, but then I remembered that Lorenzo told me I wasn't a jealous woman. But I *was* jealous.

"That sounds nice, honey," I managed, throwing aside the panty hose I had just taken off. "What time will she be here?"

"Around eight. After her workshops are done. And don't worry about cooking. I took care of the food."

"I didn't know you were so diligent."

"I guess you only remember the bad," he said, pulling me onto the bed, and onto my back, his dark-brown skin meshing with my light brown. "Do you remember how much you love having your pussy eaten?"

"Definitely," I said, trying to sound lighthearted and fun. But I was more concerned about the visitor. How was I supposed to behave? Was she coming for him, me, or us both? Was I to be a part of his "date" or to remain unseen?

He pulled the crotch of my black panties to the side and covered my pussy lips with his thick lips, softly sucking my clit. My desire swelled as he tossed my legs open wider and moved his neck in circles like he was just warming up. He flicked my clit with his tongue, over and over again.

"Lorenzo," I moaned, as he slurped my juices and probed his tongue into my pussy hole. His tongue darted into my ass. "Yes! Lick my asshole! Lick it good!"

My shirt was restrictive, and as I began to unbutton it, the doorbell rang. I lay frozen. My heart raced when Lorenzo got up. The outline of his humongous boner jutted out of his pants.

He didn't bother to wipe my secretions from his face. A few seconds later, I heard talking in the living room and began to dress.

"Why so soon?" A voice called to me from the bedroom door. The carpet had concealed the sound of her footsteps. "I know I'm early but I have a good reason for it. I wanted to invite you all to an impromptu gathering tonight, so our other plans will have to wait."

"But—"

"There will be food," she said, as if that addressed all of my concerns.

She invited herself in and stood beside the bed. She was dressed in a white, button-down, collared shirt similar to mine, a tan knee-length skirt, coffee-colored stockings, and tan pumps with pointy toes. Her hair was pulled into a bun. She sat on the edge of the bed and reached for my breast.

I drew back, breaking the gaze she had drawn me into. Her eyes never left mine as she put her hand out again. "Come here."

I scooted closer, watching the door for Lorenzo, who was missing in action. She finished unbuttoning my shirt and removed my bra. Moving ever so slowly toward me, she placed her tongue in my mouth and kissed me gingerly at first; then with growing intensity, as if I was an old lover she missed.

She explored my body with her hands as we kissed, ran her hands across my shoulders and down my arms, fondled my orbs. I couldn't remain indifferent. With each whirl of our tongues, I enjoyed more of her. I finally leaned in closer and pressed my body into hers.

She released the kiss and looked at me pensively. I felt sexy sitting before her, bare-breasted, with my back straight. She rested a gentle hand on my right breast before her left hand followed. Cupping both breasts, she moistened her lips and lowered her mouth to them. I inhaled deeply before her painted lips even made contact with my hardened nipples. I watched her lips cover my flesh, sucking the dark nubs like they contained the oxygen necessary to breathe. She bit my nipples lightly. The moisture in my pussy sprouted up like the water fountains in Centennial Olympic Park.

If this was why I had been bisexual, it certainly made sense.

Despite Lorenzo's claim that I had always been bisexual, the feeling I received from this stunning woman was completely new. I wanted her to put her hands between my legs as she sucked my tits, but I wasn't assertive enough to tell her so. Maybe I *was* bisexual. Maybe I secretly longed for a woman's touch. The rigid material of her sleeve scrunched as I grazed my hand across it. Lorenzo returned, drying his face with a towel. The clothes he had on while we were fooling around had been readjusted.

"Are we ready to go?" he asked.

Under the woman's spell, I found my voice and told him yes, although I really meant no. I had no idea where we were going, and I wanted to stay there, with her, feeling good.

• • •

A smooth, black, twelve-passenger limo was parked in the street outside our home, with a chauffeur in a black tuxedo standing beside the open door.

"Am I underdressed for the occasion?" I asked before stepping in.

"You're fine, hon," the woman replied.

"Then why'd you rent a limo?"

"I always have a driver," she said.

Lorenzo and I sat beside each other and when we were settled in, he said, "So you really don't remember Celeste? I was just kidding when I said I had met her at the CNN Center."

"Why?"

"Because it's fun! I didn't really think you'd forget our girlfriend. She's only been out of town for two weeks!"

"Our *girlfriend*?"

"We've all been together for three years now," Celeste said.

"Three years? All three of us in a relationship?"

"Well, no. You and Lorenzo are married. I'm just a third. I come over whenever you all want me, and tonight Lorenzo wanted me."

There went the cadence in my chest again. It sped up as she moved from the couch across from us and sat between us, resting one hand on Lorenzo's thigh and the other on mine. "I love to touch pussy and dick at the same time."

Since she had convinced me to leave my panties at home, it was effortless for her to stick her middle finger into my snatch while gripping Lorenzo's meat. Celeste was coordinated, finger-fucking me in and out while jerking him up and down. We were both moaning from the sensations, winding our pelvises like dancehall reggae dancers. I was on the verge of coming, but my jealousy welled up when she covered Lorenzo's mouth with her own, and they began to kiss.

She moved herself into his lap, facing him. She lifted her skirt and lowered her pussy onto his overgrown dick. She bounced up and down on it, throwing her head back and closing her eyes. Not bothering with the buttons, Lorenzo lifted her shirt and bra and began to suck her heaving tits.

"Join us," she said.

I hesitated.

"Touch my pussy, Patrice."

Looking Lorenzo in the eye, I placed my hand on Celeste's stomach and slid it down her body until I felt the brittle edges of her pubic hair. When my fingers met her clit, she cried out, "Rub it! Rub my clit! Make me come!"

Lorenzo pumped into her faster, feeling on her boobs and breathing hard. When the car stopped at a light, I pulled Celeste onto the other couch on top of me. I stuffed her titties in my mouth, then leaned up to kiss her, while she ground her pussy on mine. Lorenzo got up and squeezed behind her. Her eyes rolled back as he penetrated her. I grabbed her healthy ass, and we all rocked together, groaning and fucking in a frenzy of body parts. He pulled his dick out of her and put it in me while Celeste kissed my neck and thumbed my nipples. I hadn't remembered his dick ever feeling so good, filling my entire hole. I bucked hard as Lorenzo fucked me and Celeste rode me. Her fingers fumbled for my clit. My fingers fumbled for hers. I hoped the limo was soundproof because none of us could contain our joy.

We all came long before we arrived at our destination, one by one, then drifting off to sleep.

• • •

In the mountains of North Georgia, we stepped out of the limo and walked toward a log cabin the length of two or three homes. Several vehicles were in the wide driveway and on the grass. Lorenzo led us into the house without knocking. Most of the women inside were either topless or completely nude. The men were equally exposed. Several couples made out in the cozy living room in full view while others fucked ravenously in clusters.

Lorenzo led us into the kitchen and greeted the host, who wore a sleeveless green shirt and black basketball shorts.

"Troy, you know my wife, Patrice, and our girlfriend, Celeste."

"I know you?" I asked the tall, muscular man. He loosened the drawstring on his cotton shorts and pulled out the longest, thickest, blackest dick I had ever seen. He gripped it tightly then said, "You could never forget this."

Maybe I was a freak, because I wanted to jump on that dick and ride it like it could take me somewhere. Troy invited us to drink from the punch bowl on the counter, which Celeste and I did. We finished our drinks quickly, lingering in front of the bowl, while Troy and Lorenzo continued their small talk. I went to join their conversation but Celeste pulled me back. "You don't remember anything, do you? We have to join the women's circle before we can be with the men."

"The women's circle? What's that?"

"It's designed to warm us up."

"I'm already warm. In fact, I'm hot!"

Leaving the men in the kitchen, Celeste guided me down a long hallway. We stopped outside the last room. Sounds of euphoria seeped from inside.

"So we've been here before?" I asked.

Celeste's hand was on the knob but she didn't turn it. She sighed. "I don't know if I can do this."

"Do what?"

"Continue to deceive you like this."

She ran her hand across her forehead and stepped back. It was weird but she was so uniquely gorgeous that I felt blessed to have her as a girlfriend. She had come back from her trip and helped me release the sexual inhibitions I had developed as a result of my fall. There was no way I could repay her for that.

I leaned in to kiss her but she pulled back.

"Okay, how are you deceiving me?" I asked, kissing her hand.

Celeste let out a breath, then looked down the hall. "All of this is a setup."

"What kind of setup?"

She hesitated and sighed again. "For me and Lorenzo to keep seeing each other without sneaking." She looked down the hall again.

"I've been seeing him behind your back for three years. This place is a sexual retreat for swingers. We come every couple of months. *I'm* the one who's bisexual, but he always wished you were, so your amnesia was the perfect way to turn you into one—a bisexual swinger, that is."

I knew that was the part where the tears were supposed to spring forth, but I couldn't get them to come forward. I don't know why. I felt hurt, but not as deeply as I probably should have. Perhaps it was because I had just had sex with both of them and it was good. Or maybe it was because I didn't remember loving Lorenzo as much as a wife probably should.

"Now that you know the truth, what do you wanna do?" Celeste asked.

"What do you think?" I pulled her close and kissed her. "I wanna get some pussy."

I opened the door to the spacious room. Everything was wooden except for the wide window and colorful throw rugs. When we stepped in, a pair of naked women pleasing each other in the sixty-nine position disconnected themselves. Another kissing couple stopped and smiled. Soon, a dozen or so women formed a circle around us. Celeste led me into the middle, saying, "There's a special welcome for first-timers."

A skinny white woman extended her hand and introduced herself as Cara, the hostess. She was also Troy's wife. She lay on her back while the other women undressed me. Once my clothes were off, hands swept my arms, legs, and thighs; squeezed my tits and tweaked my nipples. There was a finger in my pussy. A thumb on my clit. Nipples pressed against my back. Fingers grazed my neck. Hands palmed my ass. Just as my knees began to buckle, Celeste said, "Lower her."

The women lowered me to Cara's face and she lapped my pussy while the other women massaged and sucked my breasts.

"It feels so good! I've never felt . . ." My body shuddered and I couldn't say anything more.

After my first orgasm, I was free to do whatever I wanted with whomever I wanted, and who I wanted was a dark-skinned woman with pointy tits. She was already making love to another woman. I went over and kissed her dark neck. She turned and gave me tongue while gyrating against her lover.

The three of us formed a sandwich on the floor, grinding, stroking, and groping one another. Before long, another woman joined us. She had a huge ass that looked fantastic. I left the sandwich and got onto my back like Cara had.

The big booty queen squatted above me, her sex scent reaching my nose before her wet pussy landed on my mouth. For my first taste, I ejected my tongue slowly, teasing her pussy lips tentatively before sucking her big clit.

The woman began wriggling her hips, spreading her pussy juices across my mouth. Each time I flicked her love button with my tongue, a moan came out. Soon, my entire face was wet and someone's head was between my legs.

Celeste was ready to go, explaining that while going into the women's circle was mandatory before going to be with the men, some women opted to stay in the women's circle. She wasn't one of them.

We left our clothes in the women's room and ventured into the living room.

Now that Celeste had told me the truth, I wasn't shocked to see my husband's dick plunging into a full-figured woman bent over the couch. She rubbed her clit as he stood behind her and dipped into her snatch in long, slippery strokes.

She shouted, "Fuck me, Lorenzo! Hard like you always do! Yeah, fuck me, baby! Fuck me hard!"

The host, Troy, sat on the couch nearby, handling his enormous tool while he watched. I kneeled before him and took as much of him into my mouth as I could. Lorenzo stopped fucking and asked to speak to me.

I said, "I can't! Don't you remember? I always suck Troy's dick, then fuck him when I come out of the women's circle. We don't need to break the routine today!"

Celeste joined me on my knees, stuffing Troy's balls into her mouth. He directed both of our heads and was loud about expressing his pleasure. He pumped his dick into my mouth while I kept it wet with saliva, licking its length and teasing its sensitive head.

Celeste released his balls and sucked his head with me. We kissed, letting our tongues swirl over his thick dick head while he shouted in a high pitch.

I was first to sit upon his dick, riding it facing him, while he smacked my ass and pumped into me. My tits were a mouthful for him, and he made my nipples feel incredible.

Lorenzo came over and tried to put his dick in my ass. It was too big, long, and wet to resist, so I helped him get it in. The men fucked both of my holes while Troy nursed on my tits. Celeste fed me her tits.

I came hard as the two men filled my holes with come. Celeste still hadn't come, so I used my new skills to eat her sweet pussy out. She came hard, then jumped up and grabbed my hand.

"I'm ready to go," she said, pulling me toward the bathroom. Once we were inside, she closed the door and said, "I think I'm jealous."

"Of what?"

"I realize I don't really know you, but I know a lot about you from Lorenzo. I've always liked the pictures he showed me but I never knew I'd feel like *this*."

I laughed. "So you mean you want me for yourself?"

"Yes."

"That's ridiculous. How can I believe that?"

"You gotta have trust."

"Trust *you*?" I scoffed. "My husband's mistress, who helped him convince me I was bisexual?"

"Well, you are."

Touché.

"As exciting as this has all been, I really don't like to share."

"You don't have to share, but you do need pussy. Look, I'll

stop seeing Lorenzo, okay? Just give me a chance. I'm sure we can work something out between us girls."

Embracing my new adventurous side, I smiled and said, "Okay."

Later, when the limo pulled up to my home, Celeste and I were locked in a deep kiss, our breasts out and hands scrambling for each other's pussies. Lorenzo couldn't hide his hard-on when he got out of the car, or his anger for not being involved in our display of affection.

We told him to go into the house but he insisted on waiting for us. Finally, I rolled down the window and said, "Hey, Lorenzo, I wanna thank you for playing these mind games with me. You helped me remember that I'm not straight and I'm not bi. Now I remember I'm a full-fledged lesbian, and that I've always wanted to get out of my heterosexual relationship with you."

Lorenzo looked confused. "But—"

"I have always loved Celeste. And now she's with me!"

"But, Patrice—"

"Am I lying?" I asked Celeste.

"No, pumpkin." She leaned out the window. "We're in love."

"Or at least in lust," I clarified.

"But—"

"I'll be in touch," I said, rolling up the window.

Lorenzo pleaded for me to get out of the car. He yelled for Celeste, but we told the driver to pull off.

Celeste kissed my neck and said, "I thought you were finished with him and only wanted me. Are you really going to get in touch with him?"

"Maybe," I said, returning her kiss. "It depends on my memory."

Sweet Chocolate's First Taste

Richard Burns

Columbus, Georgia: April 1979

I was training as an infantryman in the U.S. Army at North Harmony Church, Fort Benning, Georgia. I was seventeen years old and regrettably at the time, still a virgin. We were two weeks from graduation, and my buddies Ed Bristol and Juan Garcia took a weekend pass to visit Columbus, Georgia. A typical GI town of the late seventies, Columbus offered an endless selection of strip joints, tattoo parlors, and pawnshops. They catered to young inexperienced soldiers like me from Tinytown, Kansas; Nowhere, Oklahoma; and Jerkwater, Nevada.

We checked into a cheap, dreary motel near the cornucopia of strip joints, eager for our weekend of fun and freedom. Juan left to get "supplies," while Ed and I unpacked. The motel was a dump located on Victory Drive, with threadbare carpets, thin walls and drapes, and even thinner towels that felt as comfortable against your skin as twenty grit sandpaper. I would say it was clean, but the roaches would probably take offense. We were watching one of those pathetic seventies sitcoms when Juan abruptly returned. Grinning, he immediately began unbuttoning his shirt. Following Juan was a surprisingly beautiful black woman. I was caught completely off guard.

She closed the door behind her. I watched intently as her breasts swayed and jiggled ever so delicately. Her eyes were downcast as if she was embarrassed. She followed Juan into the room. At the sight of us her eyes went wide and she gave a shrug of her shoulders and a tip of her head, as if to say, *"Oh, well . . ."* To me, it all said: bashful.

Instantly I was captivated, and a little intimidated by both her age, which appeared to be almost thirty, and her luscious beauty. The woman—and she was a *real* woman, not a kid—had a pleasant round face with high cheekbones that gave it depth. She was tall, but still several inches shorter than my six feet, and I was struck by her very dark, coffee-brown complexion, which seemed at odds with her flowing, shiny curls of gorgeous shoulder-length hair. My palms were sweaty at the thought of getting them on her beautiful, perfectly proportioned breasts. Those breasts seemed to call to me with each sway and bounce. Her soft white cotton dress fit her form sensationally, hugging her upper body alluringly, accentuating the breadth of her torso before tapering down to her narrow waist, then loosely flowing over the graceful, but sweeping curve of her hips. My arms wanted to encircle that narrow waist, to lay my hand atop that scrumptious, perfectly developed ass, and then pull her body to mine. To press our chests and hips together; to meld into a single being; to feel her softness pressed against my hardness. To feel the slope and curve of her back as those glorious breasts press against my chest. She was perhaps the most beautiful black woman I had ever met. All of these thoughts vanished quickly with my growing anxiety at my impending moment.

Still frantically undressing, Juan said, "Hey guys, I need the room for a while."

"Hey ya'll." She gave us a wave of her hand. "He and I have

an . . . arrangement. If you guys want to make a similar arrangement, we're talking about forty dollars. Apiece."

Until that moment, I had no idea she was a hooker. This intimidated me also. After all, she was a *professional,* while I was the most rank of amateurs. I was seventeen, remember, and a virgin.

Ed and I both jumped to our feet. Ed was first out with his wallet. "Well, that sounds like a fair price to me." He handed over the money. I was fast on his heels with two twenties.

"Okay, now if you guys don't mind waiting outside?" Juan groaned.

We grabbed a beer each and left to wait on the balcony. We drank our beers, smoked, and waited our respective turns. I was actually very, *very* nervous. So I let Ed go before me.

Having never been away from home for longer than a two-week summer camp, I was naïve. Ed, Juan, and I had decided to share a motel room on our first weekend pass. As a private in 1979, my take-home pay was about 287 dollars a month, so we decided to share the expense.

Now, standing out on the balcony, I wished we weren't sharing a room. I feverishly wished I had my own room. I wished desperately for privacy.

Juan came out after twenty minutes or so and joined me for a beer and a smoke, while Ed went in for his turn "at bat." When Ed came out, the girl was peeking out from behind the door and gave me a wave of her hand. "Okay, you're next."

As I sat and bent over to untie my shoes, she dashed for the bed and promptly sat down. Strangely, she covered herself. Somewhat. *Shy? Is all this for real, or just an act? Surely, a hooker would've gotten well beyond being shy?*

She was already naked. She leaned against the headboard and smoked, with one leg bent and raised on the mattress. Her arms were hooked around her knee, effectively concealing her breasts from my gaze. Her other foot was on the floor; her luscious leg leaned against the side of the mattress, concealing the elusive, mysterious opening to her center. I could see the top of the sparse, neatly shaven hair on her pubis, a very narrow strip about two inches wide. The remainder of her sacred region was as smooth as glass. This was the era when women were just starting to groom themselves that way. *And what a Great Day it was!*

In an effort to hide my anxiety, I tried to make small talk. "What's your name?"

"Trisha." She sounded surprised. "What's yours?" She smiled at me, seemed genuinely glad for the conversation, and was suddenly more relaxed.

"Rick."

For some reason, it all seemed very conspiratorial. Or perhaps it was an unintended intimacy to the moment, but we still spoke in whispers.

"Hi, Rick. I'm happy to meet you."

She surprised me by putting her hand out; I shook it. It was then I was treated to my first glance at the bounty of her breasts. They were so perfectly proportioned, they were . . . mesmerizing. *Oh, dear God.* They were so *beautiful,* so large, so firm, so high . . . gravity defying, and capped with bright pink, nearly red nipples. I expected a shade darker than her very dark, brown complexion. Such a contrast.

"Likewise, Trisha." I did my best to sound relaxed. Once I was naked, I asked, "So where do we begin?"

She gave me a wry grin and opened her legs slightly, patting the mattress between them. "Have a seat."

My eyes ravaged her body while I moved in. I was nervous beyond belief.

She said to me, "You're trembling. Are you all right?"

I feebly replied, "Oh, yeah, I'm okay. I'm just . . . really nervous."

"Nervous? Why?"

Still not ready to let my secret out, I replied, "I'm just . . . new to this . . ."

"What are you saying? That you've never been with a hooker before?"

"No, I haven't. In fact, I've never been with *any* girl before."

"Really?" she asked incredulously. "Really? This is your first time? I'm going to get your cherry?" Her voice was barely a whisper.

"Yep, it's all yours. For what it's worth," I said, as my knees shook.

"Oh, my goodness. That's worth *a lot*. Well, then, I have to make this extra special for you."

What could I say? After all, she was the professional.

Her eyes suddenly became less guarded and while she chewed on her lower lip, I watched as her smile slowly grew into a beaming fountain of light. She turned to face me, leaning back, offering me her chest.

My heart was pounding so loud, I thought for sure she could hear it. But my desire managed to override my anxiety. With my right hand, I took one of those glorious breasts. It filled my hand to overflowing. *First contact! Oh, dear God* . . . As my breathing became deeper, I began to gently squeeze her breast, quickly consumed by the fantastic twins. My face was only a foot away from them. I was amazed by the warmth of her moist skin and how easily my pale white fingers sank into her dark softness. I was surprised at just how long her nipples were and they were still growing. I reveled in her breasts, their heavenly weight, and the contrast of black and white as my fingers pressed into her flesh. I placed my left hand on her stomach and felt her breathe for a moment. *Yep, she's real.*

Trisha took my left hand and slowly moistened my fingertips with her tongue. *Oh, dear God! How arousing.* She slowly pushed my hand south, through her curls, down to her center. "Do you feel that, Rick? That little nub? That's my clitoris. Just keep stroking it, like this . . ." she said, as she guided my fingers. She closed her eyes and embraced the sensation. Almost imperceptibly, she brought her hand to the half-hard root between my legs and stroked me. Gradually, while my organ grew in length, girth, and strength, I felt her clitoris swell to what felt like four or five times its original size. Soon, it was at least a half-inch in length.

Then after a minute, "A little faster," she instructed me.

Then, after another minute, "Now . . . stay gentle, now . . . a little harder . . . oh . . . oh . . . oh, that's it . . ." she gasped.

Her hips began to undulate against my fingertips. *Could that be because of me?* I kept my palm against that thin strip of hair, while her hips seemed to move independently of the rest of her. They swayed and turned, twisting and pressing against my fingers on my left hand. Her hands came up to her breasts; her fingers guided my right hand, showing me where she wanted more attention. Instructing me when and with what pressure she wanted me to squeeze, when and where to pinch, and how lightly or how firmly. When she opened her eyes again, I noticed there were gold flecks in her irises, which added depth to her face and an intensity to her smile. Her smooth, deep dark skin glowed. Her face was radiant. *If the eyes really are the mirror to the soul . . . what does this say about her soul?*

In the warmth of that humid Georgia night, the temperature

seemed to climb by ten degrees, as anxiety gave way to lust. Desire rose within me, consumed me, and filled the room to bursting capacity. Tiny beads of sweat began to form on the finest hairs of her skin between her breasts. I watched while the twins rose and fell with such delicate grace. She took a deep breath, expanding her diaphragm. They were so . . . *breathtaking.* Captivating. Her nipples seemed almost painfully hard now and her gorgeous body seemed to shimmer and shine with a fine sheen of sweat. My hands glided over her smooth,, moist skin.

"Do you like my tits?" she asked, almost breathless. I loved that she called them "tits," the same way guys do.

"They're beautiful. Better than I would've ever imagined."

"They like you, too," she said, arching her back slightly, firmly pressing her breast into my hand. Seductively she lowered a knee, opening her thighs, and closed her eyes. Her white teeth caught her succulent, red-painted lower lip. I could see the tip of her tongue, as she closed her eyes and slowly rolled her head from side to side. *From shy to seductive? So alluring!*

When the breath caught in her throat, she paused while her hips seemed to pulse. Then she groaned softly and froze. Eventually, with my hands still in place, I felt her breathe again. Finally, she opened her eyes fully and said, "Let me do something for you. Here," she said as she sat up and slid from under my hands.

"Just lean back," she guided me. I slid farther up the bed and took her place at the headboard as she lowered herself to the floor between my legs.

"I normally charge an extra twenty dollars for this, but since it's your first time, it really needs to be special. Now *this* is one great big white dick. It's *beautiful.* A perfect penis," she said. I thought, *the lady doth protest too much, methinks.* I'd seen enough men in the shower over the last several months to know I was nothing special down there. Nothing to be ashamed of either, but I knew better.

She licked at the head of my pole, then from the underside, bringing her bright pink tongue through the tiny slit at the tip. She continued licking away the drop of clear pre-come, and then swirled her tongue around the head. Trisha held my gaze as she took the head in her mouth. I felt the most incredible sensation of moist heat envelop me. She lowered her face on my shaft while she stroked me with her hand. Inch by inch she went lower, taking more of me in her mouth, staring at me much of the time, holding my gaze. It was so intimate. I was enthralled by the vision of this beautiful woman's face, the brightness of her lipstick, the darkness of her skin against my pale Irish whiteness, the shininess of my pole as it gleamed, sliding in and out of her mouth, gliding through her fist. *And . . . and . . . those incredible eyes,* I thought to myself.

Within a minute, she was moving with an energy I've never felt since. Her head and shoulders rose and fell as a single unit, with her entire upper body now twisting as she ascended and descended, her hand moving in concert. I lightly cupped her head and when I did, she looked back to my face and took me from her mouth. She began rubbing my organ over both of her breasts, circling the head over both nipples. Her head lazily fell back, while she painted the shiny slickness of my length over her breasts. "Do you like the way my breasts feel against your cock?"

"I love everything about them. Your skin is so warm and soft, your breasts so firm, nipples so hard." *So, now they weren't "tits" anymore, they were "breasts"?*

With my shaft now centered perfectly in her cleavage, she pressed those two gorgeous mounds together. I was trapped between the twins. *Surely, this is what heaven feels like.* Her body had a fine sheen of sweat and I glided easily through Trisha-flesh. As she took me in her mouth again, I saw her left hand move to her center and watched as she fingered herself. The sound of her fingers sliding on her own wet flesh was all I heard.

I felt my climax brewing as my organ suddenly swelled. God, I was hard enough to drive nails. Suddenly, I was terrified. *Surely, my cock was about to burst wide open.*

She looked at me with a glitter in her eyes, a wide smile revealed pearly white teeth, while she continued to stroke me.

"Do you like that?"

"Ahhh! I'm going to come," was my weak and feeble reply.

"Well, just come on, baby. Come for me now," she said. Then she must've felt my rod twitch because she quickly brought her mouth back over the head of my Johnson, just as I fired the first shot of my load. My orgasm crashed over me in a sudden deluge. I was drenched in magic sensations as the waves washed over my body.

Trisha's eyes snapped shut and she moaned slightly; her cheeks collapsed, sucking at my Johnson like a straw. After I stopped firing, she threw her head back and shook violently. I watched a vein in her throat intently as it throbbed while she swallowed; her left hand still at her center, moving furiously. I heard her involuntary exclamations, "Heee . . . Heeeeeeeee . . . Heeeee . . ." *She's giving herself pleasure, based on my pleasure!* I don't know why this seemed so incomprehensible for me, but it did.

"Well, how was that?" she asked, stroking my still-hard member.

"Amazing." I was only capable of one word. *At least it was more than one syllable.*

"I'm glad you liked it. I was thinking we could take a few

minutes while . . . your battery recharged. But I don't think we need to. You feel like you're ready to go again. So how about it? Are you ready to bust your cherry?"

"You have no idea." I knew it sounded stupid, but nobody had given me a script.

She crawled up onto the bed, graceful as a cat. "Actually, I think I do."

She used my chest for leverage and rubbed her lower lips along the underside of my rod, slowly. She allowed me to see the whiteness of my skin emerge from the darkness of hers. She took a second to run her hands over my shoulders, chest, and flat stomach—the six-pack compliments of the Army's miserable diet and a few hundred thousand push-ups, sit-ups, and flutter-kicks. She ran her fingers through each of the cuts in the muscles of my stomach. Then she raised herself and placed the head of my tool at her soft wet folds. The smell of sex was so thick, it was almost tangible.

She squared her shoulders and straightened her back, allowing me a fantastic look at that beautiful black body as it gleamed and glowed, towering above me. Then she looked me in the face, to make sure I was watching as she pushed herself down upon me. The sensation of my rod sliding into her was like gliding into hot oil. It was rapture. Her head rolled back for a second and I thought I could see the vein in her throat pulse before she began an even up and down motion of her hips.

She lowered her chest down to my face and dangled her nipples over my lips. I opened my mouth and began to suckle eagerly. Our moist bodies slid together easily.

Somehow, I forgot they were attached to a woman. I nipped one a little too hard and Trisha rose up quickly.

"You need to be gentle, Rick. That hurt."

"I'm sorry, are these sensitive?" I asked, my hands stroking her breasts, trying to ease any pain.

Holding my hands to her breasts, she said, "*I'm* sensitive, Rick. And I happen to know you are, too. Just relax. Don't worry about the time. We have all night." Slowly, she lowered her breasts back to my face, where I treated them with the reverence they were due.

Until she mentioned the time, I'd almost forgotten she was a working girl.

Soon, I felt the need to push my hips into her as hard and as high as I could. She recognized this for what it was and pushed her hips down on mine, thrusting her pelvis back and forth on my rod at a blistering pace. No longer up and down. I felt my rod swell to capacity again. Back and forth, we ground together, as the only sound in the room was of wet flesh smacking against flesh. She seemed determined to impale herself on my pole so I took a hip in each hand and did my best to assist her in the endeavor: to punch a hole clear through her cervix.

She delivered a few slow, hard thrusts of her hips, with several "Ugghh! Uggghhhh! Ahhhhhh! Ahhhhhhhhhhh!" Then stopped.

But I wasn't done, so I dragged her hips back and forth, thrusting until I felt the moment start at the tip of my cock and spread over the head and down the shaft, eventually flooding over my entire body as I began to fire my seed into the walls beyond her folds.

Trisha seemed renewed. "That's it baby. *Fuck me . . . Fuck me, Rick*. Fuck me just like that . . ."

Again. This time, the sensations struck me like a freight train. Slow but powerful, a mile long, it surged through my body. I watched as Trisha thrashed about again briefly. Watching her added so much more to my climax. Her total package of eroti-cism. Amazing.

When I returned to earth, I ran my hand along the top of her thighs. I took in the contours of her slightly curved tummy, the valleys that ran from her hip bones down to her lower lips, the ridgeline of her thighs, her flat stomach that became her narrow waist, up to the heavenly C cup swell of softness . . . *Oh, dear God!* I followed the lines back to the apex of her legs, where her tummy curved down to her thin strip, to her lips, to her very center, where my semihard pole still lay buried deep inside her. The lines all ran together, to culminate at one focal point. *Oh, dear God!* Here was the center of my universe. She continued to gyrate on my organ as it gradually softened. In a moment's inspi-ration, I reached up with my left hand and took her right breast. I wet my right thumb and brought it to her clit, stroking lightly. She groaned loudly, captured my hand to her breast and insisted that my fingers pinch her nipple tighter, and then she pressed my thumb to her clit and thrashed about for a very long minute. With her head back again, I swear I saw that vein throbbing.

When she came to rest, she looked down into my face, smil-ing and still gyrating on my exhausted organ. Her smile beamed so brightly. "Did you have a good time, sweetie?" She was whis-pering still.

"Any better and I'd swear you were trying to kill me," I whis-pered.

"I had a nice time, too, Rick. It was *very* nice."

During a few minutes of postcoital bliss, I was again struck by how well spoken she was. She spoke with a Southern accent to be sure, though sometimes she enunciated, speaking so clearly.

But when you're a prostitute, time is money. And while I was grateful for every second she spent with me, it was certainly not enough. Once dressed, I joined Ed and Juan out on the balcony for another smoke while she finished getting herself together.

On her way out, she made eye contact with all of us, smiled, nodded, and turned to leave. Suddenly, she stopped and took a couple steps toward me, shook my hand again, and gave me a kiss on my cheek. She whispered, "I've *never* been anybody's first time before. I'm glad I was yours. And you were fantastic. Inspiring. I *mean* it. I wanted to say good night, Rick. Good luck to you. I'm so glad I met you." No longer shaking my hand, she held it. During those moments, looking into each other's eyes . . . into each other's souls, not a word was said, but everything that needed to be, was being said. We'd "shared the sweet taste of a moment's love."

"Good night, Trisha. It was even better to meet you," I whispered back.

Again she started to leave, and again, she stopped and stepped back for another kiss to my cheek. "You're the first one who's asked me my name."

Now, our fingers were lightly intertwining, gently stroking. Sitting here, writing this now, I can still feel that last moist peck on my cheek.

When the guys saw her kiss me, they suddenly came forward to get theirs, too, but none was to be had. Naturally, they asked me what got me the special treatment. I denied any knowledge; still not wanting to admit this was my first time.

She smiled so damn brightly, and then turned and left. Our fingers slowly parted.

The next night, we went back to where Juan originally met up with her, but she was nowhere to be found. We never saw her again.

Had I been anything other than a stupid boy, I would've better appreciated her extra efforts. Even as naïve as I was then, part of my brain read all the gyrations, the twisting, and the writhing, skeptically. But looking back from the vantage point of a man nearly fifty years old, part of my brain likes to think she was genuinely caught up in the moment. Perhaps she was emotionally invested in giving me a good time, while taking one. Could it have been an act? Of course. But why bother? Ed and Juan said she was very "vanilla." (Pun intended.) That she just sat up, wiped off, and said, "Send in the next." Ed refused, which is why she came to the door naked.

Writing this story, memories of her fly at me so fast I have to swat them away. She was so well spoken, certainly not stupid, and definitely nobody's fool. Was she a college student, working her way through to graduation? Was she just down on her luck and needed quick cash? One can go nuts thinking of the endless possibilities.

I suppose if there is any one moral to this story, it's that there is no substitute for professionalism! We've all heard clichés about the hooker with the heart of gold, or the beautiful woman down on her luck who turns to prostitution. I've dealt with many hookers over the years as a police officer in Grand Crossings district, on Chicago's South Side (never contractually), and I have never seen a prettier, classier prostitute. *Never.*

My friends and I will always jeer, "Ah, there's no such thing!" But after a moment's reflection, I always say, "Well, you know, there was this one girl, once . . . a long time ago . . ."

SOLDIER

I was that which others did not want to be.
I went where others feared to go and did what others failed to do.
I asked nothing from those who gave nothing,
and reluctantly accepted the thought of eternal loneliness,
should I fail.
I have seen the face of terror, felt the cold sting of fear,
and shared the sweet taste of a moment of love.
I have cried, pained and hoped, but most of all . . .
I have lived times others would say were best forgotten.
At least someday I will be able to say I was proud
of what I was—
A Soldier.

—Read by CSM Charles B. Morris,
Congressional Medal of Honor,
29 June 1966 RVN, at his retirement ceremony in 1985

To Protect and Serve

Shakir Rashaan

The mantra of any officer worth their shield is "to protect and to serve."

Well, I'm not an officer yet, but I've lived by that mantra ever since I was a little kid, when I stood up to a bully who tried to take my best friend's lunch money in third grade. In high school, my sheer height and size made me an imposing presence, and the female friends I had swooned and bragged over having me as a "bodyguard."

Sometimes it is better to be in the right place at the right time . . . and come to the rescue of the right person. A sexy-ass woman would be preferred, of course. You know, just in case she wanted to show her "gratitude" in her time of distress.

I never thought I would put that mantra to good use, or knew just how I would be protecting and serving.

I left my criminology class on a Friday, walking down to the parking lot to get in my car and head to my internship at the Zone 5 Precinct in downtown Atlanta. I was looking forward to some fun over the weekend, taking my mind off concentrating on criminal profiles and trends for a change. I took the internship at the Special Victims Unit because I wanted to be a detective when I graduated. I considered myself lucky to be selected as one of the interns, even though the work was tedious and repetitive. The way I saw it, this was a way in to be where I wanted to be, and it was only for half the school year, so I was cool with it.

Especially when I found out that I was assigned to Detective Berrera's detail about a week into the internship. She was one of about three female detectives in the unit, and it was lust at first sight for me.

Seeing her every day after class was well worth the trip.

Detective Berrera was a stunningly beautiful woman. She stood about five foot eight with a rich caramel complexion and had curves to die for, even though she kinda hid them under the pantsuits that she wore most of the time. I guessed it was part of the persona of the female detectives in SVU to try not to be overly sensual or sexual, considering the type of cases that they were trying to solve. She had a natural beauty, you know, the kind that makeup only enhances. She was pretty without makeup, I mean really pretty, and I had her pegged for around late thirties, early forties or so, but she definitely didn't look like it. I often found myself daydreaming during class or at the precinct about seeing her out somewhere away from work, just to see if there is a softer side to her, something more exotic, maybe even freaky.

Hey, a brotha can dream, can't he?

Anyway, I moved through traffic, trying to shake images of Detective Berrera "reading me my rights" and searching me in a way that would definitely be a violation of police procedure. I definitely enjoyed working for her, but the more I was around her, the more I preferred to be doing a lot of work under her, behind her, and on top of her.

The only problem was I couldn't get up the nerve to approach her in that manner. It wasn't like I was on the APD payroll yet, but I didn't want to put myself in a position where I could jeopardize any goodwill that I had built with her or the other detectives in the unit.

Not just to get my dick wet. I'm not *that* desperate.

Now, I know it sounds crazy that a grown man would act like a horny teenager around a woman he has an affinity for, but that's what I felt like around her. I did whatever it took to make sure she noticed me and could see that I was dedicated and serious about being a detective, hoping that I would impress her enough to earn a compliment or a "good job, Drew," or something. Even though I stood nearly a foot taller than her and had her by at least a good 75 to 100 pounds, I might as well have been five-foot-nothing with platform shoes on trying hard to see eye-to-eye with the object of my desires.

I honestly think that she noticed my desires for her because every few days or so, she would break from her usual routine of wearing pantsuits and wear a skirt to work. She would deliberately walk past my desk whenever she had to take care of a task sometimes, and there would be other times when I swore that she wanted me to get a *good* look at a pair of legs that I fantasize about spreading on at least a daily basis. It took time to adjust and function normally on those days because it felt like she purposely wore the skirts to torture me and get a reaction out of me. Sometimes she wore light makeup and lipstick, but it was never more than once every other week.

It was a cat-and-mouse game that went on for the majority of the semester.

I usually offered to escort her to her car since it was normally around one a.m. when we left the precinct. For the past few weeks, she'd politely turned me down, letting me know that she was a big girl and she could handle herself pretty well without an escort. I had no problems with her rejecting my offers. I mean, she has been a detective for a long time, so I tried to not make it look like I was begging to protect her. I'm not a stalker or anything like that.

Damn, that sounded weak, now that I thought about it. Oh, well, I'd just have to live with it until I got my nerves under control.

The evening shift came and went quickly tonight, and it almost took me by surprise that it was nearly midnight already. I was going through my usual routine of clearing out the files and reports from the week, trying to keep the workload from being too heavy when I came back on Monday night, when Detective Berrera walked by my desk. She leaned in close, giving me the impression that she didn't want a lot of ears to hear what she was about to tell me.

"I just wanted you to know that I've been watching you the last few weeks and observing the work that you've been putting in." She locked eyes with me as she spoke. "I'm impressed by your work ethic, Drew. You might be able to earn your way into the unit after you graduate next year."

I sat in my chair, stunned and unable to break the eye contact between us. I was a little bit confused, because I'd never mentioned to anyone that I would be finishing up my senior year next year. The reason I kept it to myself was that I'd dropped out of college with a year remaining because I felt college wasn't for me and that I didn't need a degree. I took a few gigs as a bouncer and some personal security here and there, but they barely paid the bills, so I eventually came back to my senses and decided to finish what I'd started so I could be legit and make some real money.

"Thank you, Detective Berrera," I responded, trying to suppress the smile that threatened to spread across my face. "I didn't realize you knew when I graduated."

Damn, kid, that was the only thing that you could come up with? I scolded myself for the weak-ass comeback. Yeah, that was real smooth, alright.

I couldn't resist the way she sat on the desk that I was working from. Tonight was that rare night that she wore a skirt, and it rode up her legs, giving me a tantalizing up-close-and-personal view of how thick they really were. I struggled to keep eye contact with her, as I didn't want to come across as if I couldn't control the heat that made its way across my body. My mind began playing tricks on me, because I thought I caught a grin on her face.

Could she have been playing me, just to see how I would react?

Her skirt kept rising, showing more of her thighs. My eyes darted back and forth, stealing glances every chance that I got, fueling my desires to have her with each peek inside. I could trace her hips with my eyes, watching them sway as she was saying something to me. If I'd been paying better attention, I would have figured out that she was trying to tell me that it was time to go home.

"Drew . . ." She called my name, breaking my thoughts. "It's time to head home. Shift's over."

Damn. This day went quicker than I wanted it to.

"I still have a few more things to finish up around here, ma'am," I replied, cooling down to regain my composure. "I should be done in about ten minutes or so."

"Alright, but don't stick around longer than that, okay?" she told me, slipping down from the desk. She leaned against the desk again, almost as if she wanted to linger a little longer.

"No problem," I answered, trying to get back to my paperwork.

As I watched her walk away from the desk, I enjoyed the
view of her hips and ass swaying away from me. I wanted to ask
for the umpteenth time if she wanted me to escort her to her
vehicle, but I decided against it. The last thing I needed to cap off
my night was another rejection from her.

I finally got things done about five minutes later. I had a sudden urge to leave and get my weekend started with a drink or
two. I got to the parking lot and was near my truck when I heard
a woman scream, *"Get off me, I'm a detective!"*

I ran in the direction of where I heard the screams, and I saw
Detective Berrera struggling to fight off a would-be mugger. He
had her pinned against the back of her SUV, a knife to her throat.

Instincts took over instantly.

My adrenaline reached sky-high levels as I ran as quickly as I
could and tackled the mugger to the ground, wrapping his arms
behind his back and taking the mask off his head. His screams of
pain didn't faze me—all I could hear was the heightened pace
of my heartbeat as I barked out orders for him to remain silent.
Once I had his arms pinned and he couldn't move, I took my cell
phone out and called for an officer to be dispatched to the area
to take the mugger to jail.

Once my senses began to return to me, I heard something
that I didn't expect to hear. Sitting against her SUV, trying to
quiet her sobs to keep me from hearing her, was Detective
Berrera.

I moved to her quickly, trying to assess her injuries and find
out if she needed an ambulance. The EMTs finally arrived at the
same time as the officers and took her to the back of the ambu-

lance. She tried to protest that she was okay, but eventually the EMTs won that battle.

After I gave the officers my statement, I walked back over to the ambulance to check on her. She was just exiting the back of the ambulance and was startled when she saw me standing in front of her.

Her eyes expressed her embarrassment that she'd let someone get the drop on her. I didn't really care, I was just glad that she was safe. I stared back, trying to express that she had not lost any respect from me. In fact, seeing her this vulnerable made her even more attractive to me.

"I'm glad I did get my work done early," I quipped, trying to lighten the moment and take her mind off the incident. I smiled at my attempt at humor, secretly wishing that she understood that I wasn't trying to make fun of her.

She managed a smile, her eyes searching mine. I couldn't imagine what she was looking for, but I needed her to stop looking at me like that. I wasn't her boyfriend or anything like that, but her body language and the look in her eyes surged through me, making me weak.

"Thank you for taking him down. I don't know how he managed to catch me off guard," Detective Berrera finally managed. "And yeah, it was a good thing that you did finish early." She licked her lips while staring at me, and it drove me crazy feeling the heat between us. I kept trying to convince myself that she was not trying to seduce me, especially after what just happened to her. I mean, this couldn't be happening, right?

I saw her trembling and wanted to wrap my arms around her to try and calm her. I hesitated, unsure of whether to touch her or not. After all, she was my supervisor.

But the rules of engagement had changed just a little bit. I guess keeping a mugger from harming someone would do that. I decided against pulling that move in case I was reading her the wrong way. I was starting to calm down from the high, and I didn't want to make any mistakes now.

It wasn't hard to ask her this time, considering she had just been roughed up a bit. "Ma'am, would you please allow me to provide an escort home? I want to make sure you're safe and sound."

Detective Berrera nodded this time, which surprised me. "Drew, thank you, I would like that very much. And please, you can call me Yvonne."

Wow, we're on a first-name basis now?

This was turning into a helluva day after all.

I helped her gather her things and get them into her SUV, closing her door while getting another look at her thighs again. It didn't bother me that they were a little bruised from the attack. She still looked good as hell to me. I felt a little ashamed that I was still lusting after her even now after such a traumatic experience, but I couldn't help myself. After her eyes connected with mine again after shutting her door, those lustful thoughts only intensified for me.

We got to her house without further incident, and once she parked in the garage, I got out of my truck to meet her just outside the garage to make a last contact before leaving.

"Drew," Yvonne called to me. "Could you help me with my bags?"

I obliged her, walking to the driver's side of the truck to open the back door.

Everything happened at once.

Yvonne pulled me against her, pressing her lips against mine before I could protest. It was all I could do to adjust to the aggression and passion in her kiss, trying desperately to get a word in to find out what provoked her to do this.

Yvonne lifted her left leg and wrapped it around the small of my back, causing her skirt to hike up over her hips this time. My instincts took over, no longer caring to know the reason; my body simply wanted to be in control. I cupped my hands under her ass, now bare except for the thong that she was wearing, pushing her into the front seat to get better leverage over her.

"Damn, boy, you want it that bad, huh?" she smirked at me, grinning as she unbuckled my jeans. "Tell me you want to fuck me, Drew. I can tell every time you look at me."

I didn't say a word, I just continued my assault on her senses, ripping her blouse open, exposing her bra. I kissed her again, this time taking the lead as I unhooked her bra to expose her nipples to the night air. I pulled her gun belt off her shoulders to keep her from feeling so tight against me.

She tried hard to stop me, but it felt like she was only doing that to bring me further to the edge, unlocking the primal nature within me to take things to the next level. She bit my neck, clawed at my back, all in an attempt to "stop" me from fucking her.

"Take it, baby, take it now!" Yvonne screamed as she reached for the garage door opener to close the door so she could really cut loose. "I want you to take it. Come on!"

I turned her around, bending her over to expose her ass to me. Slipping a condom on, I forced my shaft deep inside her wetness, growling deep as I felt her clenching tightly around me. I gripped her hips tightly, listening to her ass smacking against me as I took her hard and deep.

"*That's it, baby . . . fuck me harder!*" she squealed.

I pulled her arms behind her back as I continued to fuck her. Being in that helpless state of having her arms and hands taken from her seemed to intensify her moans and screaming. Her words became unintelligible, her body beckoning me to push it to the brink of exhaustion, wanting me to fuck her into oblivion.

Just an hour ago, she was feeling helpless, trying to figure out if she wanted me to be her protection.

Now, there was no doubt in my mind that she wanted me to take the sting of her embarrassment and remove it with nothing short of pure ecstasy. She didn't want to feel like a victim, and I was doing my best to ensure that she wouldn't feel anything except my dick driving deeper inside her by the second.

I growled loudly as I felt my orgasm cresting, releasing her hands and raking my nails down her back. I felt her yelling out that she was coming, pressing her palms against the seat to brace herself and to keep her legs from buckling under her from the strength of her orgasm.

I grabbed a handful of her hair as I felt my own climax pushing over the edge, going as hard as I could before my body betrayed me once I came. I pulled her up, my breath against her ear, telling her how sexy she was, how much I wanted to fuck her, how much she wanted to fuck me.

"Yes, yes, I wanted you!" Yvonne yelled out, her statement echoing against the walls of the garage. *"God, you feel so good, just keep fucking me!"*

My strength was slowly leaving me as I came deep within her walls, straining the latex to its extremes. I immediately grabbed the door, bracing myself against the crash that I knew would soon come after the climax. Sweat poured down my face, causing my dress shirt to stick against my skin.

Yvonne started shaking just as my explosion subsided, her

breath catching as her orgasm began to course through her body. Her knees buckled slightly, and she caught herself by leaning across the mid console in her truck, which caused me to slide out of her pussy.

After taking a few minutes to catch our breath, Yvonne finally said, "You know, I'm gonna have to have you transferred to another unit now."

"Why is that?" I queried, a little disoriented from our unexpected clandestine rendezvous.

"Because I don't normally mix business with pleasure," she confessed, turning to face me, her lips tracing my neck. "But in your case, I have no problems making an exception. At least until you're officially on the force, then I'll have to make sure you're where I want you to be."

"And where might that be, Yvonne?" I asked, trading kisses in between words.

"Under me, literally and figuratively." She smiled, trying to stir me up again. "Now, fuck me again, and that's an order from your superior, Drew."

What could I say?

My mantra was still the same . . . to protect and serve.

And I did both for my favorite detective, and I planned to for as long as she would have me.

Leading by Example

Lotus Falcon

I worked with Barry for many years and found his outward advances both refreshing and impressive. He flirted with me in a way that was both obvious and playful and I flirted right back at him, never missing a beat. We were both educators and participated in many professional organizations together. I admired his outspokenness and ability to conduct meetings and maintain control of his audiences. He was opinionated and an up-and-coming leader in the field of education and for years, I noticed his youthfulness and eagerness to get ahead in his career.

After getting to know him and after many casual conversations, the subject of sexuality came up, probably after something I initiated. After many conversations, he admitted that he was celibate and had been practicing celibacy for a while. Since I was an educator and parent, of course I thought celibacy was the noblest thing I had ever heard of. Barry wasn't ashamed of it and, even after I questioned him to death about it, he maintained his position on the virtues of celibacy and his decision to remain celibate. For months, I would use his story with my children, telling them how much I admired his decision in order to inspire them to meet young men who didn't have sex on the brain.

After that I would bump into Barry now and then at many educational functions and, like clockwork, he would flirt a little and I would flirt back and that would be that. I soon developed an interest in writing erotica and since we were in the same writing organization, he found it fascinating that I would choose to focus my talents on this genre. We soon started emailing each other professionally and then started discussing our writing interests. Eventually Barry directed me to another email address of his; he went by the name of dickslayer007. It was through this email address that I began to uncover who the real Barry was and just how much he was true to his online name.

Barry's playful advances provided me with firsthand research and story starters for my erotic stories. Our emails became more and more explicit and I felt an enormous rush every time I read his nasty thoughts. He described in detail what he wanted to do to me and I would write back with something just as provocative, matching his imagination word for word. By that time, Barry's celibacy phase was a thing of the past and his manly horniness was in full bloom.

Barry was about thirty-two and I was forty-five when I first met him, and I kept our email playfulness in its proper perspective, even when he started crossing the line by suggesting that we "get together." I never encouraged those advances at first, because it would make me a little noxious whenever I tried to do the math. I couldn't get it out of my head that, when I was thirteen, Barry was an infant or, better yet, when I was graduating from high school preparing for college, he was somewhere in elementary school making spit bubbles and learning how to print his name.

Those images would mess with my mind and, even though his advances were flattering, they were unrealistic for a woman of my standing, or so I thought. After six children and four grandchildren, I was also trying to come to terms with my body image, which was not too bad with clothes on and not as bad as a lot of sisters my age with clothes off. As far as being naked, I looked best in very low, diffused lighting and I tried to avoid frontal nudity at all costs, since I did nurse every single one of my babies for nineteen months apiece.

No one told me at that time that my breasts, stomach, and behind would all turn against me one day. One day when I was shaving my pubic hair, I stumbled across not one, not two, and certainly not three gray hairs, but a whole army growing, multiplying between my legs. The more I shaved, the more I realized I would have to go all the way bald, so my pubic hair wouldn't look like an old man's mustache.

I looked at my behind one day in a two-way mirror. For years, I'd thought I looked pretty good for my age, until I noticed now how my jam was starting to turn into jelly. Thank goodness I worked out four to five times a week and it was easy to fine-tune those areas of my body that needed a little tightening up. However, my doubts and fears about my body weren't always about body image, but sometimes about the self-consciousness I felt about the way my nipples protruded or the way my inner labia always seemed to extend outside my vagina. I was a grown woman before I actually saw what my vagina really looked like, up close and personal, and I was horrified and left wondering if any woman had one as hideous as mine, or if they were all just as ugly.

During that time I continued writing erotica and found out I was pretty good at it and later began selling sex toys, lubes, and holding workshops on sexuality. I found out that women were hungry for information on sexuality, and I was hungry for the freedom of doing something that was so much out of my character. I did a lot of "research" for my stories and workshops and started viewing numerous adult videos, and soon discovered that I wasn't the only woman with an ugly vagina and that most vaginas were pretty ugly.

I also noticed the freedom that the women in the videos displayed and the way they were so uninhibited when it came to expressing themselves and getting what they wanted sexually. The videos inspired me more than I anticipated and, for the first time in my life, I touched myself in places I had never explored before. I found that I liked it, and couldn't get enough of myself.

Whenever Barry would jokingly ask when I would let him "tap that ass," as he put it, all those preconceived notions would enter my head. But the biggest fear that I couldn't seem to shake was that he would notice the stretch marks on my stomach or the back fat above my waist or the udders on my chest that used to be breasts. The last thing I wanted to do was make him sick to his stomach when he looked at my body and compared it to the young, tight bodies he was used to being with.

For years I would put Barry off, until he made me an offer I couldn't refuse, or so he thought. Actually, I simply got to the point where I wanted to finally see for myself what he was working with. Despite those little voices in my head that said, "Sit your old ass down and pick on somebody your own age," I went for it. I was good and ready and figured I would get with Barry just that one time, for the sake of "research."

When I finally told him that we would hook up, you would have thought someone had given him a Big Wheel for his seventh birthday. That was how excited he was. His excitement made me feel like I was doing him a favor, more so than planning a rendezvous.

Barry had to have known how old I was. It wasn't a secret that I was a mature woman, but it wasn't an issue either. I was a few years younger than his parents, but he never alluded to age or referred to it. As a matter of fact, he came at me like a man, a young man, but a man just the same. I never had any daydreams of being his woman, nor of him being my man. It wasn't that kind of party and that's what I liked about our whole "arrangement." It was up-front, honest, and grown folks' business and I was down for whatever was going to happen. I soon learned of another side of Barry that was different from the domineering educator that I witnessed at planning meetings, when I discovered that he was a domineering "sexpert" that knew how to handle his business inside the bedroom as well.

When Barry and I finally got together, he was thirty-five and I was forty-eight. I never felt awkward at the thought of us finally going to "do it." However, I did find it hard to shake my nervousness that he would have to see me naked. So, in my head, I would plan different maneuvers that I would execute to keep him from looking directly at my body, if it should ever have to come to that. I figured I would go old school on him and make him turn out the lights in order to hide the unsightly body parts I didn't want him to see. Then I planned on turning up the music to drown out the disgusting body noises that seemed to have a mind of their own when you least expected.

I also had to be wary of those facial expressions I sometimes made when the lovin' started to feel too good. I would have hated for him to judge me based on the ugly faces I could make. Let's not talk about the cussin' and swearin' I have been known to generate in the heat of passion. Depending on where you're coming from, sounds of passion could be a turn-on or a turn-off or somewhere in the middle. Oh, yeah, getting completely naked was totally out of the question. If it came to that, I would have to undress myself with bra and panties slightly off, and at no time would my clothes be out of arm's reach, in case I had to make a quick getaway. By the time I got all those provisions straight in my head, I almost talked myself out of the whole ordeal.

I was going to meet Barry at his apartment, and for the life of me, I couldn't find the right thing to wear. Everything I considered putting on either made me look old, frumpy, or matronly. My body suddenly looked as if it was out of alignment, and the gray hairs on my vagina were suddenly screaming to the tune of "Old Man River."

I tried to quiet the voices in my head, but they kept saying, "What the hell do you think you're going to do, with your old-ass self?" When I tried to ignore the voices, they would get louder. I even tried to drown out the voices by convincing myself that I would do it just this one time. So the voices must have thought that was okay; they left me alone after that.

When I finally made it to Barry's apartment, he was so eager to see me, he reminded me of a little boy on Christmas morning. As I looked around his apartment, I noticed how he had clothes and shoes and stuff thrown everywhere. He noticed me looking and reassured me that his apartment didn't usually look like that and that he'd been too busy to straighten up. I had to keep my motherly instincts from kicking in. More than I wanted sex, I wanted to hang up his clothes and organize his room, but I resisted that urge and turned my attention to the hard steel that was standing at attention in front of my face. He didn't have any underwear on and said he didn't wear any in the summer because it was too hot. All I could think was, *How nasty is that!*

I had to do away with all my old school notions of foreplay and getting in the mood and all that stuff from yesteryear. Before I could get my bearings, Barry's pants were off and his rod of steel was rubbing the side of my face like a sea sponge. His boldness took me by surprise and, for a minute, I thought his directness was a little disrespectful until I had to remind myself to get out of teacher mode and just go with the flow. It was about two p.m. in the middle of the summer, and the sun was beaming strong in the windows. I assumed Barry was going to shut the blinds and close the curtains, but no chance of that. He was mounting me before I could take my shoes off.

I became accustomed to his unnecessary roughness and found it quite refreshing to be manhandled in that way, even though I did have to tell him to ease up his death grips from time to time. We did it right there on his couch from the front to the back, and before I could catch my breath again he was escorting me to his junky bedroom, where he had to throw the clothes on the floor so we could find room to lie down on the bed. I was going to stay true to my convictions and not take my clothes off, but before I could protest in that matronly way that I had practiced, he was taking off my pants with both of his hands. As I was protesting, he thought I was playing hard to get, but I was really having a mini attack. There was so much sun coming in his bedroom, I feared that all my stuff would be right out there, big and exposed and in living color, for the public to see.

The more I tried to stop him from taking my bra and underwear completely off, the more I heard them rip until I was not only naked but spread-eagle right in front of him. He lifted my legs high into the air and looked straight into my vagina as if he was going to give it mouth-to-mouth resuscitation, and that's exactly what he did. He worked his tongue in ways that made my face distort and my body go into convulsions. He worked his tongue and his fingers at the same time, to the point I had to release myself, get caught up in the feeling, and ride with it.

When he finished, I tried to close my legs, but he wouldn't let me. He did the unthinkable, which was to sit there and look straight into my vagina, while telling me how much he liked what he saw. As he talked, my legs turned from solid gold to putty, and the more he talked about how he liked my "fat lips" the more he buried his face in them. The more he buried his face in them, the wetter I got and the wetter I got, the more turned on he became, until I wrapped my legs around his head and held him prisoner.

He banged me from the front and he banged me from the back and his strokes were long and intense. When it was time for him to go for the long stroke, he would bite his lip and look at me as if he was trying to see right through me. He kept a watchful eye on me as if he wanted to see firsthand my every reaction to his constant pounding. He was brutal and I loved it and I told him so. Some of the language coming out of my mouth surprised even me and I wondered at times who that woman was inside of me. Words like "do it harder" or "just like that" seemed to provide him with enough encouragement to make him go on, round after round after sweaty round. He dripped with so much sweat I had to take a pillow and cover my face to keep from getting soaking wet. Even my locs were drenched and all he did was wipe his face and kept on stroking.

He lay on his back for a moment and, thinking he was going to catch his breath, I decided to turn the tables on him and ride him for a while. I'd gotten my second wind by then and anchored my hands on the wall in front of us while I rode him like a bucking bronco. It felt better than I have ever remembered it feeling; he knew how to move his hips as he held my waist firmly in place with his strong, black hands. When I pushed downward, he would push upward and we were in total rhythm. He was hittin' all the right spots and looked me straight in my eyes while he was doing it. He didn't want to miss a wince or a smirk from my face and wanted to critique my facial expressions firsthand.

I was in a good groove when I happened to look down and notice how my breasts reminded me of cow udders, flopping from side to side as I tried to anchor myself on him. Not wanting to ruin the mood or the visual, I strategically placed my locs over my breasts. That simple move suddenly made me feel like a stripper, but it also gave me the confidence to keep right on movin'. I buried my hips in him and grinded them into his pelvis as if I were churning butter. At times we would synchronize our movements, and at other times, he would do a little off-beat move that would take me by surprise, but all the time never missing a beat.

After the third round of him saying, "Get your dick, get your dick, get your dick," I couldn't stand it anymore and exploded all over his chest. It was warm and plentiful and must have taken him by surprise, because all he could say was, "Oh, girl, cum . . . I like it!" as he lay back on his arms to bask in the wetness of it all. He didn't want me to get up right away so he could continue to enjoy the heat coming from our bodies, the wetness coming out of me, and his heartbeat keeping in rhythm with mine. It was at that time that I noticed the open windows in his room and could only imagine how we must have sounded to the people passing by.

He wouldn't let me catch my breath, and I wondered, from time to time, what kind of Mandingo Man I was working with, but it was indeed all good. Sister girl could keep up, and the wider I would spread my legs, the deeper he would fall into them. He was like my puppet. No matter what I asked him to do, he was more than eager to oblige. When I told him to pull my hair, he pulled my hair. When I told him to spank my ass, he spanked my ass. When I told him to go slow, he went slow. When I told him to go fast, he would go fast. He was quite obedient and I liked that, but membership does have its privileges and I had to learn to be a good sport as well.

There were many times when I wanted to say, "Slow your roll," or "Get your big ass off me," but being the team player that I was learning to be, I tried to refrain from my usual "I got mine; you got yours to get" mentality and give the man what he wanted. By the time I was finished with him, my mouth was sore, my vagina was swollen, and my knees were bruised, but I hung in there like a champ. Barry never came up for air once and I prayed that he would take a time out, but no such luck. He was in it for the long haul and I had to suck it up like a big girl and count my losses later. This was indeed one of those classic moments when I needed to be careful what I asked for, because in a matter of minutes, I had gotten everything I had ever asked for and then some.

Lucky me, after about three hours of hard labor, he took a break long enough to wipe the sweat from his body, take a leak, and get in gear for round four. As he walked around his apartment, I noticed how chiseled his body was and how tight his butt was. It was refreshing to see a man with a six-pack that didn't have to be sucked in on the count of three. He felt comfortable in his nakedness and never lay down the whole time. Sex seemed to invigorate him, almost inspire him to the point where he wanted to play basketball or run around the track. All I wanted to do was take a nap, get something to eat, and start locating my underclothes for the journey home.

After taking a few deep-knee bends, Barry was ready for round four, or rather, "one for the road," as he called it. He was amazed at how wet I was and every time he touched me, I seemed to erupt in hot lady lava, so much so that the sounds of wetness were echoing loudly throughout the bedroom. If I wasn't wet enough, he would take his fingers and make me wetter by working them vigorously in and out of me. When he finished, he would lick his fingers as though he was licking homemade pudding. Being the gentleman that he was, he unselfishly offered me his fingers, one at a time, as he fed me the tasty pudding from my own body.

I was so hot I could smell the perspiration and feel the heat coming from my own body. If I didn't have locs, my hair would have been a matted mess. At that point I didn't care about my breasts, stretch marks, gray pubic hairs, or anything else, for that matter. In the end, I felt like a used-up dishrag and it felt good. I tried not to look as though I was gasping for my last breath, but I was spent, used up, and out of order. The throbbing that was coming from between my legs was both bitter and sweet, hot and cold, pain and pleasure. There was no need for cuddling, small talk, or plans for the future. It was about pure sex, animal lust, doing the nasty, and "gettin' mine."

I saw Barry off and on after that, and each time, the sex was just as "crazy, sexy, cool" as the time before. He's now thirty-nine and I'm fifty-two, and though he's getting up in years, I'm not going to hold that against him. He's worked his way up the educational ladder and I'm proud of him, and he is freakier and as sexually uninhibited as he ever was. He's tried to talk me into having threesomes and sex parties, but I'm a little more discreet than he is when it comes to things like that. We still play our email games and talk our talk, and between work and grandchildren, I fit him in whenever I can. It's sometimes weeks or maybe months until I can get with him, but it's all good whenever we can hook up.

The maternal side of me is always trying to get him to find a nice lady to settle down with, but Barry's not trying to hear that at this time, so I let it go. Many times I'm trying to convince him to let me help him clean his rattrap of an apartment, but he likes it just the way it is, so I let it go and bite my tongue. By day, Barry is still very ambitious and is making a prominent name for himself in the field of education, and I admire his drive and dedication. By night, he's still a "freak of the week" and loves to get his "freak on" whenever he's not busy trying to change the world of education.

By the time my sexual empowerment hit me like a ton of bricks, I was already a grandmother. Barry was the catalyst that helped me to see inside myself and unleash those self-inflicted barriers that kept me from fully experiencing my total sexuality and sensuality as a woman. For as long as I can remember, I denied myself full sexual freedom because of preconceived notions about my body image, as well as an overall dislike of myself and inability to understand what I needed or wanted as a sexual being. I was not complete. It's not enough to be a woman and go through the motions faking it when I should be enjoying it. That's not living, and no one is being satisfied or fulfilled. I acted like it didn't matter, but all the time I wanted to break free of myself.

The first real clitoral orgasm I experienced was with a Bullet and it was so powerful, it scared me. I never thought something so mind-blowing could be self-inflicted. The first real orgasm I had through penetration was with Barry and that was only because I was at the stage in my life when I could let go of all my inhibitions, and allow myself to fully be present in all that I was experiencing. That was a process and, by no means, do I want to give Barry more than his fair share of praise. He was a catalyst for sure, but more important, I had to undergo a revolution in my own thinking to even allow Barry to get with me in the first place.

Barry's youthfulness and vitality were indeed a plus for my ego, but there were many times when I prayed that my legs wouldn't give out on me or secretly wished that I could have a little more wait time than he was allowing me. There were also times when I forgot to cover up my breasts with my locs, only to find one facing east and one facing west. I can laugh about it now and I laughed about it then; the bottom line is, it's all about the quality of the sex and not about the stretch marks, the body noises, or the gray pubic hairs. It's all about having the best sex you can have, living in the moment, and being true to yourself and your partner.

What I experienced with Barry enabled me to carry it over into other caring relationships I have developed with my family and friends. My sex life with my husband is now tolerable and my relationship with my children has become more meaningful. Through these relationships, you can say I am leading by example. Now I am able to give fully and accept fully and in turn I'm getting the same. Whenever I need to jump-start my libido, dial up a "booty call," or take a walk on the wild side, Barry is always just an email, text, or tweet away and more than ready and able to help a sister out.

Possessed Penis

Tiffany L. Smith

I'm sleeping with the devil. I know he's a lying, manipulative bastard. But it's like an addiction. I'm under some kind of mind control. One minute, I'm disgusted and swearing to cut him loose, the next thing I know, my clothes are strewn across the bedroom floor and he's talked me into some bullshit I swore I'd never do.

This shit is wearing me thin. I'm up at two in the morning checking his cell phone. At work, I'm hacking into his email. I spend a lot of my free time and lose a lot of sleep—*searching*. Playing amateur detective so I can stay two steps ahead.

Like today. It's 2:13 in the freaking morning and I'm tiptoe-ing around my own damn condo trying to figure out where the hell he left his cell phone. First, I run my hand across the night-stand beside the bed. No luck. Then, carefully, I search the darkness for his pants and reach into his pocket.

Bingo!

I slink quietly to the bathroom and ease the door almost shut, allowing the darkness to fold in around me. Ignoring sanity yet again, I scroll through his messages.

My breath catches in my chest when I come to a picture of my Hamilton, hugged up with some cocoa brown–skinned sister. Putting a face to my nemesis. They're looking into each other's eyes the way we do. Connecting. The picture is framed in a heart and there is a voice tag attached.

I push the door completely closed and lower the volume on the phone. What I hear next makes my stomach sick.

"*Hi, Tish.*" Hamilton's mellow baritone seems to fill the tiny bathroom. The tightening in my chest is causing me to strain for air. "*Don't we make the perfect couple? I miss you and I love you.*"

I'm in a full wheeze now, blinking back tears as they begin to sting my eyes.

Five . . . four . . . three . . . I slowly count. I've got to regain control before the panic sets in.

How did I become my mother—the woman I despised? I vowed to never be that dumb, loving a cheater . . . But look at me now.

I open the cabinet and pull out the small paper I hid when I came home today. When I'm away from Hamilton, I get small snatches of clarity and write things down—affirmations. I hide them around the house, to be able to pull them out and save myself during moments like this.

Characteristics of a sociopath: manipulative and cunning, incapacity for love, infidelity, incapable of real human attachment to another.

He's sick and doesn't even know it.

I hear the bed move. Quickly, I shut the phone and wait the sixty seconds for the backlight to go off. (*I told you this shit is ridiculous!*) I slide the bathroom door open slowly and let silent feet lead me back into the bedroom. I slip his phone back into his pants and pause just a moment before I pull the covers back to get into bed.

I'm having a very familiar battle inside my head. *This has got to end.* My head falls gently against the pillow. The fighter in me doesn't want to give up. This is war.

I study his face for a long time. He sleeps so peacefully. His silhouette has an auburn glow in the moonlight. Those beautiful eyes rest undisturbed. He is beautiful. The devil himself. The nearness of his caramel skin calls to me. I nestle my head against his chest and slowly pull the sheets all the way back so I can clearly see the outline of his penis in contrast to the room's darkness. Each time he exhales, it rises almost a full two inches before settling back into its original position. The whole scene is excruciatingly erotic to me.

I squeeze my eyes tightly, trying to shut out the image of him and this "Tish." The vision of his penis penetrating her with the same piercing pleasure he gives to me causes me to ache all over.

"Aftinn, what is wrong with you, girl?" I can hear Chante's neck swinging through the phone. "You find out he's got *another* chick in the wings, and you acting like it don't even matter!"

"I *knowwww* . . ." I whine. "I don't understand. As stupid as it sounds, I just can't get him out of my system." I needed Chante to help strengthen my resolve.

"You know what it is . . ." She pauses for emphasis. I imagine she's got her arms folded and is nodding her head like she always does.

"What?"

"It's that *PP* . . . Umm hmm . . . Yep!"

"What? Girl ain't no R. Kelly going on over here!"

"Not that kind. I'm talking about the PP. Possessed Penis! Girl, get out now, before you hurt yourself!" We both fall into laughter.

"Chante, I'm *trying*. But every time that negro gets back into this house, it's like my mind goes blank and I let him lead me straight to Hell. Now he's hinting that he wants me to move in with him." I clutch the phone against my left ear and start to rub my temples.

"What!"

I didn't want to tell her, but I had to get it off my chest. "Yesterday, when we were having dinner, he commented on how stupid it is for us to pay for two places when we're always together."

"You better not even be thinking about it . . ."

The "or I'll kick your ass" lingered unspoken between us.

"I *know* . . . It's stupid! I had to actually shovel food into my mouth to keep from agreeing. It's like I'm in a trance or something!"

"Humph. It's the PP, I'm telling you! You better be careful."

"I will," I tell her. "Listen, I gotta run, but I'll hit you up later."

"Yeah. Sure you will." She knows once I get within ten feet of Hamilton, it's a wrap. I don't make calls or take calls from anyone.

After returning the phone to its cradle, I sit a few moments to think about what she'd said. Maybe she is right. Maybe his penis has some kind of voodoo power. How else can I explain this shit?

I've had plenty of men. Cute, rich, and famous.

Hell, I've had good dick before—sex so good, I was curled up in the fetal position, sucking my damn thumb afterward! But this is different. I don't know how, exactly, but Hamilton has a way of using his eyes to look through me. I'm back to being Daddy's little girl. Back to a time when a smile from Daddy's eyes could make everything better.

I've convinced myself that if only Hamilton could rid himself of all those other women, we would be happy. Somewhere deep inside him, I believe he loves me. And frighteningly enough, I sound just as dumb as my mother, praying that the lying, cheating man will one day change his ways. But wasn't it Daddy who said a leopard never changes his spots? *Ever?*

This morning after he left, I opened all the windows and threw the sheets off my bed. It's a feeble attempt to rid myself of him. Stupid, I know, but this is my ritual when he leaves. Somehow, I feel doing this will erase him from my life.

I vacuum the carpet and scrub down every inch of my bathroom. I am hurt, and try hard as I may, I can't get the vision of "Tish" with her arm wrapped around my man out of my mind. I'm not sure if it hurts more to see him with her, or that despite all of my efforts, nothing I do can stop this man from sharing what I love so much with someone else. She looked into his eyes just like I once did. The thought makes me vomit.

After I change the sheets and dust every corner of my bedroom, I still feel his presence. I jump into the shower and try in vain to remove the memory of his touch from my body.

I soap up the breasts he's caressed a million times. My nipples stand alert, seeking the warmth from his lips and tongue again. I let the bubbles run down my abdomen between my legs. I close my eyes and visions of him moving slowly in and out of me invade my thoughts. I allow the water to wash over me as my hands travel to the places he's discovered.

My obsession with Hamilton is like a disease that has infected my entire life. I'm consumed with images of his smile that reflect in his eyes. Memories of his butterfly kisses that set my soul ablaze. Thoughts of him fluidly filling me, stroke by stroke, until I burst into a million tiny unrecognizable pieces of myself.

• • •

It's Sunday morning and the sun is peeking through his blinds, tapping me on my shoulder. I hear the sounds of pots rattling in the kitchen and the familiar smell of bacon and eggs waft into his bedroom. This is what I love so much about him. It is also what makes this so difficult for me. For every time he's come home late, smelling of someone else's Rapture perfume, for every time he's silenced his cell phone in the middle of the night, I can recall a time when he's offered me a crisp, white calla lily as a thoughtful gesture, or has just been the solid kind of man I need.

Lying in his king-sized bed, lost within the sheets and goose-down blanket, I feel him surrounding me on all sides. I have to steel myself against him. I reach into my purse and pull out that folded piece of paper. Today's affirmation reads: *You determine your own destiny . . . with or without him. Love is just a casualty of war.*

I close my eyes and feel myself sinking into his domain. When we make love, he likes when I call him "King." I can't help but wonder how many others have fallen under his reign.

Quickly, I wash those doubts out of my mind and pull his oversized T-shirt over my body. He walks in with a tray full of breakfast and plants a cheerful kiss on my forehead. He plops down on the bed, grinning like a kid. I think for a moment that he doesn't even realize we're at war. But then I blink and, for a second, I see the devil rise again in his eyes.

He hands me the newspaper and switches on the TV to ESPN. This is how we spend Sunday mornings; me reading about trag-edy around the world and him watching sports.

Life is simple that way for him. Sports—you win or lose. Work—it pays the bills. Love—here today, gone tomorrow. Life—you live and then you die.

For me, life is filled with layers and various nuances that must be taken into account. Maybe under all that deceit lies the heart of a good man . . . maybe.

"So, baby, did you think any more about this living arrangement?" He takes a long sip of OJ.

"Are you planning to move your things into my condo?"

"Baby, I already told you that you live much farther from my job, and it would make more sense for you to rent out your place since my rent is much cheaper here."

"Hamilton, do you hear how crazy that sounds? Renting out my condo that I own to pay rent somewhere else?"

Carefully, he places his hand on my thigh. I feel my resolve weaken at his simple touch. He leans over and places a light kiss on my forehead. Then he slides those damn soft lips back and shows me the whites of his teeth. His smile is his secret weapon.

"Baby, don't worry about it. We'll make it work." He turns back to ESPN. I'm not even sure what just happened here. I'm hot at first because I'm mad about what he asked me but, then again, I feel the familiar heat rise between my legs and realize I'm really hot. I have to wait for *Sports Center* to end before he'll put out this damn fire.

As I turn my attention back to the newspaper, I start to pick apart what could have gone awry during his childhood to make him this way. He says he grew up like everyone else. Says Georgia in the sixties was like most any other place in the U.S. But that's odd to me. Georgia, Alabama, and Mississippi were the cradle of the Civil Rights Movement. History was in the making. How could he have missed it? For him, back then, life was about cartoons, football, and endless summers. Simple.

Just like when he says he loves me. It's simple. There was no process, no rationale behind his feelings for me. It is what it is. Nothing more. Nothing less.

As much I love Hamilton, every inch of me hates him. I sit and watch him some nights, asleep without a care in the world. I study him, looking for any flaw to break this ridiculous spell.

I hate the fact that when he touches me, every cell in my being is awakened. When he's inside me, I hear the melody of our hearts beating together. Our souls connecting. I love him, but not for the reasons you think I do. I love him simply because I hate him.

My father once told me that hate and love are one and the same emotion. An odd notion at first, but when you think about it, to hate someone you have to spend time and energy wondering if they are suffering. You're connected. Still invested in the relationship. So the more intensely I hate him, the more intense my love for him grows. *Love is a casualty of war* . . .

Daddy said the opposite of love is indifference. You're able to walk away and not look back. You go on through life unaffected by their trials or triumphs. When you're indifferent, it's like they never existed. Hamilton has become my existence. I hate him. I love him.

Back at home, I'm comforted being surrounded by my own belongings. My classic black art. My favorite wicker rocker. My office that proudly displays all my certificates, diplomas, and awards. My condo that overlooks the Atlantic Ocean. The home with my name on the deed.

For a brief moment when I walk in the room, I feel his presence. He wants me to give this up so he can be in control.

Today's affirmation reads: *Destroy or be destroyed. Today is the day.* He'll arrive here around midnight. Says he has to work late.

• • •

The clock displays 12:22 a.m. when I finally hear him turn his key in the lock. We exchanged keys about a month ago; he said he hated having to wake me. I've never shared a key with anyone else . . . but I guess by now you're not surprised at how easily he talked me into it.

Tonight, I'm wearing a white lace teddy with matching boy-cut panties—his favorite. He'll be too distracted watching my ass jiggle under the pressure of the lace undies to think about talking me into giving up my condo. *Destroy or be destroyed . . .*

When he enters my bedroom, he quickly lies across me, wrapping me in his arms. He knows I'm lying in wait for him.

As he begins to remove his shirt and slacks, I squeeze out thoughts of "Tish." His hands travel down my abdomen and I erase images of his hands touching her with the same warmth that now drives me crazy.

His tongue invades my mouth. Hot and desperately, it pleads for me to relent once again. The four bare walls of my room began to fade as he takes my breasts into his mouth. Once again, we're on the battlefield. My stereo softly sings out Sade's "Slave Song." The only things that exist now are his hands, his lips, and the bulging manhood that's making its way up my thigh. They command me to open my womb to him once again. Despite heart-shaped visions of another woman.

By now I'm intoxicated and the sounds of Sade fill the spaces between our slurping kisses. When I'm alone, I have no trouble defining the insanity of our situation. But as soon as he's near me, I'm sucked back into that vacuum, where time, space, and reality don't exist.

Slowly he undresses me. I watch his eyes travel down my breasts, to my stomach, and then to my hips, fighting my desire.

"You are so beautiful." He looks into my eyes and I pull him close to invade his mouth with my tongue. I need him. No . . . I *want* him. I try to see this distinction clearly.

Eventually, he breaks free of my embrace and resumes his visual inspection. "I just can't get enough of your chocolate skin." I decide it's definitely his eyes. They pierce through the layers of my skin. He knows my secrets. He's studied every one.

Carefully, he slides my boy-cut panties down. I can feel his warmth. I wiggle with eagerness, trying to direct him to the center of my craving. When he finally slides the fabric over my ankles, I open my legs and welcome him home. He presses his face against my left thigh and gently slides my lips apart. The anticipation is driving me crazy. I want him to taste my sweet nectar.

"I love you, baby." His voice is low and coarse. He dives in and his tongue begins a slow dance with my clit. Round and round. Slower and more deliberate with each stroke. The waves gradually rise from my toes into my legs. My heart quickens its dance as the tide washes over my hips and abdomen. When the waves reach my chest, I'm a wild woman. I want to wrap my legs around his face and smother him with my juices.

Deftly, Hamilton rises and pulls me close to his heart. My tongue seeks his again. I hungrily suck at his mouth, enjoying my taste on his lips. He turns me over and, without hesitation or fanfare, inserts himself into me. He has me where he wants me.

I have to bury my face in the pillow to muffle my cries. Filled with pain and pleasure, I press my backside into him forcefully with each firm stroke. He runs his fingers through my hair. Grabbing a handful, he lifts my face into his so we can kiss again.

This is the way it always is. Soft and loving, then rising quickly into a heated battle.

"Aftinn," he whispers into my ear. "I want you to move in with me." He punctuates his request with a slap against my ass. It stings, sending a thrill through me that makes me wiggle harder. A moan is my only response. He feels so damn good inside me.

I make a deep arch in my back and pull my legs under me the way I know he likes. *Counterattack.* I can feel him swell and drive deeper with each thrust. He's weakening.

"Did you hear me?" He grabs my face and turns me to look into his eyes. "I want you to move in with me." We kiss softly. Deeply. Then he throws my face back into the pillow and grips both my ass cheeks in his hands as he guides himself right to that spot that takes me over the edge. *Full-on assault.*

His strokes are in rapid succession now. I tense from the pain and thrust my rear back harder to bring him with me in the throes of ecstasy. I feel him explode just as my own muscles begin to contract and expand around him.

Hamilton falls against my back; sweat dripping all over me. We both lie in a heap of exhaustion. I'm full with the warmth of his loving, yet I feel terribly empty inside. I turn to wrap my arms around him. I feel his heart struggling to resume its normal pattern. This time, when I press my lips to his, his eyes are closed. His breathing becomes even and steady.

"I'll talk with the realtor tomorrow . . ." My voice sounds strange in the darkness. I'm not even sure when that decision formed in my head. Now the words were released into the air. He brushes the hair out of my face, placing a small peck on my nose.

"Baby, I love you." He lets out a slow breath. The coolness makes the fresh tears on my cheek tingle. "We make the perfect couple." His words sting.

Darkness begins to envelop us. I lay silently, praying for a miracle. Sade's "Slave Song" now plays in my head.

Tears will come that fall like rain . . .

So many times . . .

So many times.

The Rules of Sheets

Scott G.

I had recently taken the job, and within two weeks, I was traveling with my boss. I would like to preface this by saying I am definitely all man, and my boss is definitely all woman. And we are both married.

We sat apart on the plane; we had to save money for the company. That meant flying in one of those flying casket planes—you know, where if you crash, your family doesn't have to buy you a coffin.

I stand about six foot five, a cool 350 pounds of mostly muscle . . . mostly. So the flight was bad enough, squeezing into the space.

My boss, Jamilah, stands a mere five foot six with heels on. I am sure, with her thin, but not-too-thin frame, that she weighs 120 on a wet, rainy day. Anyway, she sat ever so comfortably in the seat right behind me. "It's killing me to see you suffer like this, Carl; move your seat back since I have plenty of room."

She was so nice to suggest that I let my seat back, but I declined since it's not polite to crush your boss to death.

"I'm good, but thank you anyway." Besides, after the first hour, my legs had become extremely numb, so I was good to go since I couldn't feel the pain anymore.

After the flight, we had to go right to the office to meet folks in our department since I was the new guy to the group. I was uncomfortable; I am what is called, in medical terms, a sweaty type of person. In laymen's terms, I believe it's interpreted exactly the same way. I have to change clothes if there is a possibility that I will exert more than a couple minutes of energy. Coming to Houston in the summer, where it's a sweltering 95 degrees in the shade, I was in trouble from the time I stood up to get off the plane, get my bags, and walk to where the rental car was located.

Although I had changed clothes when I arrived, I'd accidentally pulled a tank top out of my suitcase, blindly, and I did not have enough time to pull out everything to find a proper T-shirt. So I did the best I could. Tank tops don't welcome the automatic absorbency that a T-shirt provides. It wasn't pretty when I went to introduce myself to my colleagues, but I grinned and beared it like they did. At least I will be remembered in Houston. "Ah, yes, Sweaty McSmelly."

Thankfully, the workday finally ended, and we were able to go to the hotel and get cleaned up. My boss went to her room, and I went to mine. We met back in the lobby for dinner an hour later.

It wasn't awkward between us; we are each comfortably married. This allowed us to have a good time talking about life in general without having to worry about anything happening. I love my wife, and she loves her husband. It was good to see two black people coming up in a white man's business world. Victories, however small, are still victories nonetheless.

As the evening was settling on the horizon, we had gotten a very nice view of the skyline, had shared experiences, and laughed at the thought of how happy we were in our respective lives. She had shared how she met her husband. It was a great story. While watching her tell it, with a shine in her eyes, I was picturing myself in the story as the lucky man who would get to bed her regularly. She is a very beautiful woman.

Although I am truly happy, and in total love with my wife, it's automatic for men to do this. Any chance we have to put sex in our minds, it's going to happen. If we are deathly ill, we'll imagine that a buxom nurse will come give us a bath and spend more time in our crotches. If we are consoling a friend whose dog has died, we would somehow find our hands on her breasts to console her. How that happens, we don't ask, we just do this in our heads, jack off, and go about our business.

As she was recounting her experiences leading up to marriage, I was becoming heavy under the table, so I am glad that I had a very generous napkin covering my crotch. I am also glad that I was wearing dark slacks. The more energy that was given to the thought of sex, the more energy was given to the eye of my dick and letting out an involuntary spurt of juice.

Now I am not sure that my boss had the same issue when I was recollecting my story of unbridled love, but I am smart enough to know that I, at least, had her attention. She kept great eye contact throughout my story of meeting my sweetheart.

Throughout the evening, we enjoyed great music, great company, and great wine. Unfortunately, my boss had a lotta (not a typo) too much to drink, so I had to drive us back to the hotel. She swore up and down that she would be fine to get back to her room, but being the gentleman that I am, I insisted that I would see that she at least made it into her room, and I would be on my way. She frustratingly agreed.

The awkwardness was rising up for me, but it was no big deal. I kept my mind furthest from the Zane anthological possibilities to which my mind could have easily wandered.

As we walked down the hall, my boss said that she didn't feel well and was about to barf all over the hall. We were about ten suites away from her room, so I grabbed her key and swept her up with my right arm. Because I had to have the key ready for immediate entry, I had to grab her around the waist and slam her against my body.

She noticed in the process that I was, well, excited. She made a comment about something hard and big poking her. I immediately, and embarrassingly, pulled her away from me. She automatically pulled herself back into position, and said, "I didn't say I minded it!" Her flirting quickly turned to green on her face.

I got her to the door, got the card in the slot, and opened the door just in time for her to decorate the front of her dress, my clothes, and the floor immediately inside the room.

She felt horrible about what had happened, and told me to sit down. She had to finish in the bathroom what she had already started in the entryway. I felt obligated to stay because she did not feel well. Of course, with the grossness of it all, there was no more uncomfortable feeling. Sex was the furthest thing from either of our minds. At least, so I thought.

I began using the amazingly unusual amount of towels available to clean up the floor while she tended to herself. The sounds coming out of the bathroom were horrendous. I asked her if she was okay. She told me that she had drunk too much, and would be fine soon. She sounded like this was not her first time getting blitzed. So I felt better that she was going to be okay.

I told her that I had cleaned up the floor as best as I could and that since she was going to be okay, I was going to head upstairs to my room to get cleaned up. She insisted that I wait until she came out to help me clean up. I told her that I was a big boy and that I could take care of myself. She jokingly said she knew I was a big boy already.

I laughed uncomfortably, but didn't worry about it. I figured that I would head toward the door so as I was saying good night, the door would be closing on her argument against me leaving. I was about to open the entry door when she emerged from the bathroom.

She came out in a towel. My gaze immediately moved to the left and right to avoid staring at her and wondering if she had anything on under that towel. She walked toward me, and again, the uncomfortable feeling left when she began speaking and her breath was exuding negative memories of puke. To get the point across faster, I asked her if she had a toothbrush handy. She now shared the uncomfortable laugh that I had earlier. She told me not to leave yet and she brushed right in front of me. When she bent down to spit into the surprisingly low sink, her towel cropped up in the back to confirm my earlier thought. *Yep, no panties whatsoever . . . Look at that beautiful, cara-mel, no-dimple-havin' ass!* This was going bad places quickly.

I emphasized how I was the only one not clean and that I needed to go take care of it immediately. She walked up to me and said that it was not polite to let her employee walk out of her room looking a terrible mess and that it was all her fault.

She said, "We can either get you cleaned up in my room, or in your room, but it's my responsibility."

I began to get nervous again, and my little head must have heard what she said. He was standing at as much attention as he could through my underwear and pants. It was aching that my dick was being obstructed from rising to its full potential. But my boss immediately grabbed my zipper and let it free.

She said that I needed to get out of my clothes immediately so she could soak them and get the vomit out. She made sure not to touch my dick but she examined it with her breath as she pulled off my pants and underwear.

She told me to take a shower and then she would give me a towel. I did as I was told. All the time, I am remembering that we are both married. I realize that this is soooooooooooo wrong, and I would prefer to just leave with my wallet, towel, and key to my room, and I would forget the clothes. This was in order to save both our marriages from any more unfaithful actions.

When I came out in my towel, my boss was totally naked. And she approached me. My towel was the only thing between us. She grabbed my obviously hard apparatus, towel included, and guided me to the bed. I was in big dick trouble now.

I couldn't resist the advances, even though everything in me was telling me not to do it. Would I, who stood six foot five, cave to a woman who was five foot six? I hoped not, but it was feeling that way.

She pulled me to the bed. My towel came off, and we were both standing there, butt . . . ass . . . naked.

I told her, "We can't do this."

She motioned for me to be quiet. Again, who was the man in this relationship? She handed me a sheet to cover myself. She took another sheet and covered herself.

She said as long as the sheets were between us, we couldn't have sexual intercourse. We could do anything that the sheets allowed, and only that. In the world of doing right and wrong, this sounded oddly right . . . to my smaller head, of course. And so we commenced to "not having sex."

I laid her on her back, and she closed her eyes. I didn't kiss her. The rules of sheets did not allow it. I didn't lick her shoulders, as the rules of sheets did not allow it. But I placed my hands on the sheets, the sheets that covered her nipples. She inhaled and exhaled in ecstasy. My rod was at full attention by this time and it ached for release. How would she accomplish this? I was quite intrigued.

But first, I had to get creative to get her off. So I rubbed her breast sheets until she was silly with passion. Then I turned her over, and glided my hand to her surprisingly ample butt cheeks. She had more ass than I'd figured seeing it in those work slacks. They were not flattering at all, but her naked butt took care of that. She had lovely titties and a sweet ass. I felt her ass sheets for what seemed like hours. And although the sheets were constricting, we became smarter as time went on. She clenched her cheeks together, and her butt grabbed the sheets so that the sheets were hugging it nicely. It allowed me to put my hand between those beautiful buns. She winced and immediately turned over, so I played right off her actions.

I grabbed the sheet, and pulled it tight against her body, and when I saw her bush coming through the sheet, I loosened up the sheet, and began rubbing her clitoris. She was so wet, I knew it would take very few rubs before I was trying to get my hand unstuck from the sheets.

I cupped her pussy, and as her legs opened, I tried my damndest to put my finger in her pussy, but the sheets wouldn't allow it. But I was able to rub that pussy raw, and as she grabbed my shoulder while she was coming, I ripped her hand from my skin and yelled, "Rules of sheets!"

She let go, as she uh . . . let go . . . all over my hand and the bed. She was very grateful for the release. The sheets tease everyone, as I have noticed. I put my mouth down in her area and tasted her juices; the sheets allowed it.

Then she sprang up on me. She wanted to fuck me badly, but we couldn't do that. She asked me if I had any condoms.

I told her I didn't have any. "I didn't plan on playing 'Sheets' with anyone, let alone my boss!"

She cussed, "Fuck!" But she understood that she made the rules, and that I was sticking with them exactly like her sheet stuck to her.

She threw off her frustration and went right for my dick, through the sheets, of course. She started at the top of my shaft with her mouth. She spit warm water on it so that it would show through the white sheet. She didn't use cold water to avoid shock and shrinkage, and she didn't want to get my stuff too wet. She might risk shrinkage anyway. She was very impressed by my specimen. She hadn't seen anything yet. I might make my sheet stickier than hers, but indeed, the guarantee of fruit was actually up to her.

She ran her tongue up and down my shaft and it felt great. She tightened the sheet around my balls that were begging to be touched by her long nails. That always drove me wild. I wondered if I would feel it through the sheets, but I didn't have to wonder long. She spit on the sheet so much that it was like a condom now. She ran her nails up and down my balls. It felt so good.

She wanted to fuck me so bad, she decided to try and put my dick, with the sheet, in her pussy. She had removed her sheet to try this, which I did not object to since I still had mine on.

It did not work, to which she cussed again, "Fuck! I want that thing in me so bad."

"We can't do that! You have a husband, and I have a wife. It's already wrong what we are doing, but I won't do that!"

She frustratingly yelled, "Fine!" She paused for a little while, which was enough time for my member to begin its journey back to Flaccidville.

She grudgingly kept to the promise, though. She started rubbing my boy, and it instantly became a man again. She rubbed me up and down, tickled my balls, and licked them through the sheets. She kept it up until I was ready to explode. She took the sheet and wound it tightly around the top of my dick as I was coming. It was painful and awesome all at the same time. She rubbed me with one hand and kept her mouth at the top of my dick to get the sap through the sheet. I kept coming like a water-filled balloon that was pricked with a little pin. All the liquid was being forced to exit that little hole. I couldn't stop the pain, the ecstasy, or the convulsions of my dick. I must have spurted at least twenty times. She was good at the rules of sheets, even though she tried to change the rules a couple of times. This made me wonder how many others she did this with. Did she do it with her female employees as well?

When I was finally done, and she had sucked me dry, she told me that since my clothes were soaking, I would have to wait until morning to go to my room. She would lay the clothes out over the air conditioner.

The room smelled like puke, and uncompleted sex, but sex nonetheless. I was lulled into a deep sleep by her stroking my very sensitive balls with her nails, through the sheets, of course. She was hoping to get another rise from me, but I'm a one-trick pony, so I was out for the night . . .

I woke up a little while later to the feeling of my dick being ridden. I kept my eyes closed, as I realized that I wasn't dreaming, and my boss was fucking me. The mothafuckin' rules of sheets went right out the door, and as soon as she came, so did I.

Sneakin' and Peekin'

Perkdaddy

They were at it again. The rhythmic *thump, thump, thump* of the headboard against the wall told Joy that her roommate, La'Shon, and her boyfriend, Tony, were fucking yet again. Oh, they tried to be quiet. Often she would hear La'Shon chastise her lover for being too loud. Of course, she was much louder than he was. And with good reason.

The hour was late and the house was still. All the better for Joy to hear the lovers do their thing. Wearing just her nightshirt and no panties, Joy lay in her bed, taking in every sound. What she heard made her nipples stiff and she pinched them with her thumb and forefinger. Her breathing got heavy as she teased herself. Joy's pussy begged for attention, but she continued to massage her breasts until the very last moment.

"Oh, God," cried La'Shon from the next room. The thumping got faster as Tony stepped up his pace and gave La'Shon all he had to offer.

Unable to hold back any longer, Joy plunged three fingers into her sopping wet pussy and matched Tony stroke for stroke. She put a pillow over her face to muffle her screams.

"Fuck me, Tony," cried La'Shon. "Fuck this pussy." Joy knew from the inflection in her best friend's voice that she was about to cum. She pinched her clit as the thumping grew more intense and the lovers reached their climax.

"Ohhhhhhh, shit!" La'Shon screamed as she released her nectar. With a roar, Tony came, unable to control the volume of his orgasm.

"Shhh, don't wake Joy, baby," whispered La'Shon between gasps of air. Little did they know that sleep was just now creeping into Joy's mind. She would sleep soundly, thanks to the tremendous orgasm she'd just had.

It was like this almost every night. Tony and La'Shon would dance the mattress mambo and Joy would listen, following each step closely. She often fantasized about Tony fucking her, pulling her hair and smacking her ass like the men in the novels she hid in her underwear drawer.

Tony was a fine specimen. He stood six foot two and had a slim, toned body that he kept in peak condition playing basketball for Coppin State University. Tony had broad, muscular shoulders, a barrel chest, and a six-pack one could play music on.

Joy tried to ignore the ache in her pussy when she saw him, but it was so hard. She wanted this brother bad. But as much as she lusted after Tony, she never made a move on him. He was, after all, her best friend's man and she would never disrespect her sistah-girl.

Joy Kelly and La'Shon Thomas had been friends since high school and now they were seniors in college, two strong black women headed toward bright futures. When money got tight in the middle of the semester, La'Shon suggested that Joy move into her place and share expenses. She had a nice two-bedroom apartment a short drive from Coppin's campus. The walls were a little thin and Joy had to ask La'Shon, the night owl, to turn her TV down on the weekends, but all in all it was a good arrangement, until La'Shon met Tony. That's when the dynamic of their friendship changed and the first steps on a path to self-discovery were taken.

The first time La'Shon mentioned her new man, Joy knew he was something special. La'Shon had always been the more independent of the two and the more sexually adventurous. In high school, guys were constantly after her, but she was very picky about the men she dated. It was the same in college. While other girls where falling all over themselves trying to date basketball players or fraternity men, La'Shon played it cool and mature. Soon, these guys were falling over themselves trying to get to her. So when La'Shon came home gushing like an eighth grader over a certain Tony Ward, Joy realized something was up.

After a few dates, La'Shon brought Tony home for the first time. Joy was sitting on the couch, watching movies in her nightshirt and curlers, when La'Shon and Tony walked in. The first sight of him was burned into Joy's memory—what he wore, the way he smelled, the rich tone of his voice as he said hello. Joy's pussy twitched when he shook her hand. His touch was strong and captivating.

"You guys need the living room?" Joy asked, standing up.

"Naw, girl," La'Shon replied. "You sit. We're going upstairs."

"Okay," Joy sat back down. "Have a good night."

La'Shon winked. "Oh, trust and believe, girl, I will."

That night, Tony and La'Shon fucked until four in the morning. It was loud and hot. At one point, it sounded like they were right in the same room, which suited Joy fine. Joy got so turned on by what she heard that she began to masturbate. It took her by surprise that she would get so hot listening to someone have sex. Soon, Joy found that she couldn't get enough.

After a couple of months of the audio show, things were taken to another level. One night, Joy woke up having to go to the bathroom. Tony and La'Shon were going at it furiously. She didn't want to be nosy, but she really had to go and the bathroom was at the end of the hall past La'Shon's room. The floor was carpeted, so her feet made no sound as she moved down the hall, but she panicked when she saw La'Shon's door was open. Not wide open, but enough for her to see more than she expected to.

Tony was on his back and La'Shon was riding him like a Harley. Her back was to the door and she didn't see her best friend. Joy's gaze was trapped like a rabbit in a cage. The up and down movement of La'Shon's plump ass on Tony's dick seemed to hypnotize her. She was shocked to find herself aroused not only by the sex, but the sight of her friend's body. La'Shon had smooth, caramel-colored skin that contrasted beautifully with Tony's darkness. The sweat on their bodies shimmered in the soft light of the scented candle burning on the nightstand.

Joy was amazed and a little scared. In all the years she and La'Shon had known each other, she never experienced sexual feelings for her or any other woman. Maybe it was the sight of La'Shon and Tony together. Maybe it was the fact that she hadn't had sex in three months. Whatever it was, the feeling hit her right in the libido. Beads of sweat began to form on Joy's forehead as she watched her best friend fuck the hell out of her man. Tony grabbed La'Shon's plump ass cheeks as he rammed his dick deeper into her pussy.

"Fuck me!" she screamed as Tony's hand came down hard on La'Shon's ass. This was enough to send her over the top. She came with a loud cry that she tried to muffle with her pillow.

Joy could barely tear herself away from the sexy scene. Her pussy was so wet that the juice was running halfway down her leg.

"Damn," was all she could murmur to herself.

La'Shon leaned forward, breathing heavily into Tony's broad chest. Joy took this as her cue to go to the bathroom. She had forgotten all about her bladder and now raced down the hall before she had an accident. When Joy was done, she washed her hands and opened the door. A completely naked Tony Ward stood on the other side.

If her eyes were feet they would have left footprints in his skin. They wandered over his nude form and Joy almost gasped when she saw his dick, still semihard from the fucking he'd given La'Shon. She fought the urge to drop to her knees and let his chocolate melt in her mouth.

"Oh, shit, my bad," Tony said in complete shock.

"What happened?" La'Shon came into the hallway. Then she saw Joy blocking the bathroom door. The awkwardness of the situation made everyone laugh nervously.

Tony smiled at Joy. "Is it safe to go in there?"

"Uh, yeah," Joy stammered. She was still at a loss for words. Tony stood silent the full five seconds it took for Joy to realize that she was standing in his way.

"Oh!" Joy exclaimed. She moved to the side to let Tony go by. As he passed, the tip of his dick brushed Joy's stomach. She had a mini-orgasm right there in the doorway.

"Thanks." Tony stepped into the bathroom and closed the door.

Joy turned and saw La'Shon giggling.

"What?" Joy walked toward her.

"He's got a big dick, doesn't he?"

"What, girl? I didn't even notice—"

"Joy Patrice Kelly, if you don't stop lying."

Joy stopped in mid-sentence, paused, then burst out laughing.

"What the fuck was his daddy? A redwood tree?"

"Girl, I don't know. But if I ever meet his father, I'm gonna kiss him and say thank you. He passed some good shit on to that brother. Hey, we didn't wake you up, did we?"

"No, I got up to go to the bathroom and heard ya'll. But it's cool. Seems like the brother knows what he's doing."

"Does he!" La'Shon smiled.

She was about to complete her thought when Tony came out of the bathroom. He saw Joy still standing in the hall and quickly shut the door.

"No need for that, baby," La'Shon said. "The girl saw you already."

Joy smiled. "Girl, I'll see you in the morning. Good night, Tony," she called as she walked to her room.

As she closed her door, she heard Tony coming down the hallway. He and La'Shon whispered and giggled for a while before finally drifting off to sleep. Joy was far too horny to sleep. She spent the rest of the night walking her fingers through her secret garden.

That night was merely the beginning. Every time La'Shon and Tony got together, Joy would be up, listening. Her room was right next to La'Shon's so she heard everything clearly. She would rub her breasts as she heard La'Shon moan. Her juices would flow as she listened to the *smack, smack, smack* of Tony's mouth on La'Shon's pussy. She would slide her fingers deep into her wetness and match Tony's thrusts into La'Shon with her own. The orgasms were incredible.

It wasn't just the big man that Joy was fantasizing about. La'Shon would creep into her dreams as well. Joy would see herself eating La'Shon's pussy; the small bolt in her pierced tongue working magic on La'Shon's clit. She would see herself and La'Shon on their knees worshiping at the altar of Tony's magnificent cock. A threesome was what she wanted, what she craved. But she didn't know how to make it happen. Little did she know that things where about to happen on their own.

La'Shon was no dummy. She realized that Joy was up, listening. More than a few times, she'd heard sexy moans coming from her best friend's room. The thought of putting on a show for her girl really turned her on. She also harbored some feelings for Joy that she'd never told her about. How could she?

For years, La'Shon had hidden the sexual attraction she had for Joy. It started in high school. Joy was lithe and athletic. La'Shon would watch her during cheerleader practice and as they showered after gym class. During sleepovers and long phone conversations, Joy would tell her about her dreams and fantasies and La'shon would ache to make them come true. But she could never bring herself to tell her friend how she really felt. What would she say? "Joy, I know we're girls and all, but I really want to fuck you?" Joy would go running off into the night, screaming and cursing. Or so she thought.

As the months went on, hot sex could be heard nightly. Joy absorbed every sound and would masturbate until her hand got tired. She even bought a vibrator, a month's worth of batteries, and a butt plug for those nights she was feeling extra freaky.

Soon, the sounds weren't enough. Joy wanted to see the action. The visual from that first night stayed in her mind and would not budge. No matter where she was, she could close her eyes and see La'Shon's ass moving up and down on Tony's dick. The image always made her wet.

So she took to sneaking down the hall to La'Shon's door, which always seemed to be halfway open for some reason. Joy would stand there, fingering herself, trying desperately not to make a sound. Watching as La'Shon and Tony fucked each other silly.

Then one night, things got really interesting. It was a Friday night, about one in the morning. Joy was at La'Shon's door, peeking into the room, watching every move she and Tony made. They were in the middle of the queen-sized bed, with La'Shon on all fours, and Tony fucking her from behind. The candles on the dresser bathed the room in a sexy glow that made it easy for Joy to see.

Then Tony bent forward, like he was whispering something to La'Shon. Joy heard her friend giggle and say, "Yeah."

Joy was getting nervous and was about to leave when Tony turned around with a flashlight and yelled, "Gotcha!"

Joy was caught. Her head was completely in the door and two fingers were crammed into her pussy. La'Shon turned around and laughed so hard tears came to her eyes. Joy was mortified.

"Well," La'Shon said, still laughing. "Are you just gonna stand there, or are you coming in?"

This was the last thing Joy expected to hear. "What?" she said, bewildered.

"I said, are you going to stand there, or are you coming in to join us?"

Joy was shocked, but she didn't hesitate. She wanted to be the X factor in this sexy equation and La'Shon was giving her an open invitation.

Joy moved across the room and joined the lovers on the bed. Tony deftly removed Joy's nightshirt, exposing her beautiful body.

"Lie down," he said to her softly. La'Shon made room as Joy

lay on her back. She was about to say something when Tony kissed her lips and said, "Shhhh, no words. Just lie back and enjoy yourself."

Tony took Joy's nipple in his mouth and sucked on it gently. A soft moan escaped her lips. La'Shon began to caress Joy's supple body, kissing her stomach and taking her breath away. Joy squealed and moaned, enjoying the attention she was getting. Then she felt a hot tongue on her pussy. Joy looked down and saw La'Shon smiling up at her. She was between her legs, ready to take the game to a whole new level. Joy responded by putting her hand on La'Shon's head and moaning loudly as La'Shon took Joy's clit in her mouth.

Tony knew that this was a special moment and backed away to give the ladies plenty of room. La'Shon flicked her tongue back and forth on Joy's clit, making her moan and cry out loud. This is what she'd been waiting for, fantasizing about for months. Now, at last, fantasy was reality.

"Oh, yes, baby, yes." Joy could hardly believe the words coming out of her mouth. La'Shon moved her head faster and sucked Joy's clit like a baby on a good pacifier.

"Ahhhh, I'm cumming!" Joy screamed.

La'Shon licked and sucked Joy's pussy until she flooded her mouth with sweetness. Sweat rolled off her forehead, making her face glisten in the candlelight. She was trembling and could hardly catch her breath, but she was so satisfied. Joy was open now and ready for anything.

La'Shon took Joy's hand and put it on Tony's stiff dick.

"Would you like some of this?" La'Shon asked.

Now Joy knew she was dreaming. La'Shon was offering her man to her? This fine-ass hunk of chocolate with the redwood dick? This was a trick question, right? A breathy "Yes" was all she could muster the strength to say.

Tony reached into the nightstand and pulled out a Magnum. Joy watched with eager anticipation as Tony slipped the condom onto his dick. The big man positioned himself between Joy's legs and rubbed the bulbous head of his manhood against her clit. Joy bit her lip and La'Shon rubbed her man's back as he entered her.

"Oh, my God!" Joy cried. His dick had to be at least three inches around and eight inches long. It felt like it would never stop sliding into her pussy. Joy held on to Tony's broad shoulders as he fucked her with long, slow, deep strokes.

"Oh, fuck!" Joy cried over and over again. Tony took his time and gave her all the dick she could handle. La'Shon held Joy's legs in the air as Tony rocked her pussy. This was good. Oh, so good. But Joy wanted more.

"Come here, La'Shon," Joy breathed. "Sit on my face."

Now it was La'Shon's turn to be shocked. She smiled at Joy and quickly did as she was asked. With one smooth motion, La'Shon positioned herself so that her pussy landed right in Joy's hungry mouth.

"Mmmmm," Joy moaned as she tasted her friend's pussy for the first time. She swirled her tongue around La'Shon's big clit, making her moan and beg for more.

"Yessssss!" cried La'Shon, loving the fact that her girl was eating her pussy.

In that position, the amorous trio licked, sucked, and fucked each other to magnificent orgasms. They were the first of many. That night, La'Shon, Joy, and Tony threw all caution to the wind as they enjoyed each other's bodies. It was well past daybreak when they collapsed in blissful exhaustion. The noon sun sat high in the sky and found them still sleeping, a tangled mass on the bed. Joy was still smiling from the adventure.

After that night, Joy would no longer have to creep and peek. She was a welcomed addition and formed the third point to a very erotic triangle. As passion grew and lust turned to deeper friendship, La'Shon, Joy, and Tony proved that three really is a magical number.

Big Girls Need Dick, Too

Shane Allison

I had just gotten off work. I was hungry and sleepy as hell, hoping I wouldn't nod off at the wheel on my long drive back to the sticks. I usually talk to myself, which seems to help in keeping me awake. I was trying to decide what I wanted to eat. On the side of town I was leaving, my choices were fast food and . . . fast food. If I ate another cheeseburger, another chicken nugget, I was going to seriously hurt somebody.

I'm trying to watch my weight anyway. Every time I look in the mirror I notice my ass getting bigger, a second chin coming in. The only exercise I manage to get is when I'm marching up and down the stadium steps of the movie theater where I work. I figure since I'm too lazy to get off my ass to join a gym, I might as well at least try to eat right, watch what I put in this cute, God-given body of mine. Damn, I miss New York. The two years I was there, I lost a shitload of weight. I walked everywhere and I was on a strict diet of tap water and bologna sandwiches.

Even though I didn't feel like driving across town, I decided on Larry's Giant Subs. I had a hankering for one of their infamous, oven-roasted chicken sandwiches. The one on Tennessee Street was closest. When I reached that part of town, the bars and clubs were letting out. Alpha male college boys and scantily dressed college girls stumbled down the strip. Cops and EMTs stood by for the intoxicated. Larry's wasn't full, but when I arrived, a few hungry coeds started to file in.

I ordered a six-inch chicken breast sub. I had this fine, brown-skinned brother behind the counter load it up with veggies, spinach, tomatoes, bell peppers, cucumbers, olives, the works, followed by a little salt and pepper and Parmesan cheese. I cheated when I had him draw a single line of mayonnaise along the sandwich to finish it off.

"Would you like to make it a combo, ma'am, or just the sandwich?"

I didn't want any chips and wasn't thirsty enough for a drink so I told him just the sandwich. I fished my wallet out of my purse and handed him my debit card. This drunken white boy, with blond hair and bloodshot blue eyes, bumped into me.

"Sorry, baby, my bad," he said.

First thing that came to mind was, I'm not your baby and get your drunk, date-rapin' hands off me. But "It's fine, don't worry about it" were the words that stumbled out of my mouth instead. I paid for my sandwich and walked out as more and more collegiate baby birds were stumbling in, chirping away about dumb shit that only baby birds chirp about.

I strolled along the strip, grinning and laughing at them making fools out of themselves, thankful that I was no longer a twenty-something. As I drove, my eyes caught sight of someone I knew. I wasn't sure it was him at first, but the closer I got, the more of him I could make out, and sure enough . . . Brandon Mathis.

"Well, looka here!"

A smile stretched like taffy across this round, brown face of mine. He was clearly drunk off that fine, bubble-ass of his, stumbling down the street like some inebriated wino. I started to leave him alone, thinking that he would eventually get to wherever he was headed. But I thought, what if he gets hit by some kid, drunk behind the wheel? Or a bunch of rednecks wanted to mess with him, beat his ass, just for the hell of it?

Either way, I wouldn't be able to forgive myself. I drove alongside him and let down the passenger side window. "W'sup, boy!"

He looked into the car at me. "'Sup, shawty?" His white teeth juxtaposed nicely against his black velvety skin. The peach-hued sheen from the streetlights bounced off his bald head.

"You want a ride?"

"If you don't mind." Brandon opened the door and got in. I noticed the large blistered symbol on the upper part of his left arm. I had seen the same painful-looking sign branded before on another brother's skin. I recognized it as a symbol from one of the local black fraternities on the campus of Florida Southern University. Alpha Omega, I think. I had always wanted to ask Brandon about it when he worked at the theater, but we hardly said so much as boo to each other.

"Where you comin' from?" I asked.

"I walked my ass all the way from Chubby's. They had that Rick Ross concert over there."

"I know. I wanted to go, but I couldn't get anybody to cover my shift. How was it?"

"Keisha, it was off the chain."

"Whaaat?"

"Ricky Ro-zay!" he yelled out the window.

"Stop, boy, you crazy!" I tugged at him, pulling him back in the car.

"You missed a good-ass show."

"That's why I need to quit that shit. No social life."

"That's why I left, working every damn weekend. Is that where you comin' from?"

"Yeah, I just got off."

"You smell like popcorn." I tugged at my shirt and took a whiff. Brandon started laughing. "I'm playin', boo." The smell of liquor and cologne filled my silver Charger.

"So, I heard you quit because of pencil-dick Chris."

"That was part of it, but mostly because my grades were taking an ass-kickin' because of the late hours."

"So you don't miss it?"

"Hell no! I mean, I miss you and the free movies, yeah, but not getting home late and, on top of that, tryin' to study."

I knew Brandon's type. A player, a butch brand type of brother. To say that Brandon is fine as hell would be the understatement of 2012. I was always checking him out, swiping glances at his sinewy muscles, his firm booty. He would come to the theater when he was off, looking much like he looked that night in my car: muscles tight under a Hollister T-shirt, a pair of baggy jean shorts hanging just so, showing some ass under his boxers. If I didn't know any better, I would think he was doing it on purpose, teasing me, so I would walk around work the rest of my shift with a wet pussy. If that was the case, that shit was working. A day doesn't go by when I'm not fantasizing about him booty-naked, fucking me stupid over the snack bar. I thought of how lucky his girlfriend was that she could have his dick whenever the mood struck.

"So where you stay?" I asked.

"You can drop me off at the Omega House. You know where that's at?"

"Over on Wahnish Drive, right?"

"Yeah, I'll point you to it when we get up there."

Brandon went on about the Rick Ross concert. The alcohol on his breath was like a slap to my face.

Brandon kept grabbing his dick. I tried not to look, but it's like I'm programmed to zero in on dick, especially when somebody like Brandon gave attention to it. The symbol on his arm, though, was enough to keep my eyes off what he had in those baggy shorts.

"I've wanted to ask you about that right there forever," I said, pointing to it. "That must have hurt."

"Hell yeah, but only for a bit. *Alpha Omega for life, baby!*" Brandon hollered, as he formed a symbol of his frat with his skinny fingers.

"How long you been a member?"

"Pledged my sophomore year."

"What made you wanna pledge?"

"Had to keep it in the family, baby girl. All my brothers are Alphas. My daddy's an Omega and my granddaddy. Omegas for life."

"You oughta have that tattooed on your chest somewhere."

"What? Omega for life?"

"F-o-u-r life. You know, a number instead of the letter, like Tupac."

"That's not a bad idea."

"Um, jokin', damn."

"No, for real. I might do that shit."

Dudes and the crazy shit ya'll do, I thought.

"So what do ya'll do, like sit around drinkin', hazin' brothas?"

"That's what people think, but no. We do throw parties and socials and stuff, but we don't let shit get out of hand. We don't haze people. I know frats that do that, but we don't. People have a lot of misconceptions about us. A good frat brother is a gentleman; you know what I'm sayin'? Leaders in the community."

"I think people have that idea based on what they see in the movies," I said.

"Some dudes only pledge 'cause they think all frats do is drink and party, but we—and I speak for all fraternities—we are more than that. Omegas have gone on to be doctors, lawyers, teachers, guys givin' back."

I could see that Brandon was passionate about what he was saying, and sounded hell-bent on squashing the stereotypes that were always a stigma on fraternities.

"You know what? I respect that."

"That's what we try to do. Educate."

Brandon grabbed his dick again as if it was as common as batting an eyelash, pulling at it as if he sought to make room in his shorts due to its length. I wanted him to pull it out so I could go down on him right there in the car. Sleep was no longer on my mind, and neither was food. I wanted Brandon's dick. I wanted him to fuck me.

We had reached the campus, slowly cruising past big, brick buildings named after historical black scholars. "It's right up here," he said, veering off our conversation.

I pulled into a lot and parked in front of a huge brick house. Big Greek letters were posted above the entrance of the frat house. I thought of all the hot black men that lived under its roof that pranced around half-naked behind those windows. Four men were sitting out front, looking at us suspiciously like hungry buzzards, wondering who it was that had driven up.

"Damn, this place is huge."

"Wait 'til you see inside."

I had never been in a frat house before. I expected the place to be in shambles—dirty clothes, beer cans, empty pizza boxes, like in the movies about frat guys.

"It's late. I gotta be at the theater at eleven."

"Girl, stop trippin'. Come meet some of the brothers."

The men that were sitting studied me. They were of assorted tones: brown, dark chocolate, butterscotch, high yellow. There were men with braids, fades, and others with low haircuts, or bald to the scalp.

"This is Trey, Big Will, Taj, and Mike D. Keisha works at the movies."

"'Sup?" all of them said.

"Can you get us some passes, shawty?" Mike D asked.

"Damn, you always tryin' to get somethin' free." Trey grinned.

"Come by the theater. I'll hook you up."

Mike D was one of the cuter ones in the bunch, wearing jeans and a black muscle T-shirt. He had full, kissable lips and short hair combed in waves. He didn't have anything on Brandon, though.

When I followed him inside, it wasn't like I thought, but it wasn't that clean, either. There were a few men, but none of them were half-naked. There were hardly any men around. It was Saturday, so I figured they were out at the clubs.

"That's the entertainment room where we watch games, study, whatever. That's the kitchen, and right there is like our romper room."

As Brandon and I started upstairs, he kept yanking his shorts up over his booty, covering plaid boxers. "These are more rooms and bathrooms and this is my room." Brandon's was fairly clean. I looked at the bed and thought of all the women that were probably fucked in its sheets. "Sit anywhere you want. I gotta piss."

I sat in the chair at his desk where an open math book lay. Posters of shiny, pricey cars and sports figures plastered the wall. A Rihanna calendar was thumb-nailed above Brandon's desk. I heard the thick sound of piss splashing in toilet water.

"Oh, hey, you still with what'shername?"

"Who?"

"That girl you used to bring to the movies."

"Janiece? Yeah, we on and off. Mostly off."

"What do you mean?" I heard a flush and Brandon walked out with the clasp of his shorts undone.

"She trippin', talkin' about how I don't spend enough time with her and shit. All she does is nag me. I love her, but damn."

I could see the frustration in his face. The first time I met Janiece, I could tell she was crazy, one of them clingy type chicks. Poor Brandon. Poor fine-ass, Rick Ross–loving Brandon.

"You want something to drink?" He walked over to the mini-refrigerator in the corner of the room.

"Does everyone have one of those?" I asked.

"No, my daddy brought this up from Miami."

He opened it and took out two beers. Brandon twisted off the tops and handed me a bottle. I'm more of a martini girl, but whatever. We both took a drink. I veered the conversation back to the Alpha Omega Greek letter on his arm. "What made you want to do that to yourself?"

"I'm a member for life. I wanted something to show my loyalty."

"Yeah, but damn, why not a T-shirt or something?"

"It's just a part of who I am."

"I read somewhere that branding was a form of ownership during slavery."

"It goes further back than that. In Africa, some tribes would brand a boy as he entered into adulthood."

"Well, you're braver than me. I would have freaked out."

"When I'm like, eighty years old, I want to look at it."

Brandon sat his beer down at the foot of the bed and took off his shirt. *Sweet baby Jesus,* I thought. I tried not to stare. It was like my whole body had gone numb. Roll your tongue back in your head, girl. You could bounce a penny off that chest. Hell, fuck a penny, more like a wrecking ball. Once he took his T-shirt off, exposing his smooth chest, abs, and pecs, my pussy was aching for some attention. I don't know what stopped me from reaching over and laying my hands on this delicious specimen of a man. I would be lying if I said I've never thought about Brandon's dick size.

"I don't remember you looking this tight," I said.

"I started getting more in shape a few months back, doing crunches, sit-ups, liftin' weights. I lost weight when I started playing football. I don't eat fast food or fried food. I don't drink sodas and if I drink juice, I get somethin' with not a lot of sugar and shit."

"That's what I've started doin'. My problem is snacks and eating late at night when I can't burn it off."

"I've always liked big girls." Brandon chose his words carefully so I wouldn't take offense.

He took the bottle of beer and began rolling it against his chest. Did he know what he was doing to me?

"You want another beer?" He got up to head for the fridge. I was still nursing on the first one he gave me, which had turned warm.

"Don't try to get me drunk," I teased.

"I'm not, just tryin' to loosen you up. I know there's a wild girl in there somewhere."

Brandon plucked two more beers out of the fridge, popped off the tops, and handed one to me. His skinny, pussy-fucking fingers grazed against mine in the handoff.

"If I get drunk, work is the last place my ass is going."

Brandon smiled like he had gotten the best of me. "That's the idea."

I could see a little pup tent in his shorts. I played it off like I wasn't interested. "I need to get going. It's really getting late."

I took a long final drink and sat the empty bottle on the desk.

"So you just going to leave me here with blue balls?" Brandon started tugging at his dick again. The tips of my fingers tingled. I watched him as he rubbed his hard-on through his shorts. "Don't even act like you don't want this, girl."

I didn't say a word, but smiled, dropped to my knees between his legs, unzipped those baggy shorts, reached through the slit of his red and white boxers, and pulled out Brandon's dick. The thing was like a baby's arm. I mean, he was hung like a stallion. The head of his dick was a nice cashew nut—brown while the shaft was of a nice ebony hue. I pulled his shorts and boxers down to his ankles. His balls, which weren't as big, sat in his lap like a dime bag. I brought the head of his meaty dick to my mouth and eased it past my lips, making them tight around the dick head and shaft. This was it; the thing I had fantasized about during morning masturbation sessions. Here he was, sprawled out on his bed like a birthday gift. I looked up at Brandon as I sucked. I wanted him to see how I looked with his dick in my mouth. Guys like that kinda shit.

"Damn, girl!"

I slid down until his whole dick was in my mouth. His pubes itched my nose. I started to feel Brandon's hands creeping behind the back of my neck, then up behind my head, pressing it down on his pole.

"LaDarien told me you could suck a mean dick."

What? That muthafucka told? I don't know why I was surprised. Those two are thick as thieves. Brandon was not forceful like most brothers I've been with who just want to hold my head down on their dicks, trying to choke me or some shit. It's like they forget there's a person attached to the mouth that's blowing them. I acted like I was making love to Brandon's dick. When I reached up and started playing with his balls, he went bananas. I could feel his dick ballooning in my mouth. I hugged it hard with lips and tongue.

"Oh, damn!"

As I blew him, I heard the door creak. My eyes met the sound. Brandon continued to lie there, so obviously he heard nothing. He had forgotten to lock the door. I couldn't make out who was standing there, but I liked that one of his frat brothers was watching me. I'm sure had Brandon known, he would have gone ape-shit. I put on a show by starting to moan. I pulled off Brandon's shoes, slipped his shorts and boxers off to the floor from his socked feet. The covers bunched beneath him as he slid up into the bed, his dick wet from my mouth.

"You got some condoms?" I asked.

Brandon got out of bed, walked to his desk, and got a couple of rubbers. I could feel the stranger's eyes on me, watching me get undressed, my titties exposed, my pussy in his vision. Brandon tore open the cellophane, took out the lubricated latex, and rolled it slowly onto the head of his dick, down his hard shaft. Brandon's dick jutted out from his lithe, molasses-brown physique. The tips of his fingers were greasy from the lubricant. I lay on my back.

"I like it doggy-style," Brandon said. I really didn't care what position I was in. I wanted Brandon to fuck my brains out.

Whoever was watching was cool about keeping quiet. It had not occurred to Brandon to check whether the door was locked. I felt his fingers pulling at my ass; cool air kissed my pussy lips. Brandon started to press hard against me. I could feel the blunt crown of his dick sliding slowly in my coochie. I looked to the Peeping Tom at the door as Brandon slid slowly inside me, filling me with his manhood. I could feel his washboard stomach graze against my ass. He held on hard to my hips as he thrust. I groaned softly, staring directly at the stranger as Brandon dicked me down.

I wanted him to stumble in and pretend to be surprised, say something stupid like, "Oh, I didn't know anyone was in here." You know, play it out like it was some kind of porn movie. I didn't give a damn if it was one or one hundred frat boys standing there.

"Take it deep!" I said.

Brandon's hands were hard and warm as he squeezed my titties, running his fingers along my nipples. I could make out the guy in the doorway grabbing at himself, his hand caressing the tent in his shorts. I leaned back against Brandon's dick as he slid it steady in my pussy.

"You like that dick, girl?"

I rode Brandon's dick slow. My pussy devoured inch after inch as I looked at the horned-up frat boy looking in at us. I imagined the whole house assembled outside Brandon's room, men of all heights, weights, and dick sizes waiting anxiously to "freak" me.

"Gotdamn!" Oh, yeah, he was close. The smell of sex filled Brandon's room. "I'm comin'! Fuck, I'm . . ." Brandon released a long groan as he came. As I hunched over on my elbows, his dick popped out of my pussy. "Fuck," he said, breathlessly.

He slowly got up without a word being exchanged, and walked to the bathroom. I soon heard the sizzle of shower water. I showed the guy standing in the door my fucked but still hungry pussy while Brandon washed up in the bathroom. I was able to make out more of the man that had been standing there watching us. It was Mike D, the one who had asked me about getting free movie tickets. He was caressing his dick, licking his lips as he watched me play with myself. I waved for him to come in. Two fine-ass black boys in one night. It felt good to be a little slutty. Mike D walked in and closed the door. He was like a basketball player standing over me. He hooked a few fingers over the elastic of his shorts, causing his dick to pop forth, which was just as long as Brandon's. The shade of his shaft was lighter, though; a pretty candy bar–brown. Mike D had these big bull balls. I opened my mouth for his entrance. He slid it past my lips. He wet his middle finger and inserted it slowly in my pussy as I sucked on his magic stick. We knew time was against us, but were cool as long as the shower water kept running. Mike D began to pivot faster, fingering my wet, pink core. I wrapped my hand around the base of his dick as I sucked him hard. I could feel his body tensing. Seconds before, he pulled out, coming on my titties.

I felt myself growing closer as Mike D fingered me. I wanted his dick inside me, but there was no time. I climaxed seconds before the shower water stopped. Mike D pulled his finger out of me, stuck it in his mouth, and sucked my juices from his digit. With a sinister look, he worked his wet dick back into his shorts, and exited Brandon's room about as quietly as he entered. I grabbed Brandon's shirt to wipe up the mess his frat brother had made. I slid off of his bed and started to get dressed. Brandon walked out with a towel wrapped around his slim waist.

"Damn, what time is it?" I asked.

"A little bit after three." Brandon started retrieving the empty beer bottles off the floor. He opened his dresser drawer, plucked out a pair of clean boxers, and put them on under the towel. "You still at the same number?"

"Yeah, but I don't want your girl to somehow get hold of my number and start trippin'."

"I don't let anybody use my phone. Not even Janiece."

"Call me after eight. I'm usually home by then," I told him. Brandon ushered me out of the room into the hall. He gave me a good night kiss on the cheek. "I'll get you and your boys some passes."

"Remember, live to work, girl. Don't work to live."

I descended the stairs, and left the house. Mike D was sitting on the stoop, smoking a Black n' Mild like he'd just gotten the best blowjob of the damn century.

"Nice meeting you," was all I said.

"Don't forget them passes, shawty."

"I'll come by on Thursday and drop 'em off."

"That's w'sup," Mike D said. "See ya soon, new booty."

I got in my car and drove off, knowing good and damn well I would be back for more.

Heated Waters

Jewells

The pool mirrors the moon in its stillness.

I dip the tip of my foot in and watch the moon's reflection break into tiny pieces just as my life has shattered within the last twenty-four hours.

"I'm filing for divorce."

My eyes sting as a fresh batch of tears form. I do everything I can to prevent them from falling. Clear my throat, swallow, cough. Nothing helps.

His familiar scent of Sicilian citron, apple, and cedarwood tickles my nose and betrays my emotions.

"How did we get here?" I ask as I feel him standing behind me.

He doesn't answer right away. Instead he sits down next to me, rolls up the legs of his pants, and sticks his feet in the water right along with mine.

I look over at him; beg for answers with my liquid emotions.

He wipes away a tear just before it falls from my chin. "I think this is something we've both been wanting for a while. Why prolong the inevitable?"

I sigh. "It doesn't have to be this way. I . . . I don't want you to leave."

Trevor looks up at the sky, says, "Full moon. Emotions always get the best of folks on nights like this."

I lean my head against my husband's shoulder. The shoulder

that has carried the weight of my infidelity for the last two years. His love for me kept him around all this time despite my indiscretion. It wasn't intentional, wasn't planned. It was a moment of weakness. I was lonely. Married and lonely. Two words that should never be used in the same sentence. His job kept him away more than a husband should be away from his wife. Seemed like the more I spoke up about it, the more business trips he would make. One trip lasted a week longer than planned. When he came back, I had already broken my vows.

"It wasn't the way you think."

His shoulder tenses under my head when I refer to that night. He tenses and shuts down every time I try to talk about it. "It doesn't matter anymore."

"Are we really over?" I want to know, though I already know his answer. I just need to hear him say it again to make it official.

"The papers are on the dining room table. Movers will be here in the morning."

My eyes begin to burn again.

Trevor leans his head down and places his lips against my forehead. "You'll be okay. We both will."

Maybe a full moon does get the best of people because as hurt as I am, another feeling between my thighs won't let me break down the way my heart wants me to. Been fighting my hormones since he walked out smelling all good.

I lift my head; turn it in the direction of the lips that were just on my skin. I close my eyes and kiss my soon-to-be ex-husband.

"Let's not—"

"Shhhhh," I say as I try to gain some control over what happens in my life.

For a second, neither of us moves or says anything. Contemplation is in the air. Him debating if he should oblige my offer. Me wondering if I should take it off the table.

He wins.

He removes his legs from the pool and walks back in the house.

I cover my face with my hands and tremble as the floodgates of my heart break open.

Footsteps entering the shallow end of the pool silence my sobs. I open my eyes to see Trevor walking toward me. He stops right in front of me, looks me in the eyes as if to ask if I'm sure I want to go there. With my irises, I tell him yes.

He moves in between my parted legs, reaches his hands behind me, and scoots me to the edge of the pool. Scoots my heat closer to his face. Long, slender fingers creep underneath my skirt and trace the edges of my thighs and the curve of my hips until they reach the top of my panties. I raise my torso up slightly for smooth removal. My panties are tossed to the side just like this marriage after eight years, but I refuse to think about that right now.

His eyes are intense as his face nears my warmth. He licks his lips, kisses each thigh softly. Again he grabs my rear and pulls me closer than close. His tongue navigates its way around familiar territory.

My head leans back, glazed-over eyes staring up at the moon as his tongue swims to depths only his tongue can go. My inner walls tighten around his thick tongue, trying to pull him in deeper, causing me to close my eyes and bite down on my lip at the same time. A moan trembles from my lips. He's always been a gifted eater. I run my fingers through his locs, pull him closer than close.

His moans make my love below vibrate, tickle my pearl in the worst way.

I feel his eyes on me.

I put my eyes on him.

We stare.

He wants me to know this last time is personal.

I want him to know this last time is personal for me, too.

He flips me over on my stomach, throws my legs across his shoulders. Devours me from the back. His lips against mine, tongue flicking in between my folds. Smacking noises loud enough to wake up the whole neighborhood. His tongue moves in and out of me as I ride his face like Secretariat going for the Triple Crown.

My trembling makes me lose my balance. He helps me turn back around and yanks my shirt above my head. Tosses it and my bra over where he tossed my panties a while ago. He doesn't take my skirt off for whatever reason, and refrains from removing any of his clothes.

He submerges under the water, swims to the stairs on the shallow end of the pool. Sits and waits for me, pants pulled down to his ankles. I know what that means.

I go under the water and come back up with my face right in his lap. His firmness stands at attention waiting for me to salute. I lick its girth; let my tongue linger in the juices on the tip for a second before I let half of him disappear in my mouth. I know how he likes it; not too much at first. I flick my tongue up and down his shaft; take his cleanly shaven sperm holders into my mouth, let my moans vibrate against him like his did me moments ago. This time I take him all the way in my mouth, feel him slip down my throat.

He massages his fingertips against my scalp as I massage his manhood with my mouth. He thrusts deeper down my throat and then nudges my head away. The hunger in his eyes is now a look of revenge. He grabs me away from the stairs and pulls me to the wall of the pool, turns my back to him. He prefers it that way. Hasn't been able to face me as he enters me since my moment of weakness.

His hardness enters my soft spot without hesitancy.

I scream in torture and in pleasure.

"Is this how he did it to you?"

Trevor's question catches me off guard. I don't know what to say.

My silence takes him to another level as he grabs my breasts with both hands and fills my insides in a way he never has before. Pumping in and out like a drill trying to reach the bottom of the earth. If I said it didn't feel good I'd be lying.

I toot my butt out to push him outside me. I want to stare at his wrath face-to-face.

He understands.

I reach in the water and escort him back into my fiery dungeon. I shiver as he enters me again.

They say to never look an animal in the eye because they will be able to see your fear. At this moment I wish I had listened. Fear is in my eyes. Looking in Trevor's, I can see my fear of being alone. And if I can see it in his eyes, I know he can see it, too.

Alone.

The reason we are here.

I rock my hips hard; try to ride him back into this marriage.

He makes short, hard thrusts, tries to get my mind off the matters of this marriage.

We're going at it like animals. Bucking like kangaroos and howling like wolves. Going at it so hard I feel my flesh scraping against the edge of the pool. Trevor sees my pain. Without removing himself from me, he moves us back over to the stairs. He's on top of me, growing inside me, the tip of his penis trying to knock my cervix out the ballpark. I bite down on his neck until I taste blood. That excites him all the more. He puts both of my nipples in his mouth, sucks hard like he's trying to suck a thick milkshake through a too-small straw. It hurts and feels good at the same time. My fingernails claw at his back, his drill digging deeper into my earth. He's trying his damndest to leave a lasting impression in my womb.

My legs shake. Not from ecstasy. I'm in pain.

Trevor's too far gone to even realize this is no longer pleasure for me.

This is too much. This is vengeance. Not the way I want to remember my final hours with my husband.

Again, emotions get the best of me, and I lose it. I cry like I did when I confessed my adultery and saw how thin the line was between love and hate.

He wipes away my tears, wraps his arms around me. I realize it was no longer pleasurable for him either. Again he pulls me closer than close. My inner walls throb against his manhood as my outer walls crumble against his chest.

"Are you sure we can't work this out?" I hear myself plead.

He looks at me, kisses me with the love he's always had for me, the love he had before everything changed.

My answer is in his kiss. Nothing else is to be said.

I loosen my legs from around his waist. Feel life escaping from me as he withdraws from between my legs for the last time.

Going in the house is the last thing I want to do. I want to stay in the pool until the water doubles over with my tears and drowns me in my apology. Doing so would be insane. It's my fault that life has come to this point. Nobody made me do what I did. Can't blame Trevor. Can't blame circumstance. It was my actions.

I let my body drift to the bottom of the pool, but my damn skirt acts like a life preserver, refusing to let me sink.

What the hell? This is futile. I walk the floor of the pool toward the steps. With each step, the weight of my emotions decreases as less water engulfs me. My nipples harden as the air lays kisses on my wet skin. I take off my skirt and wrench the water from it, grab the rest of my clothes from the ground, and enter the house of loneliness.

"I thought you were going to stay out there forever."

I use my clothes to cover my exposed flesh. "Trevor? I thought you left."

"I did. Came back."

"Oh" is all I'm able to say.

Neither of us look at each other, both of us probably feeling a mixture of shame and remorse from where we let our emotions take us a couple of hours ago.

"Come here," he instructs with an outstretched hand.

Still holding on to my clothes, trying to cover as much of my private parts as possible, I take his hand and move to where he is.

He grabs an orange envelope from the dining room table and walks us over to the fireplace. He removes papers from the envelope, takes our ending in his hands, rips it to pieces. Tosses it on top of wood. Clicks the remote to the gas a few times until the hum of gas kicks in and fire slowly begins to burn what would have been our demise.

Our hands tighten around each other's as we watch those divorce papers turn to ashes.

Trevor turns to me, says, "This is our beginning." He clicks the remote again to shut the gas off.

Though the light from the fire diminishes, the light in my eyes glows.

Hand in hand we walk upstairs. When he opens our bedroom door, several candles are lit. Sheets are pulled back on the bed with rose petals sprinkled over it.

"Remember our honeymoon?"

I feel my cheeks spread from ear to ear. "I do."

On my pillow, petals form a heart and a letter with my name on it is in the middle of it.

"Read it," Trevor says. "When you're done, join me in the bathroom."

We decided not to write our own vows when we married. But my husband surprised me on our wedding night by putting his written vows on my pillow for my eyes only. I thought it was the sweetest thing ever. I went to a printer and had them overlay the vows over one of our wedding pictures. It's been on my nightstand ever since.

I unfold the paper to see a resignation letter to his job.

With the letter in my hand and tears streaming down my face, I join my husband in the bathroom. "You did this for me?" I ask him.

He helps me in the tub, gets in behind me. Says, "Couldn't imagine doing it for anyone else."

We settle into the tub together. His legs straddle my body. I lean my head back on his chest. "I can't believe you're letting your job go."

"It needed to be done. In order for this marriage to work, it had to be done."

Nothing else needs to be said. I understand him and he understands me.

He rubs his soapy hands up and down my arms, rubs my neck. Takes a few suds and teases my nipples. He smoothes my curls to the side, whispers in my ear, "I miss making love to my wife."

"I miss my husband making love to me."

He kisses behind my ear. His lips make love to my burnt-almond skin. He turns my face up toward his and our lips connect. My mouth opens, his tongue greets mine. I can still taste my love on his tongue from earlier. Can feel him hardening against my back as my love below coos.

"Wait," Trevor says. He fumbles in the water for a washcloth. He pours my favorite black orchid and velvet hibiscus body wash on it and lathers me up from my neck to my toes. He leaves no skin unclean. I take the washcloth and do the same to him. We jump in the stand-alone shower to rinse the suds off and run water through our hair to get rid of the chlorine. I hand him a bottle of lavender oil for him to rub me down before I pat myself dry. I take the bottle and do the same for him. He squeezes as much water out of his locs as possible, then carries me back into the bedroom.

Everything about tonight reminds me of our honeymoon. He did the same exact things the night we married.

He lays me on the bed ever so gently. "Turn over."

I do as told.

He warms oil in his hands and places them on my back. He's careful around the scratches I got from the pool. Soft kisses apologize to my tender spots. His hands work out every worry in my body, every fear, every doubt. His lips do the same thing to the opposite side of my body, starting with my face. He kisses my forehead, my eyelids, my lips. We stay mouth to mouth for a while, slowly tonguing each other with so much passion. He sucks my bottom lip before heading further south. Locs tickle my skin as his tongue traces the roundness of my nipples. He does one then does the other. Goes back and forth before putting both breasts in his mouth at the same time. He does that and I swear the rivers of life flow from between my thighs.

His lips continue down to the land of milk and honey. "Baby, you are so wet."

"You did that," I say.

Instead of draping my legs over his shoulders, I spread them wide, placing one foot on each side of his rib cage. Opens me up something serious, allows him to dive face-first into my heated waters.

He licks and sucks like I'm a double scoop of ice cream melting down his cone. Surely my juices are dripping down his chin and he doesn't want to lose one drop to the sheets.

My husband holds my hips in his hands as my freshly waxed folds grind against his face. He holds me to keep us going in the same pace. His tongue flicks my swollen clit and for a minute I lose my breath. I can't moan, can't yell, can't scream my infamous, "Shit." I fight to find air, yet I ride his face until he comes up for air.

On his way up, he stops at my breasts again and perfumes them with the scent of my love.

I feel my sweet spot revving up again, ready for round two . . . three . . . four.

He kisses me; damn near tongues me down. I try to eat my flavor off his palate. Feel myself grind against his pelvis until I find what I'm looking for. I draw him in like quicksand; feel him hit the bottom of my pit. He makes slow, deep strokes, and enters my soul in a way he never has before.

Every stroke is an apology to what went down earlier this evening. Saying, *"I'm sorry for treating you as anything less than my wife. Sorry for pushing you into the arms of another man."*

He pulls all the way out to the tip and then glides back in. Every time he does that he promises to never leave me lonely, to always listen to what my heart says, and to be a better husband.

With every rock of my hips, I apologize for not trusting in his position as the head of this household. Every tilt of my pelvis begs for forgiveness for stepping outside of this marriage for comfort and validation.

I open my eyes and see my husband's on me. I tell him, "I promise to never leave your side again."

He kisses my tears and reminds me, "This is just the beginning."

Party On

Rachel Kramer Bussel

I clutched Phil's hand lightly, digging my red nails into his palm as we entered and gave our names before being ushered into the decked-out loft space, which had been transformed into a true sex den as befitting the city's most erotically adventurous. I'd been there for sex parties before, but those felt like they'd taken place in another lifetime; since I'd started dating Phil six months before, it had just been the two of us. He'd swept me off my feet, literally—we'd met at an ice-skating rink, where I'd decided, on a whim, to try it, even though I hadn't skated since I was a little girl. I felt a little silly in my short skirt, my mocha legs bare, my little red sweater hugging my breasts, but I couldn't resist the idea of ice skating in downtown L.A. on a gloriously sunny day in a mostly empty rink.

Once I'd started, I'd found that thrill came back to me, tinged with an edge of something a bit more adult as my short black skirt fluttered in the breeze. As I was sailing along, feeling free and happy, a tall, thin white guy had skated over and offered me his hand, then proceeded to make me feel like we were in the Olympics, flying around the rink and then holding me up in a victory pose before lowering me down, our lips almost but not quite meeting.

The tension had simmered between us for the entire hour we skated. After a while, I stopped thinking about the fact that he was a stranger, that we were in public, that he was white, a rarity in my dating landscape—not because I have anything against white guys. I just don't tend to meet any I click with that often. His name was Phil and he was a writer, taking a break from being cooped up in his studio to get a little exercise. I'd taken the day off from my job in advertising on a whim. The fact that he was clearly interested in me, but not outright hitting on me endeared him to me.

By the time we took a break for hot chocolates, I was dying to kiss him, but as confident as I usually was with guys, I'd suddenly turned shy, waiting for him to make the first move. "Do you want to go on a proper date?" he asked as I blew on my drink, the steam heating my cheeks.

"I'd love to," I replied.

"Where should we go?" he asked, then blushed, clearly thinking he should've been the one to make a plan. But I didn't mind, and only at the end of that date did he live up to the promise of his full, beautiful lips. When they pressed against mine, I forgot the fact that I'd sworn off serious relationships, not to mention that I was five years older than him, because he made me tingle all the way to my toes with just a look.

Somehow, he turned me, a thirty-three-year-old woman, into a blushing teenager. I wanted to make out with him for hours, and I did, that day, before we even got a chance to go on our first official date—followed by so much more. He took every step of sex seriously, savoring the time he spent sucking on my breasts, playing with my sex, urging me not to rush when I moved to whisk our clothes off. Most of my other lovers had been eager to get to the main event, but Phil was a revelation. He managed to worship my body in a way that made me feel like a queen, and maybe that's why I had trouble thinking of him the way I was used to thinking of guys: as potential tops, men who'd treat me like the dirty girl I longed to be.

With Phil, though, I was too busy having multiple orgasms, my body on an extended high, to miss the more perverted aspects of sex. Even when we weren't together, he had a way of saying something suggestive that wormed its way into my brain and then simmered down lower and lower. We were having such a good time that I hadn't thought about adding anyone else to the mix or offering up my truly kinky side. I was beginning to think that part of me was dead until I was cleaning on a rare weekend day I wasn't spending with Phil and found my stash of porn. It featured women getting spanked by men and women, and the sight of it immediately made my heart race. I love being spanked—the harder, the better.

It has nothing to do with my upbringing; the first time a man took me across his lap, I was in college. He was ten years older than me, a scholarly black guy who ultimately deemed me too frivolous, but once he got his glasses off, he could really deliver a wallop. I liked that he couldn't rationalize or intellectualize his interest, either; he just knew he liked the way I squealed when he smacked me, liked how wet it made me.

I popped in the video, pulled out my favorite rabbit vibrator, and spent the next hour lost in sensation, remembering the feel of the men and women who'd spanked me right here in my bedroom and at the parties I used to attend before Phil. Only when I was done coming did I wonder what Phil would think of those events. First of all, I'd never taken a white guy. There were other interracial couples who attended, and everyone was totally chill. I didn't think any of them would judge me, but still—was I ready for that? Was I ready to show him that side of me, to take on any baggage he might have?

I wouldn't say he put me on a pedestal, exactly—he had no problem pulling my hair while I sucked his cock or occasionally "ordering" me into a certain position—but overall, he did treat me like a queen. He took care of me in bed and out, and to suddenly ask him to show me off like the slut I wanted to be, for the night, anyway, seemed like a bold leap. But I knew if I didn't ask him, I'd only resent him for holding me back, and that's not hot at all.

So the next night, I made him my specialty, linguine with clam sauce, and got a bottle of champagne. "What's all this?" he asked, leaning down to give me a kiss that seemed to go on forever. I relaxed into his arms, then pulled back.

"Well, there's something I want to talk to you about."

"Uh oh, should I be sitting down?" he asked. I couldn't totally tell what he was thinking; he has much more of a poker face than I do. Then again, I could've been poised to tell him anything from wanting to break up to being knocked up.

"Sure—but it's nothing bad, at least, I hope not." He sat down, and I impulsively decided to sit on his lap. I seem to fit there so well. He put his arm around me and I smiled at him, then bit my lower lip.

"Well . . . there's something I want to share with you. I don't know exactly why I haven't already. I guess, because I didn't want you to judge me. But here goes; I'm into spanking. I mean, I like to be spanked. And I used to go to these sex parties, play parties, really, where people do that, and get tied up, and watch each other. And there's one coming up on Saturday and I thought maybe we could go together." I finished the last sentence all in a rush. I was tempted to shut my eyes as I awaited what felt like a verdict, but I didn't. If I was going to be fully myself with my boyfriend, to let him see all of me, then I had to be bold and brave.

He looked at me steadily, his blue eyes searching my brown ones. "Oh, honey . . . that's your big secret? That's nothing to be ashamed of. In fact, I'm, well, I'm interested in it also. I've never done it, but I've thought about spanking women before. Thought about it a lot."

"You have?" I asked, shyly. Why was it so much harder to bare one's innermost thoughts than to bare one's body?

"Yes, and let me just say that you have the most gorgeous ass I've ever seen. As a guy, though, it's a tough topic to bring up, and the one time I did, my girlfriend looked at me like I was a monster."

I couldn't help giggling; that was the last reaction I'd ever have. "Thank you. I guess it's just a little hard to say, 'I want a spanking.' Especially because I've never dated a white guy before. I don't know why it's different; I was just nervous. You treated me with such respect it seemed rude to almost ask you to, well, do the opposite." I did know why, deep down—I had fears, buried so deep I almost couldn't access them, that he'd suddenly decide I wasn't the kind of girl he wanted to be with, that spanking would be pushing things too far. I've had those thoughts with black guys, too, but I always got over them. Maybe I was just so into Phil I didn't want to mess things up.

"So . . . what do we do now?" I asked timidly, daring to face him once more.

"I think you know exactly what to do, Christine." Suddenly his voice was much deeper than usual, stern, almost like someone else's. When I didn't move, he said, "You're going to take off every stitch of clothing you have on and get on your hands and knees right here. You're going to show me what's between those pretty legs and especially show me that nice, juicy ass of yours, the one you so badly want me to spank."

And just like that, all my nervousness about him being uptight or judgmental melted away. I was trembling, but with excitement. This was Phil, my Phil, but with an edge, a toughness that made me want to see how far I could push him. I stood up and began slowly, sensuously, removing my clothes, making sure he was watching my every move. I wasn't wearing much, so it didn't take long, and then I got on the ground, on all fours, as he'd instructed me. This is the part that always makes me the wettest, even more than being spanked—exposing myself.

"I see all of you, Christine. I see your pink pussy lips between your legs. I see how you've got your sweet ass in the air, just waiting for me. Smack that pretty bottom for me with your hand." I did it instinctively, shocked at how doing as he said turned me on, a prelude to the present he was about to give me. Soon Phil was on the floor with me, pulling me across his lap. He was clothed, I was naked, but somehow it felt so right. "I want you to count for me, baby, but I'm not going to tell you how many smacks you're going to get. You'll just have to trust that I know what you want. Say 'halt' if you want me to stop; that's your safe word."

"Okay, sir," I said, the word slipping out. I'd figured that would be too loaded, too much, but Phil wasn't just any white guy; he was *my* white guy. He knew me inside out by then, and I was ready to go there with him.

"One!" I called out as the pain settled into my bottom, quickly morphing into pleasure. Someone who doesn't like to be spanked would only feel the former, but for me it feels like heaven.

"Two!" I shouted, and struggled to keep up as the next few land fast and furiously. By the time we got to twenty, I was tingling, aching, unsure whether I wanted more or a break. He gave me the latter, lifting me up and carrying me into my bedroom. He licked my pussy, telling me how much he loved spanking me. "I love how you feel when I hit you," he said, then, for good measure, landed an extra blow to my sweet spot, the part where my cheeks meet, before planting me on top of him, grabbing my hips, and slamming me down onto his very hard dick. The combination of his forcefulness and the way my ass ached brought me over the edge, and I came as he filled me all the way. His hands crafted my warm cheeks as he continued until he couldn't hold back any longer, giving me his hot cream right where I wanted it.

So there we were, our worlds voluntarily colliding, as my fingers pressed into his hand and I ushered him into my kinky home away from home. I was grateful we'd been practicing our role-playing; much more than spanking was going on in the room. There were floggings, men and women on leashes, and a woman being dripped with hot wax—with a ball gag in her mouth! A tremor of excitement ran through me at what I was witnessing, maximized by the fact that I got to share it with Phil. With the reassurance of his hand clutched in mine, I forgot about what anyone might think. I was with the man I loved, and if someone had a problem with that, it was precisely their problem, not mine.

"How do you feel?" he asked after we'd signed in and had gotten sodas. I was sitting on his lap on a bar stool and could feel his hardness beneath me. I knew what he was really asking: Was I nervous, bored, aroused? Did I want to simply watch or partake? Now that I was here, in a space that was not just mine, but ours, I wanted to make the most of it, to show off just how horny he made me when he took me over his knee.

I turned to him and raised any eyebrow. "I want to be a bad girl."

Phil's hand slid down to my ass, massaging it, lifting up my skirt and placing his hand under my panties. I'd worn them only to make sure I didn't drip onto the leather seat of his car. "How bad do you want to be? How hard of a spanking do you need, Christine?"

I whimpered; I felt heads turn when he said that. It had been a long time since anyone at these events had seen me, let alone seen me get spanked, and, truth be told, I didn't have half the chemistry with any of my previous boyfriends as I did with Phil.

"Or do you want me to answer that?" he continued. I nodded. "You want me to tell you that you're the naughtiest girl in the room, and that you need more than my hand tonight? You want me to take off my belt and make you give it a kiss, and then slice it in the air so everyone can hear?" I gulped, feeling tears racing to my eyes. I bit my lip and swallowed hard, nodding again. "You want me to strike your ass hard, show them all what you can take, what your pretty bottom looks like after it's been beaten?"

Phil was certainly not the shy boy I'd feared he was at first. Once he'd gotten into being my dom, he'd taken to it brilliantly, so much so that I wondered how he held those two sides of himself in: the sweet, considerate Phil and the mean, stern, top Phil. I guess the same way I did, able to be a ballbuster at work when I needed to but wanting to take orders and get naked on command within our relationship.

"I'm going to make you do something for me, first, though, Christine. You don't just get to beg to be spanked and have it happen, not with me. I'm going to find a man whose cock I want you to suck. I know how much you love getting on your knees and taking a big, fat cock all the way down between those pretty lips, don't you?"

"Yes," I managed, because it was true. I do love going down on a man; I love everything about it. I don't know why, exactly, but giving a blowjob makes me feel so sexy, and makes my pussy want to explode. Even more than the prospect of being watched while I sucked a stranger's cock, though, was my excitement at having Phil be the one to choose the man.

"Good. Now I'm going to put this on you to signify that you're mine for the night, and you're going to take everything else off," he said, pulling a collar from his jeans pocket. It was almost like a necklace, except it came with a chain.

"Can you do that for me, Christine?" He leaned down and whispered, giving me a final chance to back off, to settle into safe, familiar territory. But that wasn't what I wanted, not when I knew the thrilling promise that waited for me on the other end of the chain.

"Yes, sir," I said, and this time, it was Phil who took my clothes off. No matter how many sex parties I attend, I'll never get used to the sensation of being totally bare, wearing just my birthday suit, brown skin gleaming, nipples high and alert, in a room full of people. It's like the world's gone topsy-turvy, even if there are other bare folks of all colors around us. It's freeing in a way even the most risqué clothes can never be, and as Phil slipped the collar around my neck, I felt myself relax into sub mode.

I trusted him, and was suddenly hungry for whatever cock he was going to pick out for me. If I knew Phil, it was going to be big. "On your knees," he said, and I immediately got in position, crawling after him, knowing everyone could see me like this. It was a risk, to so boldly claim this side of me, but I knew I was among friends, or at least, friendly perverts.

I followed Phil into a room where the sounds and smells of sex permeated the air. "Hello," I heard Phil say. "This is my sub, Christine, and she's looking for a cock to suck. She's very good, I can assure you." Hearing myself talked about in the third person sent a wave of desire through me; my pussy got even wetter. It sank in, at that moment, that I'd literally given Phil the power to select which man I'd wrap my lips around.

"I could handle that," the man said, and then I felt something being slipped over my eyes. Phil had blindfolded me, so I wouldn't even get to experience the pleasure of watching the cock I was about to devour. Yet, even as he took away this joy, he gave me another, the joy of pure devotion. I was trusting him with more and more as this party went on.

"Show him a good time, Christine. Show him what a good cocksucker you are, and you'll get a very special spanking," Phil whispered in my ear. I didn't know the man's name or anything about him, just that suddenly his hard cock was before my lips. I opened them instinctively, having to stretch wide to accommodate him. Then I felt something unexpected: a man who I thought was Phil pressing against my pussy!

All of a sudden, Phil's cock was deep inside me, and I was being pushed forward against mystery man's large shaft. I focused completely on taking it down my throat and moaned against him. His hand moved to my cheek; at first I cringed but he was being gentle, urging me on. I smiled as best I could with a cock in my mouth because this is what these parties are all about: the unexpected, the new, the wanton. They're about doing things I couldn't even conceive of at home when it's just me and Phil, cozy and intimate. Getting fucked by two cocks at once, while I was collared and blindfolded, was intimate in its own way, though. I realized that as I came, shaking and trembling, while the man I loved and a man I might never even meet, used me.

"Party on, man," the guy said to Phil as he thrust into my mouth. I shivered because I knew now I'd get the beating I'd been promised with Phil's perfectly vicious, beautiful belt. Party on. Exactly.

Mea Culpa

Zane

This is my confession.

I'll admit it. I used to be one of the main people talking shit about trifling-ass men and how they can never manage to keep their dicks in their pants. All of my girlfriends, aunts, and female cousins had a variety of dogs lying up in their cribs. My aunt Delores had a black and tan coonhound named Thomas. Black hair, tan skin. He was powerful and agile, at times outgoing and stable, but when it came to keeping his dick in his pants, he was aggressive and vicious. He had something crazy like five kids outside of their eight-year relationship. I wondered when the hell he had time to fuck her if he was doing all that raw-dogging.

My cousin Sheila had a Brazilian Terrier named Davi, imported straight from Santa Catarina—they met while she was on vacation in Brazil. Once she moved his ass to the States, he became restless and started hunting small game, a.k.a. petite, thirsty chicks. Three weeks after she helped him obtain his green card, he left her for a four-foot-eleven, 90-pound, nineteen-year-old who, according to him, didn't have a gag reflex while sucking his dick like Sheila did. Can you imagine a man coming home and saying some shit like that while he is packing? He wouldn't have had to pack shit up in my crib; I would have tossed his ass right out the damn window!

Then there was the Alaskan Malamute my best friend, Judy,

had on a leash for a hot second. She assumed that since his well-muscled, heavy-bone behind had spent his early years out in the middle of nowhere, chilling in igloos and riding bobsleds to school, that he would be devoted and trustworthy. Not! He was the alpha male of all motherfucking alpha males and when she bored him, he was prone to aggression. In other words, he started beating her ass. Now, by this point, she was completely dick-whipped and no one could tell her a thing about her relationship without practically getting their head snapped clean off. I spoke my mind once and left the entire display of "fuckery" alone. I loved my girl but if she wanted to deal with Kuvageegai—hell of a name, right?—instead of sending his ass back home to hunt seals, it was on her.

Eventually, Judy learned her lesson; they all did. They ended up jumping from man to man, looking for that pipe dream of a financially and mentally stable soul mate that would be exclusive to their pussies. I used to believe in fairy tales, too—for a hot minute. But I came to my senses after I went through a quick, successive series of breeds—a Boston Terrier, an Australian Kelpie, and a Chesapeake Bay Retriever. Then I decided I simply wanted to go to work every day, make a good life for myself, and fuck whom I wanted when I wanted.

However, even that should have had its limits and it's the reason why I need to confess. After Judy got rid of "the motherfucker with the long-ass name," she went through about nine or ten guys and then ended up shacking, within a matter of months, with William. Now, William had it going on, in all areas. He was about six foot two and beautiful, way past handsome. I couldn't even call him that. He had this smooth, dark skin that was like being gifted a year's worth of Godiva Chocolates. He had this kinky, black hair that screamed for a sister to run her hands through it. And, most important, it was obvious that he was hung like a barnacle. Yes, a barnacle. Most women go around bragging about how their men are hung like horses or mules, but check this out. They're not even in the top of the game. Damn shame I know this, but the barnacle has the biggest dick of any animal, followed by the Argentine blue-bill duck, a banana slug, a greater hooked squid, an African elephant, *Colymbosathon ecplecticos,* and a blue whale. Okay, so I was bored one day and looked that shit up. If I was going to be giving brothers mad props, I decided to get my knowledge straight.

Anyway, Judy had William, who was hung like a barnacle, and I was mad jealous. And I *never* got jealous. I'm not even sure how that happened, other than I was over their place one day, in the kitchen helping Judy peel some red potatoes to boil and mash for dinner, and that's when I saw him; saw it. He was sitting on the sofa, at a good vantage point from where I was standing, drinking a beer while ESPN was playing, and staring dead at me. I almost cut my finger off with the potato peeler, I was so distracted by his mesmerizing eyes.

Our eyes locked while Judy was busy singing "We Found Love" by Rihanna. Little did I realize then that, like Rihanna, I was about to find love in a hopeless place. William broke our gaze and lowered his eyes to his crotch. I followed them and his dick was bouncing up and down in his pants like it had a mind of its own. Then again, I guess all men's dicks have minds of their own. His was speaking to me . . . in tongues. It was calling my name, beckoning me to it and, if I hadn't quickly regained my senses, I would've been over on that sofa in thirty seconds, ripping it out, and swallowing as much of it as I could cram into my mouth.

Somehow, we managed to get through dinner and then Judy

and I went into the basement, curled up in a couple of throws, and watched two tearjerkers—*Beaches* and *Imitation of Life*—together, as we always did. It felt good to cry together during movies about women who had much bigger issues than us and managed to overcome them. It helped us keep things in perspective when horrific things happened, like our Facebook or Twitter accounts being locked for twenty-four hours because we requested too many friends or "twatchers," or the nail salon having a two-hour waiting list for pedicures.

Judy dozed off halfway through *The Stoning of Soraya M.* and I realized that she was out for the night. There are people who sleep lightly and can be awakened by a moth pissing on a cotton ball inside the drywall and others who sleep so hard that someone would have to slam their heads with a hammer three or four times to get their attention. Judy was one of those.

I should have kept my ass right down there and finished watching the movie, or I could have taken my ass home but . . . I heard William rattling some pans around in the kitchen. *Damn, was hung like a barnacle and did dishes, too!* Hearing his footsteps and knowing that he was up there alone, both him and that huge tumor between his legs, made my pussy get the hiccups. My menstrual cycle was a day or two away so I was extremely emotional and even more horny that time of the month.

I cleared my throat, making sure Judy was as knocked out as I thought she was. She didn't move. I took a few kernels of kettle corn and tossed them at her forehead. She grunted and wiggled her nose but that was it. I stood up and stared down at her, thinking, *It's not like he wasn't going to cheat on you anyway.*

When I got upstairs, William was putting the last of the glasses from dinner in the dishwasher.

"Is there something I can help you with?" I asked from the kitchen doorway.

He seemed startled. "Oh, hey, Marilyn." He closed the dishwasher and turned it on. "No, I'm good, but thanks for offering."

I put my hands on my hips and licked my lips seductively. "I have a lot of *offerings*."

He blushed. *Damn, dimples! I'm too through!*

He didn't respond but there was no need. It was obvious we were on the same page. I walked over to him by the sink and flicked the tip of my tongue over his lips. He spread them for me and I went in. *Damn, and a fucking thick tongue to suck on my pussy!*

We did a dance with both our bodies and our tongues for a few minutes. I debated about leading him to the bedroom but then decided, if I was going to go for it, why not the kitchen? After all, a lot of life-altering shit happens in kitchens across the globe. People make major life-decisions, they fight and argue, and even break up in kitchens. I had done all of the above in my lifetime but, as crazy as it sounded, I have never fucked in one. Now my pussy had the hiccups and asthma.

I broke the kiss and pulled William over by the table.

"Marilyn, we shouldn't do this," he protested . . . but only with his words.

I yanked his pants and boxers down in one swift movement. Then I sat down and gazed up into his eyes. "Are you telling me that you don't want me to suck the skin off your dick?"

He sighed in defeat as I pushed his ass on the table, positioning him between my legs. The game was on. I grabbed his dick with both hands, spread my mouth open as far as I could and stuffed it with some delicious, protein-infused trouser snake.

"Ummm, ummm, ummm," I moaned with delight, hardly believing how good he tasted to my palate. I took the mushroom head out for a minute. "You have an incredible dick, boo."

"Glad you like it." He glanced at the doorway. "You can have as much of this dick as you want."

"I want it all, shit!"

William wanted some more of my good head and started motivating me by making it thump. I moved my mouth up, down, and around, trying to capture it, hands-free. Then I had to grab it again to steady it and continue my feast fit for the saints. I had to charm that damn snake into submission.

I sucked, licked, sucked, licked, sucked on balls, sucked, licked, tongue-flicked some ass, and then sucked and licked again until William couldn't take it anymore. When I realized that he was about to shoot the mother lode, I quickly grabbed the small bowl of sugar on the table and caught all of his semen in it.

William looked shocked, even though he was trying to catch his breath. "What are you going to do with that?"

"Watch."

I rose up from the table and switched over to the fridge. I opened the door and got out the small crate of strawberries that I had spotted in the drawer earlier when I retrieved the red potatoes. I took one out and smeared it in William's cum, held it up so that I could gaze at its beauty, and then sucked on the end of it before biting it off.

"Shit! You get down like that!" William exclaimed.

"Oh, sugar, you haven't seen a damn thing yet." I dipped the strawberry again and took another bite. "I'm about to show you some shit you've never seen before."

William chuckled. "Well, let's pray I can handle it."

I walked back over to the table and pushed him down into the chair that I had vacated. Then I pulled my sundress over my head in one swoop, exposing my banging black lace bra and panty set.

I ran my fingers down over my body. "Do you think this body can bring you pleasure? *Immense* pleasure?"

"Damn sure looks like it," he replied as I lowered my bra straps and fed him one of my taut nipples. He circled it with his tongue. "Um, tasty."

I took a strawberry and let the juice drip on my chest and over my breasts; then he licked it off. This went on for a good five minutes, William devouring my breasts like a starved man.

Meanwhile, at some point, my panties had dropped and were dangling around my right ankle. William started fingering my pussy and then he got creative like me. While he still had my left breast on lock with his mouth, suckling on it like a pacifier, he reached around me, got a strawberry from the crate, and swirled it in my pussy; some of the juice trickled down the inside of my thighs. It felt sticky but oh, so good.

That shit motivated me! I sat on the table and, since the kitchen was rather small, I stretched my right foot over to brace it on the side of the sink, high-heeled pump and all. That allowed William more access to the pussy, which he wasted no time digging into.

"Shit!" I shuddered when he started licking my clit. "Work that tongue, baby."

He buried his face in my pussy and I started moving my hips back and forth like a pendulum, feeding him my ambrosia. Then I grabbed the back of his head and finally ran my fingers through his hair, like I had been craving to do since the day I had first laid eyes on him.

I came quickly and fell back on the table, still moving my hips so he could get his fill of me. I managed to whimper, not whisper, "I want you to fuck the shit out of me."

William stood and glanced toward the doorway again. Damn shame that I had forgotten all about Judy. There I was sucking dick and feeding her man my pussy in her kitchen, begging for a massive dick down from him. I realize that made me a stank ho, by the definition of most, but I could not help myself. I did not believe in living my life with regrets and if he was willing to give up the dick, I was willing to intake it.

"Maybe we should go to your place," William said, obviously either feeling guilty, or nervous. It had to be nerves. Guilt would have told him to put my clothes back on. He wanted to take the sexcapade to a different location. "Judy might come upstairs."

"She's knocked," I replied and pulled him toward me by the hips. "Like you need to be knocking out the bottom of this pussy."

The dirty talk did it. William turned into a beast; a *barbarian*. He reached down, grabbed both of my ankles, slid my ass back on the table and pushed my ankles toward both sides of my head. Then he rammed the barnacle dick all up in my snatch.

It was a shock to my system; a revelation; a freaking gift from heaven above.

William grunted and his eyes rolled back in his head. "Oh, my damn!"

I started squirming my ass around on the table. This was too much but I dared him to stop. This was the dick that I needed to reminisce about in my rocking chair; *the one*.

William started grinding into me slowly . . . at first. It was like he was probing my pussy with a miniature flashlight. But that Maglite quickly turned into a floodlight. It was like his dick expanded once it hit my g-spot, and hit it, it did. The tip of his dick hit my "ledge" and I had to stifle a scream. I lost all control of my nervous system for about ten seconds.

"Are you okay, Marilyn?" William inquired, concerned. "I don't want to hurt you."

"Fuck . . . that . . ." I whispered. "Hurt me. Demolish this pussy like a wrecking crane."

William truly went for broke then. He started pounding me like a jackhammer to the point that I literally almost shit on myself. Those mashed potatoes from dinner started gurgling in my stomach and I had to prairie dog them from coming out. That might sound nasty but, let's not front, one sign of hellified, over-the-top sex is having to control your bowels like a woman has to do when she's pushing out a seven-pound baby.

William kept it up for a good thirty minutes, the pussy probe. After a while, I almost blacked out but managed to stay coherent somehow.

Finally, I asked, "William, do you ever come?"

He grinned and kept tearing it up.

A few minutes later, he took his dick out, and I was able to exhale the breath that I had been holding in. My eyes were watery and my heart had palpitations. *It's over, thank goodness!*

Um, not!

William started pulling me off the table by my thighs.

"What the hell are you doing?" I exclaimed. "I can't take any more."

"You said you wanted this dick. I'm not done," he said, the fucking barbarian.

I was like a rag doll as he turned me around, pressed my breasts and stomach down on the table and then lifted my legs up on both sides of his thighs and started fucking me with my ass and legs suspended in midair.

"Oh, hell naw!" I screamed. The dick action was too . . . fucking . . . much.

"Shh, you'll wake her up," William cautioned. "Let's . . . get . . . it . . . in." He thrust into me with each word.

"I can't feel my legs," I murmured. "I can't feel my legs, William."

That motherfucker with the barnacle dick could not have cared less. He rammed into me so hard that his balls were damn near inside my pussy with his elephantine dick.

"You asked for the dick. You're getting the dick," he said, about *ten* minutes in. "I'm not stopping until I bust this nut."

Breathless, I eked out, "How long does it take to bust one damn nut?"

"When you sucked the first one out of me, you set your own ass up. It takes me forever to get my second one."

I grabbed on to the sides of the table for more traction. "Oh, fuck!" Then I knew I was crazy. I started yelling for Judy to come help me. "Judy! Judy, come get this beast off me!"

William laughed. "Naw, don't start trying to be all cool with Judy again. She isn't going to save you. You should have kept your ass downstairs. But no, you came up here to get your back blown out." He grunted and thrust harder. "You came up here for me to knock the bottom out this pussy, remember?" He really went for broke then. "I was up here, minding my business, doing the dishes, and you came up here to get some of this, you back stabber."

Did he just call me a back stabber? What the fuck is he?

I was heated. Pissed off with a creaming pussy. I was angry but, at the same time, William was giving me the fuck of a life-time.

"Umph, I can't believe I fell asleep." Judy sat up and stretched. "How long have I been out?"

"I'm not sure. I passed out, too," I lied. "But the movie's over."

I was back downstairs, pussy sore, every muscle in my body aching, after William had finally busted that damn nut. We must have fucked for two freaking hours.

"Sorry I fell asleep on you. I guess you think I'm such a bad friend. Every time we have movie night, I doze off."

I smirked, the guilt setting in.

"How was *The Stoning of Soraya M.*?"

"Excellent," I lied again. "You have to make sure you check it out."

Judy stood and walked over to the DVD player and TV to cut them off.

I was hoping she couldn't smell the sex on me. I had cum smothered from my breasts and stomach to my thighs and ass cheeks. Plus, no doubt I had some serious dick breath. You cannot swallow something that monstrous whole and not have an aftertaste.

"I better go check on William," Judy said, and I panicked.

"Oh, he came down a little while ago, saw that you were asleep, and said he was going to grab a shower and hit the sack."

"He's not asleep. He never goes to sleep without getting some pussy. He's like an animal in bed."

Don't I know it! I thought. *And I never even made it out the kitchen. I can't imagine the shit he does in the bedroom.*

No doubt about it, I had met my match sexually. I thought I was impressing somebody with the strawberries and semen in the sugar bowl. Not! He tore my insides up, damn near gutted me. As much as I *thought* I was jealous of Judy, now I realized that was a bunch of bullshit. There was no way I could deal with that barnacle dick every night.

Judy and I talked for another twenty minutes or so. I was in too much pain to get back up off the chair right away. I finally managed to get up and we went upstairs.

"Marilyn, you sure you don't want to spend the night? It's awfully late and the streets are pitch-black."

"No, I'm good. I'd rather sleep in my own bed. You know, the whole 'no place like home' thing."

She walked me to the front door. "Thanks for coming over. You're such a good friend."

I turned to her and was about to hug her and give her a kiss on the cheek but thought better of it. Didn't want the fuck scent to hit her nostrils.

"I love you, Judy. Good night."

I was wrong for that. Dead wrong for it, but I did love her. She was my best friend.

As I sat in my car, waiting for the air in my seats to kick up to cool my sore ass off, I glanced up at their bedroom window and saw the silhouette of Judy getting undressed and climbing into bed with William.

"Good luck," I said to myself as "Straight Fuckin'" by Tyrese blared through my Bose system. "I don't even want to *think* about the third nut."

I pulled out of the driveway and cruised slowly down the

street, having learned my lesson but good. Sometimes it's better to let your friends handle their own dick action.

Then again, there was that time with my other best friend Gina's man: the Bullmastiff. But that is another confession for another time.

I really need to do better.

Mea culpa! *My bad!*

About the Contributors

Shane Allison has had stories published in *Las Vegas Noir* and *Best Black Gay Erotica*. His collection of poetry, *Slut Machine*, is out from Rebel Satori Press and his book-length poem/memoir is out from Future Tense Books. He is at work on his first novel. He can be reached at sdallison01@hotmail.com.

Abdul-Qaadir Taariq Bakari-Muhammad is a writer and recent college graduate with a B.A. in history from Norfolk State University (behold the green and gold). His areas of preference include erotica, science fiction, historical events, and poetry. He has been married for seventeen years and has three beautiful children. If it weren't for the love of his mother and father, none of this would have been possible.

Tenille Brown's erotic fiction has been widely published since 2003, online and in dozens of print anthologies including *Best Women's Erotica 2004*, *Chocolate Flava*, *Do Not Disturb*, *Making the Hook-Up*, *Iridescence*, *Best Bondage Erotica 2011* and *2012*, and

Curvy Girls. She is a proud Southerner, wife, and mother of twins who blogs at http://thesteppingstone.blogspot.com and tweets @TheRealTenille.

Richard Burns grew up in Chicago and later became a police officer on the South Side. He later became a federal agent and was transferred to Detroit, where he now lives. He holds a Bachelor's degree from Regents College in New York. He retired from the army with more than thirty years in Special Forces and the 82nd Airborne Division. With his vast experience, he's become a master storyteller and writer, having written a fast-paced, action-packed spy thriller based on his last tour in Afghanistan in 2009, to be released in March 2012, called *Say Good Night: My 2009 Adventures in Afghanistan.* All of his stories and books are available on RichardBurnsBooks.com. His work can also be found on MostEroticBook.com.

Rachel Kramer Bussel (rachelkramerbussel.com) is a writer, editor, blogger, and event organizer. She is the editor of over forty anthologies, including *Suite Encounters, Spanked, Curvy Girls, Going Down, Women in Lust, Orgasmic, Fast Girls, Tasting Him, Tasting Her, The Mile High Club,* and *Best Bondage Erotica 2012,* and writes widely about sex, dating, books, and pop culture, including a sex column for SexIsMagazine. She blogs at http://lustylady.blogspot.com and http://cupcakestakethecake.blogspot.com.

Cairo is the author of *Man Swappers, The Kat Trap, The Man Handler, Daddy Long Stroke, Deep Throat Diva,* and *Kitty-Kitty, Bang-Bang.* He currently divides his time between northern New Jersey and California, where he is working on his next literary masterpiece.

His travels to Egypt are what inspired his pen name. If you'd like to know more about the man behind the pen, you can visit him at www.Facebook.com/cairoblacktheauthor, www.planetzane .org., or on his website at www.booksbycairo.com.

Lotus Falcon is a native of Washington, D.C., who holds a Bachelor's degree in education and a Master's degree in public administration. She is an educator in a public school system that also leads women's empowerment/sexuality workshops and sells adult toys and products in her spare time. She is currently writing several projects for children and has published several stories in various anthologies. Lotus Falcon is married with seven children and two grandchildren.

Scott G.'s philosophy for writing stories is simple. "I let the idea introduce itself to me from what I learn, see, and experience. From there, the story writes itself. I am just the vessel through which the words make it to the paper." He wasn't always fascinated by reading or writing until "I picked up a fictional book in my twenties, and I realized that ideas begat ideas, and then I was hooked." He hopes that there will be readers out there who will one day "begat" an idea from something he has written. He resides in Matthews, North Carolina, with his wife and two boys.

Tigress Healy is an African-American erotica writer who writes for lesbian and bisexual women who are married to men. Her work appears in Zane's *Succulent: Chocolate Flava II; Purple Panties; Missionary No More: Purple Panties 2;* in Rachel Kramer Bussel's *Gotta Have It: 69 Stories of Sudden Sex;* in Sacchi Green's *Gotta Have*

It: 69 Stories of Sudden Sex for Lesbians; and in several online publications. She can be reached at TigressHealy@TigressHealy.com.

Allison Hobbs is the writer whom Zane calls "the only woman on the planet freakier than me." She is the national bestselling author of *Brick, Scandalicious, Put a Ring on It, Stealing Candy, Pure Paradise, Double Dippin', Lipstick Hustla, Dangerously in Love, Insatiable, One Taste, Pandora's Box, The Enchantress, The Sorceress, The Climax, Big Juicy Lips, A Bona Fide Gold Digger,* and *Disciplined.* Ms. Hobbs lives in Philadelphia, Pennsylvania.

Candy Jackson hails from Prince George's County, Maryland. Although reading is her first love, writing has been her life's passion, and she thanks God for the blessings of opportunity. You can read more from Candy including her debut novella, *Pink and Patent Leather,* on www.AChapterAMonth.com.

Jewells is a storyteller who simply loves telling tales about what happens in relationships when people aren't honest with themselves, and how to put the pieces back together once the truth is revealed. Columbia, South Carolina, is where she currently resides with her eleven-year-old cat, Kayla, who thinks she's part horse. Jewells would love to hear from you at julias blues@gmail.com or visit her at JuliaBlues.com.

Lynn Lake's writing credits include *Hustler Fantasies, Leg Sex, 18eighteen, Desire, On Our Backs, Desdmona.com, Feminine Zone, Read-erotica,* and stories in the anthologies *Truckers, After Midnight, Sex & Seduction, Sex & Submission, Five-Minute Fantasies, Spank Me, Satisfy Me, Ultimate Sins, Ultimate Uniforms, Seriously Sexy, Girl Fun, Sex at*

Work, Best of Both, Wanton Women, Dark Desires, Partner Swap, Explicit Encounters, Purple Panties 2, Indecent Proposals, Hot Under the Collar, The Mammoth Book of Lesbian Erotica, and *The Mammoth Book of Erotic Confessions.*

Patt Mihailoff, a former New Yorker, makes her home in New Jersey and is employed by a county law enforcement agency. Writing is her passion and she will do it until she can't do it anymore. She is ever thankful for the opportunities afforded her by this and other publishers.

N'Tyse is a Dallas, Texas, native and bestselling author of *My Secrets Your Lies, Stud Princess,* and *Twisted Seduction.* She currently juggles her writing career with her roles as wife, new mom, college student, and full-time personal banker. You may find her on Facebook, Twitter, Myspace, Linkedin, and www.ntyse.com.

Perkdaddy, an up-and-coming author born and raised in Harlem, New York, taught fourth grade in the Baltimore City public school system, worked telephone sales, and was a collection agent before pursuing his passion of writing. "Sneakin' and Peekin'" is part of a larger collection he's written called *Satisfied: Bedtime Stories for the Grown and Sexy.* Perk describes himself as a down-to-earth brother who is strong enough to lead, yet humble enough to ask for directions. He is divorced and currently resides in the city of Baltimore.

Rae resides in Richmond, Virginia, with her son. She works as a freelance writer. Visit her at Facebook.com/DomainRae. She is the author of the Zane Presents novel *Abnormal Lives.*

Shakir Rashaan currently lives in Fairburn, Georgia, a suburb of Atlanta, with his wife and two children. Rashaan's body of work includes two book series—*Chronicles of the Nubian Underworld,* which includes *The Awakening: Book One* and *Legacy: Book Two;* and the *Deviant Intent* series, which includes *Obsession* and the upcoming *Deception* in 2012—and a novel under his alterego, Curtis Alexander Hamilton, titled *All I Want . . . Is You.* Other credits include the anthologies *Making the Hookup: Edgy Sex with Soul* and *Erotic Snapshots Vol. 5* and *Vol. 6.*

Eroticist **Giselle Renarde** is a proud Canadian, supporter of the arts, and activist for women's and LGBT rights. For information on Giselle and her work, visit her website, www.wix.com/gisellerenarde/erotica, or her blog, donutsdesires.blogspot.com. Ms. Renarde lives across from a park with two bilingual cats who sleep on her head.

Thomas Slater is a native of Detroit, Michigan. In 1997 he picked up a pen and scribbled for three months, producing his debut title, *Run with the Pack,* an urban crime thriller. Fed up with the lack of attention street literature was receiving at the time, Thomas switched genre in 2004. His debut novel under Strebor is *Show Stoppah.* He is the author of *No More Time-Outs* and *Take One for the Team.* Thomas Slater hopes to create a footprint by stepping off into the cement of literary greatness. Visit the author at www.slaterboyfiction.com, Twitter@thomasEslater, and Facebook.com/thomaseslater.

Tiffany L. Smith is a longtime resident of Virginia Beach, Virginia. She began pursuing her dream of writing at the age of ten, having penned several short stories and a collection of poetry. She has an associate's degree in business and works as an executive assistant for municipal government. She volunteers her time to a number of nonprofit and civic organizations including A Thousand Shoes for a Thousand Smiles, the Conference of Minority Public Administrators (COMPA), and the National Forum for Black Public Administrators (NFBPA). However, her true passion is literary arts. She is a former Board Member of the Southeastern Virginia Arts Association (SEVAA), former chair of AFRAM Festival's renowned Literary Café, founder of the SEVAA Literary Guild, and probably best known for her antics as co-host of one of the hottest literary hours on the Internet, "3 Chicks on Lit." She touts herself as a literary "enthusiast." Her greatest pride is passing on her passion for reading to her two beautiful daughters.

She currently is working on two novels, which she plans to complete in Fall 2012.

Tabitha Strong has enough ideas knocking around her curly head to satisfy every whim of her personality. She began putting them on paper when the compulsion to express herself proved too strong to ignore. A writer of erotica and erotic romance, she pursues complex storylines where strong characters battle their flaws and embrace their vulnerabilities in order to find satisfaction, whatever it may be. A spoiled-rotten dog and her very own alpha male get to have her the rest of the time.

Pat Tucker is the author of eight novels and a contributor to three anthologies. She is a radio news director in Houston, Texas, and co-host of the *Cover to Cover* show with *Essence* bestselling author ReShonda Tate Billingsley. She is the author of three Zane Presents titles: *Daddy by Default, Football Widows,* and *Party Girl.*

Alegra Verde (pseudonym for Esperanza Cintrón) lives, writes, and teaches literature at a college in Detroit. Virgin Blacklace first published her erotic short stories "The Student" and "The Judge" in their anthologies *Misbehaviour* and *The Affair* in 2009. In 2010, "The Pub Owner's Daughter" was featured in *Fairy Tale Lust,* and "Things I Used to Do" was published in *Too Much Boogie.* Her ebook series *Taking Her Boss* (April 2011) and *Tempting the New Guy* (December 2011) were published by Mira Spice.

Kweli Walker is the author of *Walkin' Pussy,* a collection of Af-roerotic short stories. Her latest novel is *Fire Blue.* Her short stories have been included in *The Best American Erotica 2006; From the Streets to the Sheets;* a European erotic anthology, *Scharfe Stellen;* Long Beach Authors for Authors; Maxim Jakubowski's *Illustrated Kama Sutra;* and most recently, Cole Riley's *Making the Hookup.* She is currently completing *The Maker,* an Afroerotic thriller about love, lust, fetish, phobia, design, and espionage.

Zander is the biological son of Zane. He is a trained mechanic and website designer and owns two businesses: an auto shop where he builds race cars and installs audio/visual on cars and boats; and a graphics design company. He is an avid sportsman and an adrenaline junkie who snowboards, surfs, hunts, races cars and motorcycles, golfs, skydives, and plays softball and ice hockey. He resides in the Baltimore, Maryland, area. His upcoming debut novel is titled *The Angle of the Dangle.*

Zane is the *New York Times* bestselling author and editor of dozens of titles; the publisher of Strebor Books, a division of Atria Books/Simon & Schuster; and the creator/scriptwriter/executive producer of "Zane's Sex Chronicles" and "Zane's The Jump Off" on the Cinemax network. She resides in the Washington, D.C., area.